BECAUSE OF HIM

New Hope Falls: Book 2

By

KIMBERLY RAE
JORDAN

THREE**STRAND**
P R E S S

A CORD OF THREE STRANDS IS NOT EASILY BROKEN.

A man, a woman & their God.
Three Strand Press publishes Christian Romance stories
that intertwine love, faith and family. Always clean.
Always heartwarming. Always uplifting.

Book Layout © 2014 BookDesignTemplates.com

Because of Him/ Kimberly Rae Jordan. -- 1st ed.
ISBN-13: 978-1-988409-33-7

CHAPTER ONE

Kieran Sutherland only just managed to keep from lifting his arm and elbowing the detective seated beside him in the face. The only thing stopping him was knowing that, in the long run, such an action would do more harm than good, especially for the man seated across from them.

"A relationship between a teenage boy and girl, and the girl is the one pressuring for sex? Yeah, that's a likely story." The detective didn't bother to keep the sneer from his tone. "You really expect me to believe that?"

Elijah McNamara shrugged. "I don't expect you to believe anything. You asked me about my relationship with Sheila and why it was deteriorating. That was one of the reasons."

"Okay. Let's say I believe you." The detective clicked the pen in his hand in a rhythm that was just off enough that Kieran couldn't predict when he'd click it again. It made him want to grab the pen and snap it in two. "What's the other reason?"

"She wanted to leave New Hope."

"And you didn't?"

"No."

"Again, I find that hard to believe. Aren't most kids eager to get out of this podunk town?"

Kieran clenched his fists, but still, he didn't say anything. He absolutely had to keep his mouth shut. He knew without a doubt that the detective was waiting for him to breathe wrong, so he'd have the excuse to kick Kieran out of the interview room. The man had made no secret of the fact that he didn't want Kieran there and only tolerated his presence because his boss had told him he had to.

For Eli's sake—as well as the others they'd be interviewing—Kieran needed to make sure that he could continue to be present when the detective questioned them. So he bit his tongue and hoped that Eli would understand.

"Sure, some kids were eager to leave, but not me."

"What made you the exception?"

Eli shifted in his seat and reached for his glass of water. After a sip, he cleared his throat. "A short time before Sheila disappeared, my dad took off. Even if I'd wanted to leave New Hope, I couldn't have. My mom and sisters needed me."

"So she wanted sex, and you didn't. She wanted to leave, you didn't. Any other things she wanted that you didn't that were causing your relationship to fall apart?"

"We were young," Eli said. "I don't think either of us really knew what love was, so at the first signs of trouble, we began to struggle."

"So where were you the night Sheila disappeared?" the detective asked. *Click. Click. Click-click.*

Eli's gaze dropped to the detective's hands, obviously as annoyed by the noise as Kieran was. "I was at the house of one of my friends. Four of us were there."

"And you were there all night?"

"Yep. We were having a sleepover. Playing video games. Watching movies."

"Were the other three guys awake all night with you?" the detective asked. "Could they verify that you were in that house the whole night?"

"I don't know if the others were awake all night. I fell asleep during the second movie, so I'm not sure when the other guys did. When I woke up the next morning, a couple of them were up already. We were having breakfast when Coral called to ask if we'd seen Sheila."

"And what did you tell her?"

"We all told her the same thing. The last time we'd seen her was at the Festival when she and I met up with the guys. She wasn't happy that I was going to spend time with them."

"Oh...yet another reason why things were ending between you guys?"

"I guess." Eli leaned back in his seat, crossing his arms. "She usually didn't mind me spending time with the boys, so I'm not sure why she was so upset that night. We'd planned to meet up the next afternoon to go on the rides."

"And she never showed?"

"No."

"And she didn't answer her phone?"

"She didn't have one," Eli said. "Her parents had said she didn't need one. My folks hadn't gotten me one either, for that matter. Honestly, most of our friend group didn't have phones then."

"You wouldn't survive in this day and age," the detective scoffed.

"It was a different time back then," Eli replied.

Kieran hoped that the interview was almost over because he needed a coffee in the worst way. Instead, it dragged on for another hour, and by the end, he was ready to strangle someone. Preferably the detective. He was glad for Eli's sake that the interview was over, but unfortunately, another round of questions was just beginning. Only this time, they were directed at him.

"So, do you really believe the stuff he was spouting?" the detective said as he walked toward the coffee pot after Eli left the police station.

"What are you having trouble believing?" Kieran asked. He poured himself a cup of coffee as well and took a sip. Usually, he was fine with the coffee at the station, but right then, it tasted like swill.

"That crap about her pressuring him to have sex." The man shook his head as they walked into Kieran's office. "I mean, really? He expected us to buy that?"

"It might not make sense to you, but to anyone aware of Eli's religious background, it would."

"How's that relevant?" the detective asked as he sat down in the chair across the desk from Kieran. He slouched back in his chair, his stomach bulging out from between the edges of his brown suit coat. Setting his cup of coffee on Kieran's desk, he pulled a pack of cigarettes from his inside pocket and took one out.

Kieran kinda hoped the guy was dumb enough to light up so he could tell him to take it outside. Instead, the guy just returned the pack to his pocket and settled back in the chair after picking up his coffee. He stuck the cigarette between his lips, but he didn't make any move to light it, just pulled it out long enough to take a sip of coffee before putting it back in his mouth.

"The church Eli and Sheila attended as teens taught the youth that they shouldn't have sex before marriage."

"Religious nuts, eh?"

"They're not nuts," Kieran said, trying to keep his voice calm.

The detective gave him a curious look over his coffee mug. "Is that how you were raised as well?"

Kieran wanted to deny it, but instead, he gave a quick nod. "And I attended the same church for awhile."

The detective's brows drew together as he lowered his mug. "Were the two of you friends? Because if you were, your presence at the questioning shouldn't have been allowed."

"No. We weren't friends. I'm a few years older than Eli. By the time he was in high school, I was long gone."

The detective's frown faded and was replaced with a curious look. "So, are you married, Sutherland?"

"Me?" Kieran asked. "Nope."

"So, you're still a virgin?"

"What?" Kieran stared at him. "Why would you even ask that?"

"Just following the course of logic. You said that Eli and Sheila were taught that sex outside marriage was wrong, then you said that you were taught the same thing. Ergo, if you aren't married, you must still be a virgin."

"That is none of your business," Kieran said through clenched teeth. "And it has absolutely no bearing on this case."

The detective laughed. "I'm not sure I believe that, but I'll let it go for now."

He went on to touch on a few other issues he had with Eli's interview. Nothing Eli had said had made Kieran reconsider his earlier opinion—and also that of his uncle who had been the police chief at the time—that Eli hadn't played a role in Sheila's disappearance.

His irritation with the detective continued to mount as the man blathered on and on about the theories he had pertaining to the case. By the time he finally gathered up his stuff and left the station, Kieran was beyond happy to see him gone, but the irritation lingered like an itch under his skin because he knew his relief was only short-lived. The man would be back in a couple of days for more interviews.

That thought had Kieran storming out of the station. Right then, his focus was on getting something to hopefully improve his day and stop the anger that was coursing through his bloodstream.

He was heading toward the bakery to grab something that would sweeten his day when he spotted Eli leaving his aunt's restaurant. Jogging across the street, he called the man's name, catching up to him when he stopped and turned around.

"You doing okay?" Kieran asked as he came to a stop in front of him.

Eli shrugged, the strain showing on his face. "As good as I can be when I'm being forced to relive stuff from ten years ago. Stuff that I've tried *not* to think about in all those years."

"I was told that I could observe but not participate in the interview, and if I tried, they would boot me out. I wanted to make sure that I could stay, so that's why I didn't say anything."

"I thought that was probably the case," Eli said. "Thanks for explaining, though. Do you think I'll need to be interviewed again?"

"No clue. This detective is playing it close to his chest on certain things."

"I guess I'd better just anticipate it."

"I would say that's probably for the best."

The frown on Eli's face deepened. "Is there any more news on the vandalism?"

"Nope." And that admission added to the frustration already eating at him. "There's been nothing more?"

"Nothing since Anna moved into the lodge."

"I suppose that's a good thing," Kieran said. "But until something more happens, we have nothing to help us determine who is responsible."

"I don't really want anything more to happen, but I also don't like the idea that someone isn't being held responsible for what they've done."

When Kieran's phone rang, he pulled it out and looked at the screen. "I gotta go. I'll talk to you later." He began to walk away as he answered the call. "Lisa? What's up?"

"Mary Albridge just called. Apparently she had a break-in at her place."

"Her house?"

"No, her shop."

Kieran glanced across the street to the antique shop that Mary Albridge owned. "Okay. I'm heading over right now."

After looking both ways, Kieran jogged across the street and knocked on the glass door of the shop. Mary appeared and quickly unlocked the door.

"Hello there, Kieran." She greeted him with a warm smile. "I didn't expect to see you so soon."

"I was just across the street talking to Eli when Lisa called me." Kieran stepped inside and let her lock the door behind him. "She said you had a break-in."

"I did," Mary said as she began to walk toward the back of the store. "Would you like a cup of tea?"

"You know I'm more of a coffee person, but thank you." Kieran looked around the shop as he followed her. It was even more crowded than the last time he'd been in there. Antique furniture filled every corner of the shop. "What all is missing?"

She glanced over her shoulder as she moved gracefully through the shop, the loose caftan she wore flowing around her. "So far, I think it was just the cash from the safe."

"They broke into your safe?"

"Yes." She turned on her kettle then reached for a teacup and a mug. "Or no? I mean, is it a break-in if they knew the code?"

"They knew the code?" Kieran asked as he sat down on one of the antique chairs at the small table in the kitchen Mary had in the back of her shop. "That should help to narrow down the list of suspects."

"Uh...maybe?"

"How many people have you given your safe code to?" Kieran asked. He'd known the older woman for most of his life, so he was well acquainted with her quirks. "Have you ever changed it? Or the code for your security alarm?"

Mary let out a sigh as she set a mug of coffee down in front of him. "You know how I am, Kieran, sweetheart. I forget numbers so easily, and you told me not to write the passwords down."

"So you've never changed your codes at all?" Kieran asked, not really surprised at that revelation. "Can you remember who you gave them to?"

Carrying over a dainty teacup, she settled onto the chair across from him. "Maybe. I can try and give you a list."

"That would be great. In the meantime, I'll have someone come by to take fingerprints." Normally, Kieran would have asked more questions, but at this point, he'd be lucky to get the list of names from Mary.

It angered him to think that someone she might previously have trusted, had taken advantage of her. She was one of the sweetest women he knew, and he hoped he could figure this out for her.

"I'm going to change your security alarm code," Kieran said.

"Oh, but Kieran, you know I'll never remember a new one."

"What we'll do is we'll pick another code that will be easy for you to remember." Kieran paused to consider then said, "Do you remember your mother's birthday?"

"Well, of course," Mary said indignantly.

"Perfect. We're going to change it all to numerals and use those as your new code." At her nod, he gave her a stern look. "This time, you won't give it to anyone. And if someone asks you for it, you call me and let me speak to them. Deal?"

"Deal." Mary smiled and held her hand out.

Kieran gently took it in his, feeling the frailty of her fingers. "Are you going to be here for a few more hours this afternoon so that the tech can come to check for fingerprints?"

"Sure thing," Mary said with a nod.

"In the meantime, let me know if you notice anything else missing."

Mary laughed. "It might take me a little while to figure that out. In case you haven't noticed, I have a lot of stuff in this shop."

"Oh, I've noticed." Kieran gave a shake of his head as he got to his feet. "Start with looking through the stuff that would be easily transported."

"I'll do that."

She trailed him as he headed toward the entrance to the shop. "Take care of yourself, Kieran, darling."

Kieran opened the door then turned, bending to place a kiss on the older woman's cheek. She smelled of lilacs, reminding him of warm spring days. And his mom.

"You take care of yourself, too, Mary. And call me if anything else suspicious pops up, okay?"

"I will."

Kieran stepped out of the shop then turned around long enough to watch her lock the door. With a final smile and nod at the woman, he headed down the street, back toward the station to continue the day that just never seemed to end.

CHAPTER TWO

Cara Morgan guided her car along the road between Seattle, Washington and New Hope Falls. Exhausted from having been up since three that morning, she would be glad to get home. Though she'd been traveling alone, her papa had been a constant companion in her thoughts. The memory of their last conversation had played over and over in her mind.

"Promise me, carissima," he'd said, his dark gaze intense. *"You must never ever tell anyone who you are."*

"I promise, Papa. On my life, I promise."

He'd reached out and taken her hand. His grip wasn't as strong as it had once been, and there was a tremor that hadn't been present until recently.

"I am sorry you had to give up your life in Chicago, but you have a new life now, and I don't want you to lose that." His grip had tightened. *"So you* must *protect our secret. Your life depends on it."*

"I know. I understand."

"I love you so much, carissima." His gaze had softened as emotion flooded his face. *"You are my world. You and your mama meant everything to me. I already lost her. I don't want to lose you too."*

It had been five years since the incident that had taken her mama from her, and now she was facing losing her papa too. His battle against cancer had been waging for a year now, and she could see that it was taking its toll on him. His mind was as sharp as ever, but his body was failing him.

For the past couple of months, during each visit, he'd pressed the same point over and over. *Keep our secret. Be safe. Trust no one.* It was a difficult way to live, but for her papa's peace of mind, it was how she'd lived her last five years.

"You are my world, too, Papa. I love you."

His expression had turned regretful. *"I wish you could find someone else to be your world when I am no longer here."*

"That's hard to do when I can't tell them the truth about my past," she'd reminded him.

"You can embrace the parts that don't reveal your true identity. Most people won't dig too far into your past. Just don't tell them the worst parts."

She could do that...maybe. It just made her wonder how she could be in a relationship while withholding information about herself. She hadn't yet figured out to have a friendship because of her reluctance to let people close, so she wasn't sure how to manage a relationship while keeping secrets. But she'd made her promise to her papa, so that would be how she lived her life. Out of love and respect for him, she would uphold the promise she'd made to him.

When New Hope Falls finally came into view, Cara breathed a sigh of relief as the memories of the visit with her father began to fade. She was nearly home.

As she turned her car into the back lane, she pressed the button on the opener attached to her visor. By the time she reached the garage door, it was already completely up, allowing her to swing right into the garage. As soon as she was inside, she pressed the button to lower the door back into place.

She watched in her side mirror until the strip of daylight narrowed then disappeared completely as the door reached the floor. Once she was confident the garage was secure, she grabbed her phone and scrolled through the security cameras installed in her apartment, office, and the studio.

After a glance at the digital clock on her dashboard, she checked the clocks she'd set out at strategic places in front of the cameras, making sure that each of them lined up with the current time. It was a precaution she'd taken to make sure that no one was looping feed through her cameras. While it wasn't foolproof, it made her feel a bit better.

Once she was satisfied that her home was safe, Cara pushed open the car door and got out. She retrieved her suitcase from the trunk, then locked the car and headed for the doorway that led out of the garage. Bending toward the security panel there, she looked into the optical scanner.

The scanning took seconds, then a nondescript box next to the door slid open. She pressed her hand to the screen that appeared. Within moments, the lock on the door released. Without hesitation, she grabbed the handle and pulled it open to reveal a narrow staircase that led to the second floor and her home.

The door closed behind her with a thud, the locks engaging as she began to climb the stairs. Thankfully, the stairway was well lit, so a quick glance up the staircase revealed that the door at the top of the stairs was still secure. After going through one more set of scans, she was finally into her apartment.

As she set her suitcase down, Cara let out the breath it felt like she'd been holding since she'd left home three days ago. She leaned back against the door, closing her eyes and allowing herself to relax.

Finally straightening up a couple of minutes later, she unzipped first one boot and then the other before pulling them off and putting them in the small coat closet near the door. She hung up her jacket, then pulled her suitcase to the nearby door that led to her bedroom, but she didn't bother to unpack it.

First thing on her priority list was a bath. She wanted to soak off the last three days of travel and hotels. And, of course, the prison hospital.

She walked into her bathroom and turned on the faucets of her large whirlpool tub. As she waited for it to fill, she returned to the living room and stared out the floor-to-ceiling windows that looked out over Main Street. The day was cloudy and drizzly, casting a blanket of gray over the town.

After having been out in the world, dealing with people, for the past three days, she was ready to retreat from it all. With one final look at her adopted hometown, Cara hit the button to lower the motorized blinds that covered the windows. Once the world beyond them was blocked out, she returned to the bathroom and within minutes, was sinking into the warmth of the water.

This trip to visit her father had been particularly draining. Ever since his cancer diagnosis, their visits had become more emotional. For the first time, she'd forgone begging him to take treatment for the disease. Seeing how gaunt he was had made her realize how little time they actually had left together.

She hoped that she would have at least one more visit with him, but something told her that might not happen. And not just because she'd visited him in the medical center not far from the federal prison where he'd been transferred a couple of years earlier.

There had been something about his goodbye to her that suggested he knew they wouldn't see each other again. She'd resisted thinking about that on the long trip back to New Hope Falls, but now that she was here within the safety of her home, it was all she *could* think about.

It was inevitable. His death. For years, she'd worried that his enemies would find him, despite the measures that had been taken to protect him as a mobster turned witness for the prosecution. He'd worried the same for her, which was why she'd let him talk her into all the crazy security precautions that seemed like overkill in the small town of New Hope Falls. And also why his goodbyes always included variations of the promise he insisted on extracting from her.

They'd always said goodbye at the end of each visit, knowing it might well be their last. But this visit...well, it had seemed more final than any before it.

Cara sat forward in the warm water, drawing her legs close as she wrapped her arms around them. She stared at the bubbles, mesmerized by their iridescent shine while trying not to think about the dullness of her father's complexion. The tremor of his voice. It was like her father had been reduced to 2D. A piece of onion skin paper where he'd once been a vibrant painting. Larger than life. Someone people had looked up to. Admired. Feared.

But to Cara, he was simply her beloved papa. He hadn't been with her and her mother all the time, but when he had been with them, he was the man whose arms had held her when she'd had a nightmare, promising to keep all the monsters at bay. Even now, the scents of patchouli, sandalwood, and tobacco brought those memories from childhood to the forefront of her mind.

It was hard to imagine her life without him, even though their monthly face-to-face meetings over the past four and a half years had all taken place in one prison or another. Would she be safe once he was gone? Would his enemies be content with his death? Or would they want to wipe her out as well, if they realized she was still alive?

Because of who her father was, her life had always been at risk. She'd lost her mother because of decisions her father had made. She'd lost the life she'd had in Chicago because of those decisions. Sure, she'd built a life of sorts in New Hope Falls, but it wasn't anything like the life she'd once imagined for herself.

She closed her eyes and tried to take a deep breath, but the tight bands of emotion around her chest kept it from happening. Exhaling shakily, Cara tried to keep a grip on her emotions. Her father wasn't dead yet. She wouldn't mourn him prematurely.

Using her damp hands to brush away the few tears that had escaped, Cara exhaled deeply. He'd extracted another promise from the last time he'd held her in his arms as a free man. *No matter what else happens, I want you to live your life. Promise me you'll embrace the beauty of it the way your mama always did. Live for both of us.*

Often it had been a struggle for her to do that, but this time of year made it a little easier. The Fall Festival was that weekend, and her father had told her that she had to go and enjoy herself so that she could report back to him all about it. In the years since she'd come to New Hope, he'd loved hearing about all the events of the town, but the Fall Festival had been his absolute favorite.

She'd done her best to describe it all for him. The colors of autumn. The caramel apples. The harvest pie contest. The pie-eating contest. The first time she'd told him about that, his eyes had lit up, and he'd said how much he wished he could have been there for that.

So she'd buy one of the harvest pies from the church booth and eat a piece just for him. Normally, pies weren't a big thing for her, but she'd make an exception for this. For him. This year, he'd requested that she buy a peach pie.

So for now, she'd stop mourning his loss and do what he'd asked of her.

"I mithed you, Miss Cara." The five-year-old with ringlet pigtails grinned up at Cara, her wide smile revealing her missing front teeth.

"I missed you too, Sophie." Cara took the little girl's hand and smiled as she spun in a circle, the skirt she was wearing over thick tights flaring out in a circle around her. "Your spinning is terrific."

"I'th been practithing like you told uth to." Sophie dropped Cara's hand and lifted both hands above her head imitating the little ballerina she wanted to be.

"You're doing a great job. Keep it up."

"I will!" Sophie grabbed her mom's hand. "I'll thee you nexth clath."

"That you will," Cara said.

"It was nice seeing you," Sophie's mom, Allison, said.

"You too. Hope you enjoy the festival."

Cara watched as the little girl skipped away at her mother's side. She was one of the students in the beginner ballet class Cara taught at her studio. All of the students were a joy to teach since they were all as spirited as little Sophie. Her father had loved hearing about them, too.

Because she'd been unable to send him letters in between their visits due to security concerns, she'd gotten in the habit of keeping a journal, detailing the interesting parts of each day. When she'd go to visit him, she'd give him the journal to read through, to tide him over until their next visit. Well, she didn't give *him* the journal directly. It had to go through the scrutiny of a guard or warden before her father could read it, but eventually, he would receive the journal and read through it.

She moved through the crowds of people, careful to avoid bumping into anyone as she walked. It had taken her until mid-afternoon on Saturday to feel up to joining the festival instead of just watching from her window. Being that her apartment faced the street, she'd been able to observe without having to be in the midst of it. The isolation had suited her mood, but eventually, she'd had to come down from her ivory tower—so to speak.

Her building was one of a handful on Main Street that had a second floor, but as far as she knew, only a couple of them had a living space. She loved her apartment as well as her studio and office on the main floor, but sometimes it felt as much a prison as it was a sanctuary.

Even though she'd had to force herself out into the world beyond the walls of her apartment, each minute that she was out there, she felt more at ease. Women from her *Stretching for Strength* class stopped to talk to her. Moms who took her *Mommy & Me* class smiled at her as they pushed their babies in strollers. Pregnant women who participated in her weekly *Pregnancy Stretches* stopped her to share how they were feeling as their pregnancy progressed. But best of all were the kids like Sophie who greeted her with smiles and pirouettes.

By the time she found the booth with the pies, her smile was coming more readily and felt more genuine. The cloak of despondency that had weighed her down since walking away from her father had lifted. It had become easier to accept New Hope Falls when it was a place for her to spend the weeks between visits to see her father.

But now that it appeared those visits would be coming to an end in the next few months, she was struggling to decide if New Hope Falls could be a forever home.

"Hello, Cara." The young woman working at the booth gave her a friendly smile.

"Hey, Sarah. How're you doing?"

"Good. Just trying to figure out how many pieces of pie I can eat before I'll need to take another class at your studio."

Cara laughed. "I think you can enjoy a couple of pieces without too much trouble. I know I plan to."

"So you're here to buy a pie?" Sarah McNamara asked. "A whole pie?"

"Yep. A whole pie."

"Okay. What kind are you in the mood for?"

"Well, I told my dad all about the festival, and he insisted that I buy a peach pie and eat a piece for him."

Sarah's brows drew together over her light blue eyes. "Why doesn't he just come here and have a piece himself?"

"He's in the hospital in another state."

"Oh no." Sarah reached out to lay her hand on Cara's arm. "I'm so sorry to hear that. I'll be praying for him. And for you too."

Cara considered her words and offered her a small smile. "Thank you."

"Are you able to see him?" Sarah asked as she boxed up one of the peach pies.

"I go to visit him every month." Cara pulled a twenty from her wallet and held it out. When Sarah tried to give her change, she waved it off. "I'm sure the church can put it to good use."

"Thank you." Sarah slid the box across the counter. "I'd say don't eat it all in one sitting, but my aunt's pies are so good that that advice is pretty much useless."

A shriek had Cara turning around. "Isn't that Coral?"

"What?" Sarah said as she came around the booth to stand beside Cara. "Oh my word. That's Eli. And Anna. What is Coral doing?"

"It looks like she's...attacking them?"

People were standing around videoing the incident on their phones, but a few people were trying to pull Coral away from the couple in front of her. A couple of men in uniform ran past them, and within a few minutes, everything seemed to be under control.

In the midst of the uniformed men, Cara spotted the town's police chief. She'd noticed him plenty before, but it was the first time she'd seen him in action. She turned away from the sight and found Sarah watching as her brother and the woman with him walked in the opposite direction before they disappeared into the antique store.

"Oh. That explains a whole lot," Sarah murmured.

"What do you mean?" Cara said as she swung back around to look at her.

"Just that Coral's attack on Anna explains some things that have happened out at the lodge."

"Will they be okay?"

Sarah smiled. "I think they'll be just fine."

"I guess I'd better get this pie home, and maybe I'll eat a piece while I watch the fireworks."

"You have a good vantage point for that."

"The only thing is that being inside dulls the noise, and that's half the experience, isn't it?"

"Not if you're a dog or a baby," Sarah said with a grin.

"Hey Sarah," an older woman said as she stepped behind the booth with her. "It's my turn to man things here. Why don't you go have some fun?"

"Thanks, Lil." Sarah gave her a quick hug then stepped away. "I told Cece I'd go on some rides with her. I'll see you later, Cara."

"Sure thing." Cara picked up the box with her pie in it and slowly began to make her way back toward her apartment, stopping at a few more booths as she went. Once to buy a candied apple. Another time to get a cup of hot apple cider. And once to buy a chunk of rocky road fudge. Her dad may have been all about the fruit pies, but if she was going to indulge, she liked her chocolate.

There were lots of laughter and shrieks as she passed the area where the rides were set up. She hadn't gone on many rides in her life, but she had a memory of when she'd been six or seven, and her mom had taken her to an amusement park. It had just been the two of them, but her mom had accompanied Cara on every ride she'd begged to go on, and they'd had a blast together.

As she balanced all her purchases on one arm so she could unlock the front door of the studio, Cara pushed aside the sudden swell of loneliness. It was always there, lingering, but she knew it was partly her own fault. She'd chosen to keep most people around her at arm's length, so it was no surprise when she was alone at the end of each day.

Upstairs in her apartment, she cut herself a piece of fudge and a piece of pie and carried them with her hot apple cider to the small table that sat in front of the windows that overlooked Main Street.

She settled into her favorite comfy chair and picked up her cider to take a sip. She didn't turn on any lights so she could keep the blinds up in order to watch the activities on the street below and later, the fireworks.

She'd thought about videoing it all, but who was she going to show it too? Besides, maybe this was one of those times when it was more important to just live in the moment and enjoy it while it was happening.

CHAPTER THREE

A couple of days after the festival, Kieran left the bookstore and began to walk along the back lane, looking up at each of the buildings to see if they had a security camera that might have picked up some valuable footage relating to the break-ins. He wasn't holding out much hope, however, as most businesses in the area didn't feel the need for that type of expense, being a small town with relatively little crime.

Unfortunately, both crimes appeared to be an inside job, which made little to no sense. Mary Albridge and Drake Swanson and their businesses had nothing in common except that they'd both been part of New Hope for a lot of years. Both Mary and Drake could trace their lineage in the town back to the original founders. Drake's grandfather had been mayor for several years, and Mary's deceased husband had also held the position for a term or two.

Drake himself was a bit of a mystery. The man was rarely, if ever, seen in New Hope Falls. Kieran wasn't altogether sure if that was because the man traveled a lot or if it was because he was that reclusive. The only reason he knew the guy actually existed was because they'd been in school together. Drake had been a quiet kid a couple of years behind him who'd spent most his time with his nose in a book. Although Kieran had no idea what the man had done after high school since Kieran's family had left New Hope Falls before he'd hit his teens.

Andy, the young man who managed the bookstore, had been the one who'd called in the robbery, and he'd been the only person to talk to Kieran when he'd shown up.

Turning around, Kieran paused when his gaze fell on the garage door halfway down the block. When the new owner of the old bank building had taken possession a few years ago, a lot of work had begun almost immediately. The building had been gutted on both floors, and then the garage had been added on half of the lower level.

The renovations had been a topic of interest, mostly because they hadn't been done by a local company. And from the look of the cameras above the garage at the back, they took their security seriously. There was no back entrance except for the garage, so Kieran made his way to the end of the block and circled around to the front of the building.

Let's Move was written in elegant black script on a white sign that was situated above the door and picture window. The window was frosted but had figures of women and children clad in flowing skirts dancing etched into it.

After a moment's hesitation, Kieran pulled open the door and stepped inside. The atmosphere inside was different than anything he was used to. There was a light citrusy-floral scent in the air that he couldn't quite put his finger on, and the classical music playing was a long way from the worship or country music he usually had his radio tuned to.

"Hello, Chief."

Kieran turned his attention to the speaker. A teen with short jet-black hair and lips and a string of piercings in her ears sat in one of the chairs. "Hello. Do you know if the owner is in?"

"Cara?" At Kieran's nod, she said, "Yep, but she's gotta class at the moment." The girl snapped her gum as she looked down at her phone. "Should be done soon though."

"Is it okay if I wait?" Kieran asked as he gestured to the other chairs that ringed the small waiting area, not wanting to make the girl uncomfortable.

"Like I'd say no to a cop," the teen scoffed with a grin.

He gave her a smile in return as he took a seat near the door, feeling more than a little out of place. The chairs were surprisingly comfortable, but he still shifted uneasily as he waited. Maybe he should just come back another time.

Just as he got to his feet, however, the door leading to the back of the studio opened, and a slender woman stepped out. She wore a light blue leotard with a matching filmy skirt, and her light brown hair was pulled back into a bun perched high on her head.

He knew of her from church and also because her business was right on Main Street, not too far from the sheriff's station, but they'd never been officially introduced.

Her eyes widened when she saw him, and she stepped back, lifting a hand to rest just below her throat. She seemed to take a couple of quick breaths at the same time. For a moment, she hesitated before walking further into the waiting area.

"Are you Cara?" Kieran asked.

She crossed her arms over her waist, her lips pressing tightly together for a brief moment. "Yes, I am."

"Kieran Sutherland." He held his hand out.

After another brief hesitation, she placed her hand—which was surprisingly cold and trembled slightly—in his. "What can I do for you?"

"I was wondering if your security cameras were working."

She frowned for a moment, then nodded. "The last time I checked, they were."

"Excellent. Do you think I could take a look at them?"

Before Cara could answer, several women walked out of the door behind her, all in various stages of pregnancy. Cara turned toward them, smiling and chatting with them as they moved past her.

There were a couple of women who looked like they were ready to give birth any minute, and from the promise they made to Cara to let her know if they had their babies that week, they likely could.

The women all gave him curious looks. He recognized a couple of them and nodded in greeting as they headed for the door.

Once the women—including the goth teen—had said goodbye and left the studio, Cara turned to him, seeming to be more in control of herself. "So, you were asking about my cameras?"

"Yes." Kieran cleared his throat. "We've had a couple of burglaries on Main Street, and I wanted to see if there were any cameras around that might have caught some information that would be helpful to our investigation. I noticed you had cameras up on the back of your building. I wanted to see if they were the real thing and not just some fakes."

She stared at him for a moment before nodding. "Yes. They're real."

"Could I see the footage?" Kieran shifted his weight from one foot to the other. "Uh...please?"

He wasn't sure what it was about this woman that had him feeling a little out of step. Or maybe it was just everything he'd been dealing with lately that had him feeling that way.

First, the stuff with the cold case file, then the ridiculous twist that Anna Carrington's vandalism case had taken when Coral Thompson had attacked her, and now two burglaries. It was like the town had turned from being a safe refuge from the rest of the world into being just like the world.

"I suppose you could." She nodded toward another door. "We can use the computer in my office."

Kieran followed her into the small room, looking around as he did. Unlike the elegant décor of the reception area, the office was rather starkly decorated. Basically, there was just a desk and a computer and a couple of chairs.

"Have a seat," she said as she rounded the desk to sit in front of the keyboard and monitor. "Just give me a second to pull up the camera footage."

"I kind of thought this was a dance studio," Kieran said, watching as her gaze flicked to him then back to the monitor.

"It is, but it's more than just that. I teach exercise classes for adults, mainly women. One of those classes is for pregnant women. Stretching and strengthening in preparation for labor and delivery. The dance classes I teach are for children."

Kieran watched as she worked on the keyboard and mouse. He'd seen her from a distance over the past few years, but he'd never introduced himself, and now he wondered why that was. From what he'd overheard at the station, she kept pretty much to herself, but he had seen her at church fairly frequently.

"What time-frame were you wanting to look at?" Cara asked.

Kieran pulled a small notebook out of his pocket and flipped it open. He read over the information he'd gotten from Mary and gave her the dates he needed to see. She used the mouse again then turned the monitor, so it was angled toward him.

"This is going back to the start of the time period you wanted to see."

Kieran leaned forward, not happy with the angle of the camera. "Is this the only camera you have back there?"

She hesitated then clicked to bring up another angle. It wasn't any better than the previous one.

"Is that it?" Kieran asked out of desperation, even though two cameras were more than he'd ever expected to find. "No other cameras?"

When she hesitated yet again, Kieran found himself focusing more intently on her. If he didn't know better, he'd think she had secrets. Well, of course she had secrets. He didn't know her at all, but after this, he would be doing a bit of an investigation into her.

"There's one other one, but I'm afraid its angle isn't any better than the ones you just viewed."

"May I be the judge of that?" Kieran asked.

Her brows drew together, then she nodded. He could see what she meant when the picture came into focus. The camera looked straight down over the garage door. Only someone coming right up to the door would be seen.

"Did you research New Hope Falls at all before you moved here?" he asked.

"What do you mean?" Cara shifted on her chair, playing with the pen she'd picked up off the desk.

"One camera *might* have been overkill. Three definitely is," Kieran said. "Are you worried about something?"

"One can never be too safe," Cara replied. "It seems that there has been an uptick in the crime around here in the last month or so."

"Do you have another reason for being prepared beyond just in case something happens? Something I should be aware of?"

"Are you here to question me?" Cara asked.

"Well, not about a crime, obviously, but I can't help but be curious," Kieran said, making note of her deflection. "After all, you are a resident of my town. I feel as if we haven't made you feel that this is a safe place to live."

Cara's shoulders pulled back as she lifted her chin. "I knew what type of place this was before I moved here."

"So you did research the town?"

"I didn't need to. My mom lived here as a child, and she used to talk about it all the time."

That hadn't been what Kieran expected her to say. "Your mom is from around here?"

"Not from, exactly, but she and her family lived here for a couple of years when she was eight or nine, but she talked about how much she loved it." Cara's gaze turned to the monitor, but Kieran suspected she wasn't seeing the picture that sat on the screen. "When she died, I needed a change of scenery, so I chose to come where she had spent a few happy years."

As she talked, Kieran felt bad for having pushed her into an explanation that had its roots in pain. "I hope you have experienced similar happiness while you've lived here."

"It's been good." Another hesitation. "It's been where I've needed to be right now in my life."

"I'm glad to hear that," Kieran said.

Silence fell between them for a moment before Cara softly cleared her throat. "Was there anything else you needed?"

"No, I think that was all for now." He put his notebook back in his pocket and got to his feet. "Thank you for letting me see the footage."

"I'm sorry it wasn't more helpful." Cara turned the monitor back to face her then got up.

As they left the office, she pulled the door closed behind her. Kieran took one last look around the now-empty reception area then he opened the door to the street. "Thanks again."

"You're welcome."

The glass door closed behind him with a thud, and Kieran glanced over his shoulder to see Cara locking it. Their gazes met for a moment before she turned away and disappeared into the shadows of the interior of the studio.

He found himself staring at the empty space. It seemed he'd missed out on something over the past few years by not introducing himself to her sooner. Now he found the mystery of her intriguing, and it was a huge temptation to ignore all the other things he should be focusing on right then in order to delve into a search of Cara's past.

Instead, he returned to the station and followed up with the tech on the fingerprints they'd taken at both break-ins. Still, once he was at his desk, Kieran fought the urge to pull up a screen to start a search on Cara. Though he wanted to know everything about her, he acknowledged that he had no legal reason to use police resources to investigate her. Just because someone went overboard on security wasn't any reason to scrutinize their life.

No, there was only one way to get answers to the questions he had, and that was to ask them of her. He had an inexplicable urge to get to know her better that went beyond her excessive security. Maybe he'd have to ask her out on a date if he wanted to accomplish that.

That thought took him completely off-guard as he'd had no interest in dating since moving back to New Hope. Something had clearly intrigued him about the woman, but that didn't mean he had to do anything about it.

Or maybe it did.

~ * ~

As soon as she'd locked the door, Cara escaped up the stairs to her apartment. It was only when she was secure there with the alarm on that she allowed herself to relax the tight control that she'd grabbed onto when she'd seen the cop standing in her reception area.

Her first thought was that he was there to tell her that her father had died, which was ridiculous. News of her father's death would only come from one person...the only man her father had trusted throughout the dealings he'd had as he'd turned state's witness in several cases that had shaken up the crime family he'd been the head of.

Following his testimony in those cases, he'd been moved to the other side of the country and put in prison under a new identity. Her father hadn't even trusted his own attorney, so in the end, it was one man—Doug Anders, an assistant district attorney that he'd worked with—that he'd put his trust in.

To date, through all the prison changes in the first couple of years, the man had never let them down. And Cara knew that on the day her father died, she would get a visit or a phone call from Doug.

Still, seeing a law enforcement officer in her space had shaken her up a bit. Thankfully, all he'd wanted was to see her cameras. Relief had rolled through her at his request, but at the same time, she'd still been wary.

She'd never had a reason to not trust the cops, but she knew that some would take the knowledge of her identity and pass it on to people who were looking to hurt or kill her. After all, she was supposed to have been in the car with her mother when the bomb went off. Her father had moved mountains to stage her death, knowing that she was better off dead to the world than alive.

It was after her mother's death that her father had approached the district attorney to make a deal. In exchange, he was given a new identity, but more important to him, she was also given a new identity. He'd been stashing away a lot of money into several accounts for her and her mother over the years, so by the time he went to prison, she had more than enough to live on for the rest of her life.

The money had been another area that left her conflicted, knowing where her father had gained a lot of it. When she'd asked him about where he'd gotten it, he'd told her that it had come from the legitimate businesses and investments he had, but she hadn't been convinced. To that end, she gave money on a regular basis to organizations that dealt with drug addiction and human trafficking. It made it easier for her to use the money her father had given her for other things.

On more than one occasion, he'd apologized for the horror his life choices had brought her, and she knew the money was his way of trying to make things easier for her. After all she'd lost, he had wanted to provide a way for her to find new joy in her life, though it would be different from what she'd had before. He'd been so pleased when she moved to New Hope Falls and opened her dance studio.

It wasn't until she was in her teens that she'd realized that her father wasn't just away on a lot of business trips, but that he had a whole other family in New York. A wife. Sons. A position as the head of the Moretti crime family. The realization that her mother was his mistress, and that they would never be together as a real family had been devastating to her.

After everything that had happened, she was now alone. Her mother had kept their world small. No doubt because being a mistress to a crime boss wasn't something she could talk about. She'd stayed at home and homeschooled Cara, enabled by the money Cara's father had sent them each month. So it had just been the two of them—sometimes three, when her father came—but never more than that.

She'd carried on with the tendency to keep a distance from people, especially after everything that had happened.

Kieran had seemed curious about what had brought her to New Hope Falls, but had it been a normal curiosity? Or something more sinister? She'd heard about the break-ins, so she knew he hadn't been lying about those. And it made sense that since her studio was on the same side of the street as the two places that had been broken into, that he'd see her cameras and want to view the footage.

But something told her that she hadn't seen the last of the man. The question was, what would bring him back? And how was she going to deal with him? She couldn't ignore him if he came around again. There was nothing that was as likely to raise some red flags as her hiding from him.

Since Cara had no idea when Kieran was going to be back around, she pushed aside the worry and turned her focus onto the one thing guaranteed to calm her nerves. Dance.

With the studio being into its second month of the new session of classes, it was time to start putting together their Christmas recital pieces. She only did pieces for the classes she actually taught dance to, which were for girls ten and under. It wasn't that she didn't allow boys or men in her classes, but so far, only those of the female persuasion had shown an interest in anything the studio offered.

After making herself an early dinner, she cleaned up, then changed into a leotard and leggings. She had already found the music she wanted to use, so it was just a matter of choreographing the dances based on the capabilities of each age group.

It was a bit weird to be listening to Christmas music in October, but she had always loved the season. Even though it had just been the two of them for Christmas most years, her mom had always done what she could to make their celebration memorable.

They would decorate the house from top to bottom, then they'd spend several days baking and decorating dozens of Christmas cookies. It was kind of ridiculous to bake so many, but they'd given them to one of the local homeless shelters where they volunteered a few times each month. Everything they'd done had been set to Christmas music, so listening to it now brought back good memories.

She kept the lights off at the front of the studio, so no one realized she was downstairs, then she went into the room where she held all the classes. It was tempting to put on her playlist of favorite songs to dance to and lose herself in the music, but she forced herself to stay focused. Maybe if she got the recital pieces nailed down, she could reward herself.

~ * ~

Kieran held out until lunch the next day. He'd gone to pick up a sandwich from *Norma's*, and when he walked out, he paused, his gaze going to the dance studio. He had no clue what her class schedules were like, but that didn't stop him from crossing the street and tugging on the handle of the door.

He was pleasantly surprised when it swung open. Taking that as a sign, he walked into the reception area. Within a minute of stepping through the door, the woman who'd dominated his thoughts for the past twenty-four hours appeared. Her hair was pulled back from her face, and she wore a dark blue, long-sleeved fitted top and a pair of gray loose sweats that sat low on her hips. On her feet were a pair of black flats.

"Hello, Chief," she said as she walked toward him. Her hesitation from the previous day appeared to be gone, but there was still wariness in her gray gaze. "What can I help you with?"

No small talk pleasantries from her that day, Kieran realized. "Have you had lunch?"

Her brows drew together for a moment. "Lunch?"

He lifted the takeout container he held in his hand. "I have a roast beef sandwich on Norma's amazing bread."

"Okaaay?"

She still didn't seem to grasp what he was saying. "I thought you could help me eat it."

She stared at him, one eyebrow lifting slightly. "You need help eating a sandwich from *Norma's*?"

Clearly it had been way too long since he'd tried to flirt with a woman. She was looking at him like he was losing his mind. "You know what? How about you tell me what your favorite sandwich is, and I'll go get it from *Norma's*?"

Cara crossed her arms. "Why?"

"Uh, well," Kieran began. "I wanted to talk to you about something, and I thought we could do that over lunch."

"Turkey and swiss."

Kieran hesitated. "You want a turkey and swiss sandwich?"

"Yep."

"Excellent." He held out his take-out container but then jerked it back. "Are you going to lock the door once I walk out?"

Cara's eyes widened momentarily, but then she laughed, and Kieran felt his heart skip a beat.

"No. I promise I won't do that. Knowing my luck, you'd just break my door down."

"In the interest of eating lunch, I will not confirm or deny that."

She held out her hand. "I promise not to hold your sandwich hostage."

Kieran handed over the container, then, after a final look at her—and his sandwich—he left the studio.

CHAPTER FOUR

Norma gave Kieran a weird look when he walked back in. "Something wrong with your sandwich, Chief?"

"I don't know. Haven't eaten it yet."

"So what can I do for you?"

"I need another sandwich to go. Turkey and swiss."

"Turkey and swiss?"

"Yep."

"Just give me a few minutes. I'll get it ready for you." She started to walk away then turned back, a frown on her face. "This isn't for that wretched detective, is it? Because if it is, I don't care that you're the police chief, you can turn around and walk right back out of here without that sandwich."

"No worries," Kieran said. "I'm not buying that guy lunch now or anytime in the future."

"Okay. In that case, we will make you your sandwich."

As he stood there waiting, Kieran greeted a couple of people who came in. Being the police chief in a small town, people tended to know him even when he wasn't sure who they were. Still, he chatted with anyone who approached him.

It wasn't long before Norma reappeared with another takeout box. He paid for his order then left the restaurant for the second time in less than an hour. When he reached the door of the studio, he stared at it for a moment before reaching out and tugging on the handle. Despite Cara's promise, he was actually a little surprised when the door opened.

"I'm in the office," Cara called out.

Kieran made his way to the open door and found her seated at the desk, his takeout container sitting on the desk in front of the chair he'd sat on the previous day. Cara glanced up from the monitor as he walked in, her gaze briefly dropping to the container he held. He sat down in the chair and slid her sandwich toward her.

"Turkey and swiss, as requested."

"Thank you." Cara pulled the container closer but didn't open it.

Kieran, however, was too hungry to just let his sandwich sit. He popped the take-out container open and bent his head to say a quick prayer of thanks for the food. When he lifted his head, Cara was watching him with her soft gray eyes. He couldn't tell what she was thinking because her face was expressionless.

"To what do I owe the pleasure of a visit from the police chief for the second time in as many days?" Cara asked, her attention back on her monitor screen.

Kieran took a bite of his sandwich and waited until he was done chewing before he answered. He debated not broaching the subject with her since it was clear she was suspicious of his reappearance in her studio. Of course, she had a right to be. She'd lived in New Hope for several years, and even though their paths had crossed, they had done so at a distance, and he'd never introduced himself to her.

"Actually, I have a favor to ask of you."

"Of me?" Cara frowned as she leaned back in her chair, moving it around to face him more directly.

"Yes." Kieran abandoned his sandwich and sat back as well. "In light of what's been going on with the recent string of thefts, I was hoping you might consider helping me out."

"How exactly?" She rested her arms across her waist, her chair swinging slightly from side to side. When he didn't respond right away, she lifted her hand, hooking a finger on the dainty gold chain necklace she wore.

"Well, considering that you have one of the best security systems in town, I wondered if you'd be willing to redirect a couple of your cameras."

"Redirect them?"

Kieran nodded. "The cameras at the back are pretty much aimed only at your garage door. I was hoping that you might consider redirecting even just one of them. I mean, I understand you have your reasons for having the security you do."

She gave a single nod. "I do."

"I can probably find someone to help redirect them, if you're not able to do it yourself." He hesitated then asked, "Do you have any cameras at the front of your building?"

Then it was her turn to hesitate. She bit her lip as she regarded him for a moment before nodding. "I do, but there's only one that might be movable."

Kieran was beyond curious as to why she had so much security, but once again, he managed to keep from asking her about it. He had to admit it didn't sit too well with him that there was someone in his town who felt they needed as much security as Cara did.

"I would appreciate it, if you'd be willing. We just don't have any other leads on these thefts. It was frustrating when it was just the antique store break-in, but now that the bookstore has been robbed too, it's even more so. It's left us wondering if there is going to be yet another one." Kieran sighed and ran a hand down his face. "I'm just trying to get ahead of the game."

Cara stared at him for a few moments before she nodded. "Okay. But is there any way you could be the one to adjust the camera?"

"Uh, sure? I mean, I can't say for certain I'll be able to do it. These cameras look like some fancy ones that might require a special technician."

"At least try, please." Cara's brows drew together. "I'd rather it be someone I...know."

"Can you show me the one you think I could change the direction of?"

"Sure." She pushed back from her desk and stood. With graceful steps, she rounded the desk and headed for the door.

With a wistful look at his sandwich, Kieran closed the container so that it wouldn't dry out, then got to his feet and followed Cara. She stopped in front of the row of chairs in the waiting area, staring out the front window.

It was an overcast day, but so far, they hadn't had any rain. A couple of people walked by the window, but they didn't stop or look in. He came to stand next to her, his hands resting on his duty belt.

"Do you have any classes today?"

She gave him a quick look, then nodded. "I have a pregnancy stretching class this evening."

Kieran searched for a response to that, but as the silence stretched between them, he cleared his throat and asked, "So where are the cameras?"

"There's only one here that you'll be able to move." She pointed up to a corner opposite the door.

When he spotted it, he frowned. How had he not noticed that when he'd come in earlier? He glanced at Cara. It was as if the anticipation of asking about the cameras had distracted him from actually looking around.

He moved toward the camera, staring up to see if he could determine if it could be easily maneuvered. Glancing over to where Cara stood with her arms crossed, he asked, "Do you have a ladder?"

"Yes." She lowered her arms then turned around, heading toward an opening on the other side of the office.

She hadn't invited him to follow her, but Kieran did so anyway, not wanting her to have to carry the ladder. The short hallway was narrow but brightly lit and painted a soft lemon yellow. It dead-ended into another hallway that ran parallel to the dance studio. Both the hallways were lined with poster-sized black and white photos of ballet dancers in various poses.

Though Cara could traverse the hallway easily enough given how slender she was, Kieran had to move more cautiously so that he didn't brush against the photos. They were set behind frames that were nailed into the wall, but he wasn't sure if there was anything protecting them, and the last thing he wanted to do was to rip or mark them.

That hallway ended at a small landing that had two doors. Cara opened the one in front of her, bypassing the one behind them. Kieran noticed right away that it opened into the garage. Bright lights reflected off the small silver SUV parked there.

Cara hesitated on the threshold, her hand gripping the door frame. After a moment, she stepped through the doorway and turned to the right. Kieran followed her, glancing around to see that it was a neat and tidy space.

Turning, he saw Cara slide open a large weathered barn door. Behind it was an organized area with shelves and larger spaces to hang things like a mop, broom, and the ladder he needed.

"Here, let me get that," Kieran said as she reached for the ladder.

She glanced over at him, then moved aside. His arm brushed her shoulder as he grasped the edges of the aluminum ladder. It wasn't a super tall one, but it should get him close enough to the camera so he could see it more clearly. Once he had it out of the closet, she slid the door shut then led the way back into the hallway.

Back in the waiting area, Kieran set up the ladder then carefully climbed up. His uniform and duty belt made that a bit of a challenge, but he made it up to the step that would allow him to see the camera more clearly.

"Please try not to fall and break your leg," Cara said. "It wouldn't do much for the reputation of my studio if word got around that the police chief broke his leg while he was here."

Kieran looked down at Cara, a bit surprised to see a spark of humor in her eyes. The corners of her lips were tipped up ever so slightly. "Oh, we can't let that happen."

"Do you think you can move it?"

He turned his attention back to the camera. Reaching out, he gripped it to see if it would swivel or if he'd need to loosen something first. Thankfully, it moved surprisingly easy. "Does this one actually work?"

"What do you mean?" A concerned look crossed Cara's face. "They should all be working."

"It's just that from up here, I can see another camera that looks completely different than this one. It appears to be one that could be controlled remotely. Are you able to do that for some of them?"

Cara hesitated then nodded. "Yes, there are several that I can control, but that particular one isn't capable of viewing the outside."

Kieran could see that. The way it was set up almost made him think that it was a dummy camera to throw people off. But with Cara's assurance that it wasn't, he tried to angle it so that it would capture outside activity.

"Can we check the view?"

"Sure."

Kieran climbed down the ladder and followed Cara into the office again. He went around the desk and watched as she pulled up the feeds. The camera he'd readjusted gave a decent view of the front sidewalk and the road beyond it. He would have liked it to have a complete view of the buildings across the street, but that just wasn't possible because of where it was installed.

"These are the ones at the back by the garage," Cara said. "I can adjust one of them from here for you."

With a few clicks, she brought up a view of the lane behind the building. Kieran leaned one hand on the desk and directed Cara on where he wanted it to point. She was slow to follow what he said, and when he glanced at her, he saw that her lower lip was held between her teeth.

He reached out and covered her hand where it rested on the mouse. She froze for a moment, then took a deep breath. It was clear that she wasn't comfortable adjusting the cameras that she depended on for her security.

"What are you afraid of, Cara?" Kieran asked gently.

"Nothing," she said quickly. Harshly. Then more softly, "Nothing."

"Someone who isn't worried about something happening doesn't have this much security."

Her hand slipped from beneath his and clasped her other one in her lap. "I do suffer from a bit of...paranoia. But being a single woman, I don't think that's totally unrealistic."

Kieran stepped back then returned to the chair he'd abandoned earlier. "No, you're right, but New Hope is a pretty quiet town. Pretty safe."

She met his gaze, the concern gone now. At least from her face. There was no doubt in Kieran's mind that she had all this security because she anticipated something happening. The only reason a woman—or anyone, really—would have that much security in place was if they had either experienced a traumatic event or were anticipating one. For Cara, it might be both.

"Thank you for being willing to help me out with your cameras," Kieran said, realizing for the first time exactly how much it might actually be impacting her to let him redirect her security. "As soon as we've figured out who's behind the break-ins, you can move them back."

Cara nodded but didn't say anything, her brow was still furrowed.

"Are you hiding from something? Someone?" Kieran asked, pushing, even though he knew he probably shouldn't. "You know you can trust me, right? My job as a law enforcement officer requires me to protect people. Like the residents of New Hope. Like you."

Unfortunately, his words didn't have the effect that he'd hoped they would. They certainly didn't appear to comfort her at all. Usually, his presence was a reassurance for people. That didn't seem to be the case with Cara. And that bothered him.

"I'll just get out of your hair," Kieran said, uncertain of how to further their interaction. He'd had questions after his previous visit, and he'd hoped that coming back, he might get answers to some of them. Instead, he was leaving with those questions still unanswered and a whole bunch of new ones swirling in his mind.

He got to his feet and picked up his sandwich. Though he would have liked to stay and eat with her, he got the feeling that her tolerance of his presence was quickly reaching its end.

"Thanks again for your help."

Cara stood up as well. "You're welcome."

As a thought crossed his mind, Kieran set his sandwich container back on the desk. He pulled out his notebook and pen and jotted his name and personal cell phone number on a piece of paper before tearing it off. Putting it on the desk, he slid it toward her.

"That's my number. If anything happens, you give me a call. Night or day. Call me." He waited for her nod before picking his sandwich up again. "I'll see you around."

As he left the studio, the intrigue he'd felt for Cara continued to grow. As did the desire to do a little research about her. While he had access to all kinds of ways to search about a person, he knew that he had to limit his quest for information to the ones that the average person would have at their fingertips. Social media.

CHAPTER FIVE

Cara stared at the sandwich container on her desk. She wasn't sure what had possessed her to not only talk to the man but to agree to move her cameras.

Her gaze darted to the images that were visible on her second monitor. It was odd and slightly disconcerting to see new views on the screen. Her stomach knotted at the loss of security those cameras had given her.

It was ridiculous, she knew that. There were plenty of other cameras whose views would make up for the two cameras that had been moved, and really, the new views weren't bad. They broadened what she could see, but still, it felt wrong after having had the same views for so long.

To many people—and apparently to the police chief, as well—the number of security cameras she had was overkill. She had no idea what he would have thought if he'd seen the hand and optical scanner she had at the back of the building. Thankfully, they were set up in such a way that the average person wouldn't even notice them. Not that Kieran was in any way average, but he also probably hadn't thought to look for them.

She had a valid reason for cooperating with Kieran. Not cooperating would have raised even more red flags than were likely already flying in the man's mind. As a cop, being suspicious of things like her excessive security would be second nature. If she'd resisted helping him, he might have been even more suspicious.

Hopefully it would be a while before she'd see him again. He'd probably be back if there was another break-in that her cameras might provide help with, but otherwise, there was no reason for him to return to the studio.

She reached for the container Kieran had brought her and opened it. Normally, she ate a salad or maybe avocado toast for lunch. A sandwich from *Norma's* was a treat

Before picking up the sandwich, Cara bowed her head and prayed for her father then after a brief hesitation, she thanked God for the lunch Kieran had brought her. In the midst of the negativity swirling through her life, she tried to be thankful for the bright spots—large or small. And while she wasn't sure that Kieran was a bright spot necessarily, a lunch of her favorite sandwich certainly was.

If she'd thought she'd seen the last of New Hope's police chief, the next day, Cara discovered she was wrong.

"Has there been another break-in?" she asked when he walked into the waiting area as her mom and baby stretch class let out.

"Nope. Just brought some lunch." He lifted the bag he held. A paper bag with *Norma's* logo on it.

"You do realize that I have food, don't you?" she asked. "You don't have to keep buying me lunch."

He shrugged, and it was then that Cara realized he wasn't wearing his uniform. Instead, he wore a pair of faded jeans and a gray turtleneck sweater under a black leather jacket. It was odd to see him out of uniform, and perhaps a bit more dangerous. She'd always thought he was an attractive man, and without the reminder of his occupation, he was even more attractive.

"Um, go ahead and put it in the office. I'll be there in a couple of minutes."

Kieran looked a little surprised that she was acquiescing so easily. "Sounds good."

After the last of the women had left the studio, Cara hurried up to her apartment and pulled on a large sweatshirt then tugged on a pair of sweats. It was one thing to be in a leotard and leggings with the women, but she felt a bit awkward to be dressed like that around Kieran.

When she joined him again in the office, Kieran had set out the food he'd brought. She eyed it as she sat down across from him.

"I asked Missy what you ordered when you go in there for lunch, and she said that you usually got a salad with grilled chicken. Was she right?"

Cara nodded. "But I don't go in there that often. Maybe just once a week."

Kieran grinned, the skin at the corners of his eyes crinkling. "That's all it takes at *Norma's*. They remember their regulars."

The idea that Norma remembered that about her, even though she didn't go in there all that frequently, warmed Cara in a way she hadn't expected. Pulling the container closer, she said, "Well, thank you."

"You're very welcome."

"Has there been another break-in?" Cara asked as she opened her lunch. She emptied the salad dressing container over the salad.

"No. There's been nothing reported."

Cara paused in the process of lifting her fork to her mouth. So what was he doing there? She didn't ask him, though. Instead, she focused on the salad, even though Kieran's burger smelled divine and made her almost wish she had one.

"So where did you live before you moved here?" Kieran asked.

Cara was glad she'd had lots of practice in schooling her expression, so she didn't react to his question. Ignoring the knot in her stomach, she took another bite of her salad then said, "I'm a Midwest girl."

"Chicago?"

She gave a short nod, unable to lie to him, but not wanting to make a big deal out of it. "How about you? Have you lived here your whole life?"

"No. I was born here but moved to New York with my folks when I was ten. I just moved back here a few years ago."

"Were you a cop in New York, too?"

"Yep. I was a detective there. I joined the Sheriff's Department for the county when I came back to New Hope Falls. After my uncle passed away, they offered me the position of police chief for the substation here."

"Did you come back...on your own?"

Kieran shook his head. "My mom came back with me. Her family is here. Her brother—my uncle—was the previous police chief."

Cara found it curious that he didn't mention his father, but she didn't feel she had any right to ask. The last thing she needed was for him to turn the tables on her and begin to ask questions of her. And if there was one person she didn't want to talk to about her father, it was a cop. Not to mention having to explain how her mother had died.

She didn't like to lie to people, but there were certain things she just couldn't share. It was another reason why she didn't let people get too close. Explaining how she had no family...well, that wasn't entirely true. She had three half-brothers that she'd never met—and never would—because she'd heard her father telling someone that he thought a couple of them may have been behind the car bomb that killed her mom and should have killed Cara as well.

"Do you have siblings?" Kieran asked.

Given what she knew, Cara would never claim her father's other children as siblings, so she had no problem with that answer. "I'm an only child. You?"

"I have a brother." Kieran's gaze dropped to his sandwich, and he took another bite, looking as if he regretted having said that. Maybe she wasn't the only one reluctant to discuss certain things. "Have you always been a dancer? I saw the posters in the hallway. Were you a ballerina?"

And yet another touchy subject. It dawned on her then just how full of minefields her life was. Though the subject of dancing was complicated and nuanced, at least she could discuss some of it without revealing too much about the parts of her life she didn't want to discuss.

"I started taking ballet lessons when I was four and continued dancing until I was twenty-three. I mean, I'm still dancing, but not like I did then as part of a company."

Kieran regarded her for a moment then asked, "What made you stop?"

"The pressure." She jabbed at her salad with her fork, remembering when even a lunch like that would have caused her stress.

And pressure truly encompassed every reason she stopped dancing professionally. Pressure from being part of a particularly competitive dance company. Pressure from herself to always be her best. Internal pressure to conform to the physical standards of what she should look like as a ballet dancer. And finally, pressure from her father to remove herself from the public eye once he realized that she had also been a target of the car bomb. Not that she had really had any other options at that point.

The story had been planted that she'd been admitted to hospital only to die from her wounds. It bought them enough time for her father to get them both into hiding, and then he'd called the DA to make a deal that hopefully guaranteed them both safety in the years to come.

But there was no way she was going to tell Kieran that. Especially since she wasn't sure about his motives in coming back there that day. If it was because he was curious, the less info she gave him, the better. He hadn't gotten to where he was without being able to learn how to ask the right questions and get the information he wanted.

"Do you miss it?"

"Not really. I mean, I'm still dancing, and though I don't focus as much on ballet here, I do enough of it with teaching the little ones."

"Training the next generation of ballet dancers?"

Cara shrugged as she thought of the joy on the little faces of the kids in the classes she taught, and she kind of hoped they would never end up like she had. At this age, they seemed more interested in wearing cute leotards and skirts and spinning around with each other. The carefree abandon with which they approached the classes was perfectly fine as far as she was concerned.

"Do you miss New York?"

Kieran stared at her for a moment, then he shrugged. "Parts of it, I suppose, but this is where I needed to be."

That was how Cara felt about Chicago, though realistically, the death of her mother had not afforded her the option of staying there, or even going back. She had good memories of the city, but sadly, they were all eclipsed by what had happened to her mom.

I wish I could tell him everything.

Cara paused mid-chew, taken off-guard by the sudden thought that had careened through her mind. There had been plenty of times she'd wished she had a different life. One where her father hadn't been a mob boss and had been married to her mother. A life where her mom hadn't been killed by a car bomb planted by her half-brothers, who were bent on avenging their mother's honor. One where she could have handled the pressures better so she could have had the career she'd dreamed of since she'd been a young girl.

This was the first time she'd ever felt a desire to be able to tell someone all about her past—the good and the bad. Unfortunately, that wasn't going to happen. Because of the promises she'd made her father, it wasn't going to happen with anyone, but most especially not with a cop.

All it would take for her life to be over, was for someone to realize what they could gain by revealing where she was to certain people. Not that she'd necessarily end up dead, but she'd most certainly end up on the run, regretting her decision to confide in someone.

"So you said your mom lived here before?" Kieran asked.

Before Cara could respond, his phone rang, drawing his attention away from her. Setting his burger down, he pulled his phone out and glanced at the screen before answering it.

"Hi, Lisa. What's up?" Kieran leaned back in his seat, his gaze lowered as he listened to whoever was on the other end of the line. "Okay. I'll be there in a few minutes."

After he hung up, he returned his phone to his pocket. He glanced at her as he began to gather up his lunch. "I apologize, but I'm going to have to run. Someone needs to talk to me."

"That's okay." Cara got to her feet when Kieran did. "Thank you for bringing me lunch."

She followed him to the front door and held it open as he stepped through it.

"I'll see you again soon." It sounded like a promise, but there was a small part of her that took it as a threat. Like he was telling her that he wasn't done with his questions.

With a sigh, she let the door swing shut after he left, watching as he headed toward the police station. And then came the longing that she'd experienced earlier. The longing to just be normal. To allow herself to embrace the fact that she found Kieran Sutherland attractive. To embrace that reality and possibly do something about it.

Unfortunately, like with staying in Chicago, that didn't seem like an option for her. It was necessary for her to remember who she was and who Kieran was. No more giving information about herself and her family, no matter how innocent the questions he had for her appeared to be. And no matter how many meals from *Norma's* he brought her.

Still, as she sat back down at her desk and stared at the salad, Cara couldn't escape the feeling of how nice it was to have someone thinking about her and then doing something for her. Her mom had always been good about that, and her father, too, when he'd been around. It seemed like it had been an eternity since she had felt that sense of caring, no matter what the motives behind it might actually be.

She managed to finish the salad without allowing those thoughts to weigh her down. Instead, she focused on the less fun part of her business—her bookkeeping. So while she didn't exactly enjoy that part of her studio's operation, it was always good at holding her attention.

More enjoyable distractions were her afternoon stretching and strengthening classes. She ran six of them a week. Three afternoon sessions and three evening sessions.

There was a good mix of young and older women, which Cara really appreciated since the class was adaptable to all levels of fitness. That meant she didn't have to teach a bunch of different level classes. She enjoyed helping the women learn to properly stretch and strengthen their bodies in order to maximize their ability to move through their lives and accomplish what they needed to each day.

"Hey there, Cara," Sarah McNamara called out as she walked into the room. She wore a cheery smile and was dressed in a pair of leggings and a long-sleeve T-shirt.

"Hi." Cara smiled back at her, feeling the last of the heavy emotions that had come over her at lunch fade away. These women might not be her best friends, but they treated her like they were more than just mere acquaintances.

"This is Anna Carrington," Sarah said, motioning to the woman at her side. "She's been staying at the lodge, and somehow ended up as Eli's girlfriend."

Anna laughed and smiled at Cara. "Somehow."

"Well, it's nice to meet you, Anna. I'm Cara."

Anna took the hand Cara held out to her. "It's nice to meet you too. Are you sure it's okay for me to join the class?"

"The more, the merrier," Cara assured her.

"Just give me a spot in the back, so when I have to stop for a break because I've been eating too much of Nadine and Norma's wonderful food, I don't embarrass myself."

"You don't have to worry about that," Sarah said. "Cara lets us all proceed at our own pace. Believe me, the first few classes, we were *all* dying. I didn't know how difficult stretching and strengthening could be."

Anna turned to look at Sarah. "Did you actually want me to *stay* for this class? Because I'm having second, third, and fourth thoughts when you say stuff like that."

"Oh, you'll be fine," Cara told her. "Sarah's still coming, so obviously it does get easier."

"Does Leah come?" Anna asked Sarah.

The other woman laughed. "Yeah. That would be a big no."

Cara had seen Leah a lot over the course of the four years she'd lived in New Hope, but Leah seemed to avoid interacting with people with the same level of intensity that her twin sister sought them out. Both Norma and Nadine, Sarah's mom and Norma's twin sister, had popped into her classes. They weren't regulars, but they showed up every few weeks. She would have liked to see them there more frequently, but she knew they were busy.

Once the time for the start of class approached, Cara went to the front of the room and called for attention. The women quickly found spots and faced the front, smiling at her in a way that elevated that feeling of having connections in her life, regardless of how shallow they were.

She just had to remind herself—on a daily or hourly basis, if needed—that that could...would be enough.

CHAPTER SIX

"I hear you've been by the dance studio."

Kieran looked up from the roast chicken he was carving. "Where did you hear that?"

His mom hesitated, her gaze sliding away for a moment. "Uh. Mary?"

"Let me guess. She was at Norma's and saw me or something."

His mom shrugged. "Were you there?"

"Yep." He put pieces of chicken on the platter that his mom had set next to him on the counter. "I was asking her about something pertaining to the break-ins in town."

"Two days in a row?"

Kieran sighed. "Yes. Two days in a row."

"For lunch each day?"

"Yes, Mom, for lunch." He carried the roast over to the small table that was set for their dinner. "It was a good time to catch her since she has classes at other times during the day."

His mom sat down in her usual spot. "That's Cara, right?"

"Yes, her name is Cara."

"Mary said she's nice. Is she?"

"I haven't spent much time with her," Kieran said as he poured water into each of their glasses. "But she seems nice. I would imagine she wouldn't have much of a business if she wasn't."

His mom stopped her questioning long enough to say thanks for the food, but Kieran knew better than to assume she was done. She was the human equivalent of a dog they'd had when he was growing up. Whenever their little Bichon, Rosabelle, brought her ball and dropped it at their feet, they knew they were in for an endless round of fetch. And there was no sense in trying to stop the game because it wasn't over until Rosabelle sank down on her bed and conked out.

It was the same with his mom. She wouldn't drop the subject until she was good and ready to. And that was especially true when it came to a woman. She was bound and determined to see him married with children. It wasn't that Kieran was averse to the idea, but since his engagement had ended before his return to New Hope Falls, he was a bit gun shy.

Plus, he'd been focused on the job since coming back, not on finding a wife. No woman he'd met during his time back in New Hope Falls had been interesting enough to distract him from work. Until Cara.

"So do you think you might ask her out on a date?"

Kieran knew better than to give his mom even an ounce of hope. She had taken his broken engagement almost as hard as he had. She'd loved his fiancée and had had great hopes of them marrying and having children. In the space of six months, she'd lost her youngest son, her husband, and then her dreams of having a daughter-in-law and grandchildren.

"Right now, dating isn't an option."

And it wasn't. No matter how interested he might be, he needed to be careful. He didn't think he'd imagined the wariness in Cara's interactions with him. She had been reluctant to allow him too close.

"But you need to start dating again soon," his mother insisted. "You can't just stop living because of what happened with Toni."

"I've hardly stopped living, Mom." Kieran plopped a spoonful of mashed potatoes on his plate. "You know that I've needed to focus on my job since taking over. We might not have a lot of crime around here, but I do have plenty of other responsibilities."

"Your father had lots of responsibilities, but he still made time for me."

Kieran wasn't going to argue with her about that, even though he didn't really think that his dad had given priority to his wife or his sons. His job had definitely come first, and a lot of days, it had felt to Kieran like his buddies on the force had come second. Several times a week, he'd gone out for drinks after his shift, while his wife and kids waited for him at home.

It was probably why his mom had devoted so much of her time to her sons. He loved her for that, but at the same time, he felt badly for her. He was aware that no one deserved anything—good or bad—in their life, but there was a big part of him that felt that his mom deserved more than what she'd ended up with.

Unfortunately, if anyone had stopped living, it was his mom. She lived in the small house that had been left to her when her brother—the previous police chief—had died of a heart attack. The only times she left the house were to attend church and to sometimes go to her friend Mary's house. He came to have dinner with her three or four times a week, and he took care of anything she needed done around the house.

Other than that, his once social mom stayed holed up in the house. She was better now than when they'd first returned from New York, but at any given time, he was more likely to find her at home than out doing stuff. She read lots and had her favorite shows on television. Somewhere along the line, she'd taken up quilting and had figured out how to order the fabric she wanted online, so she didn't even need to leave the house for that.

"All I'm saying is that I want you to have someone," his mom said, her words soft and tremulous.

It wasn't that he didn't want that for himself, but at the same time, he'd already thought he'd found his someone only to have the relationship fall apart. There would be no guarantee that if he found another someone that she wouldn't walk away too. Maybe he was doing himself and any potential dates a favor by staying single.

"I'm fine, Mom. I'm trusting that if God has someone for me, He'll make it clear to both me and to her that it's His will for us to enter into relationship. In the meantime, I will continue to live my life as I have been."

His mom sighed, then nodded. She wouldn't argue with that since she'd been the one to always teach him and Sean to trust God. Even though his dad had rarely gone to church, his mom had remained true to the faith she'd been raised with and had tried her best to raise her sons to have faith in God as well. Sadly, he and Sean hadn't always been receptive to her efforts in their younger years.

By the time he left, he was ready to call it a day. Even though he only lived a block away, he drove home since he'd driven his car downtown earlier that day, before coming to his Mom's. His house was a rental since he hadn't yet found a house that he wanted to buy. Not that New Hope Falls had a lot of options that fit his budget, but he held out hope that a house he liked and could afford would come available one of these days.

In the meantime, the two-bedroom single story ranch style house was more than adequate. As he approached it, he pressed the button to open his garage. Once parked, he entered the house through the mudroom. There was a bedroom to the right that served as an office of sorts with a chair, a desk, and a printer. He tended to use his laptop while in the recliner or in bed, so the office didn't get much use.

He made his way to his bedroom and gathered up his laundry, then carried it to the laundry room just off the kitchen. After he'd loaded the washer, he turned on the television to break up the silence. With the sound of *Bluebloods* playing on the TV, he finished cleaning up the kitchen.

Realistically, he shouldn't have much cleaning to do since he lived alone, but he had a bad habit of putting it off until it had piled up more than it should have. On any given day, he would have preferred to be outside, mowing the grass or pulling weeds. Not scraping food off plates before putting them in the dishwasher.

By the time he was done, it was time to switch over his laundry. Then he was ready to settle into his recliner with a cup of decaf coffee and his laptop. His attention was half on the television and half on the laptop's screen.

So far, his searches through social media for Cara's information had been fruitless. That made him even more curious because, in this day and age, who didn't have at least one account? Okay, so maybe Eli McNamara didn't, but his girlfriend, Arianna Carrington-Harder, certainly made up for it by having a huge social media following.

He considered that for a moment...the reason why Eli didn't have a social media presence. That made sense given his situation as a person of interest in the disappearance of his high school girlfriend ten years earlier. So did that mean that Cara had a reason like that to keep herself off social media?

That idea sank into Kieran's brain, and he knew he was going to have to fight *hard* not to plug her name into a few searches at the station. He had no reason other than purely personal curiosity. She hadn't given him any legal reason to delve into her life or her background. Until it came to that point, he wouldn't cross that line.

That decision, however, didn't clear his mind of thoughts of Cara. He could still see her soft gray eyes, watching him. Unreadable, but not completely closed off. She might be hiding parts of her life from him—from people in general—but she wasn't totally removed from the town where she'd made her life.

Kieran's attention came back to the present in time to see the credits roll on the large television in front of him. He'd have to watch the show again another time to see how the episode ended.

With a sigh, he used the remote to shut off the television then pushed up out of the recliner. He took his empty coffee mug into the kitchen and added it to the other dirty dishes in the dishwasher before turning it on. He pulled his laundry out of the dryer hanging up the shirts he'd need to iron before he wore them. Ironing was yet another chore he wasn't thrilled to have to do, but it was a necessary evil considering his profession.

As he crawled into bed a short time later, he resolved to keep his distance from Cara. He needed to not be distracted from other things, like the interview he was going to have to sit through with the detective from Everett the next day.

Three days later, he found himself back at the dance studio. He'd eaten his lunch at *Norma's* while sitting in a booth that overlooked the street and also the studio. When he was done, he made his way across the street, hoping Cara would be available. There hadn't been any sign of movement through the glass window while he ate, but he decided to take a chance on her availability anyway.

When he reached the door, he tugged on the handle, but it didn't move. He rapped on the glass and waited, hoping he'd see her come out from her office. When she didn't appear after the second time he knocked, Kieran stared at the window. It took him a couple of seconds to focus in on the small black numbers under the shadow dancers on the glass.

He pulled his phone out and punched the number in before lifting the phone to his ear. It rang twice before Cara's voice came over the line with the name of her studio.

"Hey, Cara, this is Kieran."

"Kieran?"

"Uh, yeah. Kieran Sutherland."

There was a whisper of a laugh before she said, "I know who you are. I was just surprised you had this number."

"It's on your window," he pointed out.

"So it is." She paused. "What can I do for you, Chief?"

"I need another look at your camera footage, if you have the time."

"Was there another break-in?"

"No. This is something different."

"Okay?"

"Are you in your office?"

"Not at the moment. I'm upstairs in my apartment."

"Would you have a few minutes now, or should I come back later?"

"Are you downstairs?"

"Yep. I'm loitering around in front of your door."

"Isn't there a law against that?"

Kieran laughed. "Not that I'd tell you about. I'd hate to have to ask one of my guys to arrest me."

He could have sworn she giggled before saying, "I'll be right down."

Kieran hung up then turned around when he heard someone call his name. He lifted his hand in greeting before the older man headed into *Norma's*, hoping that the news that he was once again at the dance studio didn't get back to his mom. She hadn't brought the subject up when he'd been at her house for dinner the previous night, but that didn't mean she wouldn't pick it up again.

"Kieran?"

He swung back around to see Cara standing with the door open. Her hair was down, and she wore a light pink turtleneck sweater, and her long legs were encased in a pair of fitted black jeans. No matter what she wore, she looked like a dancer and moved with graceful steps.

"Hey."

"C'mon in." Cara stepped back as he walked toward her.

Once he was inside the waiting area, she pulled the door closed and turned the lock. With a nod of her head, she walked toward the office.

"So, what are we looking for this time if it's not a break-in?" she asked once she'd settled in front of her monitor.

"Did you happen to hear anything yesterday afternoon?"

"Hear anything?"

"Apparently there was a run-in between a couple of cars out in front of your studio."

She looked over at him, her eyebrows raised. "This is about a car accident?"

Kieran sighed. "Yeah. Two of our elderly residents tried to occupy the same space with their vehicles. Unfortunately, they're each blaming the other for the mishap, and I'm getting conflicting statements from witnesses. I'm hoping for video proof of what actually happened, so I don't have to rely on those witnesses."

Cara was still staring at him with a look akin to bewilderment. "You need footage to determine which of two elderly people is at fault in a car accident?"

"Actually, more like a bumper tap."

She laughed then, giving a small shake of her head. "Do these crimes keep you awake at night, Chief?"

"Oh, you know it." Kieran leaned back in his chair, lacing his fingers across his stomach. "I'm up 'til all hours trying to solve them."

"Good to know," she said with a smile. "So what time of day are you looking at?"

Kieran gave her the approximate time then waited as she brought up the footage on the screen. When she angled the monitor toward him, he sat forward to watch the scene play out. As he'd suspected, the parked car had pulled into the path of the oncoming vehicle. The driver of the parked car had vehemently denied being in the wrong. It wasn't a big deal, and he could have solved it eventually, but having video evidence would just bring the altercation to an end that much quicker.

"Can you send me the file with that footage?" Kieran asked.

Cara's brows drew together for a moment. "I've never done that before, but I'll see if I can figure it out."

"I might have a tech guy that could help you out if need be."

She shook her head without hesitation. "No. I'll figure it out."

Knowing that she was touchy about her security, Kieran decided to just let her handle it. It wasn't like this was a murder that required timely information in order to solve it. Maybe if she had a problem with it, she'd call him, and he could come back again.

No...nope. He wasn't supposed to be thinking that way about her.

"Well, if you change your mind, just let me know."

"I will," Cara said. "Was there anything else?"

"No." Kieran pulled his legs in and got to his feet, knowing he shouldn't linger. "Thanks for your help with this."

"You're welcome." Cara tapped a few more keys then stood up. As they walked to the front door, she said, "Maybe the town needs to invest in some CCTV cameras to help settle disputes and solve break-ins."

"You might have a point. I might bring that up to the mayor and the town council at our next meeting."

"Really?" Cara sounded surprised he was taking her suggestion seriously.

"Why not? It seems like crime is picking up around here."

"One can never have too many cameras."

Given the number she had, Kieran figured that perhaps that was her life's motto. He said goodbye then headed back toward his office, inordinately proud of the fact that he'd managed to not only *not* buy her lunch, but that he'd left without spending too much time with her. Certainly not as much time as he'd wanted.

He made his way down the sidewalk toward the station, greeting people as he walked. He wondered how many of the people knew Cara by name. She'd been in New Hope a few years now. That should have been enough time for people to get to know her, provided she'd been willing to let people get that close to her.

Of course, in the years since she'd been there, he hadn't gotten to know her. That was changing now, though. She was a member of his town, and he planned to treat her like he did every other resident of New Hope Falls.

CHAPTER SEVEN

Cara stared at the monitor and tried to figure out how to save just the one section of the video. She'd googled it but found nothing helpful. In the end, she just saved the day's video since she'd been able to figure that much out. Unfortunately, the file was too big to send to the email address Kieran had given her.

Finally, she went upstairs and dug through her junk drawer to find a USB drive. Once she found one, she went back down to her office, transferred the file from her computer to the drive, then debated what to do with the drive. She could call Kieran to come back and get it, but she was finding that having him in her space was a little too enjoyable.

Maybe it was time to take a little more control by going to his place of work. Then she could leave when she wanted to.

Mind made up, she went upstairs again and changed her shoes, switching out her flats for a pair of boots. She grabbed a jacket then left the studio, arming the alarm before locking the door.

Standing in front of the studio, she glanced around, taking note of the vehicles parked on the street and the people walking on the sidewalk. It was something she did each time she left the studio. It had become a habit over the past few years, but if anyone had asked her what she was actually looking for, she wasn't sure she could have answered them. A car with an out-of-state license plate? A guy that looked like a mafia goon? Someone with a gun?

She hoped that it would be something like that, but in truth, it was more likely to be something—someone—a lot more subtle. If...when...someone found her, she, in all likelihood, wouldn't see them coming until it was too late. All she hoped was that no one else was caught in the crossfire.

With a sigh, she gripped the USB drive more tightly in her hand and headed down the sidewalk. She got a whiff of freshly baked pastries when the door of the bakery swung open as she passed by. The two young women who walked out gave her friendly smiles before turning and walking in the opposite direction.

She loved Main Street, and right then, she was glad she'd made the decision to come to New Hope Falls. Settling in a large city might have allowed her to get lost in the crowd, but she would have felt that she had lost a part of herself as well. Being in New Hope Falls might not allow her to blend in, but now, a few years after moving there, she was surrounded by familiar faces even if she couldn't put a name to all those faces.

The beauty of the town and its warmth enveloped her, making her feel like she was a part of it even though she kept herself at a bit of a distance. It was like the town didn't care how she might hold herself apart, it was going to surround and embrace her, regardless. She knew the cadence of the town, the flow of its lifeblood. The town was adorned in the beauty of autumn colors with fall flowers and the changing trees.

A breeze swept over Cara from behind, causing her to shove her hands into the pockets of her jacket and lift her shoulders. She quickened her steps, and when she reached the station, she pulled the door open without any hesitation.

The woman seated behind the reception desk looked at her over the narrow rectangle-shaped glasses she wore. With a practiced move, she removed them and shoved them into the pile of curls on top of her head.

"Hello, there," she said with a smile. "You're Cara, right? From the dance studio?"

In the months following her arrival, observations like that would have freaked her out, but now she just smiled and nodded. As she approached the desk, she said, "Is Ki—the chief in?"

The woman's eyebrows rose slightly. "Sure. I'll just let him know you're here."

She picked up the phone on her desk and relayed the information that Cara was there then hung up. "I'm Lisa, by the way."

Cara shook the hand the woman held out to her. "Nice to meet you."

"So," Lisa began. "Do you have a place in your dance studio for someone like me?"

"Someone like you?" Cara asked, trying to figure out what, in particular, the woman might be referring to.

"You know....old, out of shape."

Cara smiled. "First of all, you're not old, and second, if you feel you're out of shape, don't let that hold you back. I don't run aerobic-style classes. My classes are more about stretching and strengthening."

"Yoga?" Lisa asked.

"No, not per se. My classes aren't focused on meditation or anything like that, though I do play nice spa music as we stretch. My goal is to help build flexibility and also to help women strengthen their core. Being limber and strong in the core helps to prevent injuries."

"Huh. So no dancing?"

"Oh, I do have dance classes, but they're for kids, mostly. I knew that I wanted a place that was more than just dance, so I took a bunch of courses to learn about the muscles in our body and how to take care of them."

"So maybe you do have a place for someone like me."

"Women of all ages and shapes come to my classes. There's probably only two of the adult classes you wouldn't qualify for."

Lisa arched a brow. "What would those be?"

"Those would be my pre and post-natal classes."

The other woman laughed. "Oh yes. I'm so far post-natal, I barely remember the natal part."

Cara couldn't help but join in her laughter. "So anyway, aside from those two classes and the kids dance classes, you're welcome at any of the others."

"Do you have a website or a Facebook page?"

"Just a simple website with class descriptions, times, and prices. You can look it up with the studio name."

"I'll do that," Lisa assured her.

A nearby door opened, and Cara turned to see Kieran walking toward them. He gave her a curious look as he smiled. "Hey there. Did you want to come on back?"

"No. I gotta get back to the studio, but I wanted to bring this to you." She held out the USB drive. "I wasn't able to download just that portion of the video you wanted, and the whole day's footage created a file that was too big to email, so I put it on this drive."

He took the drive from her, his fingers brushing against hers for a moment. "Thank you. I really appreciate you bringing this to me."

"No problem. Hope it solves the case."

The smile lines in his cheeks deepened as he laughed. "In my mind, it was already solved, but the people involved are disputing it." He lifted the USB drive. "This will help settle it for all."

"Can I be there when you show them the footage?" Lisa asked, humor lacing her words.

Kieran turned to her. "Well, of course. And I'll leave it to you to set up a room for all of them to come in and see it."

"Oh, goodie." Lisa rubbed her hands together. "Consider it done."

When Kieran looked back at her, Cara could see laughter dancing in his eyes. She found she liked that about him. It reminded her of the light-hearted moments she'd had with her dad before everything had gone so horribly wrong. She'd loved to make her dad laugh, to see his eyes dance the way Kieran's were.

She couldn't help but think that in a different world, her dad might have liked Kieran. But sadly, being on opposite sides of the law made them natural enemies. She'd often wondered if her dad would make different decisions in his life, if he'd had the chance. In the end, he'd given up his freedom to ensure her safety, so maybe he would have.

"Well, I'd better head back to the studio," Cara said, feeling a need to get away from the direction her thoughts were headed, fueled by the closeness to Kieran.

"Thanks again for dropping this by."

"You're welcome." She gave him a smile, then turned her attention to Lisa. "And if you ever feel like attending a class, you can just drop-in to try it out."

"I might take you up on that," Lisa said. "Goodness knows I could probably use it."

After saying goodbye to the two of them, Cara left the station. That hadn't gone as expected, she mused as she made her way down the sidewalk, her hands once again tucked into her pockets. So much for hoping that going to the station would give her control of their interaction.

Well, she had been able to leave when she wanted, but in the meantime, she'd discovered one more thing that she found attractive about the man. She didn't want that. Her goal was to put more distance between them, but that hadn't really happened.

Feeling a bit frustrated with herself and the situation, Cara made a quick decision and headed toward the door of the bakery. She wasn't one to indulge too often in sugary drinks and treats, but she felt in definite need right then.

"Hi Cara." The woman behind the bakery counter greeted her with a smile.

"Hello, Cecelia." Cara returned her greeting then glanced down at the glass-covered shelves.

"Looking for something in particular?"

"Not really. Just wanted something...sweet."

"We have fresh cinnamon buns or brownies. But I'm partial to the macarons."

"Oh, those sound good," Cara said as she bent to look at the flavor labels.

Though she probably should only have gotten a couple, she ended up getting a dozen of them, plus a mocha latte. She told herself she was helping to support the local businesses. Anything to justify the huge number of calories she was planning to ingest.

After paying, she said goodbye to Cecelia and made her way back to the studio, sipping on her latte. Once inside, she climbed the stairs to her apartment and set her sweet treats on the table by the large front windows. After removing her boots and hanging up her jacket, she settled herself in a comfortable chair at the table.

Staring out the window, she watched the traffic on Main Street. She took small sips of her latte as she rested her elbows on the table. A part of her really wanted to write about everything that was going on with Kieran in the journal she was working on for her dad. However, she wasn't sure that would be a good idea. In spite of everything, she knew her dad wanted her to find a life partner. To find a love like the one he'd shared with her mom. However, she had a feeling he'd prefer it not be with a law enforcement officer.

Instead, she picked up the pen and began to describe in as much detail as she could the beauty of the fall season, the delicious taste of the latte, her visit to the bakery, and the delicate flavors of the macarons she'd picked up. She wrote about the classes she'd had taught so far that week, then gave her dad some details about the dances she was creating for the Christmas recital. As she wrote, she sipped on her drink and ate a few of the macarons.

When the alarm on her phone beeped, she got up and went to get changed. She had a class at four o'clock that included girls ages eight to ten. It was probably her favorite age group to teach because they had more control of their bodies than the younger girls did, and most of them had an appreciation for ballet and a desire to improve.

Those ages were also a time in her life she remembered quite clearly. In fact, some of her best childhood memories came from those years. That was the period of her life before she realized that her parents weren't married and that her father was a mafia boss. Everything had seemed so much simpler then. Ballet had still been fun. Her mom had been her best friend. Her papa doted on her whenever he came home.

She'd had no idea about how complicated her world actually was. That knowledge had come later, and it had left her confused and angry. She was glad that she'd moved past her anger so that she and her mother had become close again in the years before her mom's death. It would have devastated her to lose either of her parents while she'd still been so angry.

After Cara had dressed in a black leotard, tights, and a gauzy wrap skirt that ended just above her knees, she went to her mirror and quickly put her hair up in the bun she wore when teaching. The only jewelry she wore was a gold necklace with three small diamond encrusted interlocking hearts that her dad had bought for her after her mother's death.

Finally, she touched up the foundation she always wore on the inside of her wrists. When she was satisfied that it covered the skin there, she put on her satin ballet slippers then headed downstairs to the studio.

With a little over an hour to go until the first students arrived, Cara pulled up a YouTube video on her phone. One of the things she missed from her time with the ballet company was the daily class. Thankfully, there were several ballet companies who participated in World Ballet Day each year by streaming their company class, among other things. It meant she could warm up using a video from different companies like The Royal Ballet in London or The Australian Ballet in Melbourne.

A few times a week, usually before her classes with the older girls, Cara followed along with different videos. It was easy to get lost in the memory of the times she'd attended the daily classes at her own company. The live piano accompaniment. The class teacher's instruction guiding the class through positions and movements.

Plié. Tendu. Soutenu. Glissade. All terms that were as familiar to her as breathing. Though the instructions from the teacher might not make sense to people outside the ballet world, they were perfectly clear to her, allowing her to move through the class without hesitation.

Some days, she even put on her pointe shoes, though that wasn't as frequent since wearing them was not as comfortable as it had once been. The callouses she'd built up while wearing the pointe shoes on an almost daily basis weren't as thick as they'd once been, plus the muscles required for dancing en pointe weren't as strong as when she'd worked with the ballet company.

Still, she loved stepping back into that world, even if it was by way of a YouTube video, and when her hour was up, she felt limber and in the right mindset to teach her class.

She'd barely unlocked the door when the first of her students arrived with her mother. School had ended at three-thirty, so most the girls came directly from school. It sometimes meant that they had a little extra energy to burn, but the four o'clock time seemed to be what worked best for the moms, so Cara accommodated them.

"Hi, Miss Cara," a little girl with dark hair and bright blue eyes called out excitedly as she walked in, holding her mom's hand.

Cara smiled at her, then greeted her mother. She repeated the greeting several more times until all the girls had arrived. Cara allowed the mothers to sit in on the class as long as they didn't interrupt. So far, they'd all been really good about just watching and keeping conversation to a minimum.

Once everyone was in the mirrored room, Cara had the girls line up at the barre and began to have them go through their warm-up exercises—a less intense version of how she'd warmed up earlier. Music played softly in the background as they followed her instructions. She walked up and down the line, correcting posture or positioning, and offering words of encouragement.

The class was only an hour in length, and it went by quite quickly as she began to teach them the choreography for the Christmas recital. The girls were so excited about it, and their mothers appeared to be excited as well. Cara was happy to see that as it made her job easier.

When the class was over, the girls ran to their mothers. As one mom spun her daughter around, dancing with her, a bolt of grief stabbed Cara in the heart, robbing her of breath for a moment. Her hand went to her necklace, pressing it into her skin as she wrapped her other hand around her wrist.

On trembling legs, she made her way over to where she'd left her phone after she'd pulled up the music she'd needed for the class. She took several deep breaths and willed away the emotion that was threatening to engulf her as she tried to compose herself to say goodbye to the class. Hearing voices nearing where she stood, she forced a smile and turned to face them.

It didn't take long for the studio to empty out, and then she was alone with her thoughts. Alone with her grief and struggling to breathe past the tightness in her chest.

She hated how, even after all these years, the grief could still catch her off-guard. She knew part of this was the fear that her father was facing his final days, and the memory of loss had risen up within her once again.

Without even realizing it, her steps took her back into the studio. She stared down at her phone for a moment before pulling up the one song that allowed her to pour out all her emotions. To purge the grief in the only way she knew how so that she could breathe again.

She set the phone down and moved to the center of the room. Head bent, she let the opening chords of *Without You* wash over her, then as Mariah Carey's voice came through the speakers hidden in the room, surrounding her with music, Cara let go. She moved her body, letting her emotions and her tears push up through her movements to meet the music. To meet it then draw it into herself.

The song had spoken to her in the days following her mother's death when she hadn't known how she'd be able to go on without her. She had managed it, but now she was facing another loss, one that would cut as deeply as her mother's death had. And then she would well and truly be alone.

As the last strains of the song faded away, Cara sank to her knees. Wrapping her arms across her waist, she leaned forward. Her breaths came in harsh, ragged inhales and exhales. When the pain in her chest eased enough that she could take a deep breath, she straightened and began to rub frantically at the foundation on the inside of her wrists.

Finally, enough had been rubbed away that she could see what she was searching for. On each wrist, she had the words *I love you* tattooed in black ink. The words on her left wrist were in her father's handwriting, and on her right, they were in her mother's.

She didn't hide the tattoos because she was ashamed of them, but she didn't feel the need to share them with the world. Their meaning was for her and her alone. Staring at them, she was reminded of all the things her parents had wanted for her. And they would never have wanted her to stop living her life because they weren't around anymore.

No, after all they'd done for her, she owed them a life lived well. She may have constraints on what she could do, but what she couldn't do was to allow grief to stop her from living.

Cara pressed her wrists to her cheek as she whispered, "I love you, too."

CHAPTER EIGHT

As he stared at the USB on his desk, Kieran acknowledged that he was looking for any excuse to go see Cara again.

He'd heard her tell Lisa about the studio's website, and when he'd gotten back to his desk, he'd looked it up and noticed that she had a class at four but then nothing else scheduled afterward. Deciding it would be the perfect time to return the USB drive since he'd transferred the video file over to his computer already, he'd left the station a little before five after telling Lisa he wouldn't be back.

As he walked down the sidewalk, he saw the students and their mothers leaving the studio. He stopped to talk to the wife of one of the guys who worked at the station, then he approached the studio. He thought maybe the door would be locked, but it opened when he pulled on the handle, so he took that as a sign.

Cara wasn't in the waiting area, and he was just about to call out her name when he heard music start playing. He hesitated for a couple of moments then followed the sound to the door of the studio.

Kieran didn't know what he expected, but it wasn't to have his heart broken by the grief that poured out of Cara as she danced. He wasn't prepared to witness such grace and beauty in the midst of such heartrending passion.

He wanted to go to her and gather her into his arms. Her obvious pain and the song she danced to reached deep into his heart and touched him at the very core of his being. He knew in that moment that she'd suffered loss the way he'd suffered loss.

A loss that had shattered her heart the way his had been shattered, and the pieces hadn't yet all been fitted back into their rightful places. He didn't know what had shattered her, but just knowing that something had, made him want to protect her, to make sure that nothing hurt her that way again.

As the song had come to an end, he backed away from the doorway as quietly as he could, then after a brief hesitation he left the studio. But leaving didn't still the turbulent emotions within him.

"Chief? You okay?"

Kieran looked up and saw one of his men standing a few feet away, concern on his face. No doubt, he'd been trying to figure out why his boss was standing on the sidewalk, staring down at the concrete surface.

"Yeah. I'm fine." Kieran gave him a smile that felt weak but that he hoped didn't appear that way. "Just heading home."

The man's brow furrowed, but he didn't comment on the fact that Kieran's Jeep was parked in front of the station a block away. "See you tomorrow."

"Yep. Have a good evening."

After the man had walked away, Kieran looked in the direction of the station and his vehicle, but he found he wasn't ready to go home just yet. Instead, he decided to go to *Norma's* to get some dinner. Mary was joining his mom for supper that night, so he was on his own. Rather than cook for himself—and then have to clean up afterward—he decided to let someone else take care of feeding him.

Norma greeted him with a welcoming smile when he walked in. Thankfully, the restaurant wasn't too busy, so he was able to sit in a booth along the front where he had a clear view of Main Street.

"Do you ever take a break from watching the town," Norma asked as she handed him a menu.

"Kinda hard to get a break when I'm still in town." Kieran wasn't going to admit that he was actually keeping an eye on a particular part of town that day.

Norma patted his shoulder. "Well, I'll leave ya to it."

Missy appeared to take his order, placing a glass of water in front of him. "Meatloaf and mashed for you?"

"You know it. Heaven forbid, I'm anything but predictable."

"Brace yourself," she said with a grin. "Mom's looking to add a few more items to the menu."

"Oh really? Is she looking for ideas?"

Missy shrugged. "Not sure, but you can always try."

"Well, if she needs a taste-tester, I volunteer."

"I'll pass that on to her, but in the meantime, I'll get your meatloaf."

Kieran looked out toward the studio, but there was no sign of movement in or out of the building. The windows of the second floor gleamed in such a way that he couldn't see through them, and he doubted that with all the security Cara had, that she would have installed windows that gave the outside world a glimpse into her home.

He thought about calling her to see if she was home so he could drop the USB drive off, but honestly, he was feeling a little raw, and he had no doubt that she was as well. He'd try again the next day. In the meantime, he tucked the memory of those moments he'd watched Cara dance into his heart, knowing that it had been a precious gift that she hadn't intended for him, but one that he would forever cherish regardless.

When he got back to home, Kieran felt an unusual restlessness. He roamed the house, looking for things to do. Laundry. Dishes. He even cleaned the bathroom. When he couldn't find anything else to do, he dropped down into his recliner and stared blankly at the show playing on his television. He'd turned it on to help break up the silence in the house, but he really wasn't interested in watching it.

Truthfully, he wasn't interested in much of anything but Cara right then. Needing a distraction from the thoughts that had followed him from the doorway of Cara's studio, Kieran pulled out his phone and opened up his Facebook app. It wasn't often that he went on his account, but occasionally he posted pictures of the scenery around New Hope.

He'd barely begun to skim his timeline when it felt as if he'd been hit in the heart for the second time that day. Though he'd known that this day would come, he hadn't expected to feel the impact of it the way he just had.

He wasn't connected to his ex-fiancée on any of his social media accounts anymore, but they still had mutual friends, and the congratulations of those friends to Toni on her recent engagement were bleeding all over his timeline. It was actually something of a surprise to Kieran that it had taken her so long to get to this point again. He'd assumed awhile ago that she'd probably moved on to another relationship, but now it was there for his own eyes to see.

The ache in his chest intensified as he dropped his head back against the recliner. He closed his eyes and let out a long breath. It wasn't that he still loved her. Those feelings had faded over the past few years until they'd finally disappeared altogether. It was rare that she entered his thoughts unless his mom mentioned her.

What hurt was that getting engaged to her hadn't just been about making a statement that they were going to get married, it had been about moving on to the next part of his life. The part where he'd have a wife and kids. It was what he'd wanted. He'd hoped to fill the roles of husband and father better than his own dad had.

So when she'd ended their engagement, she hadn't just shut down their relationship but had also robbed him of the dream he'd had for them. He'd asked her so many times before they'd gotten serious—and even right before they'd gotten engaged—if she really could handle being a cop's wife. She'd assured him over and over that she could. That she loved him enough that she'd accept his job even with its dangers.

But then his father had been killed in the line of duty, and the reality of it had been brought home in a harsh way. She'd seen his grief, but more than that, she'd seen his mother grieve the loss of her husband. At some point in all of that, Toni had apparently put herself into his mom's shoes and decided that wasn't a journey she wanted to take with him.

Kieran had no idea what the man she was now going to marry did for a living, but he was willing to bet it was a safe job. One where she'd never get a call saying he'd taken a bullet during an armed stand-off with some gang members. Or one where she'd never hear that her husband had died a hero trying to rescue a child from a burning building. No, her husband-to-be was probably someone who sat behind a desk for eight hours a day, then went home at the end of the day with nothing more serious than a paper cut.

Not everyone was cut out to be the spouse of the people who served in dangerous professions, Kieran knew that. He just wished that Toni had figured that out before they had gotten so deeply involved with each other. Before they'd begun to plan a future to-gether.

He still didn't know how to find a woman who'd be willing to accept the risks that came with his job. Things were safer in New Hope Falls than they'd been in New York, but that didn't mean that some of the crime wouldn't spill over from the larger cities around them.

Kieran pushed up out of his recliner and went to his room to change into his running clothes. Though it was already dark, he knew his running route well enough that it didn't matter. There was a bit of a chill that late in the day, so he pulled on a windbreaker with reflective strips on it before leaving his house.

As he ran down the familiar streets, passing in and out of puddles of light cast by the overhead streetlamps, Kieran tried to blank out his thoughts. Tried to mask the pain in his chest by pushing himself to the point where the ache could be passed off as the strain of trying to draw breath while exerting himself.

Normally, he kept his runs to around forty-five minutes in length, but he passed his usual turning point and kept going. He ran like the past was chasing him, or maybe he was trying to catch an elusive future that he wasn't sure would ever be his.

When he finally dragged himself back through his door, he had been through sixty minutes of intense exertion, and he barely had the strength left in his legs to get through his shower. Thankfully, the run achieved what he'd hoped, and when he fell into bed a short time later, his body's exhaustion overrode his brain and pulled him into sleep quite quickly.

Unfortunately, he didn't stay asleep. Several times during the night, he woke with a start, the ache in his chest still there. In between full wakings had been plenty of tossing and turning. It was the worst night he'd had in quite some time.

When his alarm finally went off, Kieran knew he was going to pay the price for his hard workout and his restless night. His legs ached as he got out of bed, and he felt a general weakness in his body, but that was nothing compared to the ache that still pulsed in his heart.

"You look like you should be home in bed," Lisa said with an assessing look when he walked into the office a short time later. "You sick?"

"No, not sick. Just overdid it on my workout and didn't sleep very well."

She shook her head. "You need to remember you aren't as young as you used to be. I mean, you're still younger than me, but since everyone in this office is, that doesn't say much."

"Gotta stay in shape," Kieran told her. "I don't want to be the one left behind if we have to chase down a perp."

Lisa laughed. "Please make sure I'm around if that ever happens."

"It's too early for this." Kieran ran a hand down his face. "I need the coffee pot."

"Lucky for you, I made the coffee this morning, so it's not going to taste like that swill the boys like."

"Thank you, Lisa. You know I appreciate your fine touch with the coffee machine even if the other guys don't."

"You're welcome." He was heading for the door leading to the back of the building when she called after him. "Don't forget that detective is coming in this morning to interview Pete."

Kieran groaned. He'd completely forgotten, or maybe he'd pushed it from his mind on purpose. All he knew was that the last thing he wanted was to have to sit next to that guy again and listen while he grilled a man who had had to endure too much over the past few weeks as it was.

"Buzz me when he gets here."

"I wouldn't be too upset if the coffee pot was completely empty by the time he shows," Lisa said.

"I'll see what I can do," Kieran replied with a laugh.

He detoured into his office and snagged his travel mug, which held more coffee than his usual mug, then headed for their small break room. The pot was half gone already, so he was able to almost drain it by filling his travel mug as well as a normal mug. Lucky for him, the travel mug would keep the coffee warm, so if the guys made more coffee to suit their taste, he would still have the better tasting stuff to tide him over.

It looked like it would be lunchtime before he'd be able to head over to Cara's. While he waited for the detective to show up, he checked her website to see what her schedule was that day. It looked like she had a morning and an afternoon class, so hopefully she'd be available around lunch time.

He wanted to say something to her about what he'd seen the day before, but it had looked like such an intensely personal moment, he figured she might get upset if he mentioned it. And the last thing he wanted was for her to be upset by his revelation. Hopefully, just seeing her would reassure him that she was okay. That whatever emotions had overflowed for her hadn't continued to plague her the way they had him.

He just wanted to make sure she was all right.

CHAPTER NINE

Cara said goodbye to the last of the moms who'd been there with their babies for her postpartum stretch class. One of the ladies from her prenatal class had delivered a few weeks ago and had shown up for the first time with her baby that morning. Cara had spent a few minutes cuddling the newborn, listening as the mom had shared how her labor and delivery had gone.

She still carried a melancholy ache within her from her emotional meltdown and holding the baby didn't help to ease it at all. If anything, it had deepened the ache. Some days she wondered if she'd ever have a baby of her own, but right then, her sadness was tied to the realization that even if she did have a baby, her dad wouldn't get to see it. Her baby wouldn't know either of its grandparents on her side.

As she stood watching the moms walk down the sidewalk, some pushing strollers, others carrying car seats to nearby cars, another figure came into view. Through the glass of the front window, her gaze met and held Kieran's. For the first time, a smile didn't readily appear on his face, and she wondered if something bad had happened.

She hadn't had time to lock the door, so he was able to pull it open and step inside. As he came closer, she could see dark smudges beneath his eyes, and his jaw was tensely set.

"Is everything all right?" she asked before she could stop herself.

Kieran's look darkened further as he frowned. "What?"

"You just look...tense. Unhappy about something."

He took his hat off and ran his hand over his closely cropped hair. Rather than put his hat back on, he just held it in his hands. "Yeah, I'm a bit unhappy. Just had another interview about Sheila Thompson's disappearance. This one with her father."

"Oh. I'm sure that was difficult."

"It was, and not just because the detective asked questions that made it seem like he thought Pete had something to do with his daughter's disappearance, but also because of everything that's gone down with Coral."

For some reason, seeing him so weighed down called to something within Cara. "Did you want to come into the office and sit for a minute?"

His eyebrows rose as if he was surprised by her invitation. Well, considering it surprised her too, his response made sense. She figured she was already in for a penny, so she might as well go for the pound.

"I was just going to run to *Norma's* to get some lunch. Can I pick you up something as well?"

Kieran turned in a full circle before facing her again. "Just looking for the flying pigs."

"What?"

"Oh, I just figured pigs would fly before you'd initiate sharing lunch."

There was a spark of humor in his eyes that was gratifying, and she found she wanted to see more of it. The tense set of his face earlier hadn't sat well with her.

"Well, hell hasn't frozen over either, but the offer still stands."

"Sure. A roast beef sandwich would go a long way to improving this day."

"Let me just grab my stuff, and I'll go get it." She went into her office and pulled on the sweatpants and jacket she'd been wearing over her leotard and tights earlier. Unlocking her desk drawer, she pulled out her wallet then returned to the waiting area. "You can wait in my office, if you want. I'll be back in a few minutes."

Kieran nodded, then headed for her office. She supposed that they could have just gone to *Norma's* together, but it seemed that he was just as happy to eat in her office. And honestly, appearing together in public would surely start rumors that she didn't want, and likely, he didn't either.

Once at *Norma's*, Cara greeted the woman then went to the counter to place her order with Missy.

"To go?" Missy asked once Cara had recited what she wanted.

"Yep. And could you add a couple of milkshakes? One chocolate and one vanilla?"

Missy's brows lifted at that. "I happen to know his favorite is the chocolate mint."

"Whose?" Cara asked, realizing that maybe her original order could be passed off as being for one person, but two milkshakes? Yeah, that was kind of a giveaway that she was buying for more than one person.

Missy leaned over the counter toward her and whispered, "Kieran's." She drew back and grinned. "So should I make one of those a chocolate mint?"

Considering how stressed he'd looked, it seemed wrong to not get him his favorite milkshake. She sighed and gave an exasperated shake of her head. "Yeah. Okay. One chocolate mint and one chocolate."

"I can add some oatmeal chocolate chip cookies onto that as well. We just took a batch out of the oven."

With a laugh, Cara waved her hand. "Sure. And if you've got his favorite soup, you might as well throw that in too."

"Perfect," Missy said with a nod.

"It's a working lunch," Cara said, though she wasn't sure that was entirely true. However, he hadn't just shown up out of the blue for no reason yet.

"Oh, you can call it whatever you want, but you might as well eat what you enjoy while you work."

Cara hoped that this wasn't going to start a rumor and create issues for Kieran. She didn't care much what people said about her, but her position in the town wasn't as important as Kieran's.

It didn't take too long for Missy to come back with their food. Cara took it along with the bill to the front where Norma rang her up. Thankfully, it was busy enough that Norma didn't make any comments aside from a friendly greeting.

Back in the studio, Cara locked the front door before making her way into the office. Kieran was seated in the chair he'd used before, his legs stretched out in front of him. He was leaning back, his chin pressed to his chest. It looked like he was asleep.

She quietly moved around the desk and set the bag and drink tray down. As she settled in her chair, his head came up, and his eyes opened. He stared at her for a moment before blinking.

"Did you really fall asleep in the short time I was gone?" Cara asked. She normally struggled to fall asleep, so she was a bit jealous that he could drop off so quickly.

He gave a huff of laughter as he pulled his legs in and straightened in the chair, reaching for his hat where he'd left it on her desk, then leaning to put it on the floor. "Yeah. I guess I did."

"Lucky you," she said as she pulled one of the milkshakes free of the drink tray.

When she set it down in front of him, Kieran looked at it then up at her. "A milkshake?"

"Yeah. Seemed like maybe you could use it." She hesitated then confessed, "Missy seemed to know I was getting food for you, too, so we ended up with quite the order."

"Really?" Kieran didn't look upset by her revelation. "Not a shock, I suppose. If you placed basically the same order that I did when I was in last week, I'm not surprised she put two and two together. Some of the people in this town put clues together faster than a detective."

"Well, in addition to your sandwich, you've got a bowl of soup and cookies."

"Can't say I'm upset by this news," Kieran said, a full smile finally spreading across his face.

Cara separated out their food then watched as he bowed his head for a moment. She knew he was saying thanks for his food, and she bowed her head as well. There were days she went back and forth on how she felt about her faith, which had been the case since she was a teen.

Part of her confusion over her faith had come from her mom. When it was just the two of them, they'd attended church regularly. It was a large church, and they'd never gotten overly involved, but her mom had insisted they go and had been persistent in teaching Cara about the faith she'd been raised with.

What Cara hadn't been able to grasp, once she'd understood the situation with her dad, was how her mom could continue to be with him when they weren't married, especially given who her father was. It was only later, as an adult, that she'd come to realize that some people clung to their sin. Despite wanting to live a life pleasing to God, there were things they still gave greater importance in their life than Him. Justifying their reasons for allowing that sin to continue. For her mom, that was her love for Cara's father.

So while she'd become a Christian at a young age, her relationship with the church and her own personal faith had been slow to grow, really only flourishing in the past few years. Not that she hadn't continued to have ups and downs in her spiritual walk. The downs usually came about because of her past and the conflict she still felt within her heart over who her father was and the relationship her mother had had with him.

On the one hand, she longed to feel the peace and security that the pastor's messages seemed to promise to those who trusted in

God. Yet there was a part of her that wondered about trusting in a God who hadn't kept her mother safe from those who had wanted to harm them, and who was now allowing her father to die of a painful disease which would leave her all alone in the world.

She knew her father was where he belonged—she'd heard enough about his crimes to know that. So it wasn't that she thought God should have spared him from prison, but losing both parents made it feel like she was the one being punished for her father's sins.

In spite of feeling confused at times, she still read her Bible like her mother had taught her, and she still went to church—or watched the livestream if she couldn't make it in person. But a lot of the time, she struggled to feel peaceful about the whole situation with her parents.

Cara eyed Kieran again as he lifted his sandwich and took a bite. He seemed to be lacking the spark he'd shown in their previous meetings. And him falling asleep like that in her office? Definitely strange. He didn't strike her as someone who let his guard down like that.

In some ways, his listless movements echoed how she felt. After her emotional meltdown the night before, she'd had to pull herself together to lead her morning class with the same energy she usually exhibited.

"So, what do you do to get your mind off a difficult day?" Cara asked as she lifted her milkshake and took a sip.

Kieran angled her a brief look before focusing back on his food. "Usually I go running, but I already did that last night, and I think my body would hate me if I tried that again today. Sometimes I pray while I run, or I listen to music. If I don't run, I read the Bible or listen to an encouraging podcast. I have a few that I don't mind listening to over and over." He looked at her again. "How about you?"

"I dance. My mom said that even when I was really little, music could always cheer me up. And she said that I could never sit still whenever I heard music. Fast or slow, I'd move to it." She lifted one shoulder in a half-hearted shrug. "That's still the case for me, and sometimes dancing is the only way to set the emotions inside me free. Happy or sad, it's the only way I can get them out."

Kieran's gaze was focused on her then, his half-eaten sandwich sitting in its container in front of him. "Do you perform anymore?"

"No. My dancing is a private thing now." Something crossed his face, but it was gone in the blink of an eye. "The dancing I used to perform when I was part of the ballet company is completely different from my personal dancing. That was choreographed by someone else to fit a certain piece of music. That's not how I like to dance anymore. I mean, I'll show my ballet classes steps from a dance that I've performed, but for my own enjoyment, I don't dance that way."

He seemed to be about to say something, but instead, he just nodded like he understood, then he picked his sandwich up and took another bite. They ate in silence for a few minutes. It was a weighted silence, like they both had things they wanted to say or to ask, but something held them back. It was just shy of being uncomfortable, so Cara still felt an increasing pressure to say something to break the building awkwardness.

Kieran, however, didn't seem bothered by the silence, but maybe that was because his thoughts were clearly elsewhere. Cara couldn't help but wonder what had brought him to her door once again. She didn't think for a minute that he'd just been wandering down Main Street and then decided to stop in and see how she was doing.

She paused mid-chew as she realized how much she liked that idea. She liked it way too much. The idea of him wandering down Main Street, saying hi to people as he went before coming into the studio to see her, was appealing.

As she sat there, it struck her that she didn't actually know if he had a girlfriend or someone he was interested in. All she knew for certain was that he wasn't married, and maybe from the way Missy had reacted, he didn't have a girlfriend. Or at least not one that the town knew about.

Kieran had just finished his sandwich when his phone rang. Frowning, he pulled it out and stared at the screen for a moment before his expression cleared. He tapped the screen then lifted it to his ear.

"Hey, Mom." The affection in his voice was unmistakable as was the way his expression softened as he spoke.

Cara shifted in her seat, not sure she should be listening as he talked with his mom. He didn't seem to have any issue with it however, since he could have gotten up and left her office to take the call. She stared down at her food and tried not to make it obvious she was focused on his side of the conversation.

"Yep, I plan to be there. Did you need me to pick up anything for you?" He listened for a moment then said, "Send me a text with whatever you need. I'm not at my desk at the moment, so I can't make a list."

As she listened to Kieran talk to his mom, she could tell he loved her. Her mom had always said that how a man treated his mom was a good indicator of how he'd treat a wife. Cara knew it wasn't a perfect way of determining that since every mother-son relationship was different, but if a man could be respectful and loving to his mother, it was a good sign.

Not that it matters, she reminded herself. *It doesn't matter. It can't matter.*

She concentrated on finishing her salad, then put her soup aside to take upstairs. It would be good for supper since she was already full and still had a class to teach that afternoon.

"Sorry," Kieran said as he slid his phone back into his pocket. "My mom worries if I don't answer the phone. If I hadn't answered, she would have phoned Lisa, and then there would have been a BOLO put out on me."

"A BOLO?"

"A *be on the lookout*. Basically, Lisa and my mom would be telling everyone to be on the lookout for me." A smile lifted the corner of Kieran's mouth. "It's bad enough being in a small town, but being the single son of an overprotective mom in a small town is even worse."

Cara could imagine how that would be. Her mom would have been just like that. She envied Kieran and his mom. She'd thought she'd have a lifetime with her mom, but that wasn't how it had happened. And now, her mom was frozen in Cara's memory at the age of fifty.

"Do you see your mom a lot?"

"I go to her place for dinner three or four times a week." A smile tipped up the corners of his mouth. "And no, I don't live with her."

"I'm sure she must enjoy having you close by."

"She does, and I'm glad I can be there to help her with things."

Again she wondered where his dad was, but she figured that if he wanted her to know, he'd tell her. Just like if she wanted him to know more about her parents, she'd tell him. Not that that was going to happen.

As Kieran finished his soup, he shared a bit more about his mom, and it dawned on Cara that it was possible that their mothers might have known each other as children. She didn't mention that though, because digging up the past might put her life in jeopardy. Kieran was the only person she'd told about her mother's time in New Hope, and she probably shouldn't have done even that.

He'd finished his soup and was sipping on his milkshake when he suddenly stretched his leg out and reached into the pocket of his pants. Pulling something out, he put it on the desk in front of her.

"I originally came by to drop this off," he said, sliding the USB toward her. "I was able to pull the file off of it, so I figured I'd bring it back to you."

"You didn't have to do that, but thank you."

"Thank *you*. I have a meeting with all the involved parties this afternoon, and with that video as evidence, I'm hoping this case will be closed."

"It seems that it's a bit more complicated than it should be," Cara commented.

Kieran scoffed. "Well, the unfortunate part is that the parties involved have had bad blood between them going back years and years."

"Really?"

"Yeah, really." Kieran shook his head. "To hear people tell it, the woman who backed out of the parking spot has long held a grudge against the wife of the man who was driving the other car. Apparently she was supposed to marry that man, but when the other woman arrived in town, the man became absolutely smitten—not my word, just for the record—and ended their engagement so he could court the new woman."

"How many years ago would that have been?"

"I would guess fifty or sixty? Like I said...long held grudge."

"How did they survive being in the same town for that long?"

"No clue. And not just the same town, but the same church."

"Did the woman ever marry someone else?"

"Yes, she did, and went on to have a family of her own, but her husband passed away a couple of years ago. It seems that his death brought the grudge back to the surface for her. Anyway, I just want to show them the video and tell them the case is closed. There wasn't enough damage to warrant all this hoopla." Kieran gave a huff of laughter. "This was not what I imagined I'd be doing back when I started on the force."

"I'm sure your mom is happy that you're dealing with those sorts of things instead of something more dangerous."

Kieran looked away, his expression sobering. "Yeah. She is."

Cara knew all about loving someone in a dangerous profession. She had asked her mom how she could love her papa, knowing that at any moment, someone could take him out. Even all these years later, she could remember her mom's response.

I'd rather have your papa to love for a short time than to not have him at all.

Of course, in the end, it had been her papa who'd had to grieve the loss of the love of his life. But he, too, had said he was grateful for the years they'd had together, though Cara had seen the burden of guilt he'd carried, knowing it had been because of him that her mom had lost her life. It was no doubt why he'd been so determined to protect Cara.

"Well, I guess I'd better get back to work. Get myself ready for that meeting." He sighed as he got to his feet. "I will be glad when this day's over."

He seemed a bit more at ease as he prepared to leave her office than when he'd arrived, which made her feel good, but she still wondered what had stressed him out so much.

"Don't forget your cookies," Cara said as she gathered up their trash.

"Oh, I don't want to take them all. You need to keep a few for yourself."

Cara thought about arguing, but honestly, she loved Norma's cookies. She still had macarons upstairs in her fridge, but that didn't stop her from taking a couple of the cookies from the bag before giving the rest to Kieran.

"Thanks for letting me hide out for a bit." He picked up his hat, milkshake, and the bag with his cookies. "I needed a break from the office and didn't feel like being out in public."

Cara almost told him that he was welcome to come to hide out there anytime, but she bit her tongue. They were already treading a fine line that would be too easy to cross. She hadn't had a serious boyfriend in a lot of years, but she didn't think she was misreading his interest in her. Whether it was something serious or just in passing didn't really matter.

She walked with him to the door and unlocked it, then, after saying goodbye, she locked it again and returned to her office. She didn't linger to watch him walk away this time, though it took everything within her not to.

Unless another burglary occurred—or an accident in front of her studio—he didn't have any reason to return. She knew that was for the best, even though it didn't feel like it was.

CHAPTER TEN

Kieran took his time walking back to the office, sipping the milkshake Cara had brought back from *Norma's*. He felt infinitely better now than he had when he'd made his way to the studio earlier.

The interview with Pete had been gut-wrenching. The man had walked in looking worn out, his face showing the strain of the last few weeks. It was apparent as he'd answered the detective's initial questions that Pete had been eager to help the investigation.

As the questions became more invasive and pointed, Kieran had seen the bewilderment on Pete's face. The man darted confused glances at him as he'd struggled to understand what the detective was inferring. Namely, that he was, in some way, responsible for his daughter's disappearance.

Kieran had kept quiet once again because more than ever, he felt the need to know what direction the detective was moving in. However, with him treating everyone he interviewed as a suspect, Kieran was none the wiser. He could only imagine what the man would ask when he finally got around to interviewing Sheila's mother, Coral.

So, in addition to feeling worn out from his restless night, he'd been feeling slightly ill from the whole interview. He hadn't anticipated that the visit to Cara's to drop off the USB would change any of that. But when she'd offered to get them lunch, he hadn't had any desire to say no.

The quiet of Cara's office, along with the soft lavender scent that drifted in the air, had unwound the knot of tension he'd been carrying around since the previous night. He hadn't planned to fall asleep, just to close his eyes for a few minutes, but even though it had been super short, the catnap had been refreshing. And spending some time with Cara was just icing on the cake.

There had been nothing spectacular about their time together, but it had been nice to talk with her, especially after the disaster of a morning he'd had to endure. The break had been rejuvenating, allowing him to consider the meeting that afternoon without the dread he'd been harboring. Good food, good company, and a catnap had helped to turn his day around, and he didn't plan to let the bickering of the people involved in the bumper tap bring him down.

He had to remind himself of that when he walked into the small conference room Lisa had set up for the meeting. He'd been able to hear the arguing all the way down the hall, and it only increased as he stepped into the room. Lisa was there, but she made no move to interrupt the heated discussion going on between the two groups.

The involved parties were on opposite sides of the table, but judging from the way they were shouting at each other, you would have thought they were on opposite sides of the building. Even his presence in the room didn't quiet them down.

With a sigh, Kieran made his way to the head of the table beside the television that was cued up to play the footage Cara had given him. Crossing his arms, he waited...and waited. When they still didn't quiet down, he turned and pressed a button to begin playing the footage.

"Where did you get that?" a shrill voice asked, plunging the whole room into silence.

"This footage was taken from a security camera mounted in front of where the accident occurred." Kieran let the footage of the event run all the way through. "Do I need to play it again, or should we just consider this matter settled?"

Voices erupted again, and Kieran fought the urge to roll his eyes. Finally, the man who'd been driving the car that had been struck leaned over and said something to his wife. The two of them then got to their feet before looking to where Kieran stood. The man gave Kieran a nod, then offered his wife his arm. The family members that had come with them stopped their angry discord with the opposite side of the table.

With a quick glance amongst themselves, they got up and followed the man and his wife, leaving the other driver and her family to stare after them. The woman turned to Kieran, and when it looked like she was going to argue with him, he arched a brow at her. With a huff, she snatched up her purse and got to her feet. Not saying a word to the people who'd come with her, she stormed from the room.

Kieran waited to see if her family would say anything to him, but they also just collected their things and left, Lisa trailing behind them. He breathed a sigh of relief then made his way back to his office.

It wasn't that he minded dealing with the residents of his town, but when his time was wasted because a decades-old feud refused to allow a cut and dried case to settle, he wasn't having any of it. And now that it was over, he was only too happy to retreat to his office and focus on more important things—like the speech he was going to be giving to one of the classes at the elementary school the following week. It was one of the parts of the job that he really enjoyed.

He usually spoke at one of the town's three schools every other month or so. And when the career symposium at the high school rolled around in the new year, he'd be there to speak to the students about the jobs available in his field. He'd joined the force because of his dad and his uncle, but he hoped to influence some of the kids to consider a career in law enforcement.

Though Kieran enjoyed the actual policing side of things, he really liked the community outreach side as well. He liked meeting with the people of his town when they weren't stressed out about something that had happened to them or a loved one. It was fun to chat about something other than a crime.

It was a bit odd that in all his interactions over the past couple of years, he hadn't spoken with Cara. Given that they both worked on the same street, just a couple of blocks from each other, and frequented a lot of the same places, it was strange that their paths hadn't crossed more than just a glance across a room or seeing each other on the opposite side of the street.

If he didn't know better, he might have thought she had gone out of her way to avoid him. But then, he didn't really know better, did he? If he hadn't approached her, it was likely that they would still be like two ships passing in the dark. Cara had definitely been reserved during the first couple of times he'd visited the studio, but his visit that day had been different. Though they hadn't had a long, personal conversation, for the first time, she seemed more relaxed with him.

Kieran sighed as he found himself wondering what she'd say if he asked her out. He wasn't sure how to broach the subject of his job and a potential future without scaring her off before they even went out for the first time. It wasn't like he could just say, "Oh, by the way, how do you feel about having a relationship—and potentially marrying—a cop?" before asking her out on a date.

He'd discovered early on that he fell for a woman way too quickly. While some men might be able to go out with someone for a couple months or more, and then if things didn't work out, they could just walk away, Kieran wasn't like that. He had to really like someone before he even asked them out, and from that point on, things tended to move quickly for him.

His interest in Cara was piqued, and he was already wondering about a possible future with her. The unfortunate part was that even if she said she was fine with dating a cop, her decision could change at a later date. That's how it had happened with Toni.

Despite all her assurances that she was fine with it, when push came to shove, she'd walked away.

So what did he do?

Kieran leaned back in his chair and swung around to face the narrow windows that looked out over the trees that separated the station from the building next door. What if he asked Cara on a date, and she said no? That would make things awkward, but maybe not intolerable. It wasn't like their lives had been all that entwined prior to the past couple of weeks. They could just go back to how things had been.

But maybe he should wait just a bit longer before asking her out to see how their next few interactions went. Just because the one that day had gone well didn't mean all future ones would. The only problem was, now he had no excuse to seek her out, and he really didn't want it to be another robbery that prompted him to go visit her again.

"Hey, boss." The words were accompanied by a knock on his door.

Abandoning his thoughts of Cara and what their future may or may not hold, Kieran swung back around to spot one of his officers in the doorway. "What's up?"

"Can I talk to you for a minute?"

"Sure." Kieran waved him in as he leaned forward.

When the young man shut the door behind him, Kieran knew this was probably going to be a personal talk. Which was fine. He wanted the people he supervised to feel comfortable coming to him with anything. If they were struggling off the job, it was likely to impact their on-the-job performance, and even though they worked in a town with relatively little risk for violence, he didn't want them distracted, if he could help it.

Once he was done talking to the young man who had just learned his wife was pregnant with their first child, Kieran focused his attention on his email. He didn't need to make a decision right then on whether or not to ask Cara for a date. He'd spend some time praying about it, trusting that if it was God's will, the right moment would present itself. And hopefully, he wouldn't shy away from following through if that moment came.

~ * ~

A couple of days later, Cara watched as women began to filter into the studio for her morning class. She noticed that Mary Albridge had walked in with someone new. The woman looked to be about the same age as Mary, but while Mary had a more bohemian style of dress, her friend was dressed more simply in a pair of sweats and a T-shirt.

She had a rounded figure, and Cara could see her glancing around the room as if she was trying to gauge how well she fit in. Hoping to put her at ease, Cara walked to where the women stood against the wall.

"Hello, Mary," Cara said with a smile. "It's nice to see you here again."

"I'm sorry to have missed a couple of classes, but I've had other things going on."

"I heard about the break-in. I'm so sorry that happened to you."

Mary frowned for a moment then shrugged. "It is what it is. No one was hurt, so I'll count it a win."

Cara reached out to touch her arm briefly. "You have a great attitude about it."

"Getting too upset about it would only add more stress to my life, and you know I'm not a fan of stress."

Not many people were, but Mary somehow managed to brush it aside when many others would have internalized it. Cara included.

"By the way, this is my friend, Rose. She wanted to see what all the hype was about."

Cara held out her hand. "It's a pleasure to meet you, Rose. I'm glad you decided to join us."

"It's a pleasure to meet you, too." Rose smiled at her as she shook her hand. "Just stick me in the back row, in case I make a fool of myself this first time."

"You won't make a fool of yourself," Cara assured her. "I encourage people to just do what they can. We all had to start somewhere."

As Rose's smile grew, Cara felt a sense of familiarity but couldn't place why. She'd probably just seen her in town at some point. Since she'd been there for four years, she'd probably seen everyone at least once even though she hadn't spoken to most of them.

When someone called her name, she gave Rose an encouraging smile then moved away to talk to another woman. Once it looked like the majority of the class was there, Cara had them find spots while she went to turn on the music she'd chosen.

Some of the women had been coming long enough that they probably could have done all the stretches on their own, at home, but for some reason, most kept coming back. She figured part of it was that she kept her rates fairly reasonable. She wasn't necessarily in business to make money hand over fist, though she did want to make enough to cover the bills. There was money in her account she could dip into, but she tried not to because if she had to leave town in a hurry, she needed to know she had money available to re-establish her life.

Though if that should happen, she didn't think she'd go to the lengths she'd gone to in New Hope to set up a new life for herself. She hoped that the steps her father had taken to stage her death and get her a new identity would be enough to allow her to live the remainder of her life the way she wanted without running again.

As the class progressed, she walked among the women, offering encouragement along with instruction. For all her worries, Rose didn't seem to struggle much with the stretches. She wasn't as limber as some, but that was something that would improve if she continued to come.

When the class ended, Rose came to speak to her again while Mary was talking to one of the other women.

"I survived." Her broad smile brought one to Cara's face as well.

"I'm so glad. I haven't had anyone die yet from one of my classes."

"I think I'll definitely be back. So how do I pay for the classes?"

"Why don't we go out front, and I'll explain how that works." Cara led her out of the studio and to the reception desk in the waiting area. "You can just pay a walk-in rate, if you want, or if you'd prefer, you can buy credits, then each time you come in, you can use one of the credits."

Rose seemed to consider the options before she said, "I think I'll just go with the walk-in for now."

Cara sat down at the desk. "That's what most people start out with."

"Perfect. Do you take debit?"

"Yep." Cara opened the drawer and pulled out the debit machine. "Also, be sure to check the website before you come as there are times that I have to cancel a class. I try to give advance notice, but I have a sick family member that I try to visit every few weeks. That sometimes necessitates me canceling a class. Alternatively, if you want to give me your email address, I'll add it to the list I use to let everyone know when that happens."

"Sure. I can do that." Rose accepted the pen and printed card that Cara handed her then moved to the side to fill it out when someone else came up to pay.

After she'd finished with the two other women who'd needed to pay, Cara turned back to where Rose waited. When the woman handed her the card, Cara looked down at it to make sure it was legible. The printing was all very clear—clear enough that the last name jumped right out at her. *Sutherland.*

She tried not to show her surprise, though her fingers tightened on the card. Instead, she looked up and smiled at Rose. "Thanks again for joining us today. I hope you felt comfortable enough that you'll return."

"I did, and Mary was right about how good it would feel. Plus, the whole atmosphere was so relaxed, I could have taken a nap."

As the woman spoke, Cara could now see the features she shared with Kieran. Was this his mom or another relative? She seemed to remember him talking about having family in the town, so it was possible she was an aunt.

"Ready to go, Rose?" Mary asked when she joined them.

"I am. Kieran's coming for supper, and I need to stop at the store to get a few things for that."

Well, that answered that question. Mom, it was. She willed herself not to react to the sound of his name. It did strike her as rather odd that within the space of two weeks, two Sutherlands had entered her life. She wondered if it would be naïve of her to chalk it up to a coincidence.

With a final wave, the two friends followed the last of the women out of the studio. Cara sat for a moment, pondering the alternative to a coincidence. It was entirely possible that Rose had gotten wind that her son had stopped in to see her on more than one occasion and had made some assumptions.

Were rumors circulating that something was going on between her and Kieran? What if Rose had been there to check Cara out?

Her cheeks burned at the thought. She didn't usually spend much time worrying over what people thought about her. The only people whose opinions had ever mattered to her were her parents and, at an earlier point in her life, the people at the dance company. Though she wanted the people of New Hope Falls to think well of her as a dance teacher and businesswoman, she hadn't let anyone get close enough to judge her personal life—such as it was.

If Rose thought Cara wanted a relationship with Kieran, she'd definitely want to see beyond her dance teacher role. The thought made Cara feel a little queasy. She had been so used to her life being just her that she forgot, sometimes, that others came with more people involved in their lives.

Kieran had roots in this town beyond just his relationship with his mom. Rose wouldn't be the only person looking at Cara and judging whether or not she was good enough for their police chief. The thought of being under that type of scrutiny made her feel a little sick.

If any part of her had been contemplating the thought of something more with Kieran, it died a quick death at that moment. In her mind, anyways. Her heart stubbornly refused to give up the desire to share everything about her life with him. Her stupid, blind heart. It wasn't that easy. Nothing about her life since her mother's death had been easy.

Suddenly, worried that Kieran might show up again, Cara got to her feet and hurried to lock the front door and turn off the lights. She could still see well enough to clear up the desk, then she carried the money and the card Rose had filled out into her office. After she inputted the information into her client file, she updated her program with the payments she'd received.

She took the money upstairs with her, not that it would be a huge loss if someone broke in, but she preferred not to reward them for their efforts. Hopefully they would be smart enough to realize that since she didn't actually sell anything, she didn't have a lot of cash on hand.

In the sanctuary of her apartment, Cara sat down to check her email. Doug Anders had taken to emailing her each day with an update on her father's condition. It seemed that for the moment, he was holding his own. Not getting any better but also not deteriorating. She hoped that meant he'd still be there when her next visit came in two weeks' time.

Still, she knew that any day, she could receive a phone call that would irrevocably change her life once again. But she tried her best not to dwell on that thought. Her worrying over it wouldn't keep it from happening, so she tried to keep it from dominating her mind. She succeeded...most of the time.

It was just too bad that she needed to avoid thinking about Kieran now too.

~ * ~

Kieran hated getting to church late, but it happened sometimes. Usually for things beyond his control. A call in the early morning hours from one of his officers had woken him to let him know there had been an accident on the road leading out of New Hope to the east. It was a beautiful road with towering trees on either side and the mountains nearby, but it could be deadly when people weren't careful when driving along it, especially in the dark.

It was a narrow road that necessitated a cautious drive at the best of times, but in the dark, it could be a challenge, particularly for people who weren't familiar with it. Unfortunately, that had been the case earlier when someone took a turn too fast and skidded out of control, hitting a car coming in the opposite direction.

He'd gone as soon as he'd heard what had happened. The ambulance arrived shortly after he had, taking away the driver and passenger of the one car. Unfortunately, the other driver had been declared dead at the scene.

Death was something Kieran had never gotten used to seeing, despite his years working in New York, where he'd seen it far too frequently. Knowing all too well the pain of being told that a loved one had passed away, Kieran felt weighed down by the echoes of grief as he walked into the church.

He could hear singing from the sanctuary, so he went ahead and opened the door and slipped inside. The usher inside the door smiled at him, then handed him a bulletin. Kieran gave him a nod of thanks, then slid into the back pew even though he usually sat closer to the front with his mom.

There were other people in the pew, so he glanced over to acknowledge them, pausing when he noticed the person closest to him, about halfway down the pew, was Cara. Her gaze was on the words of the song that were projected onto the big screen at the front of the sanctuary, but she wasn't singing.

He shifted a bit closer to her but made sure to leave plenty of space between them. If he moved to stand right next to her, rumors would start raging for sure. Not that there weren't a few already circulating.

It had been a couple of weeks since he'd last seen her, but he'd been hearing plenty about her from his mom. She'd started going to classes at Cara's studio and made sure that Kieran knew how much she liked her. While that was all well and good, Kieran hadn't run into Cara again after that day she'd gotten him lunch from *Norma's.* He didn't want to think she was avoiding him, but he had to wonder.

CHAPTER ELEVEN

Kieran's mom had mentioned that Cara had been out of town for a couple of days to visit a sick family member, so maybe she wasn't avoiding him. He hoped that was the case.

He hadn't been intentionally avoiding Cara, but his days had been tied up with more interviews and meetings with the detective. Kieran had been a bit surprised at how aggressively the man had continued to pursue solving the case of Sheila's disappearance. He had believed that with Coral having been arrested for the vandalism on Anna's car, the investigation would lose some steam since she'd been the driving force behind it. But that had definitely not been the case.

With no new leads, Kieran felt a bit like it was a waste of their time. It wasn't that he didn't want the case to be solved, but they had absolutely no new leads. Even the detective's aggressive questioning of people recently hadn't led to any new information.

Eli still maintained his innocence, backed up by the guys with whom he's spent the night. Pete also had an alibi that held up. None of the others interviewed had been able to give them any new leads.

The main office had received a call from a television show asking if they'd be willing to be interviewed for a documentary they were doing on Sheila's case. The detective had agreed, as long as certain boundaries were respected. Kieran actually hoped that the documentary would bring new information to light. If they weren't making progress with the people who had been in New Hope at the time of Sheila's disappearance, maybe it was time to broaden their search field.

Somewhere, someone knew what had happened to Sheila. The best-case scenario was that Sheila had actually run away and established a new life elsewhere in the country. If that was really what had happened, he hoped that she'd see the show and realize that even if she didn't want to come back to New Hope Falls, she needed to let someone know she was okay. Too many people's lives were being negatively affected by not having this case solved.

But while his stress had been outwardly focused, it seemed that Cara's might have been more personal. She stood ramrod straight, her hands gripping the chair in front of her as they stood. Her intent focus on the words on the screen drew Kieran's there as well.

It was a familiar hymn, one he'd sung in the church for as long as he could remember. It was also one his mom had played over and over after she'd lost her son and then her husband. He'd venture to guess that it had become her favorite hymn.

When the song was over, Pastor Evans slowly climbed the stairs to the stage. He shook hands with the man who'd been leading the singing then moved to stand behind the podium, placing his large worn Bible on it.

"It's not often that I abandon a sermon I've been working on all week, but I'm doing just that this morning." The man moved to stand beside the podium, resting his hand on the edge of it. "At some point in the night, I woke up with that song in my head and a verse on my heart. I tried to go back to sleep but soon realized that wasn't going to happen. So I got up and began to pray because it was clear that God wanted me to speak on a topic completely different from what I'd planned."

The pastor stopped and let his gaze travel over the congregation, and when he came to Kieran, Kieran tipped his head out of respect. He knew from experience that Pastor Evans was a man with a heart for God and a heart for the people who he believed he'd been called to shepherd.

"At first, I thought I was supposed to bring a message of hope and comfort for those who might be hurting in our congregation, but as I prayed, these verses showed me that it was more than that." He turned back to the podium and picked up his Bible. "I'm sorry that I don't have the verses up on the screen like I usually do, so I'll give you time to find Second Corinthians chapter one verse three in your Bible or on your phone."

Kieran pulled his phone out and opened his Bible app. He was more used to using it for his daily reading than actually looking up a specific scripture, so it took him a minute to find the verse. When he'd found it, he looked up to see Pastor Evans once again watching the congregation.

He glanced over at Cara and saw she had a Bible open on her lap. Normally, he would have had his Bible as well, but he hadn't had time to stop by the house to pick it up. This was the first time he'd sat so close to her during a service, and he had to wonder if she was always so tense, or if it was just something that had happened recently to make her that way.

"Second Corinthians one verses three and four," Pastor Evans said. "*Blessed be the God and Father of our Lord Jesus Christ, the Father of mercies and God of all comfort, who comforts us in all our tribulation, that we may be able to comfort those who are in any trouble, with the comfort with which we ourselves are comforted by God.*"

Kieran thought of the fatal car accident and the families that had been affected by it. Someone else had taken care of the family notifications since the one driver had been from Seattle, and the other one had been with her husband, who had survived the accident. Still, he knew that if he'd been called on to make those notifications that he would have struggled to comfort the family in their grief without having his own rise to the surface again.

"I know that there are some here today who are hurting or are in trouble, and it's not because I know each of you and know your situation. It's because I know we live in a fallen and hurting world. And as Christians, we aren't exempt from hurt or troubles. Verse four speaks to that directly when it talks about God comforting us in all our tribulation. Our trials. Our suffering. Our pain. If Christians were exempt from all of that, this verse wouldn't talk about how God comforts us.

"The difference between those of us who know and love God and the world that doesn't, is that we know He is there to comfort us in those difficult times. We never face hopeless situations alone because our hope is in God. We only have to turn to Him during those times to experience His comfort. But it's not enough for us to seek comfort from Him, we must also then comfort those who are in trouble or are hurting. Let people see the comfort of God through the comfort we offer them."

Kieran looked down at the verse on the screen of his phone again. He used the feature to highlight the verses then tapped to make a note of what Pastor Evans was sharing. Having read through the New Testament in the past year, he knew he'd read those verses, but they hadn't stuck with him the way he knew they would now.

Pastor Evans shared other verses that he seemed to pull right off the top of his head, and Kieran added them to his notes, planning to look them up and highlight them later.

Though the man usually spoke for more than half an hour most Sundays, that day, he ended after just twenty minutes. Instead of sitting back down, however, he walked down the stairs to stand on the floor in front of the stage. Since he wore a wireless mic, they were still able to hear him when he spoke again.

"I want to have a time of prayer for those who are in need of comfort today. You can stay in your seat and just raise your hand if you would like to let me know you need prayer. Or, you can come to the front if you wish to have someone pray with you. I'd like to ask the members of the board if they'd come forward.

However, I don't want to limit the opportunity to pray just to the board. If you have experienced God's comfort and would like to share that with someone today, then I would invite you to come forward as well. Let us become an instrument of comfort to those around us, not a source of pain."

He paused, waiting as the members of the board made their way to the front and took up positions at his side. Soft music from the piano began to drift through the sanctuary as the pastor bowed his head.

"Father, we come before you today in need of comfort. You promised us in Your word that You are a God of comfort, and in turn, we are encouraged to comfort those around us who are facing trouble and tribulation. Let us feel your presence here today, Father, as we gather together, those of us in need of comfort and those who are offering it. May our actions bring honor and glory to You."

Silence settled over the congregation for a moment, with only the piano playing softly in the background.

"Raise your hand or come to the front if you would like prayer today. We don't need to know the details. It is enough for you to say *I'm hurting*. God knows what it is that's causing you pain and hurt, and as we offer our comfort, He will also comfort you."

Kieran looked up, his gaze landing on the empty wooden cross that stood at the front of the sanctuary. It momentarily went out of focus. He swallowed hard and blinked to clear his gaze.

He saw movement out of the corner of his eye and turned enough to see that Cara had lifted her hand. Her head remained bent, and her hand didn't stay up for long, lowering as soon as Pastor Evans said, "I've seen your hand, sister, and I'll be praying for you."

At first, no one was moving to the front of the sanctuary, but then a young man got up and walked to the front before sinking down on his knees. He'd barely settled when another young person got up and went to his side, and the youth pastor joined them both.

The courage of the young man seemed to reach out to others in the congregation because soon, more people began to make their way forward.

Some were clearly there seeking prayer, but just as many were going forward to come alongside them, slipping an arm around their shoulders as they bowed their heads together. Kieran bowed his head, choosing to stay in his seat and pray for Cara as well as the people who'd gone forward.

It seemed pretty clear that Cara wasn't comfortable going to the front, but she'd acknowledged she wanted prayer, so he would do that for her even if he couldn't comfort her the way he might want to.

He folded his hands together and let them rest between his knees as he prayed for God to comfort Cara and help her through whatever it was that she was enduring. Though he wished he knew the details, Pastor Evans' words rang in his head. *God knows, and that's all that matters.*

After a while, people began returning to their seats, and Pastor Evans said, "I know we sang this before the sermon, but I'd like to sing it again as a reminder. I'd encourage you to read up on the background of this particular hymn and what Horatio Spafford was going through when he wrote it."

The worship leader walked behind the podium as the words came up on the screen again.

When peace, like a river, attendeth my way,
When sorrows like sea billows roll;
Whatever my lot, Thou hast taught me to say,
It is well, it is well with my soul.

> *It is well with my soul,*
> *It is well, it is well with my soul.*

Though Satan should buffet, though trials should come,
Let this blest assurance control,

That Christ hath regarded my helpless estate,
And hath shed His own blood for my soul.
My sin—oh, the bliss of this glorious thought!—
My sin, not in part but the whole,
Is nailed to the cross, and I bear it no more,
Praise the Lord, praise the Lord, O my soul!
And Lord, haste the day when my faith shall be sight,
The clouds be rolled back as a scroll;
The trump shall resound, and the Lord shall descend,
Even so, it is well with my soul.

When the song ended, Pastor Evans moved to the front to pray. Kieran bowed his head, listening as the man prayed a blessing on the congregation. After echoing his amen, Kieran straightened and turned toward Cara...only to find she wasn't there.

Spinning around, he looked to the back of the sanctuary, but there was no sign of her. He had hoped to talk to her, to make sure that she was okay, but it seemed she hadn't been interested in interacting with anyone. Or had it just been him? Had she realized that he was in the pew beside her?

"Kieran." His mom's voice drew his attention from the doors of the sanctuary. She came to stand next to him in the pew. "Are you okay?"

"I'm fine." He'd texted her earlier to let her know about the accident and that he was going to try and grab a quick nap before church. "Just tired."

"Do you want to come for lunch with Mary and me?"

"Actually, Mom. I think I'm just going to go home and try to get some rest."

She didn't argue with him, knowing the toll something like the accident would take on him. She also didn't ask for details. After being married to a cop, she knew that sometimes she didn't need to hear the details. She never pushed for him to talk about what he'd seen, but Kieran knew that if he ever wanted to talk, she would have been there to listen.

Right then, however, there was someone Kieran wished would talk to *him*. He was coming to realize that the gentle, friendly face Cara showed to the world hid a depth that seemed to be causing her pain. Did she have anyone in town who she considered a close enough friend that she could confide in?

Kieran slipped out the door of the church and jogged down the cement steps to the sidewalk that ran in front of the building. He glanced around, hoping that he might spot Cara, but she wasn't anywhere to be seen. As he walked to his vehicle, he debated heading to her place to check on her.

He shut that idea down as quickly as it had popped up. She might not have close friends in town, but that didn't automatically mean she'd talk to him. In fact, it spoke volumes that she'd lived in New Hope Falls for several years, and yet he couldn't remember ever having seen her hanging out with anyone. Whenever he had seen her at a distance, she'd always been on her own. All the evidence pointed to the fact that she was a loner because she wanted to be.

With a sigh, Kieran slid behind the wheel of his Jeep and started it up. Though the temptation was strong to go to Cara's, he ignored it and turned toward his own place. Once there, he changed out of his uniform into something more comfortable then he made himself a sandwich. He took it with a drink into the living room where he set it on the table next to his recliner.

Needing a distraction, he used the remote to turn on his television then settled into his chair to eat while he watched the NASCAR race that was on that afternoon. He didn't follow the sport religiously, but he enjoyed watching it. He had a feeling, however, that he'd end up missing part of the race that day as his early morning rise was rapidly catching up with him.

~ * ~

Cara stared out the window at the town. She'd been sitting in the same spot since she'd come home from church, trying to wrap her head around the emotions and thoughts that had been circling through her mind ever since she'd gotten back from visiting her dad.

After her last trip, she'd been certain that she wouldn't have another visit with him, and yet, when the time had rolled around again, he'd still been there. She wasn't sure if Doug Anders, the ADA, had pulled strings or what, but her dad had been moved to a small private room, which meant she'd been able to spend more time with him.

Much of that time had been spent with her reading from her journal. He'd been too weak to read it for himself, but he'd wanted to hear about her month. It had been something she'd been only too happy to do.

The surprise of the visit had been her dad's revelation that he'd become a Christian. In the past, he'd brushed aside her mom's attempts to get him to come to church with them. After her mom's death, Cara had tried to talk to him about it again, but he'd angrily brushed her attempts. Not wanting to cloud their times together, she'd eventually stopped trying and had just prayed that somehow God would reach her papa before he died.

But this time around, he'd had a definite message for her. *I want to see you again, carissima. I'm certain that I'm going to heaven now. I want you to be certain too. Promise me.*

She wanted him to talk more about how he was certain, but talking beyond the promises he'd once again extracted from her had seemed to require more energy than he had available. He had gripped her hand tightly as he struggled with the words, only relaxing when she'd assured him that she was certain. Probably more certain than she'd been at any point previously in her life.

And that assurance was the reason she'd gone to church that day instead of watching the service online. She'd sat in the back row, as she had every time she'd gone, and listened as the pastor talked about hurting people and God's comfort. It had been hard to admit that she really wanted that comfort. She'd been determined to be strong. To make her parents proud by being able to handle everything life threw at her without crumbling.

And she'd done okay for the last few years, but in recent months, though outwardly it looked like she was doing fine, inwardly, she was crumbling. She walked around with a constant ache in her heart, and nothing could keep her mind from worrying over the coming loss. Which was why the sermon had been timely.

Cara watched as the town's lights began to wink on. It had been a gray and dreary day, so twilight seemed like it was coming earlier than usual. The days were already getting shorter as they moved through November. In a few weeks, it would be Thanksgiving. Usually, she tried to be with her dad around that time, but she wasn't sure if that would happen that year, given his condition.

Though she hadn't planned to tell him about Kieran and her interest in him, she hadn't been able to keep that news from spilling out. Her dad had been in and out of consciousness throughout their visit, and she'd begun to tell him about Kieran while he'd been asleep. She just felt the need to talk to *someone* about what had been going on with him.

Partway through, her father's eyes had opened, and his dark gaze had been focused and intent on her.

"Do you love him, carissima?"

"No." She'd thought of Kieran and the care and concern he'd shown her, then added, *"But I think I might be able to."*

"Don't hold yourself from love." Even though she'd explained that he was a cop, her father had insisted. *"Your mother could have chosen not to love me because of who I was. We would have missed so much joy and happiness—and you—had she not given me a chance."*

Before he'd gotten so sick, they'd talked at length about his complicated relationships and the fact that he'd never divorced his wife in order to marry her mother. It had taken a long time for Cara to understand and accept his rationale. In her mind, if he'd loved her mom that much, he should have been willing to let go of his old life.

She hadn't realized that her dad had made the choices he did in hopes of protecting her and her mom. Of course, in the end, that hadn't worked. He might as well have divorced his wife and married her mom. Hindsight was everything.

Would that happen to her? If she decided to keep her distance from Kieran, would she look back and wish she'd made a different decision? Of course, the opposite could be true too. She could decide to see where things went and then come to regret that in the future. There were no guarantees that one choice was better than the other.

Though he'd never encouraged her to date, Cara knew it would give her father peace of mind if he thought she had someone to love her after he passed. But still, he'd extracted a promise from her.

Love him, but never tell him about your past. Consider it done. Like it never happened. You can remember your mama and me, but never give details of our other life. Especially if he's a cop. For the sake of your happiness, he must never know. Promise me.

And once again, she'd promised because it gave her hope that perhaps she could have a romantic relationship. Before Kieran, she wouldn't have considered dating or even having the future of a family, but since meeting him, that had changed. The only thing was that he hadn't been around much in the last couple of weeks. Maybe he really had only come around because he'd needed her cameras.

As she stared out at the houses that glowed warmly in the encroaching night, she resolved to let things unfold as they came. She wasn't going to force anything, but with her dad's blessing, she would accept any overtures from Kieran.

CHAPTER TWELVE

It was past the lunch rush already when Kieran walked into *Norma's,* and, as was his habit, he glanced around to see who was there. He spotted Arianna and Eli at a table near the back, seemingly unaware of everyone else in the restaurant. It was good to see that things were working out for Eli. At least on the personal front. Kieran was sure the investigation was weighing heavily on him but having Arianna in his life appeared to be making him happy in spite of what was going on around him.

Arianna smiled at Eli when he reached out and touched her cheek with his fingertips. The connection they had was clear in their body language and the smiles on their faces. It wasn't a look he'd seen on Eli's face before.

A longing blossomed in his chest as he watched them. He let out a sigh and looked away from the couple, only to have his gaze land on Cara, where she sat in a booth in front of the windows. She was looking down at something on the table and didn't appear to have noticed him come in.

"You here to eat, Chief?" Norma asked, drawing his attention from Cara. "Or are you taking out?"

"I think I'm going to eat in," Kieran said.

She gave him a knowing smile and nodded toward Cara. "I'll let you seat yourself. Do you need a menu?"

Kieran chuckled. "I think I'll be okay."

As Norma turned to greet a couple of people who'd just walked in, he headed to where Cara was seated. He slid into the booth opposite her, smiling when she looked up.

"May I join you?"

She hesitated for only a moment before nodding. "Are you here for lunch?"

"Yep. I was going to take it back to the office, but then I saw you here. Thought I'd see how you were doing."

"I'm doing fine." She gave him a small smile. "How about you?"

"Had a bit of a rough start to the week with a bad accident on Sunday."

"I heard about that."

Before she could say more, Missy appeared at the table. She put a glass of iced tea in front of him with a smile. "What can I get you, Chief?"

"I'll have a roast beef sandwich and a bowl of your soup-of-the-day." Though there had been splashes of sunshine throughout the morning, it was still cool, so soup was appealing.

Missy didn't even write anything down. Just said, "Sounds good." Then she left them alone again.

"I heard that people passed away in the accident."

Kieran sat back in the booth. "Yes. Unfortunately, two people died, one at the scene and one later in hospital."

"Were they from here? Did you know them?"

"The woman who passed away was from New Hope. She owned the florist shop just around the corner from *Norma's* on Semple. Her husband was also badly injured, but last I heard, he was stable. The man who passed away wasn't from around here."

"That's really sad. It's hard to lose a family member so unex-pectedly."

Remembering her emotional dancing, it dawned on him that perhaps she had personal experience with sudden loss. Of course, he did too. "Yes, it is. My mom mentioned that you've been out of town visiting a sick family member."

She stared at him for a moment before nodding. He waited for her to expound on the person and the situation, but she didn't say anything more. It was just one more thing that intrigued him about her.

Every time they were together, he got the feeling that she wasn't keen to share too much about herself. It made him suspicious, but then, he wasn't revealing everything about himself either. He just needed to chill out and not try to force things this early in their acquaintance.

It was a downside to his job. Just because someone didn't share everything with him, didn't mean they were guilty of something. If Cara were a suspect, however, he definitely would think she was hiding something. But she wasn't, so he needed to not look too deeply into what she wasn't saying.

"Have classes been going well?" Kieran asked. "My mom seems to really enjoy them."

"I'm glad to hear that. I was pleased she decided to come. I'm still waiting to see if Lisa will show up."

Kieran smiled at that. "Well, it's not really a surprise that she hasn't. Lisa always jokes that she's allergic to exercise."

He wasn't going to tell Cara that his mom had had an ulterior motive for attending the classes. Surprisingly enough, despite her initial motivation, his mom had recently been talking about how she was finding it easier to move, and she credited Cara's classes with that. Whatever might have drawn her there in the first place, she was definitely sticking around because she felt it benefited her overall well-being.

"I'm working with the kids' dance classes to prepare them for the Christmas program."

"That's neat. I bet the kids are excited about that. They probably have a lot of fun in your classes."

Cara tilted her head. "How do you know they have fun?"

"I can't imagine that your classes for the kids would be anything but." Kieran shifted forward, leaning his arms on the table. "I get the feeling that you want the kids to love what they're doing, and in order for that to happen, they need to have fun learning. I bet if I came to watch you teach, I'd see a bunch of kids who absolutely adore their teacher."

A light flush crept over Cara's cheeks, and her head dipped before she glanced up through her lashes. "I do try and make it fun for them. I've had both super strict teachers and teachers who were more fun, and though I learned from both types, I definitely enjoyed the teachers who were encouraging and fun."

As he looked at her, the memory of her dancing alone in her studio came into sharp focus. The emotion. The athleticism. The beauty. He wished he could tell her how talented he thought she was, but that would require him revealing that he'd watched her without an invitation to do so.

"I'll have to come and watch the program. Is it open to everyone? Where do you have it?"

"We use the theater at the high school, and while it's open to everyone, we don't usually have too big of a crowd. It's usually just the family of the kids performing."

"Let me know the date and time, and I'll be there."

Her smile at that was the biggest so far. "I'm sure the kids would love to see the chief there."

Missy reappeared with his food, and Kieran sat back to allow her to slide it onto the table in front of him. After she checked if Cara needed anything more, she left them alone again.

"So have there been any more break-ins?" Cara asked after he'd bowed his head and said a quick prayer of thanks for his food.

"Nope. Which is weird. To have two happen like that, and then nothing more is odd." He took a mouthful of the soup. "Not that I'm complaining because I'd rather not have any more break-ins, but we currently have no leads on either case."

They talked a bit more about the businesses that had been targeted as Kieran ate his sandwich. Their conversation moved on to other crimes that had been committed in the area since he'd taken over the position of chief. Once again, there was no personal conversation, but he figured what they had was better than nothing.

Though she'd finished her food ahead of him, Cara didn't seem to be in any hurry to end their time together. He found that as long as the conversation wasn't centered on her, she was happy to talk at length with him. Maybe they just needed to spend more time together, and hopefully, she'd become more at ease with him and open up.

When he'd finished eating, Missy came to clear away their dishes and asked if they wanted dessert.

"Not today," Kieran said with a pat of his stomach. "Going to Mom's tonight, so I have to space myself."

"I'm fine too," Cara told her. "It was all very delicious."

When Missy laid their bills on the table, Kieran picked them both up. Cara protested, but he just shook his head.

"This wasn't even planned," she said. "I don't expect you to pay for my meal."

"I know you don't, but it's my pleasure." He paused, then said, "Think we might share a meal that was planned one day?"

Her eyes widened a bit before she gave what was quite obviously a hesitant nod.

"In that case, would you be willing to go out Friday night?"

"Go out? For dinner?"

"Sure. Dinner. Coffee. Movie. Whatever you're comfortable with."

"Oh. Well, anything would be okay."

"Anything?" Kieran asked. "Like, are you into sports or escape rooms?"

"I'm not a big fan of any sport, but I don't mind watching them on occasion. Never been to an escape room."

"Me neither, but I keep hearing about them." Kieran regarded Cara for a second, then said, "So it's settled? Friday night."

"Okay. Friday night."

"Once I've settled on the plans, I'll let you know." He hesitated, eyeing her closely. "Are you going to back out?"

Her brows rose slightly at his question. "That's not my intention. At least not without good reason."

"I just have to say I'm a bit surprised you've agreed." He really should stop talking. The last thing he wanted to do was to talk her out of going out with him.

She shrugged. "I'm a bit surprised too, but honestly, life's too short to hold myself back from things."

"So it has nothing to do with my charismatic personality and stunning good looks?"

Laughter tumbled from her lips. From her reaction, his comment had caught her totally off-guard. "It might have a little to do with that too."

Kieran grinned at her, and when she smiled back at him, he felt hope flare in his chest. If she really did believe that life was too short, then that might mean she'd be willing to take a chance on him for more than just a date, despite his job.

"Well, I'd better get back to work." With great reluctance, he got to his feet. "It was a real pleasure to have lunch together."

"It was," Cara agreed. "And thank you for treating me."

"You're welcome." Before turning away, he added, "I'll see you Friday."

At her nod and smile, he was able to leave the restaurant confident that she wasn't going to bail on him before they even had a chance for their first date.

~ * ~

Cara couldn't believe that she was actually getting ready for a date. Her first date in years. She wasn't going to count the few times she'd tried to date before her mom had been killed. A couple of those dates had been as a result of a dating app, and they'd crashed

BECAUSE OF HIM · 127

and burned within minutes of the meeting when she realized the men had really misrepresented themselves on the app.

The others had been attempts to date within the ballet company, which she quickly realized wasn't wise. Too much gossip. Too much togetherness. Too much jealousy.

She was sure people would laugh at the idea that she'd reached the age of twenty-six without ever having had a serious relationship, but her life over the past few years had just not been conducive to long-term dating. And okay, maybe there was a little bit of fear mixed in with it too.

Still was, if she was honest. Over the past few days, she'd tried to figure out the best way to talk about her family if Kieran came right out and asked her about them. Obviously she'd had parents at some point, so she had to figure out the best way to share about them without going into details. As far as Kieran knew—and as far as he'd ever know—she was Cara Morgan. Carolina Jameson had died as the result of a car bomb.

The federal agent who'd worked with her to set up her new identification had said that anyone looking into her past would find enough information to not raise red flags. The last thing they wanted was for someone to look and see that Cara Morgan had come to life just four years earlier.

No one needed to know that her father was in prison or that her mother had passed away from an act of extreme violence. Or that her own half-brothers had been responsible for her mother's death.

Standing in front of her full-length mirror, Cara took in her appearance. Kieran had said to dress comfortably, so she'd decided to go with a pair of fitted jeans and a loose sweater. It was what she felt most comfortable in, and when she wasn't dressed for her classes, it was what she tended to wear.

At one time, she'd enjoyed dressing up, donning skirts, pretty blouses, and high heels. But after everything that had happened with her mom's death, her dad's arrest, and the move to New Hope Falls, her desire to dress up had been muted. And really, her life in her new hometown hadn't required she resurrect that old style. She had been perfectly happy to live in more casual clothes.

Turning from the mirror, Cara put her wallet and phone into the purse she'd chosen for the evening. Nerves fluttered in her stomach as she made her way downstairs. Even though she'd promised Kieran that she wouldn't cancel, she had to admit that the thought had crossed her mind. Several times.

She wasn't ignorant of the fact that she was taking a big risk. Not just by dating in general, but by dating a cop. The average man wouldn't have access to searches that could lead him to find any holes in her new identity. The agent may have said it was foolproof, but she hadn't tested the theory.

But what she'd realized was that her heart was telling her that Kieran was worth the risk. Her response to her father's question lingered in her mind. She might not love Kieran yet, but as she learned more about him, it was easy to think that she could.

His devotion to his mother and his town made her think that, given the opportunity, he would be devoted to her as well. Also, she appreciated his sense of humor, and even though he could be intense, particularly about his work, she'd glimpsed a more chill easygoing side of him.

The only possible negative was his career. Who her father was put them on opposite sides of the law, but once her father passed away, her last tie to that past would be gone. She wouldn't have to go to the prison for visits any longer. She'd never forget her parents, but she knew her father wanted her to move forward. They wouldn't want the violence and crimes that had directed her journey to this point in her life, to hold her prisoner in the future.

As she stood near the garage door waiting for Kieran's text to let her know he was there, Cara resolved to do her best to honor the sacrifices her parents had made for her. She would at least try to

live her life. For the past few years, she'd hesitated to make connections in the town, but as the end of her father's life loomed, she
knew it was time to reach out. She needed something to anchor
her in her life. Maybe...hopefully...Kieran would just be the start.

Her phone buzzed with a message from Kieran. When she
opened the garage door, she saw his Jeep idling in the back lane.
She stepped out and hit the button to close the door behind her.

Kieran climbed out of the car and greeted her with a smile. He
walked around the vehicle with her and opened her door so she
could slide into the passenger seat. While she waited for him to
join her in the car, Cara used her phone to arm the security system
for the whole building.

"Ready for an evening of fun?" Kieran asked as he buckled his
seatbelt and put the car in gear.

"I think so." Cara gave him a curious look. "Where are we going?"

"It's a surprise. I thought we'd go do something first and then
maybe grab a bite to eat afterward. Sound okay?"

Kieran guided the Jeep onto the road leaving the town. It was a
single lane in each direction, and there was a steady flow of cars
toward the town. She knew that people lived in New Hope and
worked in some of the surrounding towns and cities, so no doubt
some of these cars were bringing people back to their homes after
a day at work.

The day had turned cloudy a short time earlier, and with the
sunset coming in less than an hour, twilight had settled over New
Hope Falls and the surrounding area. Cara enjoyed that part of the
day, especially seeing the warm glow of lights in the houses that
lined the road. As she watched them slip by, she imagined the lives
of the people who called those houses, home.

"Did you have a good week?"

Kieran's question drew her attention from the view to the man
himself. "Yes, it was good. How about yours?"

"Seems it was about the same as others lately. More interviews with the detective overseeing Sheila's case. I followed up on the accident from last Sunday. Spoke at the elementary school about stranger danger. Did some training with some first responders. A little bit of everything."

"Do you enjoy that?"

He glanced over at her. "Enjoy what?"

"Having something different happening all the time."

"Sure. Keeps things from getting boring. How about you?"

"My life is pretty scheduled. My classes happen at the same time every week."

"So if I want to do stuff with you, I guess I need to give you some advance notice and not just try for spur of the moment outings?"

She smiled. "Well, maybe?"

"I can do that," Kieran said with a nod. "As long as I know that's what you prefer, I'll keep that in mind."

Cara wasn't sure what to think or say to Kieran's response. She'd kind of thought he'd say she needed to loosen up. Learn to live in the moment. It touched her that he understood that was how she functioned, and he didn't seem inclined to make her change.

"We're going to an escape room?" Cara asked as he turned into a parking lot in front of a one-story building. He'd mentioned escape rooms as a possibility, so ending up there wasn't a big surprise.

"Yep." He parked the car then turned to her. "Is that okay?"

"It's fine. Never been, but I'm sure it will be fun."

"Great. Our reservation is at six, but they said to be here fifteen minutes early. I think we have to fill out a waiver of some sort."

As they approached the building, Cara glanced around and saw there were a few cars in the lot, so obviously they weren't the only ones there. Kieran pulled the door open, his hand lingering briefly on her back before he followed her into the building.

There were a few other people in the waiting area who looked over when they walked in. Cara edged closer to Kieran as a woman approached them with a broad smile and welcomed them to the escape room experience.

They were asked to complete a waiver that was available online, so Cara pulled out her phone and sat down next to Kieran on a nearby padded bench. She worked her way through the form on her phone, listening to the chatter and laughter of the people who had apparently already completed their waivers.

Once they had both submitted their waivers, the woman came to stand in front of all of them and began to explain what to expect and gave them some rules for their time in the room. Cara realized, as she listened to the woman, that they were going to be playing the escape room with the other people who were sitting there.

She had to wonder how that was going to go because she was pretty sure she and Kieran were older than most of the others by several years, plus they all seemed to be together as a group. Finally, they were taken into the room they were going to have to escape from by solving a mystery.

"Did you choose this one specifically?" Cara asked as they stepped into the room.

He lifted an eyebrow for a moment before a smile curled one corner of his mouth. "Maybe?"

She laughed softly as they stood next to each other, waiting for their time to start. "I hope this doesn't aggravate you."

He glanced around the room. "Yeah. It might not have been my best choice."

She leaned closer to him, bumping her shoulder against his arm. "I think it will be fine."

Kieran looked down at her, close enough that she could see the dark gray flecks in his blue-gray irises. She was captured by his nearness, the scent of his cologne, and the steadiness of his gaze.

"You two gonna help us out?"

The question from one of the other guys had Cara shifting her attention from Kieran to the people in the room. They were watching them with varying degrees of interest. Most of the guys had turned their attention to the puzzles in the room, while the teenage girls giggled, casting them curious glances.

"Guess we'd better get to work," Kieran murmured.

CHAPTER THIRTEEN

"Okay. That was ridiculous." Kieran rested his hand lightly on her back as he held the door open for her.

Cara tried to hold back a laugh, but it was hard. Kieran's frustration had grown throughout the hour. Some of the group they'd been with hadn't been all that interested in working together to solve the puzzles. The girls had giggled and flirted, distracting the guys from what they needed to do.

In the end, they had failed to escape the room.

"Next time, we'll bring our own group." Kieran opened the Jeep door for Cara. "Seriously. That was not how I expected our first escape room experience to go."

Cara settled into the passenger seat. "I know you expected to escape, but you know what? I had fun regardless."

Kieran gripped the door in one hand and the frame in the other as he looked at her. They were parked under a streetlamp, so she was able to see the skepticism on his face.

"I guess that's what counts," he finally said. "But I really hope dinner turns out better."

Cara reached out and touched his arm. "It will be fine."

"I had an idea of how I wanted the evening to unfold, and so far, it's not really working out like I'd hoped."

"Really, it's fine. I'm having fun."

He stared at her for a moment before nodding. "Okay. Let's go have some dinner."

"Let's," Cara agreed.

Kieran shut her door then rounded the vehicle to slide behind the wheel. They ended up at a small out-of-the-way pub-style restaurant that wasn't too busy. The hostess quickly seated them in a booth against the wall. The sides of the booth were high, so they had a bit of privacy for their meal, which was lovely.

The restaurant specialized in home-style comfort food, which seemed to be something Kieran favored, if his appreciation of *Norma's* was anything to judge by. It was clear Kieran had been at the restaurant before because he had no trouble deciding what he wanted. The mac and cheese he'd ordered with his meatloaf sounded good, but she was more in the mood for chicken, so she ended up ordering fried chicken with mac and cheese.

Once the waitress had taken their orders, Kieran began to talk about the escape room again, detailing what he would have done differently if he'd had a team who was actually focused on escaping. Cara found it interesting listening to him. He was a very methodical thinker, and he remembered parts of the puzzle better than she did. She had no doubt that if they did come again with a better group, they would escape.

"Would you be interested in trying again if I could get a group together?" Kieran asked.

Cara found that she would have agreed to go with him once a week if that was what he wanted. "I think that would be fun."

Kieran nodded as if he'd made up his mind. "I think one or two guys from work might be interested."

When the waitress returned with their food a short time later, Kieran said grace, then they began to eat. Their conversation flowed more smoothly than Cara would have anticipated. Though their conversation was more personal, it circled around things they enjoyed doing and what they did in their spare time and thankfully steered clear of discussions about their families.

"So you used to run, but you don't anymore?" Kieran asked when they got onto the subject of exercise.

"It's not that I don't run, I just choose to do it indoors on my treadmill now."

"I understand that. I usually run early in the morning, though sometimes I need to decompress at the end of a bad day, and running is how I do that." He sat back as the waitress returned to refill their water glasses. When she left them alone again, he said, "Would you like to run together sometime?"

It wasn't something she'd ever done with someone before, but that had more to do with lack of opportunity rather than lack of desire. "Sure. That might be more fun than running on my own."

"Have you done any hiking on the trails around here?"

"No. I've been a bit reluctant to do that kind of exploring by myself." She gave him a rueful smile. "As I'm sure you're finding out, I don't tend to venture out too much on my own."

"That's not a bad thing. I mean, my mom is kind of like that, but if there *is* something you'd like to do but don't want to do it on your own, just let me know. Maybe we can work it out to do together."

His words sent warmth spiraling through Cara. After losing her mother and then giving up her identity, she hadn't spent time cultivating relationships that would give her friends she could do things with. Even as one chapter was coming to an end with her father's terminal illness, another was starting, and she knew that how it unfolded was up to her in a lot of ways. Whether she chose to remain distant from the town and its residents being one of them.

Once they'd finished their meal, the waitress cleared away their dishes then offered them dessert. Normally after such a filling meal, Cara would turn down dessert, but when it seemed like Kieran was interested in something, she couldn't resist. In the end, they decided to have coffee and share a piece of peanut butter chocolate cheesecake.

It was the best evening Cara had experienced in years, and she was glad she'd decided to take the risk of agreeing to a date with Kieran. It was probably too soon to admit to any sort of romantic feelings, but for the first time in a long time, she was willing to at least consider opening her heart to someone.

After they'd finished at the restaurant, Kieran took his time driving back to New Hope. Cara was glad that he wasn't in a rush as she found herself reluctant to have the evening end, leaving her to face the quiet of her apartment.

When he pulled up to the back of the building, Cara had to fight the urge to check her phone to make sure everything was okay in her apartment. However, she didn't want to have to explain her obsession to Kieran, so instead, she climbed out of the Jeep without digging her phone out of her purse.

Kieran came to stand next to her, the lights she'd mounted above her garage illuminating him. "I had a really good time—even though we didn't escape like I would have liked."

"It was wonderful. Thank you for planning it for us."

"It was absolutely my pleasure," Kieran assured her.

They stood close, and for a moment, Cara thought he might kiss her. But instead of pressing his lips to hers, he just brushed a kiss against her cheek. With him so close, she wished he'd wrap his arms around her and hold her tight. It felt like it had been forever since someone had last fully hugged her.

"Will I see you at church again this Sunday?" Kieran asked as he stepped back.

She was grateful that he hadn't brought up the previous Sunday. Part of her wanted to be embarrassed that he'd seen her in such a vulnerable state, but she decided she wasn't going to be. If they were going to have any sort of relationship—whether it be a romantic one or just a friendship—she had to allow herself to become more open with people.

"Yes. I plan to go."

A smile transformed Kieran's face. "Wonderful. I'll see you there."

She returned his smile, then reached into her purse for the device that would disarm the garage alarm and open the door. After she stepped inside, she gave Kieran a final look before she pressed it again to lower the door. It wasn't until the door was fully down that she heard the Jeep's engine roar then fade a minute later.

Before moving further into the building, she pulled her phone out to do her normal checks. After verifying that all looked good, she reset the garage door alarm, then disarmed everything else and climbed the stairs to her apartment. She had lights programmed to come on at certain times, so the apartment wasn't dark when she let herself in.

Still feeling the lightness of having had such a wonderful evening, she headed into her bedroom to change into her pajamas. And even though she knew that her father would likely never read any more of what she shared about her life, Cara found she couldn't go to bed without recording her thoughts and feelings about her time with Kieran. She wanted to have it written down in case she got the opportunity to share one more visit with him. But more than that, she wanted to be able to look back on this evening and remember it clearly.

~ * ~

Kieran parked his vehicle then let himself into the house, whistling as he walked. He hadn't allowed himself to have very high expectations for the evening, not knowing how comfortable Cara would be as they went on their first date. While he hadn't been thrilled with how things had unfolded at the escape room, Cara's obvious pleasure in the evening made him feel good.

He'd wanted her to be able to relax and enjoy herself, and if she was being honest, it seemed that she had. Out of the times they'd spent together so far, she had been the most at ease during their date. That was encouraging for him, and it made him hope that maybe...just maybe...there might be the possibility of a more serious relationship with her.

The only thing he didn't know was when he should mention his date with Cara to his mom. He hadn't told her about their plans, just in case things hadn't gone well. But since they hadn't just gone well, but had gone terrifically well, he found himself wanting to share about it with her. However, it was bad enough that his own hopes were being raised, he just didn't want the same thing for his mom until they had a couple dates under their belts.

Kieran didn't think that the evening had been a fluke, but he'd feel more confident sharing things with his mom if they'd had at least two or three dates that had turned out as well as the first one. Of course, now he had to come up with more ideas. Creative dates had never been his strong suit, so it would take some effort, but he was fine with working on that.

When Kieran walked into church on Sunday morning, he glanced around, hoping to see Cara. Unfortunately, she didn't appear to have arrived yet. He hung around at the back for a few minutes, talking with people as they approached him, all the while keeping an eye on the door.

Just a few minutes before the service was to start, the worship team made their way onto the stage. Kieran contemplated sitting at the back, but in the end, he made his way to the row where his mom was sitting with Mary. He leaned down to give her a kiss on the cheek, then took a seat beside her.

He had to remind himself that first and foremost, he was at the service to worship. It would be nice to do that while sitting next to Cara, but her presence—or lack of it—shouldn't influence his ability to focus. Sadly, however, because he was human, he did find himself wondering why she hadn't shown up.

When they stood up to sing after the welcome, he glanced back over his shoulder but still didn't see her there. Disappointment swirled through him as he tried to prepare his heart and his mind for worship. It wasn't the end of the world that she hadn't made it. They'd still see each other another time.

After the sermon was over, the worship team led them in another song as the pastor walked to the back of the sanctuary to stand by the door. At the close of the service, Kieran stood to talk with a couple in the row in front of him.

When their conversation drew to a close, his mom said, "I ended up putting on a roast. Did you want to come over for lunch? Mary said she'd come."

Kieran glanced to the back of the church, his gaze landing on Cara where she stood talking with Pastor Evans. "I'm going to have to take a rain check on that, Mom."

"Okay, sweetie." She gave him a quick hug. "See you sometime this week."

Kieran walked to the outside of the row, then made his way back to where the pastor stood chatting with Cara. They looked like they were having an actual conversation as opposed to the normal shaking of hands and quick greeting most people engaged in as they left the sanctuary, eager to get home or wherever they were going for lunch.

He stopped a few feet away to give them privacy, smiling at Eli and Anna as they walked past. Leah was with them and gave him a quick nod but no smile. He knew what had happened with her dad, even though that had occurred while he was still in New York. He wasn't sure how much that played a role in her demeanor or if she really was just the total opposite of her twin sister even though they were identical in appearance. The only reason he was able to tell them apart was that Sarah always had a smile for him while Leah never did.

"Hi."

Kieran looked over to see Cara standing next to him. "Hey."

"Sorry I was late getting here," she said with a grimace, but she didn't offer any explanation.

"No problem. Just figured you weren't able to make it."

"I debated not coming, but I had told you I would."

And now what were they supposed to do? Kieran realized he hadn't really thought through what they'd do after church. Provided she wanted to do something.

"It's a nice day out," he said. "Would you like to go for a little drive? Maybe grab some lunch?"

"Sure, I'd like that." She gestured to her clothes. "Should I change?"

"We'll be outside if you're up for it, so it just depends how comfortable you are."

"Maybe I'll change."

"Sounds good. I'll swing by *Norma's* and grab us some lunch. Sandwiches okay?"

She nodded. "And some cookies?"

"Of course," he said with a grin. "Always cookies. Do you want a milkshake as well?"

"If you're going to get one, sure."

As they left the church, Kieran didn't look around to see who might be noticing them together. For all he knew, his mom was watching them. No doubt he'd hear from her sooner rather than later if she was.

They went their separate ways outside the church with a plan for Kieran to come by to pick her up after he'd gotten their lunch from the restaurant. He had a destination in mind. He just hoped it wasn't too busy since it was such a nice day.

It was about half an hour before he finally pulled up behind her building. When he texted he was there, the garage door opened, and Cara stepped out. As he hopped out to open the Jeep door for her, Kieran wondered why she didn't have a back door. Granted, if she was worried about security, a single-entry point was easier to secure than two.

"Oh, the food smells great. Did you get more than just sandwiches?"

"I might have picked up a couple of orders of fries."

"That's definitely what I'm smelling."

"I couldn't resist."

The drive to the park where he wanted to go didn't take too long as it wasn't far from the town. It didn't have any spots for camping or a nice beach area, but it had plenty of picnic tables that overlooked the nearby river. It wasn't a big river, and people often swam at other spots along it.

There were only a handful of cars in the small parking lot when he pulled in, so it didn't look like it would be too busy. He climbed out and retrieved their food from the floor behind his seat. Cara came around and took the drink tray from him.

"I've never been here before," Cara said. "I didn't even know this place existed."

"It's a nice spot that isn't too busy most of the time." Kieran didn't share that he'd found it on one of his long runs as he'd tried to deal with his grief and the disintegration of his relationship with Toni when he'd first come back to New Hope after his father's death. There had been plenty of times he'd sat at one of the tables in the dark, trying to figure out how to move forward with his life.

They walked through the grass to an empty table close to the water. The water made a soothing sound as it flowed by, tumbling over and around the rocks.

"This is so beautiful." Cara set the drink tray down and turned to look at the river and the thick forest on the other side.

Kieran had seen the view many times, so he kept his gaze on Cara. She'd changed into a pair of skinny jeans and a large sweatshirt along with a pair of flat ankle boots. Her hair was loose, and it ruffled in the light breeze that picked up for a moment. Kieran fought the urge to tuck the errant strands behind her ear.

She turned away from the river and settled down on the bench of the picnic table. "I really don't know much about the area around here. I've been so busy trying to get my studio up and running and dealing with some personal stuff that I haven't taken the time to explore."

Kieran sat down across from her. "Well, I will happily play tour guide for you and show you the sites."

She smiled and said, "I look forward to that."

He did too, Kieran thought as he opened the bag and began to pull out the food. He set a container of fries in front of Cara while she worked the milkshakes free from the tray. Once they had their food, Kieran said a prayer of thanks.

"Ketchup?" he asked as he fished several packets out of the bag.

"Nope. Norma's fries are the perfect amount of salty, so I rarely eat them with ketchup."

"Perfect. All the more for me."

"Ketchup fan?"

"To hear my mother tell it, ketchup was the only condiment I was interested in for the first five years of my life, and I ate it on everything. I even ate cheese and ketchup sandwiches."

Cara made a gagging sound. "Seriously?"

"Yep. Can't say I'm a fan of them now. I usually confine my ketchup use to fries, meatloaf, and scrambled eggs. Oh, and hash browns."

"Well, it's a relief to learn that your tastes refined with age."

Kieran laughed. "Do you never eat ketchup? It sounds a bit like you have a dislike for it."

"About the only thing I eat ketchup on is bad fries."

"Is there such a thing?" Kieran asked with an arched brow.

"I take back what I said about your tastes refining. There is definitely such a thing as bad fries."

"What is your definition of bad fries?"

"Some of the fast-food ones are definitely bad, and good fries can become bad if they get cold and soggy."

"That's what the microwave is for."

Cara wrinkled her nose. "Microwave can't fix soggy."

"Have you always been a connoisseur of French fries?"

"I kind of became one." Cara ate a fry before continuing. "I had to watch what I ate when I was dancing, so that meant that if I was going to indulge in something like fries, I wanted to make sure I got the very best ones. I hated wasting a cheat meal on bad food, so if I found something I liked, I stuck with it."

"Are you as careful about what you eat now?"

Cara gave him a look. "Is that a serious question?"

Kieran shrugged. "Why wouldn't it be?"

"Because you've eaten with me several times, and I'd have thought you'd know the answer to that question."

"I don't know. You've eaten pretty healthily, at least as far as I could tell." He paused. "Okay, maybe the fried chicken and mac and cheese last night wasn't exactly healthy."

"Don't forget the cheesecake," she reminded him.

"I understand that people need to eat a certain way for a variety of reasons, but I also believe life's too short to completely deprive yourself of something you enjoy. Moderation and all that."

"It took me a while to accept that mindset. As long as my career was the most important thing in my life, the more willing I was to avoid certain foods. Even things I really wanted. Now, I try to eat healthy most the time, with occasional lapses. I don't feel the need to restrict myself the way I once did."

He was glad to hear that because he liked that she was willing to enjoy the meals they shared together. One of his mom's ways of showing her love and care was to cook tasty food and treats for him. As kids, if he or Sean had a bad day at school, she'd offer them cookies and then make their favorite meal.

It was a wonder he didn't have a weight problem, given his love of food. Thankfully, he also had a love of running, which helped to offset his enjoyment of food.

As they ate, a few more people showed up with kids in tow. From the shrieks of laughter as the kids ran around, it appeared they were enjoying their time out in the fresh air too.

They'd just finished their meal when the sky began to darken, and the breeze became more than just a gentle brush across his skin. Cara hugged herself as she looked up at the clouds.

"You cold?"

"A little. It was so nice earlier that I didn't bother to bring a jacket."

Kieran laughed. "Top tip for living in New Hope...always take a jacket with you."

"I know. You're right. It's just that it was so nice..."

"Do you still want to stay for a bit? If so, I can grab you one of my jackets from the Jeep. I always have one or two with me."

"If you don't mind me borrowing one, I'd love to stay for a little longer. Or until it starts to rain."

He had no problem at all with loaning her one. Especially if it meant they could stay there together awhile longer. "I'll be right back."

CHAPTER FOURTEEN

Kieran picked up the bag that contained the remnants of their lunch and dropped it in the garbage can as he walked back to the car. He found a windbreaker and a heavier zip-up hoodie on the back seat. He grabbed them both and headed back to where Cara sat. She had her phone out and appeared to be taking a picture of the river. He didn't blame her for wanting to capture the view. It truly was beautiful.

"Here you go," he said as he set the hoodie on the table. "I think that will be warmer, but if you'd prefer the windbreaker, you can have it instead."

"Maybe you should take the hoodie since you're not wearing a warm shirt."

"I'm fine," Kieran assured her as he tugged on the windbreaker before sitting back down across from her. He would have liked to sit close to her, maybe wrap his arm around her to help her warm up, but he didn't think they were quite at that point in things yet.

"Thank you." She put the hoodie on, not bothering to zip up, just tucking her hands into the pockets and pulling the sides across the front of her body. "That's much better."

Kieran was glad she'd said she wanted to stay for a bit longer in spite of the shift in the weather and the possibility of rain. Strands of her hair blew across her face, and she pulled her hand from her pocket to tuck them behind her ear.

"Do you just work Monday to Friday?" Cara asked.

"Those are my normal hours, but I suppose, technically, I'm on call all the time. If a situation arises or my officers need me for something, they know they can always call me. Like with the accident last week. They called to let me know, and I decided to head out there and see what was going on."

"Do you ever get vacation time?"

Kieran shrugged. "I do get it, but I haven't really utilized it much. I've taken a handful of days, but I haven't needed much more than that. It helps that the job here isn't as high stress as, say, working in Seattle or Portland might be. I don't feel the pressing need to take time off."

The last time he'd put in for more than a few days had been when he'd requested time off for his honeymoon. He'd ended up needing time off following his father's death, and then his original request for holidays hadn't mattered because the honeymoon, along with the wedding, had been canceled.

When his mom had made known her desire to return to New Hope Falls, he'd been only too happy to leave New York and the violence that had taken the lives of his brother and father and left him and his mom with the heartache and grief that had torn their lives apart.

"Are you okay?" Cara asked.

Realizing that he'd gotten lost in his thoughts, he gave her a smile. "Yeah, just trying to remember the last time I'd actually taken a full-on holiday. It's been a while."

He didn't count the month or so he'd taken off to move back to New Hope Falls. That hadn't been a break at all.

"Yeah. It's been a while for me too. Thankfully, I love my job, so not having a vacation isn't a big deal."

"Where would you go if you did decide to take a couple of weeks off?"

"Good question. I moved here because I liked being near the mountains and also close to the water. The best of both worlds within a short drive. I think if I had to choose one place, it might be somewhere like New Zealand. Has anyone who's watched *The Lord of the Rings* not dreamed of visiting that beautiful country?"

"I would have thought you'd like to go somewhere that has a renowned ballet company."

Cara's gaze went distant as she stared past him. He didn't like that his question had created that response in her, and he wondered what exactly had set it off.

When her gaze came back into focus, she gave him a small smile. "You would think that, right? But it's hard to think about going anywhere ballet related because that was a plan I'd had with my mom. We were going to visit as many of the major companies as we could. Paris. London. New York. Moscow. Just to name a few."

"What happened to your mom?"

She hesitated just briefly before saying, "She was in a car accident. It killed her instantly."

"I'm sorry to hear that." Kieran knew all too well the pain of losing a parent unexpectedly. "That must have been a huge shock."

"It was," Cara said, her gaze once again moving from his. "It was horrible."

Their conversation had ended up as dark as the sky, and Kieran wanted to steer it back into happier territory.

Apparently Cara wanted to as well, because she said, "Where would you like to go if you took a vacation?"

Kieran didn't have an immediate answer. For their honeymoon, Toni had wanted to go somewhere with a beach, and since he hadn't had a strong preference for anything different, he'd agreed. They'd ended up booked into an all-inclusive resort in the Bahamas.

"If it were up to me, and I didn't have to take anyone else's preferences into account, I'd probably end up going to Daytona or Talladega for a NASCAR race."

Her eyes widened at that. "You're into racing?"

"Well, I wouldn't say I'm a die-hard fan, but I enjoy watching the races and would love to see one in person some day."

"I can't say I've ever watched a race."

"We might have to remedy that one day. Unfortunately, there are only a few races left in this season, but it starts up again in February."

"Do you watch any other sports?"

"I'll watch whatever's on, but I prefer football or baseball. Basketball, in a pinch, but hockey isn't really my sport at all."

"Do you know how to skate?"

Kieran laughed. "Nope. I never had any desire to balance on a thin blade while sliding around on the ice."

She smiled at him, her eyes lighting up. "But skating is so beautiful."

"Let me guess. You know how to figure skate."

"I do. I took lessons for a few years but then decided I was more interested in ballet."

"I bet you were a beautiful skater. As beautiful as you are a dancer."

Her expression turned curious with a tinge of something else Kieran couldn't quite put his finger on. "How would you know that?"

"Just a wild guess that the black and white photos on the wall of your hallway are of you."

"Oh. Right. I forgot you'd seen those."

"Even if I hadn't, I still would have known you were a beautiful ballerina. I mean, you're a beautiful woman, so it only stands to reason."

Cara laughed and dropped her gaze, her cheeks turning pink. "Thank you for the compliment."

"You're welcome. I call 'em as I see 'em."

"Though I do have to say that the definition of a beautiful ballerina in the ballet world is different from yours. Though I can't say I object to that."

They both laughed, and Kieran found he enjoyed hearing her laugh and seeing her eyes twinkle with merriment. He knew they would have many serious conversations if things moved forward—*please, yes!*—but he hoped they had even more lighthearted moments filled with laughter.

"Those photos were taken quite a few years ago. My mom had them hanging in her house, so I brought them with me when I moved."

"They really were quite stunning. Especially since they're in black and white like that."

"It was a fun photoshoot. My mom set it all up, wanting to have them for her home."

Kieran could see her mood dipping again, and though he didn't want to discourage her from speaking about her mother, it hurt him to see the sadness on her face. "Did she know that you planned to set up a dance studio?"

Cara shook her head. "I only decided to do that after she passed away, but I think she would have understood the change in direction my career took."

"And your father?"

Another hesitation. "He was very supportive of my move to New Hope, and he loves to hear about the studio."

"Has he ever visited you here?"

"No. He wasn't able to make it before his health began to fail."

"Have you been able to see him regularly since he's been sick?"

She nodded. "I try to make it to see him every few weeks."

"Where does he live?"

Her gaze dropped again, and she pulled the hoodie's edges more tightly to her body. "Texas. He moved there after my mom died."

Kieran wondered why she hadn't moved there with her father, but given the fact that the subject seemed to be a difficult one for her, he decided to let it go. Maybe another day she'd be willing to share more. It was only the second time they'd hung out together with the goal of getting to know each other. He could save further questions on the difficult subject of her father for a different time.

Though he wanted to know all about her, he wasn't quite sure he was ready to talk about what had happened in his own past. At least not yet.

He glanced around, seeing that most of the people who had been there earlier had left. With the sun behind the clouds, people were retreating to the protection of the indoors. Most of the time, it was a fifty-fifty shot if they'd get rain once the day darkened like it had. People who didn't live in the area often thought it rained every single day, but the reality was, that it didn't. In fact, depending on the time of year, they didn't get as much rain as people attributed to them.

Yes, they probably had more rainy days in a year than sunny ones, but it wasn't by an overwhelming majority. Still, it wasn't a big surprise when he felt the first splatter of rain on his cheek.

"Guess it's time to head back," he said with a grimace. "I'm surprised the rain held off this long."

"We did get lucky, didn't we?" Cara said as they got up from the table. "It's been lovely."

When the rain began to increase in intensity as they made their way back to the Jeep, Kieran reached out and took Cara's hand. "Let's make a run for it."

Cara grasped his hand tightly as they made quick work of the distance to the parking lot. He unlocked the doors then opened her door for her. Cara didn't hesitate to quickly duck inside. Kieran shut the door and jogged around to the driver's side.

"Hope your seats will survive this," Cara said as she buckled her seatbelt.

"They'll be fine. This isn't the first time they've gotten a little wet." Kieran started the Jeep.

He was in no hurry to get home, so he continued on the road away from New Hope. It would be the first step in letting her in on the splendor of the region. For Kieran, the beauty of New Hope and the surrounding area was its biggest draw.

The rain made it difficult to truly appreciate the sights, but Cara didn't comment about the fact that they weren't heading back to the town. The radio played music from a local Christian radio station softly in the background.

Their conversation centered on the areas he was driving through. Cara appeared to be interested in the little stories he shared of things he'd seen because of his job.

He still wondered if she'd given any real thought to what dating him might mean. Though he wanted to know, he was a little afraid to ask. Maybe after a couple more dates, if things were still going well, he'd initiate the conversation and pray that she would be receptive to continuing to date him despite his career. He wasn't prepared to give up his job, so all he could do was hope that the woman he'd set his heart on would accept all of him, including what he did for a living.

~ * ~

Cara relaxed back in her seat, pulling the hoodie tight around her. She loved being wrapped up in the warmth of it and catching the lingering scent of Kieran's cologne. Ensconced within Kieran's Jeep, she appreciated the light conversation set against the softly playing music.

It gave her a glimpse of what it might be like to have a relationship in her life. To be able to spend time with someone, just the two of them, sharing a meal and conversation. Learning about each other. Sharing their lives.

The only thing that gave her a moment's pause was his job. She supposed some would say she should be worried about the danger of his profession, but that didn't concern her at all. First of all, New

Hope wasn't necessarily a hotbed of violent crime. Second, if she came to love him like her mom and dad had loved each other, she would be grateful for any time they had together, be it short or long.

It was more of a concern that his job gave him access to tools that might reveal her past, and now that she'd had a taste of being with Kieran, she didn't want to risk losing him.

One thing she'd realized earlier when Kieran had taken her hand was that she missed that physical connection. After living the first couple decades of her life being lavished with love and affection by both parents, it had been hard to basically lose all of that in the space of a few months. Her mom's death had been the first blow, but then when her father had gone to prison, all that easy physical affection had stopped completely.

She wanted to have those affectionate and loving touches again. Hugs. Hand holding. Kisses. And being with Kieran was bringing that desire to the surface in an intensity she hadn't felt since the days following her father's incarceration. Cara knew she shouldn't rush things on a physical level, but she couldn't help the pull she felt to Kieran.

"Did I lose you?"

Kieran's question brought her thoughts back to the cozy atmosphere inside the car. "Sorry. My thoughts drifted just a bit. What did I miss?"

Kieran chuckled. "Nothing important. You just kind of zoned out."

"Yes, I did, and I do apologize for that. Every once in awhile, my mind catches on something, and I focus in on it. Sometimes to the exclusion of things around me."

"I think we all have those moments." He looked at her briefly, giving her a warm smile. "Don't worry about it. I didn't take offense."

Cara was glad to hear that because the last thing she wanted was to upset him. He'd been so good to her, and she didn't want him to think she wasn't enjoying the time they spent together, because she really did.

When his phone rang a minute later, she could see from the display on the dash that it was his mom. He pressed the screen to answer it without hesitating, and she wondered if he did that because he was worried something might be wrong.

"Hey, Mom."

"Hi, honey. Where are you?"

"Out for a bit of a drive."

"Oh. Are you okay?"

"I'm fine. Just wanted to get out of town for a little while."

Cara noticed he wasn't saying anything about her, and while someone else might have taken offense at that, she didn't. Living in a small town, she was aware that speculation and rumors sometimes traveled at lightning speed. Even though she'd run into a few people—like Missy—speculating about how things were between her and Kieran, she wasn't quite ready for the scrutiny of the townspeople. Even Kieran's mom.

"Are *you* okay?" he asked. "Did something happen?"

"No, nothing has happened. I just wondered if you planned to come over this week for Sean's birthday."

Kieran gave Cara a quick look before he answered. "Of course, Mom. I wouldn't miss it, you know that."

"It's hard to believe it's been almost six years. He would have been thirty this year."

"I know."

Cara's curiosity was piqued as she listened to them talk, wondering who Sean was. Like when he'd taken his mom's call in her office, it felt a bit awkward listening in on a personal conversation— both sides of it this time. But short of digging out her earbuds and her phone, she had no way to avoid it.

Instead, she turned her attention out the window, but not before noticing that Kieran's easygoing demeanor had given way to tension. Where he'd only loosely held the steering wheel earlier, he now had a firm grip on it.

"Listen, Mom. Can I give you a call when I get home? We can talk more about it then."

"Of course, honey. I didn't mean to bring this all up while you were enjoying some peace and quiet. Just give me a call when you want to talk."

"Thanks, Mom. I'll call you in a little while."

They said goodbye, then Kieran ended the call. "Sean was my younger brother. He was killed."

Cara focused more fully on him. "I'm sorry to hear that. Was he a cop too?"

Kieran gave a humorless laugh. "No. He was definitely not a cop. He got caught up with the wrong crowd and was in the wrong place at the wrong time."

"That must have been horrible to deal with."

"It was. There were only two of us, so suddenly I was an only child. Helping my mom through losing her youngest son was rough. His death nearly ended her life."

"I can't imagine. I don't think any parent plans to outlive their children."

"No, they don't. That was something my mom said a lot in those early days. That we were supposed to be the ones burying her, not her burying one of us."

"I'm sorry this will be a difficult week for you."

Kieran's shoulder slumped a bit. "To be honest, I had kind of forgotten that it was his birthday. I would never tell my mom that, and it's not because I've forgotten him. It had just been a long time since we'd celebrated his birthday with him even before he was killed. We didn't celebrate if he wasn't there, and in the years before he passed, he wasn't around much. I mean, not that we're celebrating his birthday this week. It's more about remembrance.

Remembering the man he was before he decided to go his own way, making far too many bad decisions in the process."

"No one can blame you for not living your life firmly entrenched in the past. It's a bit different for your mom. I mean, she would remember having given birth to him. She would have memories of how his birth changed her life."

Kieran nodded, not saying anything for a moment, but then he glanced at her again. "I hope you're not upset that I didn't tell Mom you were with me."

Cara reached out to lay her hand on his arm, letting it rest there a moment before tucking it back in the pocket of the hoodie. "I'm not upset at all. In fact, I'm kind of glad. It's better if it's just the two of us in this...getting to know each other and things we've got going on."

She felt relieved when the corner of Kieran's mouth lifted slightly. "I would agree."

"I figure if we end up spending more time together, people will undoubtedly start to weigh in with their thoughts on the situation, so we might as well enjoy the privacy while we can."

"I see you've figured out how things work in New Hope," he said with a laugh.

"Kind of. I've heard lots about Eli's situation, then about him and Anna, not to mention the opinions on a few divorces that have taken place in the time I've lived here."

"Welcome to New Hope Falls, where your business is everyone's business."

"Is there anything off-limits when it comes to gossip?"

"Not really. There are some who will share rumors or gossip about everything. Then there are others who won't gossip about anything. Most fall in the middle, where they might chat about you, but if it were something really serious, they wouldn't say anything."

"I don't suppose people would do me a favor and wear labels to let me know which one they are."

"No, probably not. They wouldn't see the fun in that, because how would they get you to share your deepest, darkest secrets with them if you think they'll turn around and share them."

Cara thought about her deepest, darkest secrets, and she was confident that she wouldn't be sharing those with anyone.

"I think it's best to just not share those sorts of things until you know a person really well."

"Good plan. There are only three people that I can absolutely vouch for not being gossips. One, of course, is me. Another is Eli because he knows how hurtful gossip can be, and he's said he'd never inflict that on anyone. The final person is Pastor Evans. That man has held a lot of confidences over the years. Ask anyone who's ever spoken with him, and they'll tell you that he is a trustworthy holder of secrets."

"That's good since I would assume that would almost be part of his job description."

"Yes, it would be," Kieran agreed.

She'd spoken to the man for a few minutes after the service, thanking him for his message that day as well as his prayers the previous week. The man's caring nature had shown through in his gentle smile and warm gaze. She could see why people found it easy to confide in him.

She didn't realize that Kieran had turned them around at some point until a sign for New Hope appeared. Though she was disappointed that their time together was ending, at least it was ending on a slightly more upbeat note.

"Sorry we couldn't spend more time together, but I think I should drop in and see if Mom's okay. I'm sure she is, but—"

"No. Don't feel you have to explain it to me. In your shoes, I'd want to check in on her too." When he pulled up behind her building, she reached into her purse and pushed the button to open the garage door as she said, "I'm assuming we'll have more opportunities to hang out?"

"Definitely." He smiled at her, the earlier tension disappearing from his face. "Most definitely."

"You've got my number." She pushed open her door. "I look forward to hearing from you."

CHAPTER FIFTEEN

It was still raining, so Cara darted for the open doorway. Before closing the door, she waved at him one more time, wishing that they were already at the point where a hug and a kiss were part of their goodbyes. She closed the garage door, listening as he drove away. As she turned to disarm the main alarm, she realized she was still wearing his hoodie.

Cara felt a bit like a teenager as she lifted the edge of it to her nose and sniffed, once again appreciating the whiff of his cologne. She didn't know the name of it, but its scent lingered as she climbed the stairs to her apartment. It was only as she walked in the door that she realized she hadn't taken time to look at her cameras, which was something she hadn't done since she'd moved into the building.

As much as she enjoyed her time with Kieran, she couldn't allow herself to become distracted to the point where she didn't pay attention to her surroundings. Thankfully, this time around, it appeared that nothing had happened while she'd been out.

She wandered over to the window and stared out at the gray clouds hanging low over the town. A shiver went through her as she watched raindrops slide down the glass. As the sky continued to darken, shadows crept into the apartment. Moving through the room, Cara snapped on a couple of lamps, providing just enough light to keep the room from being too dark.

After she got herself a mug of coffee, she made her way to the small table near the front window where she sat to journal. She set her mug down then used her phone to queue up her favorite playlist, smiling contentedly as soft music played through the hidden speakers in the room. Settling into her chair, she picked up her notebook and pen from the table.

Drawing her legs up, Cara gazed out the window as she tried to figure out what she wanted to write. When she realized the answer was *everything*, she bent her head and set her pen to the paper. Words flowed as she tried to capture all the feelings she'd been experiencing while spending time with Kieran. Knowing that what she wrote in the journal would now be for her own memory-keeping rather than for her to read to her papa, she didn't hesitate to write down everything she'd felt.

As her words shifted from what had happened to what she hoped the future would hold, Cara looked up and stared unseeing out the window. For the first time since her mom's death, she felt hope and the freedom to dream about a future.

She hadn't consciously realized that hope had slipped away. There had been so much else going on that she hadn't been able to focus too much on what she wanted for the rest of her life.

Since meeting Kieran, however, she was finding that her hopes and dreams were coming to life once again. The joy she'd once felt before suffering so much loss was coming back to her. And it wasn't just Kieran who was responsible for that.

There had also been something about her father the last time she'd seen him. A peace she hadn't witnessed before. Up until that moment, his worry about what would happen to her after he passed had caused him untold amounts of stress. This time, he hadn't seemed resigned to his fate but more at peace with it.

Cara sank back against the chair, realizing that while her papa was at peace with what was to come for him, she didn't feel entirely the same way. It was hard to feel at peace when his passing would mean both of her beloved parents would be gone.

The idea that she'd be on her own at that point still weighed heavily on her, but perhaps not as heavily as it once had. Maybe that was because she knew that all she had to do was open herself up to the people around her, and she wouldn't be alone. Maybe it was accepting, in a way she never had before, that God was with her. Even in her darkest moment, He would be there for her.

Feeling drained of words, Cara flipped the journal closed and put it back on the table with the pen. She picked her mug up and took a sip of the now lukewarm coffee.

Leaning back against the chair, she angled her head so she could see out the window. It eased some of the constant ache within her to know that when the time came to grieve her papa's passing, Kieran would be there for her.

~ * ~

"Chief! You need to come."

Kieran looked up from the file he'd been reading at the request of a detective in Everett. Every once in awhile, one of the guys he knew in Everett would ask for his input on a case, aware that Kieran had previous detective experience from his time of service with the NYPD.

Without waiting for an explanation, Kieran got to his feet, grabbed his hat, and followed the officer, knowing that none of his staff were prone to hysterics. If they said he needed to come, he would follow them.

When they reached the main entrance, he saw Lisa tending to a young woman who sat bent forward, a young man hovering at her side.

"What's going on?" Kieran asked, keeping his voice low and steady.

The young man glanced up, and Kieran could see that he was shaken. "We found a body."

Kieran's stomach knotted when he heard the words. "Where?"

After he listened to the man stumble over his words trying to describe where they'd been, he finally said, "How about you take us to where you found it?"

The man glanced at the woman sitting on the seat next to Lisa.

"I'll take good care of her," Lisa said, giving him a reassuring smile. "Go with the chief and show him what you found."

The man nodded, then bent down to talk to the woman. "I'll be back, babe. Just wait for me here, okay?"

She nodded and lifted her head to look at him. He gave her a quick kiss before straightening. "I'm ready."

Kieran wasn't sure he was. The thought that kept going through his head was whether this was the body of a recently deceased person or if it might have been there a long time...like from ten years ago when Sheila had disappeared.

"Carl, follow me in your car," he said to the officer who'd first called him from his office. Turning to another officer who'd come to the front of the station, he added, "Let Everett know we're going to need help. I'll phone you with an update as soon as I have one."

He walked out the front door of the station with the young man at his side. Kieran got behind the wheel of his official SUV and waited as the man climbed in next to him.

As they drove, he got some basic information, mostly about the couple and what they'd been doing in the area. The man—Steve—guided him northeast of the town, up the road that led into the mountains. He pointed out the lot where they'd parked to do some hiking.

Kieran pulled into a spot then waited for Carl to park next to him. Together, they followed Steve as he led the way up a trail then showed them where they'd gone off the path to take some pictures.

"We were just over there," Steve said. "Then we noticed bones and clothes."

Bones and clothes. A chill swept down Kieran's spine. He hoped he wasn't going to have to make a death notification to Pete, but he supposed at least then their wondering about what had happened to Sheila would be over. But he couldn't make an official notification until they knew for sure who the victim was, and by that time, Pete would probably have already heard that a body had been found.

Pushing aside everything but the facts—of which there were none just yet—Kieran pulled out his phone and made the call to update his boss in Everett. He wanted to approach the remains to see if he could find anything that might identify the body as Sheila's, but he stayed back. If this was, in fact, a murder, the deceased deserved to have their killer found, so Kieran wouldn't do anything to disturb the crime scene.

After he'd given detailed directions to the scene to the Everett detective, Kieran told Carl to take Steve back to the station and get a statement from both him and his girlfriend. Though he cautioned them both about not speaking to anyone about the finding, he knew it was only a matter of time before word began to spread. The vehicles from Everett would have to pass through the town, and some eagle-eyed resident was sure to recognize them for what they were.

Alone in the quiet of the woods, he said a prayer for the family of the victim, whoever it was. There was a part of him that had a hard time believing it could be anyone but Sheila. After all, to his knowledge, they hadn't had any other missing person reports in the past few decades.

If it was Sheila, and she'd been murdered, then they had a killer who'd been on the loose for ten years. And he knew this would impact Eli, but he still had no doubt of the man's innocence. It was just too bad the detective wasn't as certain of it, which meant Eli would be called back in for questioning yet again.

The beauty of nature surrounded him, but right then, he couldn't appreciate it. Death had marred the beauty and left him with questions, the answers to which he wasn't sure he wanted to know. Even if it wasn't Sheila, the fact would remain that someone had either died there in the woods or been brought there to be buried. Neither scenario was great, and both would leave the people of the area shaken.

Kieran took off his hat and ran his hand through his hair, then settled himself on a nearby rock to await the arrival of the crime scene technicians from Everett. He kind of doubted that there would be much to find beyond the body itself. If it really was just bones, that meant it had been out there far longer than a few weeks, which also likely meant that any evidence of the killer was probably long gone. It would make it that much harder to solve the case, but they would do their best.

The peacefulness of the forest was broken a short time later when Carl arrived back with the first of the crime scene team. Kieran met them and relayed what he knew so far about the body and where it was located.

Kieran sighed when his not-so-favorite detective showed up about a half an hour after everyone else had arrived.

"You think it's our girl?" he asked as he lit a cigarette then put it between his lips.

"No clue," Kieran said. "We don't even know if the body is male or female yet. We'll just have to wait until the coroner or the forensic pathologist has a look."

The detective grunted as he took a drag from the cigarette, his gaze on the group of people working within the taped off area.

The coroner arrived a short time later and, after greeting them, made his way to the crime scene. Kieran could feel the tension rolling off the detective, but thankfully, the man was keeping his thoughts to himself. They weren't what Kieran wanted to hear right then. He had plenty of his own thoughts, and none of them were good.

Remembering that he'd told Cara that he might come by the studio for lunch, Kieran pulled his phone out and tapped a message to her.

I'm not going to be able to make lunch today. Something's come up at work.

Cara: *I'm sorry to hear that. Hope it's nothing too serious.*

Unfortunately, it is kind of serious. I'll talk to you about it later.

Cara: *Stay safe.*

Kieran sighed as he read the words. In this particular situation, he wasn't concerned about his safety or that of the people around him, but that might not always be the case. There might come a day when his personal safety was a concern, and he couldn't help but wonder—again—how Cara might react to that. It was a conversation they needed to have soon. He needed to tell her about his past with Toni and what had led to them breaking up.

When the coroner approached them awhile later, he said, "It appears to be an adult female. Cause of death, I'm going to assume, because of the knife between her ribs, is a stabbing."

"The murder weapon is still there?" Kieran asked as he watched the team carry the body bag toward the trail leading to the parking lot.

"I'll have more details once I get the body back to the morgue. I didn't see any sign of a gunshot wound, just the knife." The man ran a hand through his snowy hair. "We'll probably need the forensic anthropologist on this since all we're left with is bones."

"How long will that take?" the detective asked.

The coroner shrugged. "At this point, I have no clue. I'll have to talk to her and see what her schedule is like."

"Where there any clothes or jewelry with the body?"

"All that's been bagged. You'll have to talk to the crime scene team to see what they found."

The detective gave a huff of impatience, and for once, Kieran agreed with the man. He wanted answers sooner rather than later, but in this particular case, he knew the answers were going to be slow coming. There would be no fingerprints, at least not on the victim, and he didn't think they'd get lucky and find any on the knife. The fact that the knife had been left with the body told him that the perpetrator had probably known they weren't leaving anything behind that could be traced back to them.

They'd need dental records to positively identify the person, though the clothing might be helpful. No one had been able to say with one hundred percent certainty what Sheila had been wearing the night she'd disappeared, though Eli had been able to remember what she'd had on the last time he'd seen her, as had Coral.

"I'm heading back now," the coroner said.

"Me, too." The detective dropped his cigarette butt and ground it out with his heel.

"Hope you plan to pick that up," the coroner remarked as he walked past him. "The last thing we need is a forest fire."

Kieran fought the urge to smile as the detective bent and picked up the cigarette butt, muttering curses under his breath as he followed the coroner. Though he would have liked to head out too, he stayed there until the last person had left, then finally, he headed back to the station.

He wished that this would be his case to work, but while he'd probably be a part of the team and would get regular updates, another detective would take the lead. Possibly even the detective who was working on Sheila's case.

As Kieran drove back to the station, he took his time, needing the drive to quiet his mind. It was rare they had such a horrific crime in the area, and whether he wanted to admit it or not, this had shaken him a bit. At one time, something like this wouldn't have made him blink. He would have taken it all in stride and not even thought twice about it. However, he'd become very accustomed to the slower pace of New Hope in the years he'd been there.

He found that all he wanted to do was to go see Cara. She was a light in his life these days, and just being with her brought him a sense of peace. They'd even gone running a couple of times together. That was something Toni had never been interested in. She'd always said that if he ever saw her running, it was because something was chasing her or there was a good sale on at Neiman Marcus.

It was nice that Cara enjoyed doing something that he also enjoyed. It was just one more opportunity to spend time together. Maybe, if he didn't need to stay at the station too late, he'd see if she wanted to go into Everett and grab a bite to eat. He wasn't up for anything more than some good conversation and a good meal, but he didn't think Cara would mind.

Back in his office a short time later, Kieran made a few phone calls to follow up on the case. He was invited to attend the briefing the next morning, which he definitely planned to do. If the body ended up being Sheila's, he wanted to know what was going on with the investigation.

Once it looked like he'd be out of the office at a decent hour, he called Cara, and she quickly agreed to go with him for a late dinner. They didn't go anywhere special. He'd just wanted to go somewhere that was open late, so they weren't rushed.

"Did your day turn out okay?" Cara asked once they'd given the waitress their order.

"Well, what happened today was just the start of an investigation." He told her about what had transpired, knowing that he could trust her to not spread information about it.

"So you don't know if it's Sheila?"

"Not yet." Kieran hesitated for a minute then said, "Can I talk to you about something else?"

When she gave him a weird look, he realized how dumb the question was. "Of course you can."

"I'm just curious how you feel about my job."

Her dark brows rise slightly. "Your job?"

"Yes. Some people have not-so-great feelings about cops and the risks they have to take on the job."

"Oh." She sat back in her chair and regarded him with her soft gray eyes. "Maybe I'd feel differently if you worked in a city with more dangerous crime. I mean, undoubtedly I'd worry more than I do at the moment, but my life has taught me that any of us can die at any time. My mom was a stay-at-home mom who home-schooled me. I mean, could you find a less dangerous life? And yet, one day, she was gone. Taken away while she was in her car, doing something most people do without ever considering it to be dangerous."

Her gaze remained on him, but Kieran had a feeling that she was seeing something else. Someone else. Sadness took over her expression, and he wished he could do something to take it from her.

"What I learned was that we need to make the most of our days, and to let those we love know how much we care about them." Her gaze came back into focus. "I asked my dad if he would have chosen not to love my mom, knowing that she would be taken like that, and his answer was no. He wouldn't have given up all the days he did have with her even though she was taken away from us far too soon."

"I was engaged before."

Her eyes widened in surprise, but she didn't say anything.

"When we first started dating, my girlfriend said she could handle my career. We ended up getting engaged, and we were just a couple of months away from the wedding when my dad was killed in the line of duty. That really shook her up, and she ended up calling everything off. I guess seeing firsthand how my dad's death affected my mom brought home the danger of the job in a way it hadn't occurred to her before."

"I'm sorry you had to go through that," Cara said, her gaze sympathetic.

"I won't lie. It was hard. My brother had died only a short time before that, so in the space of a few months, I lost my brother, my father, and my fiancée." He sighed. "I'm not glad that my father died the way he did, but at least his death stopped Toni and me from making a mistake. It showed her before our wedding that she couldn't handle the danger the way she thought she could. Quite possibly we would have ended up in divorce if she'd realized that after the wedding."

He paused then gave her a half-hearted smile before adding, "I'm not proposing marriage or anything like that, but I...like you, and I needed to know where you stood before we let our relationship get any more serious. Provided that's what you want."

A smile curved Cara's lips, and her expression softened. "It *is* what I want."

"Just talk to me about any concerns you might have, okay? If you're worried about something to do with my job, tell me. I'd rather have it all out in the open between us. Communication is important, especially about something like that."

"I promise I'll talk to you about it."

"Good. Thank you." He gave her a relieved smile, feeling as if a weight had been lifted from his shoulders. "I really wasn't looking for a relationship, and honestly, I'm not sure why it took me so long to notice you like this, but I feel so comfortable spending time with you and getting to know you." Reaching across the table, he covered her hand with his. "I like you a lot."

She turned her hand over, so they were palm to palm and gave him a smile that made his heart skip a beat. "I like you a lot too."

It wasn't quite the L-word, but it was close, and Kieran knew it was only a matter of time before it became love for him. He'd been a bit more cautious with Cara. With Toni, they'd exchanged *I love you's* within weeks of meeting each other. Despite the short time they'd been dating, he'd known that he'd loved her and had been looking forward to the life they'd have together.

Things with Cara were moving slowly, and yet he knew his emotions were as deeply engaged with her as they had been with Toni, maybe even more so because they connected in ways he never had with Toni. All he knew was that he'd almost given up on the idea of finding love again, but somehow Cara had entered his life after being on the periphery of it for a few years, and her gentle nature had drawn him in.

When the waitress reappeared with their food, Kieran reluctantly released her hand and sat back in his seat. Over their meal, he learned a bit more about her childhood and how close she'd been to her mom. How it was often just the two of them because her father had traveled a lot on business. In return, he shared about his early years growing up in New Hope Falls before moving to New York City, so they could be close to his dad's family.

He liked the times when their world narrowed down to just the two of them, and they could learn even more about each other. Though there would be plenty of people with opinions about their relationship, what was important were the moments when it was just the two of them.

It was almost ten before they headed back to New Hope. When he got back to town, he pulled into the back lane behind her building and put his Jeep in park. He jumped out and came around to the passenger side as the garage door began to rise.

He opened Cara's door, and when she got out, she hesitated in front of him for a moment. Kieran reached out and cupped her cheek with his hand.

"May I kiss you?" he asked, his voice low.

They'd hugged before, but he hadn't felt like they were in a position for anything more intimate. After having the conversation they'd had earlier that evening, however, their emotional closeness had led them to a place where a bit more physical intimacy felt natural.

Instead of answering, she stepped closer and lifted her face to his. Her hands moved up his arms to his shoulders as he lowered his head to brush his lips against hers. He slid his arms around her back, holding her loosely.

Their kiss was a soft and gentle press of lips, and Kieran felt their connection deepen and take a firm hold on his heart. He wanted this with her more than he'd wanted anything in a long time. When the kiss ended with a final brush of his lips against hers, he prayed that their relationship would only continue to grow and strengthen.

"Have a good night," he said softly.

She rested her hand against his face, her touch gentle. "You too."

His arms slid from around her waist as she stepped back toward the open garage.

"I'll give you a call tomorrow."

"I look forward to it," she said with a smile. "Thank you for tonight."

"It was my pleasure."

As the garage door began to lower, she gave him a quick wave. Kieran waited until the door was completely closed before he went around the Jeep to get back behind the wheel. He couldn't keep the smile from his face as he drove home.

The day may have started out badly, but it was certainly ending on a high note. He hadn't woken up that morning with any plan to talk to Cara about the future, but he was so glad he had. It gave him hope that he might be able to attain the family he'd thought he'd lost when Toni had called off their engagement and wedding.

It was odd that before getting to know Cara, whenever Kieran had tried to imagine being in a relationship after what had happened with Toni, he'd had a hard time picturing how it would be. Toni had been his first serious relationship, so he'd never experienced the differences of relationships with different women. All he could imagine was that another relationship would be similar to how his had been with Toni.

And yet that was totally not how things were with Cara. Though Cara had been a bit reserved and aloof at the beginning, the more time they spent together, the more at ease she became. She was so easy to be with, and Kieran hadn't realized how much he needed that. Her being so easygoing meant that he was more relaxed too. He wasn't constantly worried if she was okay, or if he'd chosen the wrong restaurant, or if she wouldn't approve of the plans he'd made.

So far, she seemed to have enjoyed everything they'd done together, and that made him happy. Making her happy made him happy. And he hoped he could do that every single day.

CHAPTER SIXTEEN

Cara snickered as she listened to Kieran complain once again about the group they'd ended up with on their latest venture to the escape room.

"I thought we weren't going to rely on random groups again," she said as Kieran turned out of the parking lot onto the street.

Kieran sighed. "I know, but since we haven't really made our relationship public, it's kind of hard to find people to go with us."

Cara wondered how long he wanted to wait before they made things a little more official. Lately, she'd become even more convinced that she wanted something serious with Kieran. After their conversation a couple of nights prior, she was confident that he wanted that too. But when would the time be right to let the people of New Hope Falls in on the secret of their relationship?

Since he would be more impacted than her by people finding out, Cara was leaving that decision up to him. She wasn't going to pressure him. She couldn't blame him for wanting to make sure that things were a go for them before sharing the news with others, especially his mom.

She was planning another trip to see her dad in a couple of days, and she intended to tell him all about Kieran and what had developed between them since her previous visit. It was hard to believe that her dad was still hanging in there despite the cancer ravaging his body, but he was, and she was beyond grateful for that.

"How do you feel about meeting me at *Norma's* for dinner tomorrow night?"

Cara turned to look at him, wishing the streetlights did a better job of illuminating his expression. Had she said part of her internal monologue out loud? "What?"

He shifted both hands to the top of the steering wheel and gave her a quick glance. "Well, unless you'd rather not."

She reached out and rested her hand on his arm, giving his forearm a light squeeze. "No, I would like that very much."

"Are you sure?"

"I *am* sure, and I've been sure for a couple of weeks now."

"So, you want to make it official?"

Cara laughed softly. "New Hope Falls official?

"Yes, and that's even more important than Facebook official." He moved his hand from the wheel and took hold of hers, interlacing their fingers. "Though we could make it official there too."

"I don't have Facebook, though I suppose I could sign up for it if you want it to be official on social media as well."

Kieran lifted their joined hands and pressed a kiss to the back of her hand. "I don't need that at all, babe."

Babe. The endearment warmed her, and she tightened her fingers around his. "I'd set up an account just for you, though. I probably won't ever post on it, but I'd set one up."

"I've had my account for ages, but I really don't post much. I think my mom just likes to have a way to share silly animal videos with me, and occasionally tag me in pictures." He looked over at her. "You didn't have any friends you wanted to keep in contact with after you moved?"

And those were the questions that put her in the uncomfortable position of having to lie as long as she didn't tell him the whole truth about her previous life. "As a kid, I didn't have a whole lot of friends since my mom homeschooled me, and even though I had friends in the ballet company, when I left it, we lost touch, since, to be honest, ballet was pretty much all we had in common."

That probably would have been true even if she'd left the company of her own volition instead of them thinking she'd died as a result of a horrific car bombing.

"You're probably one of the smart ones who hasn't let social media take over your life."

"I think one could find a happy medium, though. It shouldn't have to be all or nothing."

"True, and to be honest, it's been good for my mom. She's been able to keep in touch with old friends and family in New York as well as her friends and family here."

"I should confess that I do have Instagram, though I rarely post on it either. I just like to look at pretty pictures. And at this time of year, I follow accounts that post lots of holiday stuff."

"That's one platform I have never used," Kieran said.

For the first time since her "death," Cara considered setting up a Facebook account because she found herself wanting to forge connections with people. Perhaps she'd surprise him with a friend request later that night. Then maybe after their dinner at *Norma's* where they made their relationship New Hope Falls official, they could also make it Facebook official.

Making that decision brought a smile to her face, and excitement filled her at the thought of people knowing that she and Kieran were a couple. That they belonged together. Now that they were committed to each other, she wanted everyone to know.

When Kieran pulled up behind her garage, Cara didn't want their evening to end. However, they both had to work the next morning, and she knew his week had been long already, and it was only half over. Though he hadn't gone into detail about the body that was found, she knew the case was stressing him out. She'd figured that it wasn't her place to know all the details of what his work entailed, but rather to give him a place to escape it if he wanted or needed to.

He might have griped about their group at the Escape Room, but she knew the main goal of the evening had been for him to get a break from what was going on at work. That he wanted her to be part of that break made her feel really good. She wanted to be the person he went to when he needed an escape from the ugliness and stresses of his job.

After turning off the Jeep, he got out and came around to her door. She slid out of the car to stand in front of him, her heart thudding in her chest as he reached to take her into his arms. She slid her hands up behind his neck as she tilted her head back to meet his kiss.

His strong hands on her back made her feel protected while the gentle way he kissed her made her feel connected...cared for. She didn't want this to end. Not the feeling of being in his arms nor the time they'd spent together.

When their kiss ended, Kieran rested his forehead against hers for a moment as he took a deep breath. "I'd better go."

She tightened her hands briefly at the back of his neck before letting go. "Thank you for another lovely evening."

He laughed. "Even though I was complaining about our group earlier?"

"Even though." She let her hand rest briefly on his cheek, his stubble prickly against her palm. "As long as I'm spending time with you, I don't mind what we're doing."

"I agree, which is why I'm looking forward to dinner with you at *Norma's* tomorrow night."

"Me too."

Kieran dipped his head to brush one more kiss across her lips. "I'll see you then. Sleep well."

"You too." He stepped back from her, his hands slowly sliding from her back. He waited beside the Jeep until she'd gone inside her garage, and the door had settled back down into place.

She was smarter this time and took the time to look over her cameras before climbing the stairs to her apartment. Once upstairs, she got herself something to drink and took it to her favorite chair. She lowered all the blinds then sat down, and though she did plan to journal about her evening, first, she needed to set up a Facebook account.

Her old account was still set up, but she hadn't logged in since the day of the car bombing. It had been imperative that everything supported the news of her death. Her laptop and everything had been replaced as part of her new life, so there would be no chance of her accidentally logging into something because of a saved password in a browser on her old laptop.

Once it was loaded, she hesitated over what photo to use. She knew it couldn't be too recognizable, so after a few minutes of hesitation, she took a selfie of her profile and then took a few more until she got one that looked natural and not too posed. Given that she wasn't one who took selfies, that was the most challenging part of setting up her account.

Once she had it all set up with a picture and a cover photo, she did a search for Kieran's profile. When she found it, she set him a friend request. She didn't know how quickly he'd accept it, so she set her laptop aside and picked up her journal.

The next day, after the students of her last class had left, Cara hurried upstairs to take a quick shower and prepare for her dinner with Kieran. She stood in front of her closet for a few minutes, trying to decide what to wear. Given that they would probably garner attention being together, she wanted to be sure that she looked nice.

In the end, she settled on a pair of fitted brown and gold plaid pants that she matched with a deep rust-colored turtleneck sweater. She liked the autumn look of the combination. Sitting down at her makeup table, she pulled her hair up into a loose knot on her head, leaving a few strands curling down around her cheeks. She applied a bit of makeup, then called it good.

She'd just pulled on a pair of brown ankle boots when her text alert sounded. Going to her bed where she'd left her phone earlier, she picked it up to read the message.

Kieran: *Ready to go public?*

Ready as I'll ever be!

Kieran: *I'm coming to the studio so we can go together.*

You know I can cross the street on my own, right?

Kieran: *Oh, I know that. I just want to walk into the restaurant holding your hand.*

Then I shall happily wait for you because I'd like that, too.

Kieran: *I'll BRT.*

Cara was smiling as she walked down the stairs and followed the hallway to the front. She waited until she saw Kieran approaching before she stepped out of the door and used her phone to arm the alarm.

"You look lovely," he said as he reached her. "Very fall-like."

"That was kind of the look I was aiming for."

Taking her hand, he leaned down to give her a quick kiss, which let her get a nice whiff of his cologne. "Time to let people have a look at us."

Together they crossed the street and walked into *Norma's*. The woman herself was standing at the podium and looked up as they stepped in front of her. For a moment, she just stared at them, then a grin spread across her face.

"Table for two?" she said, her eyes twinkling.

"Yep. Just two," Kieran told her. "And I'd prefer a booth, actually."

"Of course. Do you want one by the front window so people can see you as they walk by?"

Kieran chuckled. "Sure. Why not."

"You can't be worried about being seen since you came here," Norma remarked dryly.

"It's all part of the plan," Kieran said as they followed Norma to one of the booths that looked out over Main Street.

Kieran waited for Cara to sit down on one side of the booth before he sat on the side opposite her. "Well, that's a downside to sitting in a booth."

"What's that?" Cara asked as she took the menu Norma held out.

"I can't hold your chair for you, so that you can see my mom taught me to be a gentleman."

Norma laughed as she walked away from the table.

"You've already shown me many times that you're a gentleman." Cara hesitated then said, "Speaking of your mom...did you tell her about us already? I would hate it if she found out from someone who saw us here."

"No worries. I called her after I left work and told her." Kieran smiled. "She was *very* happy, considering she's been telling me how nice you are for weeks now."

"I'm glad she was okay with it."

Kieran reached across the table and took her hand. "You had nothing to worry about. She's been so ready for me to find someone."

"Your mom is a sweetheart. I really have enjoyed having her in the classes at the studio."

"I know she went to check you out at first, but the class has really benefitted her physically as well, which is why she keeps going back."

"That's what I like to hear."

A young woman that looked familiar but whose name Cara didn't know appeared at their booth. She put down two glasses of water then asked if they were ready to order.

"Maybe just give us a couple more minutes," Kieran said with a smile.

"Sure. I'll be right back."

Cara had been eating out more than she usually did, so she decided to just go with a salad and a bowl of soup. When the woman returned, Kieran waited as Cara told her what she wanted, then he ordered a fried chicken dinner with mashed potatoes and a salad.

They talked a bit about their day, but they hadn't even gotten their food before the first person stopped by their table. It turned out that they were just the start of an endless stream of people who came to talk to them.

"This might not have been the best idea," Kieran murmured when they had a moment to themselves. "I didn't realize that word had gotten out about the body that was found outside of town. I should have known that we wouldn't get lucky enough to not have that info leak until after they'd confirmed identity."

The women approaching them seemed most interested in the fact that they were there together, while the men had questions about the body. It was the first time since they'd started going out where it hadn't really felt like a date. She'd actually thought that it would just be about people seeing them together, not that they would actually be approached over and over again.

Part of it was that, as Kieran had noted, people were curious about the body, but it also seemed like they saw Kieran as town property, because of his job, so they had no qualms about approaching him, even if it was clear that the two of them were on a date. Something told her that if they wanted to be able to actually talk to each other, they needed to do what they'd been doing already, and that was to not go on a date anywhere in New Hope.

But their goal for the evening had been to let the town know they were in a relationship, and they'd definitely managed to do that.

They didn't linger once they'd finished eating, both clearly done with people interrupting their conversations. After they walked back to the studio, Kieran came inside.

"I wanted to do something," he said as he pulled out his phone.

Cara hadn't turned on the lights in the waiting area, so they were only illuminated by the streetlights outside the building. She moved closer to lean against his arm as he did something on his phone.

"There." He turned his head and kissed her forehead. "Accept that when you log on later. If you want to, anyway, but be prepared for a flood of friend requests if you do."

"What is it?" she asked.

"It's making us Facebook official."

"Oh. I like that." She wasn't above wanting to let the rest of the women in New Hope know that Kieran was off the market.

Kieran shifted to face her as he put his phone away. "I like that too."

He tugged her close, and she went willingly, appreciating the strength of his arms and the feeling of safety they brought her. She hadn't felt that in a very long time, but she knew that he could—and would—protect her if need be. He hadn't had to say the words, either. She had just known because she'd come to know the type of man he was. Even if he hadn't been a cop, charged with serving and protecting, she knew it would be something he'd do.

She'd never really gone out with a guy beyond a couple of dates before he'd decide that the time she had to devote to her dancing career was more than he wanted her to. Kieran was the first man she'd been with where the relationship had progressed to the point of not just physical intimacy, but emotional intimacy as well. And she felt it with Kieran, which was a good thing, but it was also leading to conflict for her.

The closer they got, the more she wanted to tell him about her past, even though she'd promised her dad to never speak about it once she set up her new life. How could she be honest with Kieran while also upholding the promise she'd made to her father?

"I gotta go," Kieran said as he lifted his head, ending their kiss.

His arms still held her close, and Cara relished it because she knew it would be ending all too soon. "Want to come by for lunch tomorrow?"

Kieran chuckled, his breath coming in puffs against her cheek. "Don't want to brave *Norma's* again?"

"Not exactly. Tonight was fine, but I'd rather be able to hold a conversation without constant interruptions."

"It was pretty bad, wasn't it? I really hadn't anticipated that. Maybe we'll limit dinners there to once every couple of weeks."

"I can live with that," Cara said, resting her head on his shoulder for a moment.

"I'll pick us up some lunch and come by here unless something comes up that keeps me from getting away from the station."

"Sounds good."

All too soon, Kieran gave her one last kiss before leaving the studio. Cara leaned against the door, watching through the glass as he walked down the street toward the station. Would there come a time when they wouldn't have to part at the end of the day?

The thought of getting to the point of being married to Kieran gave Cara a feeling of excitement, and she found that, even though they hadn't been together that long, it was something she wanted. After everything that had happened, she'd resigned herself to being alone. To not having a family, but now...her hopes and dreams had been rekindled in Kieran.

Upstairs, she logged onto her laptop and confirmed that she was in a relationship with Kieran, smiling like she was a teenage girl with her first boyfriend. She was looking forward to their lunch the next day because she would be leaving on Friday for the weekend to see her dad.

All she'd told him was that she needed to go see her dad in Texas. Thankfully, he hadn't asked too many questions about why there was so much physical distance between them, especially since her dad was dying.

At one point, she and her dad had argued over that. She'd wanted to get an apartment closer to the prison or to just stay in a nearby hotel and visit more frequently, but he refused to allow her to put herself as risk by being there for more than a couple of days. She hadn't thought there was a risk, but there had been no convincing him of that.

Though she wasn't looking forward to being away from Kieran, she was excited to talk to her dad and tell him how things were going with Kieran and all about the sermons she'd been hearing at church. She didn't know if he had access to any type of spiritual teaching, or if he was limited to visits from the chaplain. The last time she'd talked to Doug a few days earlier, he'd said that his condition had been pretty steady, and he was still fairly alert.

For safety sake, Doug was the one that was contacted with any updates. She wasn't even sure if the guards at the prison were aware of who her father was. When she signed in at the prison for a visit, she did it with a different ID to the one she used in her real life.

Each night, she went to bed, praying that she didn't get *the* call from Doug the next day, and so far, those prayers had been answered. But that couldn't go on forever. At this point, all she wanted was just one more good conversation with her dad.

CHAPTER SEVENTEEN

The next day after her morning class had finished and everyone had left, Cara went into her office and sank down on her chair. She checked her phone to see if any messages had come in during the class. Seeing none, she frowned. Though Doug didn't have a set time to send her an update each day, usually by lunchtime, she would have received something from him.

Worry settled in her stomach as she set her phone down and tried to focus on the website's calendar on her screen that she needed to update with the class cancellations for later that week. Having the calendar on her website was one way to keep people informed on the schedule of classes, and she'd also send an email to the ones who preferred to hear that way.

When Kieran appeared in her office door with a bag of food from *Norma's,* the worry eased a bit. His presence was a reminder that when the call did come, she wouldn't be alone. He set the bag down on the desk, then bent to give her a lingering kiss.

"Is your day going good so far?" he asked as he took the chair across from her.

"It is," she told him. "And it's even better now."

Kieran grinned at her. "Yep. Same for me."

As they ate, he talked about the meeting he'd had with Eli when he'd shown up to at the station. It wasn't a big surprise that Eli wanted more information about the body that had been found.

They'd just finished eating when Cara's phone rang. She picked it up and glanced at the screen, assuming it was going to be one of the women from her classes. The name she saw there made her heart pound with dread, robbing her of breath and making her dizzy.

"Cara?" Kieran's voice came from a distance.

"I need to take this." She got up and rounded the desk, tapping the screen as she walked on shaking legs to the dance room. Leaning against the wall, she swallowed hard. "Hello?"

Her voice came out thin and reedy, and the blood whooshing in her ears made it almost impossible to hear the series of words that Doug uttered to confirm that he wasn't speaking to her under duress.

"Cara?" he said when she didn't respond. "Are you there?"

"I'm here," she whispered, then recited her own set of words, knowing he wouldn't talk with her until she did. "Is he...? Is he...?"

"No, he's not, but he's not doing well. I know you were planning to come this weekend, but if you could come sooner, I think you should."

Cara turned to face the mirrored wall and rested her forehead against the smooth, cold surface. She pounded her fist once against the mirror, then left it there as she tried to breathe. How come it was so hard? She'd known this was coming. Had resigned herself to the fact that her goodbye on her previous visit might be her last one.

She should have been prepared for this, but she wasn't. She absolutely, positively wasn't prepared to lose her last remaining parent.

"Is this for real? Not a trick?"

"It's for real. I'm sorry. I got the call just an hour ago that he was declining quickly. I'm heading there myself.

"I have a flight tomorrow morning. Should I try and fly out tonight?"

"Yes." The fact that Doug didn't hesitate at all made her want to weep. "I didn't tell you this before because I didn't know until just recently, but there is more money for you that your dad let me know was available in a few other accounts. There is enough that if you were to rent a private plane to get here, the cost of doing so wouldn't put much of a dent in the funds. That way you could get around having to deal with airport hassles and airline schedules."

"Okay." She had known that there was more money. Her dad had told her that he'd left instructions for her to have access to the remaining money once he passed away.

"Let me know when you arrive, and I'll be there to pick you up." He hesitated then added, "I'm sorry I had to call you with this news."

Cara took a deep breath. She could do this. "I'll send you the flight information as soon as I have it."

"See you soon."

The line went dead, and she dropped her hand, her phone feeling like it weighed a hundred pounds. She took several deep breaths, trying to push aside the grief that wanted to well up and smother her. To drag her beneath its vicious current. But she couldn't grieve yet.

"Cara?" She heard Kieran's voice a moment before his hand landed gently on her back. "What's happened?"

She swallowed, trying to get rid of the tightness in her throat so she could talk. Finally, she just said, "My dad's dying."

When he wrapped his arms around her, she felt the urge to give in to her grief, but she couldn't. Not yet. First, she had to get her flight arranged so she could get to him as soon as possible.

"I'm so sorry, babe," Kieran whispered.

His words almost weakened her, but she took another deep breath. "I need to go to him."

"What can I do?"

"I have to book a private plane to fly me to Texas. It will take too long to get there on commercial flights."

"A private plane?" Kieran asked.

Cara nodded, well aware that this was going to create a situation where she'd need to explain a bit more about how she had access to that kind of money. "It's the only way I have a hope of getting to him before he dies."

"Okay. Do you need my help?"

She moved back enough so that she could look up at him, some of the anxiety within her easing as she saw the concern on his face. "Can you drive me to the airport once I get the flight arranged?"

"Definitely. I'm going to run to the office really quick, then I'll come back with my Jeep."

"Okay. Thank you."

He gave her a kiss then left her to make her calls. Arranging for a private plane wasn't something she'd ever done before, but thanks to her dad, once again, she had a credit card with enough space on it to cover the cost of the flight. Presumably, she could fly back commercial since that flight wouldn't be time sensitive.

Once that was arranged, she finished packing, adding a few extra outfits since she didn't know how long she'd be in Texas. She was still adding a few things to her bag when Kieran texted to let her know he was waiting out back. Through all of it, she tried not to think about what she would face when she finally reached the hospital.

She was sure that Kieran had questions, but during the drive to the airport where she'd board the private plane, all he did was hold her hand and tell her that he'd be praying for her. She was thankful for his support and strength, and it was horribly difficult to say goodbye to him at the airport when he dropped her off.

"Call me when you can, or just text to let me know how things are going, okay?" Kieran said as he gave her a tight hug. "I'm gonna miss you."

"I'll miss you too."

They kissed, and then she was leaving him behind. Once she was on the plane, Cara settled into a seat near the exit. It wasn't the fanciest plane, but fancy hadn't been important. What *had* been important was that the plane was available to get her to Texas as soon as possible.

She'd texted Doug to let him know that she was on her way and to give him her arrival information. After she'd sent that, she stared at her phone screen for several minutes, wanting to send a text to Kieran but not knowing what to say beyond what they'd already said when he'd left her at the airport earlier.

She wanted to tell him everything, and if her papa was still lucid when she arrived at his bedside, she was going to ask him to release her from her promise. She could trust Kieran, she was positive of that. She wanted to have forever with him, and it was starting to feel more and more imperative that she tell him all about herself. Where she'd once felt that she could close the door on her past and not look back, she wasn't so sure that that would be possible anymore.

But she had no idea if she would have the chance to talk to her papa, and if she didn't, she wasn't sure if she could go back on the promises he'd been adamant about her making to him.

When the crew let her know that they were ready for take-off, she gave up on trying to formulate a text to send to Kieran and set her phone to airplane mode. The flight lasted several hours, and she tried to fill them by alternately playing games on her phone or reading and praying. Anything to keep her from wondering what news would greet her at the end of her trip.

When the plane finally landed, she gathered up her bags and disembarked to find Doug waiting for her as he'd promised. He took her suitcase then led the way to a waiting vehicle.

"How was your flight?" he asked after he'd loaded her bag into the back and they were buckled in.

"Long. How is my father?"

If the man was offended by her abrupt answer, he didn't show it. "When I left him to come get you, he was hanging in there, but he hasn't regained consciousness since you and I last talked."

That wasn't what Cara had wanted to hear. "Can I see him right away?"

"Yes. He's been moved to a private room that will allow you to spend more time with him."

"At the prison hospital?"

Doug shook his head. "I got special permission to move him to a hospice when it became apparent that the end was near."

Cara was glad that her father wouldn't be spending his last days or hours surrounded by prison bars. She knew there were plenty of people who would think that was what he deserved, but as his daughter, she didn't care about what others thought right then.

It seemed to take forever—yet was probably not really all that long—to get to the hospice. The property looked more like a large home than a medical facility, and Cara found that it eased some of the tension within her as she followed Doug through the front door.

A faint scent of antiseptic hung in the air, but it faded away as she took in the homey décor. The walls were painted in soft pastels with artwork depicting various nature scenes. Some were of sunsets, others of the mountains. All of them were serene and peaceful.

"Here we go," Doug said softly as he stood next to an open doorway.

Cara came to a stop, wishing so much that Kieran by her side. She wasn't sure she had the strength to do this on her own. Doug didn't pressure her. He reached out and touched her arm and said, "I'll go on into the room. Come in when you're ready."

He stepped into the room, and she was left on her own to figure out how to say goodbye to the man who meant everything to her.

~ * ~

Kieran knew that he wasn't being fair taking his frustration out on those around him, but his mind wasn't on the job. No, his mind and his heart were hundreds of miles away with Cara. He'd gotten a text from her to say that she'd arrived safely and that her dad was still alive, but that had been the previous day.

It had been almost twenty-four hours since she'd left, and he'd kind of been hoping that she'd call him. He knew she was dealing with a lot and probably didn't have the time to call, but he wanted to let her know that he was there for her.

If she'd even given a hint that she wanted him with her, he would have found a way to request some time off to fly to join her wherever she was in Texas. Maybe their relationship was still too new for her to want to share something like this with him. He didn't feel that way, but it was possible she did.

"Why don't you call it a day, Chief?"

Kieran swung his gaze from the window he'd been staring out of to see Lisa in his doorway. "What time is it?"

"Not officially quitting time, but you've checked out already, so you might as well take the rest of the day off. If something comes up, we'll let you know."

It was tempting, but honestly, what would he do if he wasn't at the office? Maybe go for a long run? That was what he usually did when he had a lot on his mind.

Pushing back from his desk, he got to his feet. "I think I'll take you up on that suggestion."

"Have you heard from her?" Lisa asked as he pocketed his cell phone and grabbed his jacket and hat.

"Not since last night when she texted to say she'd arrived. I'm not sure if that's good or bad."

"We'll keep praying for her."

Kieran nodded his thanks. "I'm sure she'd appreciate that."

Lisa walked with him to the front door then gave him a hug. "Have a good weekend."

When he stepped out of the station, he didn't linger on the sidewalk. He went right to his Jeep and slid behind the wheel. After making the short drive home, he changed into his running clothes and headed out on a route he knew would take a couple of hours to complete.

He had his phone in a holder on his upper arm playing music, but he would also hear if any texts or calls came in. The beat of the music helped him to set a steady pace and also drowned out his thoughts for the first little while. After he had settled into his running groove, his mind began to wander a bit, and the worries he'd hoped to outrun began to filter back in.

Rather than fight them, he focused on praying for them instead. He prayed for Cara, her father, and any other loved ones who would mourn his passing. He knew what it was like to lose a father. What he didn't know was what it was like to lose both parents.

His run left him exhausted physically and mentally, but he hoped that meant that when he went to bed later, he'd be able to fall asleep right away.

It wasn't until the next day around noon that he got another message from Cara.

Cara: *He passed away this morning.*

Kieran sank down onto his front step, leaning the rake he'd been using on his lawn against the railing. *I'm so sorry to hear that, sweetheart. Call me?*

Cara: *I can't.*

He frowned at her response. Surely she could spare a few minutes so they could talk.

Why not?

Cara: *I can't hear your voice right now.*

What? That made no sense. Of course, she couldn't hear his voice. They weren't talking.

Cara: *I need to hold it together, and at the moment, I'm not sure that would be possible if I heard your voice.*

Oh...well, that sort of made sense, but at the same time, he would have preferred to have been able to talk to her. He didn't want to make things more difficult, though, so he didn't press for her to call him.

I'll be praying for you. And if you change your mind about talking, call me at any time.

Cara: *I will. I'm going to be here a few more days tying up loose ends.*

Okay. I miss you! Did you need me to do anything with the studio here?

Cara: *I'll send an email out to everyone to let them know I'm away for a bit. I'd kind of warned them about this since my dad has been failing for awhile.*

I hope everything goes smoothly for you there.

Cara: *Me too. I'm so tired. I've spent the last two nights in the hospice with Papa. I'm going to a hotel tonight.*

Kieran frowned, trying to figure out the situation. *He doesn't have a house there?*

It was a minute or so before her reply came through.

Cara: *No. He was living in a multi-resident facility before going into hospital and then hospice.*

Kieran found that for every answer she gave, he ended up with more questions. It was a reminder that they hadn't really known each other that long, but that wasn't necessarily a bad thing. He just hoped they had a chance to learn more about each other soon. He still had questions about her security, among other things.

Text me so I know how you're doing, okay? I worry.

Cara: *I don't mean to worry you. I'll be fine...just need to get through the next few days. I was expecting this but still don't feel like I was ready, you know?*

I'm not sure we're ever ready to lose a parent, no matter how much advance warning we have.

Cara: *You're right about that.*

Kieran looked up and stared out across his lawn. He didn't like texting. Their conversation usually flowed so smoothly, but this felt awkward and stilted. To know how she was truly doing, he needed to hear her voice. Her text said she was fine, but maybe that was just her trying to be strong.

He didn't want her to feel like she had to be strong when it was just the two of them. If she was struggling, he wanted her to feel that she could lean on him. But maybe it was too soon to expect that. After all, from the sound of things, she'd been on her own for the past few years. It would probably take her some time to get used to leaning on someone else.

Cara: *I'd better go. I still have some arrangements to make before I can take a nap.*

Take care of yourself. Xoxoxo

Cara: *I will. You too. Xoxoxo*

Kieran sat on his porch steps, his thoughts still on Cara and her situation. It was amazing how quickly he'd gotten used to having her nearby. Whether they were at work or at home, they were only minutes away from each other.

It was a bit disconcerting how quickly he'd gotten to this point. He probably should have been a bit more reserved with his feelings, but it was too late now.

With a sigh, Kieran pushed up to his feet and grabbed his rake. It had been a relatively nice day, so he didn't want to waste it. Plus, raking leaves gave him something useful to do while he mulled over everything.

CHAPTER EIGHTEEN

It was Tuesday before Cara finally let Kieran know that she was coming home. Much to Kieran's dismay, they'd spent the days since she left, texting. He hadn't pressured her to call him, but he'd reminded her each time that she could call if she needed to. Apparently, she hadn't needed to.

He was actually surprised that she'd agreed to have him pick her up at the airport. If she'd turned him down for that, he might have started to really worry. Thankfully, she hadn't hesitated to accept his offer.

As he drove to the airport on Wednesday afternoon just before four, Kieran worried that he wasn't going to be able to provide the support that Cara would need. Though he'd been through loss himself, he wasn't sure he knew how to be the comforter instead of the comforted. He and his mom had leaned on each other, both of them grieving and supporting at the same time. This situation with Cara felt a lot different.

He told himself that since he'd been in her position, having also lost a father, that he just needed to remember what things he'd found helpful during that time. He'd been worried enough about it that he'd phoned the pastor and asked him to pray for wisdom for him and comfort for Cara. His mom had assured Kieran of her prayers as well, so he was confident that God would provide for Cara even if he didn't know exactly how to support her himself.

After he found a parking space, he headed inside. The arrivals board said the flight was on time, but since he'd left New Hope earlier than he'd needed to, he had time to spare. Looking around, he spotted some empty seats, so he headed over there to wait.

Leaning forward, he braced his elbows on his thighs as he scrolled through his phone. He checked his Facebook and saw that several more people had commented on the change in his relationship status. Some of those were friends he shared with Toni.

He hoped that no one thought that his change of status had been prompted by Toni's engagement because nothing could be further from the truth. He had to admit, though, that as his relationship with Cara had progressed, for the first time since his engagement to Toni had ended, he was glad that things hadn't worked out for them.

He could admit now that back then, he hadn't seen the ending of their engagement as God's will. He'd thought that Toni was being selfish, even if she was being honest. It had felt like she hadn't loved him enough to take a chance on a life together. After all, the odds—if you will—were in their favor. Far fewer officers were killed on the job than were not.

Thankfully, that no longer mattered. The woman his heart was focused on now appeared to not fear the dangers of his job. He could only hope and pray she would continue to feel that way.

Kieran looked up to see people beginning to gather in the arrivals area. Getting up, he made his way to look at the board again. This time it looked like the flight was already on the ground and taxiing to the gate.

Even though it had been just a week since he'd last seen Cara, it felt like much longer. He hoped that she was looking forward to seeing him and being back in New Hope Falls as much as he was looking forward to having her back.

He shifted his weight from one foot to the other as he waited for the first glimpse of her. It wasn't until he noticed another guy show up with a bouquet of flowers in his hand that Kieran realized that maybe that was something he should have done for Cara. He had never been the greatest at romantic gestures, but he wanted to do better with her. Unfortunately, it was too late for anything this time around.

When he finally laid eyes on her, his heart began to beat a little faster. He wove his way through the crowd to greet her. The ache in his chest from missing her, finally eased when she saw him and smiled.

It was a weary smile, but after going for almost a week without hearing or seeing her, it was exactly what he needed. When she was within feet of him, he opened his arms, and she walked right into them without any hesitation.

"I've missed you," Kieran whispered against the fragrant softness of her hair as he wrapped his arms around her. "So very much."

He felt her take several deep breaths before she tipped her head back. As he gazed down at her, he could see the dark smudges beneath her eyes, and her slender face looked almost gaunt. When her hand slid up behind his neck, he dipped his head and pressed his lips to hers.

And just like that, the time they'd been apart faded to nothing. They were back together, and even though she'd felt she had to shoulder the death of her father on her own, he was there now to help her. And from the way she responded to being in his arms again, it seemed that she was ready to let him.

When the kiss ended, she gazed up at him. "I missed you too. I'm so glad to be home."

The final bit of tension and worry Kieran had been trying to ignore released at her words. "And I'm glad you're back."

"I have a bag I need to pick up," she said as she bent her head forward to rest it on his shoulder.

"Okay, sweetheart. Just tell me which one it is, and I'll grab it for you."

She held onto him for another minute before finally loosening her arms and stepping back. Hand in hand, they made their way over to the baggage claim area. It didn't take too long for bags to begin appearing on the carousel, and as they waited for hers to arrive, she kept a firm grasp on his hand and leaned her head against his shoulder.

Once they had her bag, they left the airport and walked to his Jeep. "Are you hungry?"

Cara sighed. "Not really, but I know I need to eat."

"Do you want to stop somewhere on the way home or go to *Norma's?*"

"I don't think I'm up for a meal at *Norma's,*" Cara said with a weak laugh.

"After our last meal there, I'd have to say I don't think I am either. I don't want to have to share you just yet." He glanced over as he put the Jeep in gear and caught the smile she gave him.

After a brief discussion, he turned the car in the direction of the closest Panera's. It was a little busy when they arrived, but they got their table and food without too much waiting. Kieran was glad to see her eat with some relish since he'd been afraid that she would just pick at her food after her comment about not being hungry.

She didn't appear to want to talk about her time in Texas, so Kieran told her about what had been going on in New Hope in the week she'd been gone. Not that there was much to report. They still had no positive ID on the bones that had been found, although they did say they had confirmed the coroner's initial report that they were from a female. That meant that the possibility of the bones belonging to Sheila hadn't been ruled out, but the detective had begun to comb through missing person cases to see if there were any other possibilities.

Once they'd finished their meal, they headed back to New Hope. Even though he hadn't hurried to get back, Kieran still felt that he was pulling up at Cara's garage door far too soon. After he came to a stop behind her building, he put the Jeep in park and reached out to take her hand.

"Are you going to be okay?" he asked.

She squeezed his fingers. "I'll be fine. I'm already feeling so much better now that I'm back and have spent some time with you."

"Do you feel like spending more time together?" he asked. "Tomorrow, perhaps?"

"Of course. What did you have in mind?"

"I don't know. What would you like to do?"

"How about another escape room?"

Kieran laughed. "You're determined to torture me."

Cara chuckled softly in return. "No. Not at all. It just feels like our thing, and to be honest, I need that to feel normal right now."

"In that case, sweetheart, we will definitely do an escape room tomorrow night."

"Thank you." She squeezed his hand again. "I know that you wanted me to call you this week, and I'm sorry I couldn't do that. There were things I needed to focus on, and if I'd heard your voice, I would have wanted to abandon everything and just come home. Now, though, I've dealt with it all, and I can be home without thinking of what I left undone."

"You're right. I wanted to be able to talk to you, but all that matters now is that you're back." Kieran lifted her hand and kissed it. "But I want you to know you can depend on me. If you need to talk, or you need a shoulder to cry on. Anything. I want you to know I'm here for you."

Cara shifted in her seat, leaning toward him. She lifted her hand to rest it on his cheek. "I don't know what I ever did to deserve someone like you, but I'm so grateful for you. Having someone to lean on is new to me, so have some patience if I forget."

Kieran covered her hand with his, capturing it against his cheek. He leaned closer so that he could kiss her again. "And I'm so grateful for you."

When they finally got out of the Jeep, Kieran retrieved her suitcase from the back while she got her laptop bag. "Do you need help carrying it upstairs?"

She appeared to hesitate for a moment then said, "If you wouldn't mind."

"I don't mind at all." Kieran knew he couldn't stay long because he wasn't legally parked in the back, but he was curious to get his first glimpse of her home.

After he came into the garage with her, she closed the door behind him. She glanced over at him as she walked over to the wall and leaned close, stepping back as a panel slid open. He watched in a bit of amazement as she pressed her palm to the screen. Before that moment, he'd thought her security was just alarms and cameras. He hadn't realized it went way beyond that.

He didn't say a word though, just waited for her to open the door and lead the way up to her apartment, though after having seen the authorization necessary to get into the building, he certainly had more questions than ever. At the top of the stairs, she pressed her palm against the wall again, then opened the door and walked in, pausing to hold it open for Kieran.

Though he didn't want to invade her privacy, he couldn't help but glance around. He felt like seeing her home would give him more insights into who Cara was. From where he stood in the entryway, he could see the kitchen straight ahead and a table and chairs beyond that in front of a set of large windows. At the front of the building, was the living room. He couldn't see anything through any of the large windows, and it took him a minute to realize that they were covered by blinds. And they didn't look like the cheap blinds he had covering his windows at home.

Though the apartment had high ceilings, it still had a cozy feel to it. The furniture in the living room was large and comfortable looking, and lamps cast warm light throughout the room. If he had to guess, the lamps and the soft music that played were on timers, or possibly she controlled them from her phone.

"I'll be right back," Cara said as she took the handle of her suitcase then headed through a doorway to the left of the kitchen.

Kieran moved a little further into the room, spotting a fireplace on the wall between the two sets of floor to ceiling windows. It faced the open area where the living and dining areas were situated. He noticed some photos on the mantel and shifted a little closer to look at them. There were a couple framed photos of Cara in ballet poses, but there were also a few photographs of her with other people. One showed Cara with a woman that he assumed was her mother. The resemblance was quite stunning.

The other photo showed Cara standing between a couple that Kieran figured were her parents. He couldn't see them as clearly because they were both in profile as they looked at her while she smiled with so much joy and happiness that Kieran couldn't help but smile as well. The only other thing on the mantel was a brushed nickel vase with elegant etchings around the top and bottom of it.

There appeared to be some writing on it, so Kieran leaned closer to read it.

Unable are the Loved to die
For Love is Immortality
Elizabeth Jameson

Kieran stepped back, returning to where he'd been standing earlier. He felt like he'd just intruded on something, even though they had already spoken about her mother's passing.

He didn't find it strange to see the urn there since his mom had a similar one in her home for his dad. For some reason, she hadn't been able to do anything else with his remains, and Kieran wasn't about to force her to do something she wasn't ready for. Although it had been five years since his father had been killed.

He pulled his phone out and stared at it as he waited for Cara to reappear. He wasn't sure if she wanted him to stay, but he knew that he couldn't hang around too long. Her exhaustion was very evident, and he had a feeling that being home would be the best thing for her. He hoped that she'd take time before going back to work, but he knew that getting back to work had been what had helped him keep his sanity after his father's death.

"Sorry about that," Cara said when she reappeared. "Thank you for helping me up with the bag. I'm so beat I probably would have just left it downstairs until tomorrow."

"You're welcome, and I'm going to head off so you can relax."

She smiled. "I can relax when I'm with you, but I do think I'm going to crash."

"Do you have classes tomorrow?" he asked.

"No. I've told everyone that the classes won't start back up until Monday."

"I'm glad you're taking a few days before you get back to it."

Cara nodded. "Yeah. I think I need the time." Her smile faltered, and she blinked rapidly. "I love...loved him so much. It was hard to say goodbye. My loss hits me at the strangest times, so I'm hoping a couple of extra days will help me get a handle on it."

"I think people would understand," Kieran said. "Will you give me a call tomorrow to let me know how you're doing?"

"I will." She came closer to him and reached out to wrap her fingers around his wrist as she went up on her toes to kiss him then she tucked her face against his neck. "I'm so glad to be home."

Kieran slid his free hand around her waist and held her close. She relaxed against him, their fingers interlacing as they stood there for a couple of minutes. He felt her take a deep breath before lifting her head. They kissed one more time—apparently making up for the kisses they'd missed while she was away—then moved apart.

"I pray you sleep well tonight," Kieran said. "I'll talk to you tomorrow."

Together they walked down the stairs where she opened the garage door once again for him. He climbed behind the wheel of the Jeep but waited until the door was closed before he drove away. As he headed home, he felt a wealth of relief in knowing that Cara was once again just a few minutes away from him. It felt like all was right in his world once more.

He hurt for her as she grieved the loss of her father. It was clear from everything she said that he had meant a lot to her and that they'd been close. He hadn't been that close to his own dad, but the loss had still been intense. He could only imagine how much harder it was to lose a parent with whom one had a close relationship.

Even though he didn't completely understand the depth of her grief, he knew how he'd feel if he lost his mom, so he would use that as a reference point in offering his support. And hopefully she'd let him know if there was something specific he could do for her.

~ * ~

Cara woke to the sound of her phone ringing, and she lay there for a moment, trying to figure out if she was really home, or if she was just wishing she were.

The phone stopped ringing but then rang again a couple of minutes later. Concerned it was Kieran trying to get hold of her—after all, she wouldn't be receiving calls relating to her papa any longer—she rolled over and picked her phone up from the nightstand where she'd set it the night before.

She stared at the name on her screen for a moment, trying to decide if there was any reason she should answer it. After all, with the death of her father, that chapter of her life was closed. The person who had been her contact for the past few years was no longer needed.

Finally, curiosity won out, and she tapped the screen.

"Hello, Cara. How are you doing?" Doug said when she answered.

"As well as can be expected, I would imagine."

"You have my condolences again on the passing of your father."

"Thank you." She waited for a beat then said, "What can I do for you?"

"I need to see you," he said without hesitation.

"Why? I mean, my father's gone now."

"That's precisely why I need to see you. He gave me some things with the instruction to give them to you when he passed."

"What things?" Doug had only been able to stay in Texas until the day after her father's death, but he could have still given them to her when he'd seen her there. He'd had to return to New York, though he'd kept in contact with her while she was in Texas.

"A letter and a USB drive."

She hated the idea of leaving again so soon after she'd just gotten home. "Where do you want to meet?"

"I'm coming to you," he said.

Cara shot up into a sitting position. "Uh. I don't think that's a good idea."

"It's fine, Cara. You can trust me."

Could she? Her father had trusted the man implicitly, but he was gone now. Would the loyalty Doug had had for her father transfer to her?

"Your father wanted me to continue to check in on you to make sure that you never needed anything."

Cara slid out of bed and left her darkened room. The apartment was still in darkness as well because usually by this time, she'd opened the blinds to let the daylight in. She hit the button to raise the blinds then made her way to the kitchen, all the while listening as Doug Anders shared about one of the last conversations he'd had with her dad.

She started the coffee, trying to figure out what her gut was saying. All she could hear was her father's voice telling her that she could trust this man.

"When did you want to come?"

"I'll be there early next week," he said. "I look forward to seeing you again."

His voice seemed so sincere, but Cara just wasn't one hundred percent sold on trusting anyone completely. Except maybe Kieran.

After the call ended, she took a mug from the wrought-iron mug tree next to the coffee pot and poured herself a cup. After adding some milk and sugar, she wandered back into the living room. A glance at the clock on the wall told her it was almost noon. She wasn't surprised that she'd slept that long, only waking once to use the bathroom before stumbling back to bed.

She settled into the chair by the window, thinking of her journal as she did so. It had been one of the last things she'd grabbed before heading out, and she'd filled pages of it during her time in Texas. Though her father had never regained consciousness while she'd been there, she'd spent those final hours at his bedside, reading to him from the entries in the journal.

She'd told him all about Kieran as well as what had been going on in the town. At one point, the chaplain for the hospice had come in to see if there was anything he could do for her. Though it hadn't been her intention to have a long drawn out conversation with the man, it seemed he sensed that she had questions. He'd offered her answers that had allowed her to finally feel at peace with her papa's passing. Unfortunately, it hadn't lessened the intense grief she'd felt once he'd died. She may have had the assurance of seeing him again in Heaven, but that didn't stop her from feeling the impact of his absence from her earthly life.

Staring out the window at the town that had become her home, she rubbed at the intense ache in her chest. She wondered how long it would be before the ache faded to just a dull pain. It had seemed to take forever with her mom, but she knew that was probably partly because the death had been so shocking, plus she'd lost her whole life at the same time. She'd already been grieving her father's passing, starting from the moment he'd told her that he wasn't going to be pursuing any further treatment when the first round did nothing to help him.

Soon she'd have another urn, and once it arrived, she would bury them both together in a nearby cemetery. It was what her father had requested when he'd made the arrangements for her mother's cremation. So she'd kept her mother's ashes, not knowing how long it would be before she could put them both to rest. Even though she'd known it was a possibility that someone might manage to track her father down and kill him in prison, she'd hoped that she would still have many years left with him.

With a sigh, she closed her eyes for a moment. She needed things to get back to normal, and she knew that her papa would have wanted that for her too. Everything he'd done for her had been so that she could live a full and happy life. To do anything less would be a disservice to his memory.

Setting her mug down on the table, she tapped out a message on her phone.

Good morning!

Uncertain if Kieran would be too busy to respond right away, Cara picked her mug up and took a sip. Relishing the warmth of the coffee, she took a few more sips. Part of her wished she'd told the class members that she'd be doing classes that day, but she knew she needed a couple more days to get her emotions back on an even keel.

Kieran: *Good morning, babe! You just squeaked that in under the wire.*

I know, right? How's your day going?

Kieran: *A whole lot better now that I've heard from you. Are you up for some lunch?*

A late lunch, maybe? I haven't even finished my first cup of coffee.

Kieran: *That would work for me. Or an early dinner, if that would be better for you. I kind of forgot that I have to be at the church tonight for a men's meeting, so the escape room will have to wait for another day. I hope that's alright.*

Cara was a bit disappointed, but she was glad that they were still going to be able to spend some time together.

Kieran: *I'm sorry, babe. But I did book us for tomorrow night, if that's okay.*

That's perfect!

Kieran: *I'd still love to see you at some point this afternoon though.*

After a few more back and forth texts, they finally agreed on an early dinner at four. That meant that she had a few hours to unpack, do some laundry, and get herself cleaned up. She'd hated going to bed without a shower the night before, but she'd been so exhausted.

First up, though, was grabbing a small bite to eat since her stomach was reminding her just how many hours she'd been without food. She was so glad to be back in her own home, and already she could feel herself unwinding, the tension of the past few days easing out of her body. And even though dealing with her past still appeared to be necessary, it didn't stop her from feeling like she was where she was supposed to be.

CHAPTER NINETEEN

Rather than go to a restaurant yet again, Kieran had invited her over to his place. The day had been surprisingly warm, and he'd said his back deck would be the perfect place to spend some time together. When she'd offered to make something, he'd said he'd take care of everything.

Cara couldn't arrive emptyhanded, though, so before heading to the address he'd given her, she stopped at the bakery and picked up an assortment of sweets. She'd had basically no appetite at all while in Texas, so she figured a few extra-sugary treats weren't going to negatively impact her.

When she pulled up in front of the address Kieran had given her, she was a little surprised at how quaint the house looked. The lawn was well-manicured, and his flowerbeds were full of autumn colored flowers. She walked up the steps to his front porch and rang the bell.

Kieran opened it with a smile and pulled her into his arms for a quick kiss. "Welcome to my humble abode."

Cara glanced around as he motioned her into the house and closed the door behind her. "It's nice, Kieran. Very you."

"Funny. I thought the same thing about your place."

"That it was very you?"

Kieran chuckled. "Yes, exactly that."

It was very apparent from the dark colors and masculine décor that this was a man's domain, but it also looked very comfortable. "Have you lived here long?"

"Ever since I moved back. I needed a place that was close to town, but I didn't want to be right in the thick of things. Being on the edge of town has worked out well." He motioned toward the kitchen. "I was just going to start barbecuing."

She followed him into the small kitchen where she set the bakery box down on the counter, he picked up what he needed to start barbecuing, then she followed him out onto the back deck. The deck was larger than the kitchen and looked out over a medium-size yard. The nicest thing about it was that the yard was surrounded by trees, so they had privacy even though they were outside.

"Go ahead and have a seat," he said as he motioned to the table and chairs set off to the side of the deck.

The barbecue wasn't far away, so they were able to talk as he cooked. Their conversation steered clear of heavier topics, for which Cara was grateful, though she knew that eventually she wanted to talk to Kieran about what had happened in Texas. She wanted to share with him how difficult those last couple of days with her dad had been, and she figured that, having lost his own father, he'd understand some of what she was going through.

He turned out to be pretty good with the barbecue, as the steak he cooked was done just the way she liked it and was tender as well. He'd baked a couple of potatoes and then cooked some mixed veggies on the grill as well. The desserts she'd brought were the perfect ending to their meal.

"I hate that we can't spend the rest of the evening together," Kieran said as they cleaned up the dishes once they had finished their meal.

"It's okay," she told him. "I don't expect you to abandon your plans. Plus, we still have a date tomorrow night, right?"

He grinned at her. "Yes, we do."

They joked back and forth about what they figured would happen when they got into the escape room once again and what their chances of getting out on time were. When they were done cleaning up, they walked out to her car, hand in hand.

"Dare I kiss you in public?" Kieran asked with a laugh.

Cara tugged on his hand. "I certainly hope so."

"I'll take the chance." He bent down and pressed his lips to hers.

She had missed so many things about him while she'd been gone, but since she'd been home, the unsettled feeling she'd experienced from being apart from him had calmed. She didn't know if it was a good thing that he had become so important to her, but that wasn't the only important thing that had happened. Her connection with him had strengthened her connection with the town, and she'd needed that.

"Do you think that's going to end up on social media?" she asked when the kiss ended, though they still stood close together.

Kieran groaned. "Knowing my luck, probably. Not that I'm ashamed of kissing you, but I'm not too keen on hearing about it from my mom. She'd be all up in arms over the comments on that video if she saw it."

"Oh, boy. Then I'd hear all about it from the women in my classes."

"Small town life, sweetheart. Small town life."

"Send me the link if you see it first," Cara said as she slid behind the wheel of her car.

"And vice versa."

He bent down to give her one more kiss then stepped back as she started up the car and pulled away from the curb. Her heart was lighter than it had been since she'd gotten the call about her father. She wasn't naïve enough to think she wasn't going to have her down moments in the days ahead, but she was also smart enough to embrace the high moments without feeling guilty about them.

That was what would have made her papa happy.

~ * ~

Kieran listened as Cara giggled uncontrollably as he pulled out of the parking lot of the escape room. It seemed, without fail, that each time they went, the group they ended up with was worse than the one before. This one started out pretty good, but it had quickly devolved into madness when it became clear a couple in the group had real control issues. When that was combined with Kieran's need for things to be logical and methodical, the result had been that they didn't have a hope of making it out of the room in the time allowed.

But once again, if the disaster of an escape room attempt made her laugh, he was just fine with how the evening had turned out. He kept meaning to line up some people to go with them, but he knew that neither of them would be as relaxed if they had to make conversation with people they knew.

Maybe he should see if Eli and Anna wanted to come one time. Of anyone, they might be a couple he and Cara could enjoy being with for an evening. Of course, it would be seen as a conflict of interest for him and Eli to be together since Eli was technically part of the on-going investigation. The detective was still focused on Eli as the main suspect in Sheila's disappearance, especially since the body had been discovered. Apparently he felt that even if the body wasn't Sheila's, it didn't mean Eli was innocent.

"Do you want to stop for dessert before we go home?" he asked.

They'd had dinner earlier, but they'd passed on dessert at the time. Kieran wasn't anxious for the evening to end. He knew it wasn't the best thing for them to go back to either of their places. That would be just too much of a temptation when he already knew how much he enjoyed their physical closeness.

"I think I could be convinced," Cara said. "Though I'm going to have to start working out more because honestly, I'm not used to eating like I do when I'm with you."

"Maybe we need to work out together because I'm not used to eating like this either." He felt her hand come to rest on top of his, her fingers lacing between his as he gripped the gear shift. "The offer to run with me always stands."

"I think I'll have to take you up on that."

"But in the meantime...dessert."

They ended up at a restaurant that he knew served great desserts. As they ate, Cara shared more about her dad's passing. She didn't go into a lot of details, but he could see how much she'd loved the man, and he had no doubt there would be rough moments for her in the days ahead.

"The grief kind of hits me at the weirdest moments," she said as she scooped up a piece of the berry crumble she'd ordered. "Because we didn't live very close to each other, I was already used to not seeing or talking to him on a daily basis. So it's like I forget that he's gone, you know? It isn't until I'm thinking of something I want to tell him that it hits me, he's gone. And it could be over something as simple as how good the smells coming from the bakery are."

He reached out and put his hand on her arm. "The grief definitely comes in waves. I had to learn to just ride it out."

"I thought it would be the same as when my mom died, but it's not. Her death was so sudden that I had to work through the shock and the grief at the same time. This time around, though, I had time to plan, but the grief is still intense."

"The church has a grief support group you might want to consider attending."

"Do you go to it?"

"I haven't been in a couple of years, but I think Mom goes more frequently. I'd go with you, if you'd like me to."

She took a bite of her dessert then said, "I'll keep that in mind. I haven't been one to share much of my life, to be honest. It would take some getting used to."

"You don't have to talk or share anything, but it helps to hear from others who have gone through something similar."

Though she seemed to be considering his suggestion, she didn't commit to anything, and he didn't pressure her.

Because there was church the next day, they didn't stay out too late. Cara directed the conversation away from her father's death, and Kieran let her since he knew that sometimes you just needed a break from it. He wanted her to feel that she could talk about whatever she wanted without any judgment from him.

Once they got back to town, he dropped her off, then headed for home after sharing a few goodnight kisses. He didn't like having to leave her at the end of each date, but it was necessary, and he left encouraged that they were closer than ever. The trajectory of their relationship made him excited for what was still to come.

Monday morning, Kieran was at his desk when he got a call from a fellow cop in New York that he'd been working with when his dad had passed away.

"Dude, I've got some interesting news," he said after they'd exchanged pleasantries. "Rumor has it that Marco Moretti has kicked the bucket."

Kieran sat forward, his pulse pounding. "How do you know that?"

"Apparently someone let it leak. Not sure who, but they're saying he was in a federal prison in Texas when he died."

"Did someone get to him?"

"I assume that's what happened, but who knows. All I know is that he didn't die the way he should have," the man groused. "Which is in the electric chair."

Even after the man had turned state's witness, he'd never had to face all the loved ones of the people whose deaths he'd been responsible for in one way or another. He'd testified in several trials, but he'd done so remotely—a protective measure that none of the cops thought he was entitled to—and then had promptly disappeared.

While they'd been glad that several very bad men had gone to jail as a result of Moretti's testimony, it had seemed a bit unfair that he, the mob boss, had "escaped." While he hadn't pulled the trigger for all the deaths he had ordered, he'd certainly pulled it for enough of them that he should have faced the full weight of the law. Victims' families had been assured that he wasn't off living his life in luxury somewhere, but given what the DA had gained through Moretti's testimony, no one had been truly convinced of that.

"Thanks for letting me know, man," Kieran said. "I guess we'll call that good news."

"I know this is not the ending we might have wanted for the guy, but at least he's gone now." The man sighed. "If only I could say the same for his sons."

"Are they still causing problems?"

"In some ways, they're worse than Marco. Eduardo and Antonio Moretti are two peas in a pod, which I guess is a given since they're twins, but together, they're worse than their dad."

"I still don't understand how they ended up not going to prison even after Marco testified against them while others in the organization ended up with lengthy prison sentences."

"We're pretty sure it's because they had someone on their payroll."

"A judge?"

"Possibly. Or a juror."

"So maybe there was no risk in Marco testifying against his sons if he'd made sure they wouldn't be convicted."

"I wouldn't put it past him."

"What about the other son?"

"He's not been on the scene since Marco disappeared."

"Really?" Kieran leaned back in his chair and swung around to face the window. "If he hadn't died in prison, I would have wondered if he'd taken that son with him when he went into hiding."

"I don't know. We got info just after Marco disappeared that the youngest son was in university to become an accountant. My guess is that they were hoping to have a close family member handling the money. Those guys aren't much for trust."

"So Marco's gone, but his kids are stepping up their game."

"We've lost more guys to their madness."

Kieran rubbed a hand across his forehead. The idea of more officers losing their lives because of guys like the Morettis was hard to take.

"It feels kind of like we're dealing with the hydra. We cut off one head, but two grew in its place. Still, I'd be happy to see these two sons gone."

"Wish I could help, but not much I can do from here. Stay safe."

"Always, bro. Same to you."

As the call ended, Kieran fought a battle with guilt. He had no problem staying safe in his small-town job. The cops who were dealing with mobsters like Marco Moretti and his sons were the ones putting their lives on the line. Part of him wished he could be back in New York, helping with that fight, but he couldn't do that to his mom, and he wouldn't do that to Cara.

After spending a couple of hours on phone calls regarding everything from the unidentified body to the high school principal wanting to confirm his appearance at an upcoming career day, Kieran headed over to *Norma's* to grab some lunch. Cara hadn't been able to join him as she said she had several classes plus a meeting that was going to keep her tied up for most the day.

Since he was alone, he decided to stay and eat in the restaurant. He didn't enjoy it much when Cara was with him because he preferred not being interrupted by a constant stream of people, but when he was on his own, that didn't matter as much.

He ordered a sandwich and soup from Missy then settled back into the booth. Though he wished Cara was there with him, he managed to entertain himself on his phone in between people stopping to talk to him about various things.

He'd just finished eating when he saw two familiar faces walk by the window. Stunned, he watched as the pair crossed the street and went into Cara's studio. He sat there for a moment, unsure of what to think or do.

Part of him wanted to storm into the studio to make sure that Cara was okay, but Cara had told him she was having a meeting. Was she expecting them? And if so, why? Their presence in New Hope made no sense at all. And beyond that, what were they doing with Cara?

She'd told him she was from Chicago. So what were these two men from New York coming to see her about? Unless she'd lied about where she was from.

Kieran's gut ached at the idea. He didn't want to believe something like that, but what other explanation was there? And what could possibly connect her to these two men? Also surprising—but maybe not when he thought about the conversation he'd had earlier—was the presence of these two men, not just in New Hope, but there together.

His mind was spinning with so many things as he tried to figure out what was going on, and whether he needed to brace himself for an influx of crime. He prayed that wasn't about to happen because his life was much more intimately intertwined with the people of this town than it had been in New York, and his officers here weren't used to the level of crime that was prevalent in New York. It would be a blood bath.

Sliding out of the booth, Kieran settled up with Norma then left the restaurant. He glanced at the studio but then turned in the direction of the station. There was no way he could risk going into the studio without knowing why those men were in New Hope.

Once he was behind his desk, he thought back on his conversations with Cara, and the things that had puzzled him about her.

First and foremost, her intense security. What she had installed went far beyond a simple alarm system. It was the type of security someone would have if they were afraid of bad people coming after them.

Like one of the men who'd just walked into her studio. Except if they were walking in the front door, maybe they weren't the ones she was afraid of. The thought was too much for him to consider.

He needed more information, and this time, he wasn't afraid to go digging. After a general search pulled up nothing on Cara in their systems or online, he sat for a moment, thinking of other things she'd told him, trying to find significance in those conversations beyond what he'd originally given them.

It was as he thought about her parents dying—if that was even true—that he decided to consider another angle. He didn't know her father's name, but thanks to the urn on her mantle, he knew her mother's. Her last name had been different to Cara's, but he'd just figured that she'd either kept her maiden name or that she'd divorced Cara's father and remarried. It hadn't been anything that had tripped an alarm in his head, but now, that alarm bell was clanging loudly.

Leaning forward, he typed *Elizabeth Jameson* into the search bar, hoping that he'd find, at the very least, an obituary. What he found was so much more.

Local mother and daughter killed in car bombing.

He read the article, puzzled by the information it contained. It said that Elizabeth Jameson had been killed in a car bombing, and her daughter, Carolina Jameson, had been severely injured, passing away later in the hospital. One of the pictures included with the article was *definitely* of Cara, plus it went on to talk about how Carolina had been a dancer with the Joffrey Ballet in Chicago, so Cara hadn't been lying about that.

More confused than ever, Kieran grabbed a notepad he had on his desk and began to scribble down what he was learning. It was clear that even though it had been reported that Carolina had died in the car bombing, she hadn't. That meant that her death had been faked. But why?

He wished he knew her father's name. That might have given him additional insight.

Father unknown.

Passed away in Texas.

Passed away in Texas? What had the guy said earlier? That Marco Moretti had died in a federal prison...in Texas.

Kieran shoved back from his desk and stared at his notepad. That...that was just not possible. The coincidence was too big. But more than that, he didn't want to think that Cara's father had been responsible for the deaths of his father and brother.

He bent forward, trying to draw air into his lungs. The very idea that this scenario was even a possibility was enough to cause a band to tighten around his chest and make breathing difficult.

If the scenario was, in fact, truth, it gave a new reason for why Marco had turned state's witness. He knew that Marco's wife had lived in New York, and she'd shared his name. So if he *was* Cara's father that meant her mother had been his mistress. Cara had mentioned that her father traveled a lot, which would make sense since Marco had lived in New York.

Was it possible that he'd turned state's witness in order to protect his daughter, but then he'd also done what was necessary to ensure that his sons didn't go to prison even though he'd also testified against them? It had left them free to run the organization even while he'd ended up in prison.

If all this were true, Cara was a mafia princess, the daughter of one of the most vicious mafia bosses New York City had ever known.

So what was an ADA and Marco's youngest son doing in New Hope Falls? And how did Cara factor into their visit?

He needed answers, but for the first time in his career, he was scared of what he might find out. He wasn't sure that he could be in a relationship with Cara if Marco really was her father. Not to mention that she hadn't been truthful about her past. Not that he could really blame her. There would be a target on her back if the wrong people found out she was still alive.

But he wasn't the wrong person. Even if the worst was true, he would never reveal her identity to anyone.

Feeling shattered by his thoughts, Kieran abandoned his desk. He grabbed his hat and phone and headed to the front of the station.

"I'm heading out for the day. Give me a call if something comes up."

Lisa looked at him in surprise. "Everything okay?"

"It's fine. Just need to take care of a few things. See you tomorrow."

Kieran plunked his hat on his head as he left the station, nodding to a couple of people who walked past him. Thankfully, they didn't want to talk, so he was able to climb into his Jeep and head for home. Already he knew that he wasn't going to be staying there. He planned to change into his running clothes and go for a long run.

CHAPTER TWENTY

Cara was glad that the women in her morning class didn't hang around to chat for too long. She was nervous about the upcoming meeting with Doug Anders, and she wanted a little bit of time to prepare herself for it.

After the last woman had left, Cara went upstairs to change into something besides her leotard and leggings. She wanted to look at least a little professional, so she settled on a pair of black slacks and a cream-colored sweater. Her hair was pulled back in the bun she usually put it in for her classes.

Even though it was lunchtime, she had no appetite. She would much rather be meeting Kieran for a bite at *Norma's* than having to go through this visit with Doug.

Once she was ready, she went back downstairs to her office to wait for him. When she heard the door open, she got to her feet and went to meet him.

When her gaze landed on two men instead of the one she'd been expecting, her steps faltered. And when she saw the second man, her heart started to slam against her ribs. She didn't know which one he was, but there was no denying that the second man was one of her father's sons. The likeness was uncanny. She felt like she was looking at a younger version of her dad.

The emotions that were barreling through her made it difficult to breathe let alone talk.

"Cara." Doug Anders held his hand out in a placating gesture while the other man stayed near the door.

Was he blocking her exit? If she could get into her office, she could retrieve the gun she kept locked in a drawer there and would be able to defend herself.

"We're not here to hurt you," Doug said. "I promise."

Cara stepped back toward her office door. "I only agreed to meet with *you.*"

"I know. I didn't tell you about Gio because I wanted you to speak to him yourself."

"We should have met somewhere else," Cara said, her voice tight. "You've compromised my home."

"This is what your father wanted."

Cara shook her head, unable to believe that. He'd repeatedly told her that his sons were dangerous. He wouldn't have risked her life by having Doug bring one to her safe place.

She watched closely when Doug reached into his suit coat pocket, bracing herself to dart into her office for her gun. Though she'd been leery of owning a weapon, she'd gotten one at her father's insistence, and she knew how to use it. Her father had taken her to a shooting range while she'd been in her teens, and he'd made sure that she was adept at using a gun. So while she didn't like the idea of using one, she would if it meant the difference between life and death.

Instead of a gun, however, Doug held a white envelope when he pulled his hand out of his pocket. "This is from your father."

She glanced at the man standing at the door whose dark eyes were watching her, his expression open and curious. He didn't look threatening, but then, neither had her papa. At least not to her.

After a moment's hesitation, she took the envelope. Her name was written in a familiar scrawl, and she had to blink back a sudden rush of tears.

"If you want to open it in private, we'll wait out here for you."

Cara nodded and slipped into her office, closing the door behind her. Rounding her desk, she sank down in her chair, grateful that her shaking legs no longer had to hold her weight.

With trembling hands, she opened the envelope and pulled out a piece of paper and the USB Doug had mentioned during the phone call. She sat for a moment before she unfolded the paper to read what was written on it.

Mia carissima ~ If you're reading this, it means I have passed on and am hopefully now with your mama. I'm sure you are confused at this moment, but Doug is carrying out my final wishes in bringing Gio and this letter to you.

Cara frowned as she read that sentence. So bringing Gio to meet her really had been her dad's idea?

I want you to watch the video on the USB and know that I made it without any sort of duress. These are my final wishes for you. All my love forever...Papa

She let out a shaky breath as she stared at the USB. Everything within her told her to ignore its contents and to tell Doug to leave and take Gio with him. But her love for her father compelled her to put the USB into the slot on her computer.

Watching through damp eyes as her father's image came into focus, Cara struggled to take a breath. He looked so much better than the last time they'd talked. He must have filmed this a couple of months ago. Why hadn't he just told her whatever was on the USB himself when they'd talked?

Hello mia carissima. His smile was filled with a familiar affection that made her heart ache, and she had to blink away tears. *I know you won't understand all that I'm going to tell you, but believe me when I say that I believe that this is for the best. It's what I want for you and for Gio.*

Last year, Gio reached out to Doug with some information he had on his twin brothers that could help prosecute them for several crimes, including the car bombing that killed your mama. Doug and Gio agreed that Gio would continue to work for the family while gathering more information. Soon after that, Gio asked Doug to open the lines of communication between us.

It took awhile for me to feel I could completely trust him, which was why I never mentioned him to you. I wanted to be one hundred percent certain before I was willing to introduce him to you.

He is the one who told me about God, and it is because of what he told me that you and I now share a faith. It is his desire to right the wrongs done by our family in much the same way I tried to. He has the proof that is needed to put his brothers away for your mother's murder, and he is willing to testify in order to put them in prison where they belong.

In turning against his brothers, Gio will lose his family as surely as if they had died. His mother will also turn her back on him once she realizes what he has done to her other sons. You will both be without family, and it would be my last request of you to consider him your family now. It would mean everything to me if you two could become family for each other, so that neither of you are alone.

Unlike his brothers and me, Gio never played a significant role in the criminal side of our family, so in testifying, he will not have to give up his freedom like I did. He will be able to be there with you in a way I was never able to be once I tried to make things right.

At least hear him out, my darling. Gio is now a man of God, and serving God is the direction in which he wants to move. There is a seminary near you he could attend to pursue what he believes to be his calling.

I love you with all my heart, and I truly believe that Gio will be able to give you what I couldn't.

I am sorry that I couldn't have this conversation with you myself, but I didn't want to waste any of our time together arguing over this. Please trust Doug and Gio. They mean you no harm whatsoever. I would never trust them with you if I felt otherwise.

Until we meet again in heaven, mia carissima.

As his image faded away, Cara wiped at the tears that slid down her cheeks. Her heart was so torn. If she didn't have Kieran, she would have been able to let Gio into her life more easily. But after her father had passed, she'd been looking forward to closing that chapter of her life. To cutting ties with Doug and her past.

How would she explain Gio's presence in her life after she'd already told Kieran she had no siblings? One explanation would lead to another. Neither the letter nor the video had released her from the promise she made to her dad to not reveal anything about her past. And on top of that, now she'd need Gio's permission to share anything with Kieran since her revelations would impact him as well.

Cara slumped back in her chair, pressing the palms of her hands against her eyes. She was so confused. Her love and loyalty for her father warred with her new feelings for Kieran. She worried that she couldn't have both. She might have been willing to go against her father's wishes and tell Kieran if her connection with her past had ended with his death.

But it obviously hadn't.

Her past was as firmly entrenched in her life as it had ever been, and she didn't know what to do about it.

She rubbed her hands over her face, trying to wipe away the wetness there. When the tightness in her chest had eased enough for her to take a deep breath, she got up and left her office. Uncertain of what to say to the men waiting for her, she just regarded them as they got to their feet.

"Do you have any questions?" Doug asked, his voice gentle.

"Will Gio go into hiding once he's testified?"

Doug nodded. "He'll have to, for his own safety."

"My first choice would be to come here," Gio said, speaking for the first time. "To carry out my father's wishes and be a part of your life. However, I will respect your wishes too. If you don't want me in your life, I'll walk away and never contact you again."

Cara wrapped her arms across her waist. It was hard to look at Gio and think about telling him to walk away when he looked so much like their father. There was a gentle expression on his face that was so much like the one she remembered seeing whenever her papa had looked at her.

"I would get my own place nearby, but I'd like to get to know you."

"And you'd go to school? How old are you?"

Gio took a step toward her as Doug moved back. "I'm thirty years old, and yes, I'd like to go back to school. To seminary, actually."

"Seminary? You want to be a...?"

"A pastor. A minister."

"Really?"

Gio nodded. "I became a Christian during my last year at college while I was getting my bachelor's in accounting."

"You're an accountant?"

Gio nodded again. "It was supposed to be a career that could help the organization. I managed to drag things out as long as I could. Once I graduated, I ended up working for them for a few years, but during that time, I made notes of every illegal thing that was done."

"And that's the information you're giving to Doug?"

"Yes. My goal is to take the organization to the point of being unable to function any longer. It's what our father wanted."

Cara stared out the window past Gio and Doug, wondering if New Hope could still be her home if she accepted Gio into her life. She could tell Kieran he was a half brother she'd never met before. That wasn't a lie. Presumably he'd have a new identity as well. Maybe it could work. Maybe.

"You don't have to make a decision today," Doug said. "We'll still be here for a couple of days."

"Where are you staying?"

"At the small hotel just outside of town."

"Not the lodge?"

Doug shook his head. "No. It's called the Hideaway."

"Okay. I'll call you when I've had the time to think about all of this."

Gio came closer to her, forcing her to tilt her head back a bit to meet his gaze. "Regardless of your decision, it was a pleasure to meet you. Though I do wish it had been under better circumstances."

Cara could only nod, still uncertain how she felt about this man's presence in her life. At that precise moment, all she could think about was how complicated her life had become because of him.

All she'd wanted was a quiet future in New Hope with Kieran.

Was that even possible anymore?

The men said goodbye, then headed out of the studio. Cara stood frozen as she watched them walk across to *Norma's*. How was she supposed to make this decision?

With a sigh, Cara glanced at the clock on the wall to see how much time she had before her afternoon students arrived. Seeing there was still about an hour left, she went upstairs and changed back into the outfit she always wore for leading the class. She wasn't hungry, but she forced herself to eat a sandwich since she would need to keep her energy up.

As she ate, she texted Kieran to see if they were still on for supper later that night. She wasn't sure if she wanted him to agree or not because he was sure to pick up on her state of mind and ask questions she wasn't sure she could answer. But she also really needed to see him.

He hadn't answered by the time she had to go downstairs for her class, which meant he was probably tied up in a meeting or something. The afternoon class was her pregnancy stretching class, and she usually loved to see the women at each class. It was fun to watch their bodies change over the weeks, and then to have them come back after the births, with their babies, was so special.

But that day, she just wanted the class to be over.

She'd found herself opening up more to the women in her classes over the past couple of months. It seemed the closer she got to Kieran, the closer she wanted to be to others in town. Was it possible to still have that closeness while keeping a secret from them?

"They're inducing me," one of the women said to her at the end of the class. "So I won't be here next week."

Cara smiled at her, hoping that it looked genuine since she was still feeling raw from earlier. "Well, I pray your delivery goes smoothly, and I look forward to meeting your little one."

"I'll definitely bring her by as soon as I feel up to it," the woman assured her.

"I hope you'll come to the mommy and baby class once you're ready."

"I plan to, if for no other reason than to get out of the house every once in a while."

That was one of the reasons she liked to have a progression of classes. It meant the women didn't have to stop coming to the studio once they were done with one class.

The woman left the studio a couple of minutes later, chatting with another woman who was also coming up on her due date. Cara placed a hand against her own stomach, feeling its flatness and wondering what it would be like to carry a child. Growing up, she'd planned to have kids once she was done with ballet, but then that had all faded away when her life had changed so dramatically.

It was only because of Kieran that she was once again thinking of children in her future. She didn't want to give that dream up. She didn't want to lose her chance at love and a family of her own.

~ * ~

Kieran's feet pounded the pavement as he made his way along the road that he usually took for his run. His pace was faster than what he'd usually set for that early in a run, but he needed to move. To put as much distance as he could between himself and New Hope.

His mind was a mess of thoughts and emotions as he started running, but the more demands he put on his body, the more focused his thoughts became. Not on what was going on with Cara, but on the music that was playing in his ears and controlling his breathing. His many questions and confusion would still be there when he got back, and hopefully, by then, his thoughts would be calm enough to think through what he needed to do.

He felt his phone buzz on his arm where he'd strapped it earlier, but he ignored it. If it was the station, they'd call him. The only people who tended to text him were his mom and Cara, and he didn't want to talk with either of them right then.

It was a couple of hours before he made his way up the steps to his house. He'd stopped for awhile near the edge of the river, sitting on a rock and watching the water tumble by. The turbulent water had been an accurate representation of what he was feeling inside.

Once home, he decided to take a bath instead of his usual shower because he needed to soak his muscles after that long run in the cool air. His body was getting too old for him to be pushing it so hard. He'd pay for it the next day.

It wasn't until he was out of the tub and dressed that he checked his phone. His stomach clenched as he read Cara's message.

Cara: *Are we still on for dinner tonight?*

Kieran set his phone on the counter and grabbed a glass from the cupboard. After he'd filled it with water, he took his phone and retreated to his recliner to ponder his next step, starting with how to respond to Cara.

The longer he sat in the chair, the more he felt that he couldn't be in a relationship with Cara if she really was connected with the Moretti family. It was clear from what she'd shared about her father that she was close to him, so if her father was Marco Moretti, then that meant he was the papa she loved so much.

Was she unaware of what her father had done over the course of his adult life? Did she know how many lives had been rubbed out because of the mob organization he'd led? If she did know, how did she reconcile that with loving him?

Even if he hadn't lost his brother and then his father because of the Moretti family, as a cop, he couldn't be in a relationship with someone connected to them. To do so would leave him conflicted on so many different levels.

Kieran blinked back the sudden rush of moisture in his eyes. He had to stop thinking about her as Cara, the woman he'd been falling in love with, and start thinking of her as Carolina Jameson, daughter of a notorious crime boss. Maybe if she could have convinced him she knew nothing about her father's life in New York City, they might have a chance at a future together, especially now that he was dead.

But then he had to wonder why Doug Anders and Giovanni Moretti were coming to New Hope to see her. Plus, as he thought about it, she'd been going to Texas to visit her father, which meant she had been seeing him in prison. While he may have been willing to give up the dirt on some in his organization, he was still guilty of a *lot* himself.

Kieran had always thought Doug Anders was a straight-up guy who had made sure that Moretti had had to pay for his sins even if a jury hadn't found him guilty of them. Seeing Doug with the youngest Moretti son made Kieran reconsider how straight up the man might actually be.

Finally, he lifted his phone and tapped out a message to Cara, knowing he couldn't put off the inevitable.

I can come by your place around six.

He set the phone down in his lap and leaned his head back, trying to figure out why this hurt *so* much. It wasn't like they'd been together that long. They hadn't even said they loved each other yet.

Not that Kieran doubted that that was how he felt about her. He'd known for a little while now that she had a firm grip on his heart. The only reason he hadn't said the words yet was because he'd felt it was too soon, and he'd been a bit worried that maybe she didn't feel the same way.

Now it didn't matter because their relationship was at an end. His mom would be disappointed, and he wouldn't be able to give her the real reason why it had ended, because while he might be angry that Cara had kept this a secret from him, he would keep her identity private. He didn't want to put her in any kind of danger.

A text came in a short time later, and Kieran sighed as he picked it up to read it.

Cara: *Sounds good! See you then.*

The heart she sent him was just like a kick to his gut. If she did love him, had she planned to tell him about her past eventually? Or would that have been something she kept from him forever, knowing that, as a cop, he would have struggled with the knowledge?

But what was a relationship without honesty? Not a good one, that's what.

Kieran glanced at the clock on his phone and saw that he still had an hour before he had to go to Cara's. His stomach felt tight with nerves, and he was a little nauseous at the thought of what was to come. He'd never broken things off with someone before. Toni had been his only serious relationship, and she'd been the one to put an end to their engagement.

He spent the hour rehearsing what he was going to say to her, trying to make sure he wouldn't choke when the time came. The most effective thing so far was to picture her face filled with adoration for her papa. The man who might as well have pulled the trigger on his family. The way his stomach twisted at that thought was enough to know he had to push through...no matter how much it hurt.

Their relationship was doomed if he couldn't get past that feeling. Maybe if he'd been just an average cop who knew about the Moretti family but had never experienced their brutality firsthand, he would have been able to deal with Cara's identity. Unfortunately, most cops in New York had more than just a passing knowledge of the family. Whether it was because they'd had a buddy on the force who'd been wounded or killed as the result of a run-in with some member of the family, or because they'd been directly impacted, he figured most of the guys would have a problem dating a member of the Moretti family.

When it was almost time to leave, he changed from the sweats he'd put on earlier into jeans and a sweater. He made sure his hair wasn't standing up at odd angles then gathered up his wallet, keys, and phone and left the house.

It only took him a matter of minutes to get to Cara's studio. He found a parking spot a couple of doors down, then slowly got out of the Jeep.

Steeling himself against the emotions that were running rampant through his body, Kieran walked down the sidewalk, his gaze fixed on the door to the studio. The one Doug Anders and Giovanni Moretti had walked through just hours ago.

When he reached the studio, he paused for a moment, then pulled the door open. Cara came out of the office, a smile on her face. As she neared him, he could see that the smile didn't quite reach her eyes. It seemed that perhaps the visit from the men earlier was stressing her out, too.

Before she reached him, Kieran held up a hand for her to stop. He couldn't deal with a hug or a kiss right then. Not when so much stood between them now.

She came to an abrupt halt, her brows drawing together in a frown. "What's wrong?"

Steeling himself for what was to come, he lowered his hand and said, "Is your father Marco Moretti?"

The emotions that crossed her face told him everything he needed to know. Shock. Fear. Guilt. The knot in his stomach tightened even further.

"Why are you asking?"

"Because I need to know."

She wrapped her arms across her waist as her head bent forward for a moment. When she looked back at him, her expression was resigned.

"Yes. He is...was...my father."

"So he just died in prison in Texas?"

Her eyes narrowed briefly before she nodded.

Without waiting for her to respond, he asked, "What were Doug Anders and Giovanni Moretti doing here earlier?"

Shock once again crossed her face. "How do you know them?"

Resolved to what he had to do, Kieran decided he might as well answer her question. It was the only way she'd understand why he was doing what he was.

"I knew Doug Anders as an ADA when I worked in New York. And every cop in that city knows who the members of the Moretti family are." He paused. "Except for you. They didn't know there was a mafia princess."

Her expression tightened at the term. "That's not what I am."

He was too weary to fight with her over semantics. "The main reason I know who your father and your brothers are, is because they are responsible for the deaths of *my* father and brother."

CHAPTER TWENTY-ONE

Cara's face went pale at his words. "What?"

"My brother got caught up in the world of organized crime and was one of the low guys on the totem pole in your father's organization. Do you know what that meant?" She shook her head. "It meant he was expendable. So when they sent him on a risky drug deal, they didn't care what was waiting for him at the other end. They didn't care that he was taken down in a blaze of bullets when the deal went south."

Cara stood there, her eyes wide, but she didn't say anything, which was just as well, because Kieran didn't want to hear an apology from her. And he wasn't done yet.

"Six months later, my father was filled with so much rage and grief that he confronted your father one night when they crossed paths while my dad was on a different case. Moretti's goons made sure my dad didn't get anywhere near him again and our family, which had been four, suddenly became two. Your family did that to mine."

He saw Cara take a shaky breath and lift one hand to fist it beneath her chin. "I don't know what to say."

"I don't either." Kieran rubbed a hand down his face. "But I don't think this is going to work out for us."

She blinked rapidly, but then she nodded, understanding and devastation warring for dominance on her face. "Doug Anders brought Giovanni here as a favor to my father."

Kieran stared at her. "A favor to your father?"

"I know you say that things are over for us, but can I trust you?"

Her question, laced with worry and fear, gutted him. "Yes. I will never breathe a word about who you are to anyone. I just can't forget about it myself, which means it's impossible for me to see a future with you."

She nodded, her gaze dropping. "Gio, whom I'd never met before, is preparing to testify against his brothers. He has proof that they were responsible for the car bombing that killed my mother and was supposed to kill me. He's also been working as an accountant for the organization and will be presenting enough evidence to bring the organization down."

Her words shocked Kieran. "He's turning state's witness, just like your dad did?"

"Yes, but unlike my father, he won't be going to prison because he hasn't committed any crimes."

Kieran had a hard time believing that, but he wasn't going to argue with her. If she needed to believe the man was innocent, that was her prerogative, but he knew enough about the family to have a hard time accepting that anyone with the last name Moretti was actually innocent.

"I hope he has more success with his testimony than your dad did. His sons still managed to walk away from their trials as free men."

"I think Gio's evidence is more damning than what our father had."

He really hoped that the guy could come through and that they'd get an honest judge and jury so that justice could be done for the many people who'd lost their lives because of the Moretti family. It sounded like Cara had suffered at the hands of the brothers too, having lost her mother and then her identity in order to be safe from their blood-thirsty vendetta.

For a moment, he wanted to toss all his reservations to the wind and gather Cara into his arms. If he'd only known that the kiss they'd shared the night before would be their last, he would have held her longer. But there was no going back now. He couldn't be with her for so many reasons, so it was better to back away now rather than offer some kind of false hope that maybe things could work between them.

When her beloved father was the man responsible for the death of Kieran's loved ones, there was no way to bridge that chasm.

As the reality of that thought sank into his heart, the ache intensified, and Kieran knew he had to get away from Cara.

"I need to go."

Cara took a noticeably shaky breath and blew it out as she nodded. Kieran stared at her for one more long second before he turned away and pushed open the door. It wouldn't be the last time he saw her—the town was too small for that—but he wouldn't allow himself to ever get as close to her again. That would just make things that much more difficult.

As it was, the pain only got worse as he made his way home. The more distance he put between them, the worse it hurt. How could it really hurt that badly? The pain was like losing Toni all over again, but they'd been together for a few years, not just weeks.

He'd already been off work because of his dad's death when Toni had broken up with him, so he hadn't had to try to figure out how to focus on work when his personal life was falling apart. This time around, he didn't have that same luxury. He'd have to go into work each day and hope that people would stay out of his personal life.

That was probably a vain hope because so many people had been excited to see him and Cara together. They'd all want to know what had happened. *Irreconcilable differences* had never rung truer, but he wouldn't be able to give any details beyond that.

When he'd told Cara he wouldn't reveal any of the details about her life, he'd been telling the truth. It wasn't his desire to mess with her life or livelihood. He just couldn't be a part of it any longer.

Kieran walked into his house, feeling as if the weight of the world rested on his shoulders. He wasn't sure he could handle losing love again, even if it had been his decision this time. For sure, he was done with relationships. It hurt too much when things went wrong, and for him, it seemed that when they went wrong, they went epically wrong.

With his body and heart aching, Kieran dragged himself to bed despite the early hour, hoping that even if he did toss and turn for part of the night that he'd get enough sleep so that he wouldn't look like death when he walked into the station the next day.

~ * ~

Cara watched Kieran walk out of her studio, stunned at the painful turn her life had taken in just the past few minutes. She wanted to run after him, to beg him to give them another chance, but the futility of the situation held her in place. He'd found out about her past, which, under normal circumstances, they might have been able to overcome. But finding out the horrible way in which their families were connected had put a nail in the coffin of their relationship.

On some level, she'd known that her dad hadn't been a good man even though he'd always been so gentle and loving with her. The fact that even after he'd turned state's witness, he'd still ended up in prison had told her that he'd done some pretty awful things. But knowing it and seeing the ramifications of his actions for herself were two very different things.

She knew Kieran well enough at that point to see the hurt he felt as he ended their relationship. If only they could have just forgotten all about the family connection, but that wasn't possible, and now she was left to wonder if she could even stay in New Hope.

A sob escaped her throat as she sank to the floor. She wrapped her arms around her legs and pressed her forehead to her knees. The grief she felt at having lost the man she'd come to love threatened to tear her apart. Her grief was compounded by her father's passing, which was now complicated by the feeling that she'd never really known him.

How much more loss was she supposed to have to endure in her life? She'd thought that with Kieran, she finally had hope for a future where she wasn't all by herself, but now that was gone, and she found herself alone once again.

"Cara?"

The sound of a woman's voice had Cara scrambling to her feet, dragging her hands across her cheeks. Looking up, she saw Sarah standing just inside the doorway.

"Are you okay?" Sarah asked, concern clear on her face as she walked toward her.

Cara wrapped her arms tightly across her chest and shrugged. She wasn't sure she could trust her voice not to fail her. To her horror, more tears spilled down her cheeks, and Sarah instantly closed the remaining distance between them and wrapped her arms around her.

The other woman's offer of comfort without even knowing what the problem was brought on the tears again. The last person who had held her and offered her comfort had been Kieran, and now she'd never know what it felt like to be held by him again. His strength and support were no longer there for her to lean on.

She didn't know how long she'd stood there crying in Sarah's arms before it felt like all her emotions had drained out of her, leaving her exhausted. The emotional toll of the day was over-whelming her.

Stepping back from Sarah, Cara wiped at the moisture on her cheeks and let out a long breath. "Sorry to cry all over you."

"It's okay. I don't mind, except I don't like seeing you so upset," Sarah said with a gentle smile. "What's wrong?"

Cara thought about passing it off as grief over her father, but the truth would be out sooner rather than later. In a town that size, it would spread like wildfire, and since there wasn't much chance that this was only a temporary break-up, telling Sarah what had happened seemed to make the most sense.

But saying it would make it seem so real...so official. Still, there was no going back now. "Kieran and I broke up."

"What?" Sarah's eyes widened to almost comical proportions while her mouth gaped open. "Seriously?"

Cara sighed as she nodded.

"What happened? You guys just seemed so perfect together."

Even though she'd thought she'd cried all the tears she had, another sob rose up within her. She'd thought they were perfect together too. She'd felt closer to him than to anyone except for her mom and dad, and now they were all gone from her life.

"Something came up that we just couldn't get past."

Sarah's brows drew together. "Something insurmountable? Something you guys couldn't work through?"

"Yeah. I can't go into details because it's private, but it's not something that we'll be able to move beyond. This was for the best."

"Did you call it off?"

"No, but he was right to do it."

"I refuse to believe that it was that bad." Sarah crossed her arms and lifted her chin. "I'm going to pray for you guys and hope that it's God's will for you to get back together again."

Cara wanted to tell her to save her breath, but she didn't because maybe God would make a way that she and Kieran couldn't see in their present situations. There would be no harm in Sarah praying. As long as Cara didn't harbor any hope herself, it wouldn't hurt if others wanted to pray on her and Kieran's behalf.

"You're not going to leave New Hope, are you?" Sarah asked. When Cara didn't reply right away, she frowned. "You can't. You're a part of this town. We need your classes. I'm not the only one who loves what you've brought to New Hope with your studio. Please don't go."

"The town is so small," Cara said. "And this was Kieran's home first. It will be impossible not to run into each other all the time, which will make things really difficult."

"I can understand that, but don't make any decisions yet. This just happened today, right?"

"Yeah. Just a little while ago."

"Then don't make any decisions while your emotions over it are still so fresh." Sarah gave her a fierce look. "Promise?"

"I promise."

"Besides, you can't leave before Christmas. You have the dance recital to carry-through with," Sarah reminded her. "Which is why I'm here."

"Oh no. I completely forgot you were coming over. I'm so sorry."

"No worries." Sarah patted her arm. "Do you want to discuss the scenery you wanted me to paint for the recital now? I can come back another time if you'd prefer."

"Now is good. Might help to take my mind off things."

"Good. That's what I like to hear."

"Do you want to come up to my place?" Cara asked, suddenly needing to be in the comfort and security of her home.

This was the first time she'd ever invited anyone upstairs except for Kieran, but maybe it was time to invite more people in. Although it might not matter in the long run if she did decide to leave New Hope.

"Sure."

Sarah picked up her bag from where it lay at her feet as Cara moved past her to lock the studio door. As they passed by the photos on the wall in the hallway leading to the stairs, Sarah stopped to look at them.

"This is you," she stated.

"Yes."

"You were an honest to goodness ballerina."

Cara couldn't help but smile at her words, even though it was a small smile. "Yes, I was."

"These photos are stunning." Sarah turned to look at her. "Would you let me paint you?"

"Paint me?"

"Yes. I'd love to paint you in a ballet outfit like one of these. I mean, I could even do a painting from one of these pictures if it's easier."

Cara shrugged. "I'm not sure why I'd want a painting of myself. I don't have anyone to give it to."

"Your parents?"

Swallowing down another wave of grief, she said, "They've both passed away."

"Oh, I'm so sorry."

"Thank you."

"If you'd be okay with letting me paint from one of these photos, I could change just enough so that you're not recognizable, and then I could put it in the gallery."

"I would be okay with that," Cara said. "If you're really sure you want to do that."

"I'm sure. These are gorgeous."

"We can talk more about it later." Cara led the way to the stairs then up into her apartment.

"Wow," Sarah said as she followed Cara inside. "This is also gorgeous. You brought some real class to Main Street, and we didn't even realize it."

"Oh, I think Main Street was doing just fine on class without my help."

"Maybe, but this just brings it all up to a whole new level."

"Can I get you something to drink? Coffee? Tea? Water?"

"A coffee would be nice."

"Decaf or regular?"

"Guess I should go with decaf since I have to sleep tonight in order to be able to get up in the morning to help with cabin cleaning. Leah gets grumpy if she has to do it all by herself."

"Is Anna away?"

"Yeah. She's in LA for the week. Eli is going a little crazy without...her," Sarah's words seemed to fade as she realized that hearing that might be difficult for Cara.

And she wasn't wrong. Tears threatened again as she realized that Kieran wasn't going to ever go crazy because of missing her. He'd chosen to walk away. Knowing she wasn't being fair to him, Cara tried to push aside her pain as she turned to pull down mugs to make coffee for her guest.

"I'm sorry, Cara." Cara glanced over at Sarah and saw a rueful look on her face. "That was thoughtless of me."

"You're fine." Cara tried to give her a reassuring smile, but she had a feeling she'd failed miserably. "I don't want people to feel like they have to constantly watch what they say around me now. I have to get used to it. And I'm happy for Eli and Anna. They seem to really love each other."

"They do." This time Sarah's tone was wistful.

"No one on the horizon for you?"

Sarah huffed out a laugh. "I wish. It's hard in a town this small. I mean, I've known most the guys my age since we were kids. I can't remember a time when I didn't know them, really. Not that there are that many who have stuck around New Hope."

"No new blood has come in?"

"A few, but none I've been interested in."

"How about people who come to the lodge? That's how Eli met Anna, right?"

Sarah nodded as she took the cup of coffee from Cara. "That was a bit different, though, because we got to know Anna really well since she also helped us out at the lodge. Most the people who come just do their own thing. We might see them for meals, but even then, we're usually busy helping Mom."

Cara led them to the small dining room table and motioned to one of the chairs. She found she didn't really have the stomach to be discussing the subject of men.

"Anyway," Sarah said, seeming adept at reading Cara's silence. "How about you tell me what you're looking for with regards to the backdrop you want for the Christmas recital."

Cara was only too happy to leave the previous discussion behind, even though it was hard to pull up the excitement she'd been feeling towards the Christmas event. If not for her commitment to the event, she would happily have left town for at least a month or two. At least until she could see Kieran without feeling sick with the pain of her loss.

Sarah kept the conversation focused on the topic at hand, and when they finished, she didn't linger. Cara had appreciated the company, but she was rapidly reaching the point where she needed to be alone.

"Take care of yourself," Sara whispered as she hugged Cara at the door.

Cara nodded, but she couldn't push any words past the emotion that had tightened her throat. She closed and locked the door after Sarah had left, then turned off the lights and headed back up to her apartment.

Once she was upstairs, she turned off those lights as well then made her way to her seat by the window. She stared off in the direction of Kieran's house, wondering if he was hurting like she was. Or was he so angry at her that his anger eclipsed everything that had previously been between them?

She drew her legs up and wrapped her arms tightly around them, trying to keep the pain contained. It felt like the emotions were expanding in her chest, threatening to break the band of tightness there and tear through her.

Her breaths came in short pants as she struggled to keep herself under control, but the grief and loneliness were just too much. Ragged sobs burst from deep inside her, and there was no way she could stop them.

How much pain was she supposed to survive in her life? Her father had always told her she was the strongest person he knew, but even a strong person had a breaking point. And it seemed that she'd reached hers.

She didn't want to face hurt after hurt after hurt. Loss after loss. It was just too much. And now she was well and truly alone.

When her mom had passed, her father had been there to help her grieve, and when her father's time had come, Kieran had offered his strength and understanding. But now? Now she had no one to help her keep from falling completely apart. And there would be no one there to help her pick up the pieces afterward.

She didn't feel strong at all. No, she felt weaker than she'd ever felt before in her life.

Feeling like she was going to be sick, Cara stumbled from her seat into the bathroom off her bedroom.

"Why, God? What did I ever do to deserve this pain? Why have You taken away every person I've ever loved?" Anguish drew the words from her as she bent forward, hands braced on the cool tile of the bathroom floor.

When her arms began to tremble, she leaned against the cabinet and took shaky breaths, trying to draw enough air into her lungs to calm her emotions. She didn't want to be in New Hope anymore. She didn't want to see judgment or pity on the faces of the people in the town.

She wanted to go where no one knew she was so broken inside that she knew she'd never be whole again. And she would never love again. Never again. Loving had only brought her pain.

New Hope had finally felt like home, but it was more Kieran's home than hers, and she knew that he wouldn't be leaving. And someday, he'd find another woman to love.

The thought sent Cara scrambling to the toilet to empty her stomach. She couldn't be around when that happened. She definitely wasn't strong enough for that, and she doubted she ever would be.

When her stomach was no longer endeavoring to empty itself of its contents, Cara slumped against the wall and stared blankly at the floor. With that horrible scenario stuck in her head, the only thing she could do was begin to plan her exit from New Hope.

She'd stay through the Christmas recital because she owed it to her students, but then she would leave. She wasn't sure where she'd go, but she had a few weeks to figure that out. And this time, she wouldn't be telling Doug Anders where she was going. She was as done trusting people as she was done loving them.

Cara wasn't sure how long she'd been sitting on the bathroom floor, but when her swollen eyes began to droop, she dragged herself to bed. She didn't bother to change before crawling beneath her comforter. Thankfully, her emotional exhaustion gave way to physical exhaustion, and she welcomed sleep when it came.

CHAPTER TWENTY-TWO

The next morning when her alarm went, Cara lay there for a moment, wondering if she was coming down with something. Her eyes felt puffy and gritty. Her head ached like she'd had way too much to drink the night before.

Her one and only experience with excessive alcohol consumption had been when she'd celebrated turning twenty-one, and that had been more than enough. The memory of that feeling still lingered all these years later. But she couldn't figure out why she would have been drinking because she knew Kieran didn't drink. They'd never gone to a bar, and she didn't keep alcohol in her apartment.

Swinging her legs over the bed, she leaned forward and held her head for a moment before reaching for her phone. Maybe something there would jog her memory.

Peering at the display, she saw that she had no new text messages, so she opened her app to see her last conversation with Kieran. It was only when she saw their last exchange that things began to come back to her.

"Oh no," she whispered, wishing then that she hadn't woken up.

Before anything else, she sent out a quick message to the classes she had scheduled that day to let them know she was feeling sick and apologizing for having to cancel again. It wasn't a lie either. She felt wretched, and the last thing she wanted was a lot of questions about what was wrong.

When that was done, she took a deep breath, knowing that she needed to pull herself together to face the day. She had to deal with

Doug and Giovanni first, then she had to start planning her new future.

Was she a coward for running? Sure. But honestly, she didn't have it in her to be strong anymore. At least not yet.

After a long shower where she shed a few more tears, Cara pulled on a pair of jeans and a sweater, then smoothed her hair back into a bun and applied enough makeup to cover most the damage her crying episodes had created. Feeling slightly more human—but nowhere near her normal self—she made herself a mug of tea, afraid that coffee would do nothing to calm her upset stomach.

With the mug cupped in her hands, she made her way back to the window. The view that she'd enjoyed so much since moving there brought her no joy at that moment, but she couldn't seem to stop looking at it. In fact, the sight of *Norma's* caused even more pain. She'd come to appreciate the restaurant and its owner. Norma had always had a ready smile and an encouraging word for her.

Her heart ached at the thought of leaving it all behind, but for her sake, she had to. And no doubt Kieran would be glad to see the last of her too. She'd always be a reminder of what had happened to his father and brother. The last thing she wanted was to be a negative reminder for someone.

Before all of this had happened, she'd brought a smile to Kieran's face whenever he'd seen her. She didn't think she could stomach seeing his features tighten in anger or pain whenever he saw her.

Resolutely, she took the stairs down to the garage and was soon backing out into the alley, then heading toward the road that would take her to the hotel where Doug and Giovanni were staying. It was closer to Everett than New Hope, and it was a fairly nice place.

Uncertain of their room numbers, she texted Doug as she walked into the reception area to let him know that she was there and that she wanted to talk to them. As she waited for a response, she fought the urge to look through her pictures or read her text messages from Kieran. She needed to keep her emotions under control for this conversation.

"Cara?"

She swung around and saw Doug coming toward her. He was dressed casually in a pair of jeans and a long sleeve Henley shirt.

"I need to talk to you and Giovanni."

He gave a quick nod. "We're just having some breakfast in the restaurant." He gestured toward the direction from which he'd come. "Would you like to join us?"

She wasn't hungry in the slightest, but she wasn't going to just hang around the reception area waiting while they finished eating. At her nod, he waited for her to reach his side before he turned to walk with her to the restaurant.

Gio stood as they reached the table. "Good morning."

"Morning." It was so far from good that Cara couldn't even pair the two words.

She took one of the two seats that didn't have food in front of it. A waitress appeared almost immediately, but Cara only ordered tea. She was still not sure how her stomach would tolerate coffee.

Once they were left alone, Cara turned to face Doug. "Do you know Kieran Sutherland?"

Shock crossed the man's face before he nodded. "How do you know that name?"

"Until last night, I was dating him."

"Oh man," Gio muttered.

"Yeah. Apparently he saw the two of you in town and did a little research before putting the pieces together and figuring out who I was."

"He always was a stellar detective," Doug said. "Just like his father."

"He broke up with you?" Gio asked, his dark brown gaze soft as he regarded her.

"Do you think it would have been possible for him to stay with me once he realized who my father was?" Cara swallowed against the tightening in her throat. "I don't blame him. He told me what your family did to his brother and his father."

Gio nodded slowly. "But you are not our father. You're not responsible for the things that he and others in the organization did."

The waitress returned and placed a small silver teapot and a teacup on the table in front of her. Cara waited until she'd left before saying anything more. As she prepared her tea, she said, "But see, the thing is, I'd told him all about my father. Not his name. Not that he was in prison. Not that he was responsible for a criminal organization. No, I told him all about the man *I* knew. The man *I* loved. How could he reconcile the fact that the man I loved and mourned was the one responsible for the deaths of his brother and father?"

"I see." Gio lifted his coffee and took a sip. "You and I will both have to live with the fact that the man we knew as father was different from the man others saw. The father I knew was also very different from the one my brothers knew. To many, he was a monster. To me, he was simply Papa."

Cara blinked back tears at the name Gio gave to their father. He'd been her papa too. "I had hoped that with Papa's death, I'd be able to leave our past behind and fully embrace the identity I have now."

"Had you planned to tell Kieran about your past?" Doug asked.

"I had been feeling torn about it because I'd promised Papa I wouldn't tell anyone. And because he was a cop, I thought maybe it was better he didn't know." Except she had a feeling that if they'd reached a certain point of intimacy in their relationship, she would have wanted him to know everything. And if the hurt was this powerful after only a few months of being together, she couldn't imagine what it would have been like a year or two down the road.

"Is there anything we can do?" Gio asked. "Do you want us to talk to him? Explain what's going on?"

If she'd thought it would make any difference, Cara would have jumped at the offer, but she knew it wouldn't, so she shook her head. "He said he won't say anything to anyone about what he knows about me, or that he saw you and Gio here."

"That's good," Doug said. "I know he still has friends in the department, and I'd hate for word to get back to them. The last thing we need is the wrong person finding out where you are or jeopardizing the case we're building."

"I trust that he'll be true to his word and won't say anything." She was completely certain of that. Regardless of what was going on between them, he'd given his word, and she believed him.

"I hope you're right." Doug sighed. "So what are you going to do now?"

Cara looked at him, knowing he was probably wondering if she planned to leave New Hope, but even though she did, she didn't plan to let him know that.

"I have a Christmas recital I'm planning for my students at the studio, so I'll be focusing on that."

"Have you thought anymore about what your father asked in his letter?"

"No. The bombshell that Kieran dropped last night sort of distracted me from that."

"I'll understand if you need more time," Gio said. "I just want you to know that you aren't alone. That I understand what it's like to try to reconcile the man we loved with the things he did. At least we can take comfort that in the end, he did try to do the right thing. I don't see that happening with my brothers."

Cara allowed herself to really look at the man across from her. There was hurt and grief there that she recognized. She'd never

BECAUSE OF HIM · 249

had to face the consequences of her father's actions until the previous night, but Gio had had to live with them his whole life. And not just the actions of his father, but those of his brothers as well.

She found herself a little curious about how he'd managed to not become just like her brothers. But she wasn't going to ask.

She hoped that Gio was able to see justice meted out for his brothers, and that he would one day be free to live the life he wanted. She'd had a brief taste of that in New Hope, and she wanted it again. Running might not be the answer, but it was the only way she'd get to live a life free from the stigma she faced now.

"We won't bother you about this again," Gio said, his expression stoic. "I will leave you with the information to contact me if you should wish, but I won't be bothering you. I can see now how much being associated with my family has hurt you, and I have no wish to add to your pain."

"You only have to call if you need anything," Doug added. "Your father extracted a promise from me as well. I know that it seems unlikely, but I considered him a friend. I saw the weight he carried because of his actions. I know he loved your mother deeply, Cara. It was his wish that I continue to care for you as I would my own daughter, and I will do just that."

Cara's chest tightened at the emotion in the man's words. If only Kieran had been able to see the change in her father, maybe he would have been more accepting of him. But she could hardly expect him to take her word for that. She might be moving on, but she'd never forget Kieran in the same way she'd never forget the man she knew her father to be. Because of them, she'd learned about love, and she'd carry the memory of her love for each of them with her forever.

With emotions welling up within her again, Cara pushed back from the table and got to her feet, abandoning her tea. "I'm sorry. I need to go."

Doug and Gio both stood up as well, understanding on their faces.

"Take care of yourself," Doug said as he held out his hand. "And please, call me if you need anything at all."

Gio also extended his hand once she'd shaken Doug's. "It was a pleasure to meet you, though I wish it had been under better circumstances."

Cara nodded then gave them a brief smile before she turned and walked away. She hurried out of the hotel and back to her car. Her only focus was getting back to the sanctuary of her apartment, where she could continue to privately grieve all she'd lost in the last few weeks.

She just hoped that she'd be able to find the strength to walk away from New Hope when the time came. Right then, she didn't feel strong enough to do much of anything but cry.

~ * ~

Kieran hated the idea of going into work. He wasn't ready to face anyone when he was still feeling so raw from what had happened with Cara. It would likely take just one look at his face for Lisa to know that something was horribly wrong. He figured he had until noon before his mom called him to find out what was going on.

He was tucking his wallet into his pocket in preparation for leaving his house when his phone rang. Glancing at the display, he realized that he'd underestimated the rumor mill of New Hope.

"Hi, Mom," he said as he tapped the screen to set it to speakerphone. "What's up?"

"I was just calling to see what's wrong with Cara."

His heart thumped hard in his chest at the sound of her name. "I don't know. I haven't talked to her this morning."

"She sent a text out saying that all the classes for today were canceled because she wasn't feeling well."

"I guess that's what's wrong with her then, Mom."

There was a beat of silence before she said, "Is something wrong between the two of you?"

Kieran knew he couldn't lie to his mom when she asked a direct question like that. She'd be furious if she found out what had happened from anyone else, and rightfully so. As his mother, she should be the first to know what had happened.

He sighed, then said, "We broke up."

"You *what?*"

Kieran winced at her shriek. He knew she really liked Cara, and he was going to be in an awkward position now. He didn't want to explain to her why they'd broken up. He needed to keep his word to Cara and not reveal what he knew about her past.

"What happened?" she asked, her voice a little calmer. "Everything seemed fine the other day."

Everything *had* been fine the other day. "We just agreed that it wasn't going to work out."

"That makes no sense. I'm sorry, but you two were perfect together. Anyone could see that."

Kieran winced at her words, wishing he could tell her that in a world without any outside influences, they had felt perfect, but they didn't exist in that world. He knew that if he could tell her the details, she'd agree with his decision, but since he couldn't, she'd just have to accept his vague excuses. The feelings he had for Cara hadn't died while he slept, and he didn't want anything bad to happen to her. So if that meant he kept her past a secret from his mom, he'd do that.

Logically, he knew that Cara wasn't responsible for what her father and his organization had done to his family, but he had hated her father for far longer than he'd loved her. He wasn't sure he could ever separate the two of them in his mind. Because of that, he had no doubt that at some point, her father's identity would come between them. They were both better off moving on.

"It's private, Mom. We have our reasons, and no one is going to convince us otherwise."

"Ah, honey, I'm sorry. I wish I knew what to say."

"There's nothing to say." He grabbed his hat and keys and headed out the door for his Jeep. "It is what it is."

The words came easily, but honestly, each one was like a stab in the heart. It was only now, as he was contemplating life without her that Kieran realized just how much he loved her. His first thought when he'd woken up had been of her. But that had been before reality had intruded and reminded him that she wasn't his to love anymore.

"Come to dinner tonight. I'll make your favorite."

"I don't want to talk about it, Mom."

"I understand, honey. Just let me try to help you feel better."

"I'll be over when I'm done at work."

"Hope your day goes okay. I'll be praying it does."

"Thanks, Mom. Love you."

"Love you too, Kiki."

He groaned at his childhood nickname, born of his brother, Sean, being unable to say his name when he'd first started talking. It just so happened that it was also a shortening of his first and middle names—Kieran Kingsley. When his mom pulled out the nickname, he knew that she was going to be babying him like she had when he was a kid. Though he normally would have balked at it, he was hurting too much to brush it aside.

He drove to work slowly, his gaze going to the tall building that housed Cara's studio and apartment as soon as he turned onto Main Street. How was he going to be able to heal from this break-up when he'd be seeing her at every turn?

After parking, he sat for a moment, gearing himself up for what was most likely going to be a trying day. Maybe he should see if he could make up an excuse to head into the office in Everett. It would at least guarantee he wouldn't see Cara. He enjoyed his job in New

Hope, but maybe he should consider seeing if he could get a job at the Sheriff's office there.

He'd still see her periodically since he wouldn't move. However, it wouldn't be as much as if they were working on the same street. But he liked his job in New Hope. He liked knowing the people he worked for. He didn't want to leave the station there.

With a sigh, he climbed from the Jeep and headed into the station. Thankfully, Lisa was on the phone, so he could get away with just nodding in greeting before making his way to his office.

As it turned out, he didn't have to make up an excuse to head into Everett. Not long after he'd sat down at his desk, he got a call inviting him to a meeting with an update on the body that had been discovered. He was more than happy to escape New Hope and head for Everett and the distraction the meeting would provide.

He made it two days before someone asked him about him and Cara, and no surprise, it was Lisa.

"Did you two break up?" Lisa asked when he returned to the station after picking up a lunch from *Norma's* that he wasn't sure he wanted to eat.

"Why do you say that?"

"Answering a question with a question?" Lisa arched a brow. "That's as good as confirming."

Kieran shrugged and headed for the door that led to the back of the station. He knew that he only had a brief reprieve, for as long as it took Lisa to reach his office from her desk. For a plus-size woman, she could move surprisingly fast when she wanted to.

"What happened?" she asked when she appeared in his doorway as he was hanging up his hat.

Kieran set his food on the desk then sat down. "If we wanted people to know the details, we would have given Craig an exclusive."

Lisa frowned. "I don't understand."

"Well, Craig publishes the newspaper, and if you want everyone to know something, you call him up and tell him to put it in the weekly."

"You know that's not what I meant," Lisa said as she put her hands on her hips. "I meant that I don't understand why the two of you have broken up. It makes no sense."

Kieran leaned back in his chair. "It's a good thing that it only had to make sense to Cara and me."

Lisa moved closer to his desk, her gaze pinned on him as she attempted to read his mind. He'd endured far worse attempts than hers, so he just stared back at her until she finally shook her head.

"You know that I only care about you." She hesitated then added, "And her too. She is such a sweetheart."

He couldn't argue with Lisa there, but he also couldn't reveal that Cara's father had been the monster responsible for ripping his family apart. "You don't need to take sides in this. It just wasn't meant to be."

Lisa tilted her head. "Are you sure?"

"Very." Although he did have moments where he wondered if he was sure. But they were just brief moments, and all he had to do was remember his father's broken body on the floor of the building where he'd been gunned down by Marco Moretti's body-guards to be reminded that yes, it had been the right thing to do.

With a sigh, Lisa shook her head. "Stubborn."

"No. Just private about my personal life."

Now that Lisa knew, Kieran guessed that it would be only a matter of time before others did as well. Not that he thought she'd be the one to spread the rumor, but if she was noticing that he and Cara weren't around each other anymore, others would notice, too.

CHAPTER TWENTY-THREE

The only good news Kieran had received that week was that through dental records, they'd been able to confirm that the body found in the woods, wasn't Sheila's. The detectives were still in the dark about the real identity of the body, so that wasn't a good thing because it meant that since it wasn't Sheila, they had another murder on their hands.

After Lisa had finally left him alone, Kieran tried to focus on work, but it was hard. Every day it was a struggle, and he was on edge constantly whenever he was anywhere but the station or his house, just waiting for the moment when he ran into Cara for the first time since their break-up.

He had thought that as time went by, life would get easier, but instead, it was getting more difficult. Now that the original rush of emotion caused by the breakup had faded, he was left with memories, hopes, and his love for Cara. Everywhere he turned, something reminded him of her or of something they had done together.

That hadn't been an issue when Toni had ended their engagement since he'd left New York not long after they'd broken up. He'd been able to heal without constant reminders of her everywhere he turned. It would not be so easy for him this time around.

His mom had told him that Cara had canceled a second day of classes, but she'd been back to her normal schedule that day. His mom asked if he cared if she continued to attend the class. He'd said no, but he'd also made it clear that he didn't want her to use the class as an opportunity to pump Cara for more information about their breakup.

He didn't doubt that Cara would stay mum on the details. She'd already proven she was able to keep things private. So private that she hadn't even shared them with him.

Lifting the travel mug full of coffee he'd brought with him, Kieran took a sip and resigned himself to not being able to get Cara off his mind that morning. It had been a struggle to not think of her when things were going well, but it was even worse now. He wished that he could hate her for the situation they'd ended up in, but he couldn't. He could definitely hate her father and the Moretti family, but not her. It was just too bad the two were now so intertwined in his mind.

In the days since he'd discovered her secret, he'd realized that he wasn't mad at her for what she'd kept from him. He actually understood why she had done that. Her very safety could have been at risk if she'd shared about her past with the wrong person. He hoped that had things gone differently for them, that at some point, she would have felt safe enough to tell him about who she really was.

The truth was, if he had just been the police chief of a small town without the connection to New York City and her family, he wouldn't have had a problem with her past. He wouldn't have ended things between them. After all, she couldn't help who her family was.

The sticking point wasn't just that her father had been responsible for the deaths of Sean and their dad, but that she adored that man. Her love for her father was something Kieran couldn't accept. Marco Moretti had not been an honorable man. He hadn't been worthy of Cara's love and devotion, and yet she'd given it to him without reservation.

That was what he struggled to get past. And he knew that it would always stand between them. That he wouldn't be able to look at her without remembering who her father was and what he'd done to Kieran's family.

With a sigh, Kieran reached for the phone, needing something to distract him. The detective on Sheila's case had mentioned talking to Eli again, this time about the recent body they'd found. It was like he thought Eli was responsible for that murder, too.

Up until that body had been found, it had seemed like the guy was finally accepting that Eli hadn't been involved in Sheila's disappearance. Now, he seemed positively gleeful at the opportunity to possibly pin something else on Eli.

Kieran understood the intense desire to solve a case, but this appeared to be more of an obsession that was blinding the guy to the truth.

Thankfully, the detective was happy to ramble on about his latest theories in the case, and it was enough to distract Kieran from his thoughts about Cara.

~ * ~

Cara breathed a sigh of relief when she pulled back into her garage. The past five days had reminded her a lot of her arrival in New Hope. She'd kept to herself, not interacting with anyone in the town. At least at the beginning. But eventually she'd gone into the bakery and *Norma's* and had slowly begun to acquaint herself with the people who lived in the town that was now her home.

But here she was, back to keeping to herself, trying her best to avoid running into Kieran. The only people she saw these days were the women and kids in her classes. It had been challenging, dodging the topic of the breakup. It seemed that everyone knew about it now, and they all wanted the scoop.

So far, she'd managed to shut down their questions by saying it was a mutual decision about something private. That was a bit of a lie, though, since she hadn't wanted the breakup at all, even though she understood why Kieran had.

Unfortunately, she still hadn't managed to make it through a day without crying. Her heartache over the loss of her relationship with

Kieran ran deep, flowing through her veins, carrying the pain to every part of her body. There were times she wondered how long it would be like that. How long she'd feel the bone-deep ache.

Then there were other times when she hoped it never went away. She wanted to carry a reminder of how deeply she'd loved Kieran. He was her first true love, and though their relationship had ended so badly, she didn't want to forget about him. But she did hope that one day, she could look back on these months with him and only remember the love, not the pain that had followed.

For the time being, though, she was just trying to survive the first few days without him. She'd hardly left the studio, and when she had, it had been to go into Everett to get groceries or to walk around the mall. She'd needed the break from her own company and her own thoughts.

Adding to the pain of that first week following their breakup was that Thanksgiving had been at the end of it. She was supposed to have spent the holiday with Kieran and his mom, and his mom had sweetly extended the invitation again, obviously trying hard to understand what had happened between them.

Though she'd been thankful that Rose hadn't chosen to take sides, it had just made the loss of Kieran all the more difficult. She had been so accepting and encouraging of their relationship. Cara wondered how Rose would have felt about her if she knew the truth about who she was.

In the end, even though she'd also received an invitation from Sarah to join them at the lodge, she'd chosen the solitude of her apartment. Though she'd tried to focus on all she was grateful for, it had been a challenge...as so much of life had been since her father's death.

With the breakup following so closely on the heels of her father's death, being thankful had been a bit beyond her ability. She hadn't wanted to feel sorry for herself, but again, it had been hard not to. In the end, she'd spent most the day in bed, reading and trying to escape for just a little while from the lonely thing her life had become.

Not able to handle the quiet of her apartment any longer, the next day she'd braved the Black Friday crowds and made her way to the stores in Everett. She hadn't bought anything since she had no one to buy anything for anymore. But just wandering around helped her feel less alone.

When she'd had her fill of the crowds, she'd gone to the grocery store and picked up a few things before heading home. Once there, she put away the groceries, then made herself a quick dinner, putting on some music to stave off the quietness of the apartment.

Usually at this point in the year, she would have been playing Christmas music, but her heart just wasn't in it. In years past, she'd left New Hope for Christmas to spend time with her dad in Texas, but this year she'd be somewhere else. She hadn't decided where yet, but one thing she did know was that her next destination wouldn't be a small town. She needed to be able to lose herself somewhere, and there would be no way to do that in another small town like New Hope.

The next day she woke with a headache that matched her heartache. She'd cried herself to sleep again, then tossed and turned throughout the night. Would she ever be able to sleep peacefully again?

After two days of her own company, she was kind of relieved she had some plans for Saturday, even if they would no doubt include questions about the breakup. The moms of the girls in the Christmas recital were coming to discuss costume options, and though Cara assumed there would be more questions about her and Kieran, she was kind of looking forward to having a conversation with others.

The Christmas recital was the only thing keeping her mind occupied, and since it was going to be her last one with her studio there, she planned to enjoy every minute of it. She'd hoped to be celebrating the recital and the upcoming holidays with Kieran and his mom, but instead, once the recital was done and she'd taught her last classes before the holidays, she would be gone from New Hope.

That thought lingered as she spent the day cleaning the apartment and the studio in preparation for the meeting that night. Once she was done cleaning the studio, she set up the tables and chairs they'd need in the dance room. She was grateful for the work that kept her busy until the first of the women arrived just before seven.

"How're you doing, Cara?" the woman asked as she walked in with a container of goodies in her hands. "Did you have a nice Thanksgiving?"

"It was fine. How about yours?"

Thankfully, this woman was one of the chattier ones and happily talked about the meal she'd made and everyone who had been there. By the time her conversation wound down, a couple more women had arrived and were happy to carry on the conversation.

"I'm so sorry to hear about you and the chief."

Cara turned to see a woman who was a single mom to a pair of twin girls who were in her five and six-year-old class. "Thank you."

"I know going through a breakup is a special kind of difficult in a small town like New Hope." The woman's expression was sympathetic. "People just care a little too much about what other people are going through. It will get better. Hang in there."

Cara offered her a smile that she hoped conveyed her appreciation for not prying. "Thank you. It has felt a bit weird with everyone wanting to know what happened."

"Yep, but eventually they'll drop it. Something else will come up, although I'll admit, it might take them a bit longer to get past this. Chief hasn't dated much, or at all, really, so it was big news when he started dating you, which means the breakup will be a hot topic for awhile. I'm sorry."

BECAUSE OF HIM · 261

That's what Cara had figured, so it wasn't a big surprise. "Just part of life, I guess."

The woman sighed. "I wish it weren't, but yeah, it does feel like it is. For some of us, anyway."

Before Cara could respond, the woman who'd headed up the costume committee for the past couple of years called them to attention. Since she'd already presented the music and they'd begun to rehearse, Cara didn't have to do anything but listen to the lively discussion that ensued.

It was a pleasant distraction, and for a couple of hours, she was able to pretend that life was normal. That after this meeting, she'd call Kieran and tell him about how determined the different mothers had been for their daughters to wear certain outfits.

For all the disagreements, they were able to finally come to a consensus, and an agreement to each bring their daughters' costumes to their next class. Since they'd had their coffee and tea, along with the dainties they'd brought, while the meeting was going on, they didn't hang around too long when it ended.

A couple of the women managed to ask some semi-veiled questions about how she was doing since the breakup. Cara managed to brush them off, much to their disappointment. Still, she was sad to see the last one leave since that left just her in the quiet of the studio.

As she climbed the stairs, sadness settled over her as she realized she wouldn't be here in another year to plan a recital. She had no idea what she'd be doing. If she'd try to find something related to dance, or if she'd choose a totally new direction. Maybe go back to school.

Her father had left her enough money that she wouldn't have to work right away, but she would need something to occupy her time, so she didn't completely lose herself in her heartache and grief.

When she woke the next morning, Cara lay for a moment, wondering if she should go to church. She'd been attending regularly, but now it felt a bit like she was infringing on Kieran's turf. She wanted to go, though. It had become part of her routine, and it was an activity that fed her soul in a way that attending church as a teen never had.

Deciding that she'd arrive late and leave early, Cara rolled out of bed and headed for the shower. After a check of the weather, she dressed in a pair of fitted black jeans and an oversized red sweater. The temperatures had dropped a little in the past couple of days, so once she'd finished getting ready, she grabbed a jacket and pulled on a pair of flat ankle boots.

Her stomach knotted as she approached the church, even though she was arriving a little late. She hesitated inside the doorway, glancing around the empty foyer, before making her way to the doors of the sanctuary. A peek through the slender glass window in the door showed that the congregation was standing, which was perfect.

She eased open the door and slipped inside. The greeter near the door offered her a smile and a bulletin. She took it with a nod then headed for the nearest empty seat. Long familiar music filled the air, and Cara stood with the others, but not singing as she let the music and words wash over her. Her mom had always loved Christmas time, especially at church.

Parts of the service brought back memories for her in a way she hadn't expected. She missed her mom intensely at that moment, and the ache only increased as she spotted Kieran near the front with his mom. In past weeks she'd sat in church with him, her shoulder pressed against his arm. Usually at some point, she'd end up tucked against his side, his arm around her shoulders.

She blinked back tears and exhaled quickly, trying to breathe out the emotions that were rising within her. She didn't want to have an emotional breakdown right there in the church, giving the citizens of New Hope even more to talk about.

By the time the pastor got up, she was convinced that coming had been a bad idea. Her chest was tight again, and it was all she could do to keep the tears from falling. She missed her mom. She missed her dad. She missed Kieran.

"Today is the first Sunday of Advent," the pastor said as he took his place behind the pulpit. "And as you heard from the reading earlier when Cadi lit the first candle, this week's focus is on hope. We read in the Old Testament of those who prophesied about Jesus' birth, offering hope to the nation of Israel. Their Savior was to come and save them. It was their hope of salvation, and even though Jesus has already lived His time on this earth, Christmas is a reminder of the hope His birth still offers to us."

Cara focused on Pastor Evan's words, trying to use them to keep her emotions at bay, but it was hard. She felt a sense of hopelessness. She'd just finally started to feel hope for a future for the first time since her mom's death, but she no longer felt much hope for anything. At this point, she just wanted to find a way to get through each day without crying and without the constant sick feeling in her stomach.

"Too often, we put our hope in people or circumstances. We hope that someone will hire us for a new job. We hope that our boss will give us a promotion. We hope that our relationship will work out. We hope that our children will grow up to be good people. All of those are fine things to hope for, but only if we've first put our hope in the Lord Jesus Christ and in His will for our lives."

His words sank into her mind, jarring her out of her emotional state. Her hope had definitely been on anything but God. She wasn't used to thinking of situations like that. Would putting her hope in God have made it hurt less when Kieran had broken up with her?

It felt too late to do anything about that now. The pain was well and truly entrenched in her heart, and right then, it didn't feel like it was ever going to go away.

Cara listened as the pastor continued to talk about hope, remembering how her father had expressed his hopes for her. The look of peace on her father's face as he'd spoken about his new-found faith in God filled her memory. If he was able to find peace while facing death, surely she could find peace while facing life. A new life, true, but life nonetheless. Could she find peace and hope in the midst of her grief and hurt?

"As we enter this time of celebrating the birth of Christ, let us take time to embrace the hope He brought for us. A hope that, if we place our trust in God, will sustain us, even in the darkest of hours. Though the hopes we have may be dashed at times, our hope in God will buoy us up so that we do not sink beneath the weight of those unrealized hopes and broken dreams."

Once the pastor drew his sermon to a close, the worship leader got up to lead them in a song. Cara had been prepared to leave then, but as the pianist began to play, the song once again drew her memory back to the services she'd attended with her mom.

Come, thou long-expected Jesus,
born to set thy people free;
from our fears and sins release us,
let us find our rest in thee.
Israel's strength and consolation,
hope of all the earth thou art;
dear desire of every nation,
joy of every longing heart.

Born thy people to deliver,
born a child and yet a King,
born to reign in us forever,
now thy gracious kingdom bring.

By thine own eternal spirit
rule in all our hearts alone;
by thine all sufficient merit,
raise us to thy glorious throne.

The words were not contemporary, but that drew her in even more as she'd always been drawn to historical music, particularly the music she'd danced to with the ballet company. So she lingered, singing along with the words, mulling them over.

Hope of all the earth thou art.

She wanted that hope for herself. The hope of God in her heart and her life.

As the song ended and the pastor rose for the final prayer, Cara slipped out of the row and headed for the doors leading to the foyer. She didn't want to speak to anyone right then, especially with Kieran in the vicinity.

Though the message had given her much to think about, she was a bit adrift and feeling as if pain instead of hope was the anchor she had available. She wanted hope as she moved forward with her life, as she faced the ups and downs that she knew were still to come.

Outside the church, Cara lifted her face to the sun that was peeking through the clouds. She took a deep breath and let it out, wishing the pain had gone with her breath, but knowing she just had to embrace it for now.

~ * ~

Kieran left the service feeling...he wasn't sure what. He'd missed having Cara sitting beside him, and he'd wondered if she would be there. Though he'd glanced around before and after the service, he hadn't seen her. The ache in his heart had pulsed a little stronger at that realization.

Given the topic of the sermon, it was a bit ironic for him to hope for something, but he did, even though it wasn't for himself. He hoped that Cara would continue to pursue her faith. He had accepted that they were going to have to exist in the same town, and maybe even the same church. It would be hard, but as long as he knew she was safe, he would deal with it.

As had become his habit in recent days, Kieran returned home after turning down his mom's invitation to go to *Norma's* and changed into his running clothes. His mom was harping on him that he was losing weight, which was likely true. Since the breakup, he'd had no appetite to speak of, and he'd been doing more than his usual amount of running.

It had been similar after his breakup with Toni, but that had been compounded by his grief over his dad. Things had gradually righted themselves, but it had taken awhile. Work and exercise had been all that had kept him sane.

He had a feeling it was going to be similar this time around. His connection to Cara had been strong enough that he'd started to have glimpses of what a future with her might be like. So the heartache was real. As real as it had been when things had ended with Toni.

His shoes pounded the hard surface of the road as he headed out of town. He didn't have a definite course in mind, but he soon found himself on the long route he seemed to favor these days. With music playing loud enough to drown out his thoughts, he once again tried to outrun his feelings.

By the time he made it back to his house, it was raining, and his body ached. He was fine with both those things, though, since the rain sort of reflected how he was feeling inside. It felt like his mind was covered by dark clouds, and his heart was weeping at the loss of Cara.

Instead of going inside, he settled on the top step of his porch, not caring that he was getting even more soaked than he had gotten on the run. He stared out into the misty air, feeling loneliness settle deep within him.

He missed Cara.

They might not have been dating for long, but she'd made a place for herself in his life and in his heart. So much so that when she'd been torn from his life by circumstances beyond his control, she'd left a gaping wound that refused to heal.

Kieran rubbed his hands down his face. Logically, he knew he would heal, but right then, it felt like he had a wound that would never close. He had never thought that he'd experience one heartache, let alone two, in his lifetime. After what had happened with Toni, he knew he would heal. It would take time, but healing would come.

But he didn't really care. He was now two for two when it came to serious relationships, and he wasn't sure if the third time would be the charm or if he'd strike out. And at that moment, he wasn't in any rush to find out.

CHAPTER TWENTY-FOUR

A couple of days later, while having dinner with his mom, she mentioned that the Christmas dance recital was coming up that weekend. Kieran remembered how excited Cara had been about it. His plan had been to attend it in support of her.

"I think I'd like to go," his mom said as she passed him a bowl of mashed potatoes.

She'd gone all out for their dinner that night, clearly trying to tempt him to eat more. Kieran was doing his best to satisfy her by taking good-size helpings of the roast beef, veggies, potatoes, and fresh-made rolls. It was a struggle to eat it all because his appetite was still gone, but he did his absolute best.

"Will you come with me?"

Kieran looked up from his plate. "You want me to go with you to the recital?"

His mom nodded. It was so hard to not tell her the details about their breakup, but he didn't want to turn her against Cara. He didn't want her to have to experience the heartbreaking reality that Cara's dad had been responsible for her husband and son's deaths. But most of all, he didn't want to put the burden of Cara's secret on her. He'd promised to keep that secret, and he would, even from his mom.

"I'm not sure that's a good idea."

"You *miss* her."

"I do," Kieran admitted. "But there were just things that came between us that we couldn't overcome. We truly are the epitome of irreconcilable differences."

"I wish you would tell me what happened."

"I'm sorry, Mom. It's something that Cara and I have decided to keep private."

His mom frowned. "I'm sure you know there are rumors going around."

"I'd have been more surprised if there weren't. This is New Hope Falls, after all."

"And you don't care?"

"I don't care what people are saying about the break-up. What I do care about is people saying bad things about Cara. *That* is something I'd better not hear."

His mom's brow wrinkled as she stared at him, clearly not understanding how he could care about protecting Cara from negative rumors and yet still not want to be together with her. He wished he could explain it to her, but that just wasn't possible.

Finally, his mom let the subject drop, though Kieran didn't think for one minute that he'd heard the last of it. That wasn't uppermost in his mind as he left her house a couple of hours later, though. No, the dance recital was.

His plan, originally, had been to attend the recital with a big bouquet of flowers for Cara to celebrate the evening. He couldn't get that plan out of his head, and by the time Friday rolled around, he knew that wild horses couldn't keep him away.

He dressed in a pair of black jeans and a black turtleneck, then grabbed a jacket and left the house. It didn't take long to get to the high school where he planned to sneak into the building. Hopefully without running into anyone.

Seeing Cara at something that he'd planned to attend with her was no doubt not going to help him get over her anytime soon. But he found he didn't really care about healing more quickly. He'd loved Cara...still loved her...and he wasn't eager to have that feeling leave his heart. She still meant everything to him.

His heart pounded as he walked across the rather dimly lit parking lot. He made a mental note to talk to the principal at the school about making sure that the lights in the lot were always working properly. With the days being short, any kids staying for after-school activities were leaving when it was dark outside, and that wasn't good if the area wasn't well lit.

There were quite a few cars there, which wasn't a real surprise. There were probably a lot of grandparents and aunts and uncles attending along with the parents of the little ones who would be performing. His mom was probably in there as well since the last he'd heard, she planned to attend.

He heard the music as soon as he neared the theater. It was muffled behind the closed doors of course, but he recognized it. *Jingle Bells* increased in volume as he slowly opened the door and slipped into the darkened theater.

The people in the audience were all gathered in the front part of the auditorium, which allowed him to settle in a seat in the back row without interrupting anything. A row of six little girls in shiny red costumes with bell bracelets were making their way through their choreography with varying degrees of success. One little girl in particular, kept stumbling around, bumping into her fellow dancers, which earned her a few frustrated glares from the girls who were managing to keep in step.

Kieran couldn't help but smile at the antics. When the number ended, the girls skipped off to the side, waving out at the applauding audience as they did so. From the opposite side of the stage, a group of slightly older girls, dressed in green outfits that had long sleeves and full skirts that looked to be made of matching netting with sparkles on them, appeared. After they were in position, *O Christmas Tree* started to play.

These girls were slightly more coordinated and managed to dance without actually bumping into one another. As they moved around, Kieran noticed that they had small colored balls attached to their hair buns, and there were strips of tinsel in their skirts.

They did look like little Christmas trees and danced very well to the music.

There was plenty of applause as they exited the stage. The next group was dressed in white and danced to *Let It Snow*. They were older than the two previous troupes, so they were the most coordinated of the groups so far, but it was clear when the final troupe came out, that they were the most experienced dancers of them all.

They were dressed in silver outfits with tiaras that sparkled in the overhead lights, and they moved smoothly and gracefully to *Silver Bells*. When their song ended, Kieran heard Cara begin to speak over the PA system.

"Thank you all for coming tonight. I'd like to introduce you to our beautiful dancers who have all done such a terrific job. They've been working really hard, and you can see that their diligent work has paid off."

Kieran closed his eyes as he listened to Cara introduce each of the dancers. He could hear the pride in her voice, and he so wished that things had worked out differently for them. He wanted to tell her that the girls were as good as they were because of their talented teacher. He wanted to tell her how proud he was of *her* for sharing her knowledge and experience with these young girls.

He inhaled then let out a long breath. Maybe it had been a really bad idea to come to the recital. Not maybe...probably.

It took a while to announce each of the girls since she did a little intro for each of them, too, sharing a few of their favorite things including what they hoped to get for Christmas.

And when she was done, the girls lined up again, looking very festive with the colors of the outfits all mingling together. Their final song was *We Wish You A Merry Christmas*, and Kieran stayed until just about the end of the song before standing up and slipping out of the theater.

His chest was tight, his heart aching as he walked toward his Jeep. He hadn't even seen Cara, just heard her voice, and he was an emotional mess.

All the way back to his place, Kieran tried once again to figure out if he could possibly just ignore Cara's past. Could he just ignore her connection to the worst events of his life?

His heart said yes, but his mind said no. Nothing had changed from the moment he'd realized who she really was. If only it were as easy as turning off that knowledge.

Would he rather have never known? What would have happened if she'd finally shared about her past with him later on in their relationship? If they'd been married, would he have divorced her?

He had no idea of the answer to any of those questions, but he couldn't deny that finding out the information later in their relationship would have made life infinitely more difficult. So maybe it was a blessing that the truth had come to light now. Too bad he couldn't really appreciate that blessing right then.

~ * ~

When Cara left the recital, it was with a heavy heart. Her final obligation had been fulfilled, and it was time to move on. It had taken everything in her not to fall apart as her girls had performed their last dance of the evening. They'd been beautiful, graceful, and energetic, everything she'd wanted them to be. It had been a perfect evening for them, even with the little mishaps during the younger ones' dances.

It had been hard to say goodbye to them all at the end of the evening, knowing that was probably the last time she'd see them. They didn't know that since she had yet to notify everyone that the studio was closing, and all unused credits would be refunded.

With Christmas just a couple of weeks away, she'd gone ahead and closed the studio, aware that people were going to be super busy with holiday preparations. She wasn't, of course. Unlike last year, when she'd decorated both her apartment and the studio, this year, she'd focused strictly on the studio since people would wonder why if she didn't.

She didn't want to say goodbye. She didn't want to have to explain why she was leaving. She especially didn't want to see disappointment on anyone's face. Maybe it was cowardly to run the way she planned to, but she'd said far too many goodbyes in her life. She just couldn't handle a whole bunch more.

Back in her apartment, she headed for her bedroom and the suitcases that lay open on the floor. She stood for a moment, resisting the urge to cry as she stared at the clothes she'd packed into them already. This wasn't the path she'd envisioned her life taking, but after facing so much heartache, it really shouldn't have surprised her.

She'd let her father light the flame of hope within her. She'd participated in life because of him, and when she'd voiced her reluctance to love, he'd encouraged her to not let the chance to love pass her by. He'd told her that even though it might hurt to one day lose that love, it was worth the risk.

Maybe it was only worth it when you lost that love through no fault of their own. Her dad might have lost the woman he loved, but at least he lived with the knowledge that, had she been given a choice, her mom would never have left him. It hurt like crazy to have the person you loved decide you weren't worth being with anymore.

Mafia Princess.

Even now, the disgust in Kieran's voice as he'd said the words resonated in her head. She didn't believe that he had been aiming the disgust at her directly, but it hurt nonetheless.

Turning away from the suitcases, she went into the bathroom and cleaned off her makeup. She changed into a pair of leggings and a loose sweatshirt before going to make herself a cup of tea that would hopefully help her sleep. She'd been having a horrible time with sleep lately. The tea didn't really seem to help, but she kept trying it anyway because she was just that desperate.

Leaving the lights off, she carried the mug to her favorite seat by the window and settled into it, drawing her legs up. This was how she ended each day, trying to commit to memory the town as it lay before her, sparkling in the night.

She'd also spent hours watching cars arriving, filling all the parking spots on Main Street, as people had come to town for the Christmas Market. It was something she'd planned to attend as well, but now it hadn't seemed worth the effort of putting on a happy face. And then there was always the chance she'd run into Kieran. So, in the end, she retreated into her apartment and watched it from afar. Much like she had the first year she'd been in New Hope.

Every day, more Christmas lights lit up the night sky. Main Street had lighted shapes of candy canes, angels, stars, and trees attached to lamp posts. *Norma's* had lights outlining each window, and she'd had someone come in to paint her windows with Christmas messages and decorations. Cara could have just taken pictures of it all, and she had taken a few, but she knew that a photo would never capture the heart of the town and the wonderful people who lived there.

When she heard a text alert from her phone, she turned to look over to where she'd left it earlier. There were only two people who would be texting her, and she really wasn't in the mood to chat with either of them. Doug and Giovanni had texted her periodically to check on her, and while she appreciated their concern, she still wasn't sure about continuing to maintain contact.

The one person she was fairly certain wouldn't be texting was Kieran.

She decided to ignore her phone for the time being, and just enjoy her moments taking in the sight of the town. She only had a couple more nights to do that before she'd be leaving. Though it had caused her great heartache, she'd begun looking for a place to move to a couple of weeks earlier.

She wanted to move as far away as possible, but the idea of living in the heat of Florida, with no real difference between seasons, hadn't appealed to her. New York wasn't an option, and California didn't call to her either. She quickly realized that nothing really suited her.

In the end, she'd decided to go see what Denver might be like. But first, she was going to spend Christmas in a cabin near Estes Park in Colorado. She planned to do nothing but appreciate the promised stunning views at the cabin and finding a series or two to binge-watch on Netflix. She had also been loading up her tablet with plenty of books, as well.

Part of her felt like the only way to get through Christmas that year was to ignore it, and in order to do that, she needed to be away from places that were focused on it so intently. A secluded cabin in the mountains should help achieve that. At least she hoped it would.

As lights on houses began to wink out, Cara let out a sigh and closed the blinds, then she rinsed her cup and went to her bedroom. She'd finish packing the next day, and then she'd be on the road the following morning.

Though the idea of starting over caused a spike of anxiety within her, she knew she could do it. She'd done it before, and she'd survived. However, this time around, she needed to do things differently so that she didn't have to start over again with yet another broken heart.

She'd had enough heartache to last a lifetime.

~ * ~

Kieran slid onto a chair at the counter in *Norma's*, giving Missy a weary smile as she set a mug in front of him and filled it with coffee. "Thanks."

"You're welcome." She patted his hand. "It looks like you could use a cup."

He couldn't argue with her there. He definitely did need a cup or two. Maybe even three. But first, he would start with this one.

Lifting it to his lips, he took a sip and swallowed with appreciation. He hadn't been sleeping well, so the caffeine was welcome, but also, the weather had taken a cold turn in the past day. Hot coffee definitely hit the spot.

"How're you holding up?"

Kieran glanced over to see Anna seated a couple of chairs from him. Shrugging, he turned his attention back to the mug cupped in his hands. He didn't mean to be rude, but he really didn't know how to answer her. It went against the grain to admit how much he was struggling with the breakup.

He didn't like showing weakness—something his father had drilled into him—but he figured people saw his struggle whether he put it into words or not. Or maybe they were just hoping for a tidbit of information they could pass on to others.

Not that he suspected Anna was doing that. Given her own experience with people exploiting a difficult time in her life, Kieran doubted that Anna would, in turn, exploit other people's pain.

"It's not getting any easier," he muttered. Out of the corner of his eye, he noticed that Anna shifted over to the seat next to him.

"I'm sorry to hear that," she said softly. "We've been praying for the two of you."

"Has she talked to you?" He knew he had no right to ask, but he couldn't stop the words from tumbling out.

"No, but Sarah texted her the other night to invite her over for Christmas dinner. Cara told her that she was leaving town for Christmas. We assumed she was going to spend it with family."

The thought of Cara's family knotted Kieran's stomach. He knew that at least the youngest brother was in contact with her. Had she gone to spend Christmas with him?

His reaction to the idea told him that his decision to ends things was the right one, no matter how much it still hurt. If he couldn't even hear a reference to her family from someone else without tensing up, being with her would have been impossible.

"At least she won't be alone," Kieran said with a sigh.

"The studio's been closed for the last week or so, and she hasn't given a definite date for when classes will start up again in the New Year." Anna slid her mug forward when Missy returned with the coffee carafe. "I've hardly seen her in the past month."

That was true for Kieran, as well. Given how small the town was, he'd braced himself for running into her fairly frequently. However, he'd only seen her once or twice from a distance. It had been especially painful to go from seeing her on a daily basis to seeing her only a couple of times in a month. He'd thought it would be hard to see her around town, but as it turned out, *not* seeing her was worse.

CHAPTER TWENTY-FIVE

"Where's Eli?" Kieran asked, not so sure he wanted to continue to talk about the mess his life currently was in.

"Uh...the detective called and asked him to go to the office in Everett to meet with him."

Kieran jerked his head around to look at Anna. "About Sheila?"

Her brows drew together as she nodded. "You didn't know?"

He wondered if he'd missed something. If he'd dropped the ball because of his distraction lately. "No."

"Hmmm. Well, he's supposed to be meeting me here, so maybe he can tell you about it."

Kieran wasn't sure he wanted to discuss the case in the middle of a restaurant, but for sure, he'd be phoning the detective to find out what was going on. It bugged him that the detective, after having gotten to the point of accepting the fact that Eli hadn't been involved in Sheila's disappearance, had zeroed back in on him with the recent discovery of a body.

"How is he holding up?"

"He's doing okay," Anna said. "It helps that he's resolute in his innocence."

After not having any unsolved mysteries during his tenure there so far, it was beyond frustrating to Kieran to now have three cases that hadn't reached a satisfactory conclusion. He had no further leads in in the case of the break-ins. And while Sheila's disappearance and the recent discovery of a body weren't technically his cases to solve, he still considered them as such, simply because of their connection to his town.

"Can I bring you something, Chief?" Missy asked.

He wasn't really hungry, but he knew he needed to eat something. "Just a bowl of the cream of potato soup."

"How about you, Anna?"

"I'll wait for Eli. He should be here soon."

"How are you enjoying your first Christmas in New Hope?" Kieran asked after Missy had moved away.

"It's been fantastic. Going to the beautiful Christmas market was such a thrill."

Kieran had attended it in an official capacity, which hadn't been his original plan. Before the break-up, he'd planned to take the day off so he could go to the market with Cara. He'd thought he might see her there, but in all his walking around, he'd never laid eyes on her.

She had been looking forward to attending, so he could only assume she'd changed her mind about going because of the break-up. That thought had made him sadder than he'd already been. There were so many lost opportunities because of the way things had ended between them.

"Are your parents coming?"

"No. They're doing some traveling. Christmas was never a big thing in our family."

Kieran gave a huff of laughter. "I bet it's been a shock to your system being with the McNamaras this year."

"Well, I've come to realize that they take the holiday quite seriously." Anna's smile grew as she chuckled. "Nadine is a force of nature when it comes to decorating. I'm pretty sure there isn't a surface that doesn't have some sort of decoration on it."

"Is the lodge full?"

"Surprisingly enough, yes. All the cabins are occupied as well. Being at the lodge is definitely going to be a different Christmas experience for me this year."

Kieran's plan for the holiday was going to be the same as it always was. He would go to church Christmas Eve with his mom, then he'd spend the night at her house so he'd be there Christmas morning. Despite his age, she still hung a stocking for him and gave him more presents than he really needed as an adult.

He could pretty much guess what she was going to get him each year. Usually there was a pack of socks, a bottle of his usual cologne, a gift card or two to his favorite stores, and a gift pack that included body wash, shaving cream, and a new razor. She also knitted him a scarf, beanie, and mitts each year. Sometimes she got him a book if she knew that one of his favorite authors had published a new one.

In turn, he got her a bunch of gifts that she knew to expect each year. Stuff that she used for her crafting. Her favorite toiletries. Some jewelry. Candy that she loved but would never buy for herself. Basically, they each knew what to expect from the other.

This year was supposed to have been different. They were supposed to have had someone else to buy for, and he had actually bought a couple of things for her that were now in a drawer of his desk. Kieran knew that his mom had begun to dream of their family growing beyond just the two of them. The holes in their family were never more apparent than at Christmas. Even Sean had tended to make an appearance at their Christmas celebrations.

Instead of having Cara with them, however, it would be another year of just the two of them. Mary would join them for their small Christmas dinner later in the afternoon, just as she had each year since they had moved back from New York.

He listened as Anna talked more about her plans to join the church's caroling outreach. They were a small group that visited and sang carols to people who were housebound or resident at the seniors' care home in the town. Kieran wished he could siphon off some of her excitement. Maybe even take a bit home for his mom.

Even though she had still put up all her decorations, and he'd helped her decorate the tree, he could see that she was sad. Instead of this being the best Christmas since Sean and his dad had died, it was turning out to be just as bad as that first Christmas after everything had happened.

"Hi, love."

Kieran glanced over to see Eli bending to give Anna a kiss. When the man straightened, Kieran could see the strain on his face, though the tension eased as he gazed down at the woman he loved.

"How did it go?" Anna asked.

"It went." Eli sighed as he sat down on the seat next to Anna. He looked at Kieran and gave him a weary smile. "Hey, Kieran."

"Hey. Sorry I wasn't there. I didn't know about the interview, man."

Eli shrugged. "He had me go to his office in Everett."

Kieran frowned. "I'm not sure what he's up to. I'll give him a call later."

"He seemed most interested in the likelihood that I was involved in the murder of the woman whose body was found."

That didn't surprise Kieran, but it did frustrate him. "I'm hoping we get an ID on the body soon. Hopefully, that will help with the direction of the investigation."

Eli nodded, then said, "How are you doing?"

Kieran shrugged. "I'm fine."

The man's eyebrows lifted slightly. "Glad to hear it."

Kieran was sure Eli didn't buy a word of it, but maybe if he said it often enough, it would become true.

Missy returned with his bowl of soup then turned to Anna and Eli. "You two going to eat here, or you want a table?"

"Booth please, cuz," Eli said.

"Sure thing."

"Did you want to join us?" Eli asked.

Kieran gave a short laugh. "I'm good here."

There was no way he wanted to eat his lunch with the lovebirds. His appetite still wasn't back to normal, and it would definitely disappear altogether if he had to observe their relationship up close and personal when he still wasn't over Cara.

After the two had gone to their booth, Kieran said a quick prayer before he started to eat his soup. It was hot and tasty, warming him from the inside out. Normally he'd have eaten a sandwich as well, but he was satisfied after the soup. He didn't linger, pausing on his way out of the restaurant to pay, then making his way back to the station.

Lisa didn't bother to talk to him about Cara anymore, having waved the white flag in her attempt to get any further information from him. His mom had had a similar reaction, though every once in a while, she'd subtly comment on something with regards to Cara.

The thing was, it didn't matter if people mentioned her or not, she was always in his thoughts. Always.

~ * ~

It was still dark when Cara pulled her car out of the garage. She idled in the back lane, waiting for the garage door to lower. Once it was in place, she used her phone to make sure her alarm system was armed completely. When that was done, she stared at the phone for a moment before she powered it off and leaned over and put it in the glove compartment.

She closed it with a snap then picked up the phone that was sitting in her cup holder. It was a new one that she had purchased in preparation for leaving New Hope behind, at least for the next couple of weeks.

She didn't want to know if she was or wasn't receiving texts or calls from anyone. She didn't want to read any emails from anyone. It was easier to just replace the whole phone since switching out the SIM card wouldn't have prevented her from getting messages, which was what she wanted.

After setting the GPS in her car, Cara took one last look at her building and slowly headed down the lane to the main road. It was early enough that there weren't a lot of people on the road, so she was able to take her time as she left the area she'd called home for the past four years.

It was a twenty-hour drive to the cabin she'd booked, but she planned to take three days to drive it, staying in hotels along the way. Once she was on the highway headed southeast, she instructed her phone to start playing one of the audiobooks she'd downloaded for the trip. The last thing she'd wanted was to spend the twenty hours on the road mulling over everything and crying as she drove, so she needed something to occupy her mind.

By the time Cara pulled into the parking spot of the cabin three days later, she was very tired of being in the car. She got out, leaning back, then bending forward to stretch out the muscles of her lower back. The host of the cabin had given her instructions on how to let herself in, so she didn't even have to talk to anyone.

She'd stopped in a nearby city to pick up a bunch of groceries for her time at the cabin. Her appetite still wasn't back, but she hoped she'd be able to coax it to life with the junk food she'd bought. Yeah, she'd bought some healthy stuff too, but there were also bags with chocolates, cookies, and a freezer bag with a couple of different types of ice cream.

Once she'd unlocked the door to the cabin, she carried in the bags of food then lugged her suitcases in the door, trying not to remember when Kieran had carried her bags upstairs when she'd come back from Texas after her papa's death. She hadn't done a great job in keeping her thoughts off of Kieran, but at least she'd managed to confine her tears to the hotels where she'd stayed along the way.

She'd hoped that the further away she got from New Hope and all the heartache it held, the looser the band around her chest would become. The less the ache in her heart would hurt. Unfortunately, that hadn't been the case. If anything, it had gotten worse. All she could do was hope that time would do what distance obviously hadn't.

The cabin was everything she'd hoped it would be, but as she wandered around, looking out the windows at the incredible view, all she could think about was how much Kieran would have enjoyed being there. If it had been warmer, they could have gone for runs and walks together.

And just like that, her emotions began to rise up once again, threatening to choke her as tears filled her eyes. If circumstances had been different, they could have come to this cabin. Maybe even on their honeymoon...because that's what she'd begun to imagine and hope for.

Turning away from the view, Cara began to unpack her groceries. She should have made herself some supper since she hadn't eaten anything but a bag of chips since the bagel and yogurt she'd had for breakfast that morning. Instead, she took her suitcase into the bedroom that ran the length of the back of the cabin. One section of the wall was floor to ceiling windows that looked out across the mountains.

The bed was big with heavy wooden head and footboards that suited the rustic look of the cabin. There was a bathroom at one end of the room that had a large tub in front of more floor to ceiling windows. She might have been concerned about privacy, except there were no neighbors around to see in.

She unpacked her suitcase then pulled out her tablet. After going to the kitchen to fill her water bottle, she locked up the cabin and returned to the bedroom. The bed was as comfortable as it looked, and she gratefully settled on it to read one of the books she'd loaded onto her tablet before she'd left New Hope.

As long as she could find things to distract herself, hopefully the next few days would start the healing that, as of yet, had not begun to take place in her heart.

The woman dressed in a form-fitting red suit unlocked the door and stepped into the apartment, holding the door for Cara. "As you can see, you'd have a gorgeous view of the city."

Cara followed the woman further into the apartment, agreeing it was a beautiful view. Except it wasn't the view she wanted. She smothered a sigh at the thought. Even after her week at the cabin, she was still missing New Hope and Kieran more than she wanted to admit.

"You can take possession on the fifteenth of January if all your information checks out," the woman said once they'd completed their tour of the apartment. "Will you be in town for a few days?"

"I'm here through the New Year but can stay longer if need be."

"Given the holidays, it might take a little bit longer to get all the checks done," the woman said apologetically.

"That's fine," Cara assured her. At this point, she hadn't seen anything that she liked. It wasn't that the apartments hadn't been nice. Some of them had been *very* nice, but nothing called to her. Nothing made her feel at home like her place in New Hope had.

"I get the feeling that this isn't what you're looking for," the woman said. "But don't you worry, I have one more place to show you today."

Cara gave her a rueful look. "I'm sorry."

"No need to be sorry." She waved her hand dismissively. "You need to find the place where you'll be comfortable."

Except Cara wasn't sure she was going to find such a place. "Let's see what the next one looks like."

The woman's expression brightened. "I left the best for last. I think you're really going to like it."

She could only hope, though she wasn't holding her breath. As she followed the woman from the apartment, Cara tried to figure out what she had to do in order for something to feel like it could be home. Nothing so far even felt like it had the potential.

She had a definite lack of peace about anything she'd seen so far, but she couldn't figure out why that was. Was it God trying to tell her something? Or was it her heart trying to keep her from moving on? As the woman drove her to the next apartment, Cara prayed that this one would be the one for her.

Unfortunately, it wasn't. Like the woman said, it was the best out of all they'd seen so far, but it still didn't resonate with her the way she wanted her next home to.

"Don't get discouraged," the woman said as she pulled to a stop in front of the hotel where Cara was staying. "There are more places for you to see. I'll give you a call tomorrow."

"Thank you for showing me around today," Cara said. "I really appreciated it."

"You're very welcome. Have a nice evening."

"You too." Cara gave her a smile then got out of the car. The cold air slapped her in the face, so she quickly closed the door then shoved her hands in her pockets as she hurried to the front door of the hotel.

She didn't dawdle in the lobby but made her way directly to the elevators that would take her up to her room. If she got hungry later, she'd just get room service like she had the past two nights. She'd arrived in Denver from the cabin late in the afternoon, so the day before had been her first full day there.

Her time at the cabin hadn't accomplished all that she'd hoped. While it had helped her get through her first Christmas without her dad and Kieran, it hadn't dulled her grief over the loss of both of them. The cabin hadn't been decorated for Christmas—the host had offered, but Cara had declined—so it had been easy to pretend the holiday just wasn't happening. Unfortunately, the things she'd brought to distract her from Kieran and the breakup hadn't worked so well.

With a sigh, she tossed her jacket and purse on the bed and headed to the window. Her room was on an upper floor, so she had a great view of the mountains in the distance. There was nothing wrong with the city, but she wasn't sure she could call it home.

If she couldn't find a place that gave her the feeling she wanted, Cara knew she'd just have to force herself to make a decision. Maybe wherever she ended up would grow on her. After all, it had taken her a while to feel like New Hope was home.

She really wished she still had her dad to talk to about everything, but she had a feeling that he'd tell her she just needed to tough it out. That people all over the world got over broken hearts without running away.

But Cara had to wonder if those same people had to live with the knowledge that their presence was a reminder to someone else of two of the worst days of that person's life.

CHAPTER TWENTY-SIX

Kieran stared at the fire flickering in his mom's electric fireplace. Midnight was still an hour away, and he would much rather have been home in his bed, but he and his mom always celebrated New Year's Eve together.

They'd attended a service at the church that evening as they did each year, then they'd come back to his mom's to eat a late dinner and wait to ring in the new year together. His mom sat in her favorite rocker near the fire, working on her latest knitting project.

He lifted his mug of hot chocolate—yet another tradition for many, many years —and took a small sip. "Do you hate Marco Moretti?"

"What?" From the corner of his eye, he saw his mom frown at him as her hands lowered to her lap.

"Never mind," Kieran said with a shake of his head, uncertain why he'd asked her such a dumb question.

"No."

Kieran turned his head to look at her directly. "No?"

"No, I don't hate him."

It was Kieran's turn to frown. "You don't?"

She let out a soft sigh. "When we first moved back to New Hope, I was consumed by how much I hated the man. He'd taken so much from me, how could I *not*?" Picking up her work, she began to rock again as her needles flew. "But the thing about hate is that love can't exist alongside it. The hate was growing, edging out any love I had in my heart. That included my love for God, my love for your dad and your brother, and my love for you."

Kieran stared at her. "I didn't know." Except, maybe he had, now that he thought back. In the months after their return to New Hope, his mom had retreated into herself. She'd never left the house, not even for church. He'd passed her reclusiveness off as grief, but now it seemed that there had been something else alongside the grief. Hate.

"I didn't want you to know." She looked up at him again, her expression sad. "When I realized that I was in danger of losing everything, I knew I needed help, and that's when I went to Pastor Evans. It was only in talking with him that I came to realize that I had to make a choice. Let the hate go so love could grow, which is what God wanted me to do, or let the hate grow until there was no love left. I decided I couldn't let that happen."

She sighed as her gaze went distant. "It wasn't easy, but the first thing I had to do was forgive Marco Moretti. Anytime his name came to mind, I would whisper that I forgave him, then I'd pray for his salvation."

What she shared made Kieran feel at a loss for words. And it shone a massive light on his own heart. He'd allowed his hatred for Marco Moretti to overshadow his love for Cara. Maybe he'd done a better job than his mom of compartmentalizing the hate in his heart, only really feeling it when someone talked about Sean or his dad, or the Moretti family, but it had been there all the same. His discovery about Cara had brought it roaring back to life, revealing that while the hate may not have seemed to be a huge thing in his life, its roots were deeply entrenched in his heart.

"Hate never gives us anything," she said softly. "All it does is take. It robs us of the good in our lives."

Kieran stared down at his mug, realizing he'd just lived out the truth of his mom's words. It was like a kick to the stomach when it dawned on him that his mom probably wouldn't have had the same struggle with Cara's connection to Marco Moretti that he had.

Because she'd already excised the hate she'd had for the man from her heart, it wouldn't have overshadowed how she felt about Cara.

"Can you keep a secret if I tell you something?" he asked.

"Of course, darling. I know you think I gossip, but only ever about the frivolous stuff. If it's something important, I'll never breathe a word."

"Cara is Marco Moretti's daughter."

His mom's eyebrows rose, and her mouth went slack. "Are you... Is that... Really?"

He nodded. "I found that out the same day I found out that he'd passed away in prison in Texas."

Her surprised look melted into compassion. "Oh no. That must have been hard for her. Mary said that Cara had been making regular trips to visit a sick relative for quite a while." She paused, comprehension dawning. "That's why you broke up with her."

Kieran nodded as he told his mom about Cara's background and how she'd lost her mom. "She loved her father."

"Of course she did." His mom settled back in her chair, her knitting forgotten. "There are men who the rest of the world might view as horrible, who are still kind to those they love. It wasn't her fault that he only showed her his softer, gentler side. If she didn't know about his other life until she was older, and if she was kept apart from that life, there was no reason for her to hate the man. From the sound of things, her father's older children weren't protected from the mob life like she was."

She set her chair in motion once again. "And it appeared that he paid a price for his lifestyle. From what you've said, he loved Cara's mother as well as Cara, and in the end, he lost them both. It was hard enough for me to lose Sean and your father without feeling responsible for their deaths. My guess is that it was doubly hard for him to lose the woman he loved, knowing that her death happened because of him."

Kieran rubbed at the ache in his chest that hadn't faded in the time since that day in Cara's studio. "We didn't talk much about what all she knew about her father's life."

"Kieran, darling." The look she gave him held a gentle reproof. "You've always seen things in black and white, and I suppose that's something that's served you well as a cop, but sometimes things aren't so cut and dried."

"I know, Mom." His heart pulsed with pain. "It's just that I wasn't sure we could stay together when anytime she mentioned her father, I'd be reminded of what happened to Dad and Sean. And not just that, but she loved a man that I considered to be a monster."

His mom nodded. "If you're unable to separate the two in your mind, a relationship with Cara would be difficult. But darling, it wouldn't be impossible. Your emotions made the decision to end things. Maybe it's time to look at the situation in the light of what God would have you do. And don't tell me that God wouldn't expect you to have to overlook something like that because I can tell you right now, He most definitely would. What He wouldn't do, would be to expect you to deal with it on your own. He helped me remove the hate from my heart, and He can do the same for you. Go talk to Pastor Evans. Let him guide you like he guided me."

When the clock on her mantel began to chime, they both turned toward it.

Kieran hadn't made any resolutions for the New Year yet, but maybe it was time to do just that. He looked over to see his mom leaning forward in her chair, her hand stretched out toward him. Without hesitating, he reached out to take it. She held tight to his fingers as she prayed a blessing on the year ahead, asking for wisdom for him and comfort for Cara wherever she was.

When Kieran left her house a short time later, the pain was still in his heart, but he felt lighter. Like a burden had been lifted from his shoulders.

After he got ready for the night, he sat down on the edge of his bed, phone in hand. He really wanted to phone Cara, to hear her voice after going so long without it. But if she was in New York with family, they were three hours ahead, which meant it was too late to call.

In the end, he decided to send a text. If she was already asleep, hopefully she'd see it in the morning. Deciding to send a text was the easy part. Deciding what to *say* in the text was probably the hardest thing he'd ever done. He tapped and deleted. Tapped and deleted. Tapped and deleted.

With a sigh of frustration, he closed his eyes and bent his head forward, pressing the corner of his phone against his forehead. He prayed for wisdom and that Cara might be receptive to his message. He knew he didn't deserve for her to be, but he had to start somewhere. To at least see if he'd ruined everything or if there was a hope that she'd give him a second chance.

Finally, he tapped out a short message then pressed send before he could continue to overthink it.

Cara...can we talk? I miss you.

He stared at the message, waiting for a couple of minutes to see if she might respond. But when no reply popped up, he put his phone on the nightstand and settled under his comforter. Then, for the first time since the breakup, he didn't pray for God to heal his heartache, he prayed for Him to change his heart. And the hopelessness he'd gone to sleep with on previous nights was surprisingly absent as he drifted off—despite the lack of a reply from Cara.

It took another ring from his phone before he realized what had woken him. Groaning, he reached for his phone. It felt like he'd only just fallen asleep. He blinked a couple of times before looking at his screen. Seeing a number for the station, he answered it right away.

"Sorry to bother you, chief, but we just got a call from an alarm company. They said a silent alarm was tripped at the dance studio. They tried to call Cara, but she's not answering."

Kieran flung back his covers and climbed out of bed, his heart pounding. He assumed she wasn't back in town because he hadn't seen any activity around the studio, but he didn't know for certain that she hadn't returned and was perhaps just keeping a low profile. "Head over. I'll be there in a couple of minutes."

He pulled on a pair of jeans and a sweatshirt, then grabbed his badge and a jacket. Within minutes, he was climbing into his cold Jeep and heading toward Cara's. A glance at the clock on the dashboard showed that he'd been asleep for just over an hour. Thankfully, the adrenalin pumping through him had removed any sleepiness. Along with the adrenalin, however, was a healthy dose of worry and fear. Not knowing for certain if Cara was in the apartment made him feel a little sick.

Even though Cara's building wasn't that far away, it felt like it took forever to get there. Lights blazed from the lower level, and he could see a few people standing in the waiting area.

Kieran hurriedly climbed out of the car and jogged toward the door. The people turned to look at him as he walked in. Two of his men were standing around a slight figure dressed in black. The person had their head bend, hands in the pockets of the hoodie they wore.

"What's going on here?"

The man that had called him gestured to the person. "We caught her in the office, going through the desk."

"Her?" Kieran stared at the girl. She glanced up at him, and he found himself looking into a pair of bright blue eyes, framed by black lashes and set in a face with delicate features. She looked so young. "What were you doing here?"

The girl lifted a brow at him. "If you don't know, I'm not going to tell you."

The sass almost made him smile, but instead, he directed his gaze to the officers. "No sign of Cara?"

"She's not here," Jelina said.

"And how do you know that?"

"How do you think?" she said then turned her gaze away from him.

Of course, she'd probably been staking the place out and upon realizing it was empty, decided that it was the better option for breaking into. Even though it might have less money on hand than an actual store, maybe she'd figured there would be jewelry and electronics she could fence.

No doubt she'd assumed that since it wasn't a store, there wouldn't be a security system. Had she not even bothered to look at the back of the building? And if so, had she assumed the cameras there were fake? She'd been good enough to bypass the security system for most of the main floor. She just hadn't realized that there was apparently a different system for the office part of the studio. If she'd been more experienced, she would have realized those things, and they probably wouldn't be standing there like they were

"Guess you'd better take her to the station so we can question her," Kieran said. For some reason, he got the feeling this kid knew the drill. She was clearly talented at breaking and entering. Even though she'd tripped an alarm, she'd managed to gain entrance to the building.

Clearly, she hadn't expected to run into the level of security that Cara had in place. No surprise, as there wasn't another building in town—except for maybe the bank—that had that level of security. Kieran had a feeling that the girl might also be responsible for the break-ins at Mary's and the bookstore.

He stepped to the side so one of the officers could take the girl to the station. When it was just him and the other officer, Kieran walked into Cara's office, surveying what had been going on in there, taking care not to touch anything. They'd have to get some techs out to fingerprint the scene, though if this was the same person, they likely wouldn't find any that didn't belong there. Though it was clear that the girl had been searching, she hadn't been ripping through things. Like with the previous break-ins, the crime scene was pretty clean.

"She seems young to be able to carry off this level of breaking and entering."

"Yeah," the officer said. "I'd venture to guess she's had some training."

Kieran had been thinking the same thing. "Maybe we should go see if we can figure out who might have been teaching her."

They discussed how to secure the building since Cara wasn't there. In the end, the officer decided to stay at the building until they could get hold of a locksmith to fix the lock. It was a holiday, so it was probably going to cost a pretty penny to get someone out there, but with Cara absent and not answering the calls from the alarm company, he had to make a decision.

He did a quick walkthrough to see that both the door to the garage and the one to the upstairs were closed and locked, which meant the thief hadn't gotten that far yet, thankfully. Once he was satisfied Cara's home was still secure, he headed to the station.

A few hours later, he was back at his house. At shift change, one of the officers offered to take care of finding a locksmith to get the lock changed. As it turned out, for all her sass at the crime scene, the girl had started talking not long after Kieran had taken up a seat across from her.

They'd offered her a lawyer, but she'd declined and also told them she had no parent available to speak to them. The reason why she was so eager to talk had soon become apparent when she'd revealed that she had a younger sister hiding behind a nearby building. She gave the officers a code word to say to the sister, so she'd come out of hiding with them since it was so cold out.

It hadn't taken too long to get the whole story. A father who'd been a professional cat burglar until he'd gotten caught. The girls going into hiding in hopes of avoiding the foster system. Kieran felt for the girl, and he hoped that things somehow worked out for her.

She wasn't an adult yet, so it might be possible that the judge would be lenient with her sentence. Unfortunately, her younger sister was going to end up in care. At least until things were settled with her older sister.

Kieran felt bad for both of them. What the older one had done was wrong, but she hadn't broken in to be destructive or to get rich. She'd just been trying to get money or things she could sell in order to buy food for her sister.

He was exhausted when he got home, but he took the time to call Cara since it was already morning. He wasn't too surprised when the call went to voicemail. Wearily, he told her what had happened, along with the info that they had called a locksmith and that the key for her front door would be at the station. After a brief hesitation, he asked her to call him.

Now all he could do was wait for her to make contact.

CHAPTER TWENTY-SEVEN

Cara came to a stop behind her garage then pulled her old phone from the glove compartment. She'd known there was a possibility she'd be back, but she had hoped that she'd be returning to pack up and move to her new life. Instead, she was back because nothing had felt like home in Denver.

With a sigh, she turned on her phone so she could access her security program. Alerts began pinging as soon as it powered on, and Cara frowned when she realized they were from her alarm system. She also had several missed calls from her alarm company and one from Kieran.

She glanced at her building before pulling up her security program. She logged into her cameras and scanned through them. The apartment and garage looked fine. It wasn't until she got to the office that she could see that things had been disturbed.

Had someone broken into the studio?

Satisfied that it was safe to enter the building, she opened the garage and pulled inside. Then, before she got out of her car, she listened to her voicemails. There were several from the alarm company, letting her know that one of her alarms had been tripped. After she listened to those calls, the one from Kieran began to play.

Her heart clenched at the sound of his voice, and she had to blink rapidly to clear the moisture from her eyes. He sounded tired as he relayed to her what had happened and the steps they'd taken to secure the studio after the break-in. She listened as he paused, then added, "Please call me, Cara."

That was the last voicemail, but she had several text messages. There were a few each from Giovanni and Doug, and then there was one from Kieran.

Cara...can we talk? I miss you.

She inhaled sharply at the three little words he'd tacked onto the end. Her breaths became shaky as she tried to figure out what he was saying. Did she want to talk to him? Nothing had changed in the two weeks she'd been gone. She was still Marco Moretti's daughter. She still had blood ties to the family that had killed the people he loved.

And she was definitely still struggling to get over the heartache from their breakup. What good would talking do except to prolong the inevitable? She didn't think she'd be doing either of them any favors by agreeing to contact him. For now, she needed to regroup and figure out what she was going to do.

If Denver wasn't going to work out for her, then she needed to figure out where to try next. *If* she tried somewhere else, that is. Part of her felt that she would struggle to feel at home wherever she went, even though she desperately wished that weren't the case. So should she even bother to consider relocating?

Maybe if she just kept to herself, she wouldn't have to watch Kieran move on with his life. She could attend a different church, maybe go to one of the larger ones in the city. It would be a bit of a drive each Sunday, but she could do it. That would mean she could keep her studio, and hopefully, when Kieran started to date again, she would be in a better place emotionally. One where she didn't feel like throwing up at the very idea of him with someone else.

Feeling that her building was as safe as it ever was, Cara got out of her car and went to the trunk to get her bags. She let herself in then climbed the stairs to her apartment, glad to see that despite what had happened in the office, the rest of the building was untouched.

As soon as she walked into the apartment, a weight lifted from her shoulders, but it didn't make her happy. She didn't want to be so attached to her home in New Hope that she couldn't leave it behind.

With a sigh, Cara took her things into the bedroom then returned to the kitchen to make some tea. Though she told herself not to, once she had her mug of tea, she turned off the lights that had automatically come on in her absence, then pushed the button to open the motorized blind covering the window by her favorite chair.

At her first sight of the town, still brightly lit with Christmas lights, even though it was now a few days past the new year, something within her had settled. She sank down into her chair and stared out the window. Her gaze landed on *Norma's* for a moment before it slid in the direction of the police station. Not that she could see the station since it was on the same side of the street as her building.

Forcing her gaze back to *Norma's,* she could see people seated inside. It was just past six, but the sun had set a while ago, covering the town in a blanket of darkness, broken only by the lights shining warmly from the houses and buildings.

As she sat there, she realized she needed to make a big decision. It had been her plan to close the studio, but that had been when she'd thought she'd find a place in Denver. Having not succeeded at that, she now needed to figure out her next step.

People were expecting the studio to open again soon. It was also her busiest time as women came to the studio as part of personal fitness resolutions for the new year. If she was going to close the studio permanently, she needed to let them know soon and issue refunds for unused credits.

As Cara sipped her tea, she mulled over her options, knowing that the main reason she'd wanted to leave hadn't changed: she didn't want to be around when Kieran decided to move on with his life. That felt like a bit more than she was able to handle right then, especially because she felt like her heart was never going to heal.

She had been able to make it through some days without crying, but that was only because she had managed to keep busy and to occupy her thoughts with things other than Kieran. That hadn't happened too often, however, so she still, more often than not, had at least one tearful episode a day. Usually that was at night, when there was nothing to keep her mind from remembering all she had lost. Sometimes her tears were for her papa, brought on by the intense need to be able to talk to him. To ask him what she should do.

She'd journaled extensively during her recent time away, pouring out her heart onto paper since she had nowhere else to turn. Unfortunately, she didn't see that changing anytime soon, since she was now more reticent than ever to let people close.

Her phone beeped a text alert, drawing her attention away from the window. It was her old phone since no one had her new number except for the woman who had been helping her look at apartments in Denver.

She only debated a moment before setting her mug on the small table next to her and getting to her feet and going in search of her phone. It didn't take her long to find it on the counter next to her purse.

Given that she was kind of expecting it to be Kieran again, she was a little disappointed to see it was from Giovanni.

Giovanni: *I know I said I wouldn't bother you, but I'm a bit worried that you've been out of contact with both Doug and me. Can you let me know that you're doing okay? That at least you're safe?*

Cara carried the phone back to her seat and sank down into it. Though she hadn't wanted anything to do with Gio or Doug, it warmed her heart a bit to know that he was concerned about her. Maybe it was just because their father had tasked him with making sure she was okay. Or maybe he really did feel a personal need to care for her.

After sitting there for a few minutes, she decided that maybe it wouldn't be so bad to have at least one person in her life who worried about her.

I'm fine. Safe. I've been out of town for a couple of weeks and turned my phone off. I just got back this evening.

Giovanni: *I'm glad to hear that! I can understand needing a break. It's definitely been a rough time for you. I'm sorry for that, and for any part I played in it.*

Cara wasn't sure how to respond to that. Yes, his and Doug's visit had set off a string of events that had left her broken-hearted, but there was a part of her that knew those events would have played out at some point down the road. She wasn't sure she would have been able to hold off on telling Kieran the truth indefinitely.

It is what it is. There's not much that can be done about it now.

Giovanni: *That may be true, but I pray for you each day, that God will guide and direct you and comfort you in your grief.*

Thank you.

Giovanni: *Remember that doors we might assume are closed to us may be opened by God's hand.*

Cara stared at the words, wondering what he meant by them. She could only assume he was speaking with regards to Kieran because that was really the only part of her life that he was aware of, and only because she'd told him and Doug that they'd broken up.

She'd assumed there was no path forward for her and Kieran, but then she remembered that people were praying for them. Gio had stated he was, and Sarah had said that she'd be praying for them as well. Could God work this out for them when they couldn't work things out for themselves? But to her mind, that would mean that Kieran would need to have some sort of amnesia so he could forget about her past and her family.

That just didn't seem possible.

On Sunday, Cara waffled back and forth on whether she wanted to attend church. Well, it wasn't so much about whether she wanted to because she did want to, but it was more if she should. It might be best if she went to a different church.

In the end, she decided to go to the church in New Hope. As she'd done since the break-up, she'd arrive late and leave early to prevent any potentially awkward moments. She dressed in a pair of black pants and a deep turquoise sweater with a cowl neck then pulled her hair up into a loose bun.

Nerves fluttered in her stomach as she left her apartment. They got even worse as she approached the door of the church a short time later. She almost turned around and left, but instead, she took a deep breath and pulled open the door and stepped into the foyer.

She preferred to wait until she heard singing because it meant people would be standing, and her arrival would be less likely to be noticed. There was no singing as she walked toward the doors leading into the sanctuary, and when she looked through the narrow window on the door, she saw that someone was talking, and the announcements were up on the screen at the front.

Pressing a hand against her stomach, she waited until the worship leader motioned for the congregation to stand, and the music began. She took a deep breath and opened the door enough to slip in. With a smile, she took the bulletin the usher held out to her, then made her way to a nearby seat.

At the end of the first song, the worship leader said, "I'd like to welcome each of you to church this Sunday. God has graciously given us a new year, and what better way to start it off than with those who also love Him. I'd like you to take a moment to greet those around you and let them know you're glad to be a part of God's family with them."

Cara turned to the people sitting on her left and shook hands with them. The people in front of her greeted her by name with warm smiles. She didn't have a chance to turn to anyone else when she was suddenly wrapped in a tight hug.

"I'm so glad you're back," Sarah said softly. "I was worried you'd left us for good."

Cara returned her hug, not bothering to tell her that it had been her intention. "It's good to be back."

And it was. Even when Sarah left her side, and Cara turned to the front once again, her gaze meeting Kieran's, it still was. And though her heart broke a little to see him once again, it still was.

At that moment, she knew that New Hope would always be her home, and somehow, she'd have to find a way to live there.

Cara couldn't seem to tear her gaze from Kieran's, drinking in the sight of him. Finally, the music started up again, and Kieran slowly turned back around to face the front. Had he figured she'd left town for good like Sarah had?

He'd said he missed her, but that could mean any number of things. They'd had a friendship as well as a romantic connection. Maybe he wanted them to continue on with their friendship. She couldn't imagine that working—at least not yet.

Pushing those thoughts from her mind, she kept her attention on the service. When Pastor Evans got up and preached on how they should view the year ahead, Cara was reminded again why she'd come to enjoy the church so much. She appreciated his down-to-earth, practical sermons that she could apply to her life without needing to understand a lot of complicated theology.

His underlying message, though, regardless of the subject of his sermon was how they should keep their eyes fixed on God. One of his favorite sayings was *When walking the road of life, keep your gaze on God, and He will keep you from tripping.*

She hadn't spent much time wondering if God wanted her to move, and it was only as the pastor spoke about seeking God's will for the new year that she realized she had to be better about that. It was more than clear as she listened to the pastor that even though she knew she should turn everything over to God, she was reluctant to trust Him with her heartache.

That thought weighed on her through the rest of the sermon, and as she stood up and slipped out of the sanctuary. She didn't linger in the foyer, needing to get away before anyone stopped her to talk.

She'd barely made it home when her phone beeped with a text message. It didn't surprise her at all to see it was from Kieran. His seeing her at church made it almost a given, particularly since she hadn't responded to his earlier text.

Kieran: *Can we talk?*

Part of her wanted to talk to him again. Badly. But she really wasn't sure she was strong enough for that yet.

Did you need to speak to me about the break-in?

Kieran: *Sure. We can talk about the break-in...among other things. I'll even bring by the key to the studio's front door.*

For a moment, a smile curved Cara's lips. She could almost hear Kieran saying that aloud.

Her smile faded away as she sighed. Short of giving him a flat-out no, she didn't really feel that she had a choice but to agree. She could get through it. She'd had to act when she was part of the ballet company, so she could act her way through this.

Okay.

Kieran: *I'll be there in a few minutes.*

Cara didn't bother to respond. She had no need to freshen up since she'd just gotten home, so she made her way downstairs to wait for Kieran. She wasn't sure what to say to him when he arrived, but since he was the one asking to talk, presumably, he had something in mind.

She was glad she hadn't eaten anything as her stomach felt a bit nauseous. It was taking longer than she'd expected for Kieran to get there, so she went into her office and sank down on the chair at her desk. She rubbed her palms against her thighs, wanting nothing more than to escape back up to her apartment.

There was just no way that this meeting was going to end with anything more than her heart aching even worse than it already was.

When she heard the front door open, her stomach lurched. She got to her feet, planning to meet him in the waiting area. But before she could step out from behind the desk, he appeared in the doorway, a tray of drinks in one hand.

"I brought lunch," he said, holding up a bag in the other hand.

The moment held so many shades of their first few meetings that her heart thumped hard in her chest. Kieran came further into the office and set the bag on the desk, but Cara wasn't sure she would be able to eat anything.

Slowly she sank back down onto her chair as he took the drinks from the tray and set one in front of her. As he opened the bag and began to take food out, Cara drank in the sight of him. From the look of things, the last few weeks had been as difficult for him as they had been for her.

The circles under his eyes were more pronounced, and he looked like he'd lost some weight. Though he had requested the meeting, she could see the tension in the set of his jaw as he focused on the food. He put a container that looked like it held her favorite salad on her side of the desk then looked up at her as he sat down in the chair that she'd come to think of as his.

"Thank you for agreeing to talk to me," Kieran said as he sank back in his chair. He stared at her for a moment before he exhaled deeply. "I've missed you."

Cara didn't know what to say. She'd missed him too, but she wasn't sure it would be beneficial for either of them for her to say that. Instead, she looked down at her food, reaching for her drink cup.

"I'm sorry." At his words, she looked back up. His gaze caught and held hers. "I reacted very...harshly to what I discovered."

"You had every right to," Cara murmured, even though his apology soothed some of the ache in her heart. "It was an unfortunate set of circumstances that would have been a shock to anyone."

"Still." Kieran sighed. "At that moment, I had a difficult time separating you from what had happened."

"I understand that. I'm sure that would have been the case for anyone." Maybe this was the closure she needed.

"The thing is, I've had a lot of time to think about the whole situation." He paused, his gaze dropping for a moment, then he cleared his throat. "I need to let you know that I told my mom everything."

Cara felt her stomach sink. In the time since their break-up, Rose had always continued to be kind and friendly to her. She hated to think that would change now.

Kieran shifted on his seat. "I didn't start out to tell her. I just wondered how she felt about Marco Moretti."

She hated him, Cara was sure. She didn't think Rose would betray her secret, but she had no idea how to ask Kieran about that. But maybe this was him warning her of what might be coming. She might be left with no choice but to flee, even though she'd kind of decided to stay.

"She surprised me," Kieran said. "When I asked her if she hated Marco, she said no."

Cara's eyes widened. "She doesn't hate him?"

"She did for a while, but then she came to the realization that love and hate couldn't share space in her heart. The hate was eating away at her life and eroding the love she had for God and for me. She made the choice to meet with Pastor Evans to seek his guidance on how to rid her heart of the hate."

"And she was able to do that?"

Kieran nodded. "She said she forgave Marco, then every time she thought about him after that point, she would remind herself that she had forgiven him, and then she'd pray for his salvation."

Cara gasped, pressing a hand to her mouth before saying, "My father became a Christian in the months before he died."

Kieran's brows rose. "He did?"

She nodded. "Gio is also a Christian, and it was through him that my dad became one too."

"Wow." Kieran stared at her for a moment then sat forward, an earnest expression on his face. "That's incredible. I'll have to tell my mom that. I think she'd like to know that."

Cara was still in a state of shock over the very idea that Rose had prayed for her father's salvation. It was odd that her father had played a role in the worst events of their lives, and yet his mother had played a role, through her prayers, in the most wonderful decision her father had ever made.

She wasn't sure what to stay, but it appeared that Kieran wasn't finished yet.

"After finding out that my mom didn't hate your father, I told her about what had led to our break-up. It was in talking with her about all of it that I realized that I had allowed my hate to rob me of love. She also helped me see your situation from a different perspective."

The air seemed to rush from her lungs. What was he saying? Hope flared like a small flame on a matchstick. She tried to smother it, though, because she didn't want to get her hopes up only to have them dashed again. Rather than question him about it, she kept quiet, pressing her trembling hands together.

"I knew I needed to take the same steps my mom had. I went and talked with Pastor Evans and shared what had happened between us." He gave her a small frown. "I realize I'm admitting that I've talked to two people about your situation when I said I wouldn't tell anyone. I'm sorry about that, but I trust both of them with my life—with your life—and I really needed advice."

If this might lead to a better situation for the two of them without compromising her safety, she couldn't be mad at him about it.

Kieran's gaze dropped to his hands. "I...I'm struggling with all of this, to be honest. But if these past few weeks have taught me anything, it's that you are important to me, and I don't want hate to win over love."

Cara swallowed hard against the emotions that were rising within her. "What does that mean?"

"It means that I want to work past this. To find a way for me to change how I view everything I've learned." His gaze held hers. "You're still the woman I fell in love with."

CHAPTER TWENTY-EIGHT

Kieran's words hit Cara in the chest. He loved her? He'd never said those words when they'd been together, so she hadn't known for certain how he'd felt about her. Of course, she'd never said the words to him either, even though those feelings had definitely been growing in her heart for him.

"You haven't changed. Everything that attracted me to you in the first place is all still a part of who you are. The only thing that's different now is what I know of your past. I don't want something neither of us can change to come between us."

"You want us to try again?" Cara asked, her voice soft even as her heart pounded at the thought.

"Yes. I want us to try, but more than that, I want us to succeed. Would you come with me to meet with Pastor Evans?" He paused for a moment. "If that's what you want too, of course."

Of course, it was what she wanted. But... "What if it doesn't work? What if you really can't get past who my father was and what he did?"

"I know I'm asking you to take a risk when I haven't really proven myself, but I *want* this to work. I realize now that hate blinded me to the fact that the choice I made was *not* the only one available to me. Talking to my mom was eye-opening. Gut-wrenchingly so. I'm so sorry for what I did." The earnestness of his expression tugged at Cara. "You've come to mean so much to me."

She wanted to be mad at him for what he'd done, but in truth, she'd understood that his reaction hadn't been about her specifically. But there was a part of her that wondered if what he felt for her was truly strong enough to overcome what they had to in order to make things work.

Would she be able to fully open herself up to him? Or would she spend each day wondering if that would be the one when she made a comment, or something that reminded him of who her father was, and it was just too much? She wasn't sure she could spend their relationship always second-guessing what she was going to say.

He must have read her hesitation in her expression because the hope that had been on his face faded, and his shoulders slumped. "I understand. I shouldn't have asked you to take a chance like this."

"It's just..." Cara struggled to find the right words. "Honestly, I understood your need to break up with me more than I understand this. I kind of feel like we're just setting ourselves up to fail again. I'll constantly be watching my words to make sure I don't talk about my dad for fear of upsetting you, but my dad was very important to me. I'm still grieving his death, and if I have to hide my grief, it won't work out for us long term."

"You won't have to," Kieran said. "And I know your dad was important to you. I wouldn't want you to feel you couldn't ever share memories of him."

Cara wanted to believe him. She really, really wanted to. But fear of just prolonging the hurt kept her from grabbing on to this chance with both hands.

"I had to try," Kieran said with a sigh as he reached for his drink and his container of food. "I'm sorry if I've upset you with this. I won't bother you again."

Cara's heart clenched painfully as he got up and turned for the door. "Wait."

Kieran paused and stood for a moment before turning to face her. He didn't say anything, just watched her, his expression drawn tight with pain.

"I...I can't agree to this right now, but can I think about it?"

"Of course. Take all the time you need."

"Thank you."

"I guess I'll see you around." He gave her a cautious smile, then turned and left the office.

Cara held her breath until she heard the front door close then she slumped back in her chair. She could almost believe that the pounding of her heart was in protest of her allowing Kieran to walk away, but she really did need time. This wasn't a decision to make lightly after things had ended so badly last time.

It was only as she headed out to lock the door that she realized he'd left without giving her the key. She turned the deadbolt then returned to get her food to take it upstairs. Though she wasn't hungry right that minute, she wouldn't let it go to waste when Kieran had gone to the trouble of getting it for her.

Upstairs, she changed out of her church clothes into a pair of sweats and a thick sweater. After making herself a cup of coffee, she found her tablet and settled into her favorite chair. She made an attempt at reading, but after she'd read the same page over a couple of times, she gave up.

Though she found herself staring out the window, she didn't really see the town. All she could think about were all the pros and cons of rekindling a relationship with Kieran. The biggest pro was that she loved the man and wanted to spend her life with him. The con, of course, was that he might not really be able to accept her and her past, even with God's help.

Cara wished she had someone she could talk to about everything, but the only people who knew the details about their breakup were either too close to the situation—Rose—or not close enough for her to feel comfortable talking to them—Doug or Gio. It was at times like this when she missed her dad even more. This was something she would have talked to him about...although he might not have been the most objective person to discuss it with since he would probably be upset that Kieran had dumped her in the first place.

It was a while later that Cara focused in on the view out her window and frowned. She hadn't heard that it was supposed to snow, but there were big fat flakes lazily drifting down from the sky, so clearly, she'd missed something. They didn't get a ton of snow in that area, but every once in awhile, they got enough that it stuck around for a bit.

Cara leaned closer to the window, a feeling in her gut that this was more than just a bit of snow. The clouds hanging low in the sky were gunmetal gray, and as she watched, the wind seemed to pick up, sending the snow swirling in the air. She remembered seeing clouds and snow like that in Chicago, and it usually resulted in a larger than normal snowfall.

Grateful that she had plenty of food on hand and that she'd had a backup generator installed on the roof of her building when all the renovations were being done, she got up and went to the kitchen to get another cup of coffee. She'd never had to use the back-up generator, but it had been something her father had insisted on installing when they'd discussed the plans for the building.

Even in the short time it took her to get her coffee and return to her seat, she could see that the storm was picking up. Visibility had dropped so much that she could see across the street but not much further. Shivering, even though it wasn't cold in the apartment, Cara got up and flipped the switch for the fireplace.

With her mug cupped in her hands, she stared into the flames for a few minutes. Warm air blew out of the vents of the fireplace, but the comfort it offered was not at all like the warmth of the real fireplace they'd had in their home in Chicago. But she still enjoyed it. The only thing that would have made the ambience better would have been the scent of burning wood. Of course, if she'd had that, she would have had been tempted to break out the marshmallows, chocolate bars, and graham crackers for some smores.

Though she'd planned to have classes start up that week, Cara had a feeling that might not be happening. She returned to her seat and spent the next little while watching the snow as it continued to increase in intensity. After a while, she picked up her phone to check the forecast and saw there was a warning for their area. From the look of it, the first day of school after the Christmas break was going to be a snow day.

When her lights flickered a bit, Cara glanced at them. It appeared her generator might be put to use after all. She put her mug down on the table and went to plug her phone in. She had faith in the generator...mostly. But the last thing she wanted was to be caught with her electronics not charged if it happened to fail. She had a couple of power blocks to charge as well.

Next, she pulled out a couple of pitchers to fill with water. She had a water dispenser downstairs in the studio along with three extra jugs, so she wouldn't run out, but she didn't want to have to run downstairs if she needed water.

Once she was sure she was as prepared as she was going to be, Cara took the container of food Kieran had brought her and went back to her seat. After saying a prayer of thanks for the food, she opened the box and saw that he'd gotten her the salad he knew she liked.

With a sigh, she stared at the salad, feeling deeply her resolve to take time to think over her decision. He'd said he loved her, but even without the words, he'd shown her time and time again that he did. But was it enough?

She really wanted it to be.

~ * ~

Kieran hung up his phone and tossed it on the couch beside him. He'd had to call his officers to make sure they were all aware of what was headed their way. The storm was supposed to have stayed well to the east of them in the mountains, but somehow it had slid far enough west to hit them, and from the look of things, it was going to a doozy.

He'd been in contact with the mayor as well as the administrator of the senior care home already. His biggest concern was what would happen if they lost power. Some places, like the care home, the station, and the community center, had backup generators, but there were a lot of people who wouldn't have power if electricity went out. And not everyone had wood-burning fireplaces to keep their homes warm without electricity.

Though he knew he needed to be focused on the town as a whole, Kieran couldn't help but be concerned about the two women who meant the most to him. Picking up his phone again, he called his mom to check on her and to make sure that she'd filled some containers with water and had charged her phone and tablet.

Though he wanted to call Cara, he wasn't sure his call would be well received after the way things had ended between them earlier. He was pretty sure that he wouldn't be able to hold off calling her much longer, though, since he needed to be sure that she had what she would need should the electricity go off.

He was praying hard that the power wouldn't go out because it would make his job a lot harder. His phone rang, and seeing that it was the mayor, Kieran answered. Without any pleasantries, she asked him to come to a meeting with herself, the fire chief and a few other town officials.

Once that call was over, Kieran went to his room to change into his uniform. He had a feeling this would end up being a long night, even if the power didn't go off. People had been cautioned to stay off the roads, but he knew that for every ten that would heed that advice, there would be one who didn't. And that one would get stuck and need to be rescued...

Knowing he might be tied up for a while, he decided to phone Cara on his way to the meeting. Already the roads were starting to get clogged with snow, and Kieran wasn't looking forward to having to shovel snow in the coming hours.

"Hello?" Cara's voice washed over him as he slowly guided his Jeep down the street.

"Hey. I just wanted to touch base and make sure that you were ready for the storm. Have you charged up your phone?"

"Yes, I've got my phone, tablet, and a couple of power banks all plugged in."

Of course she did. That was one of the things he liked about her. She thought for herself, and even though he'd always want to check on her in situations like this, it would only be because of a need within himself, not because he actually thought she wouldn't be prepared.

"There's a possibility that we might lose power. Is your fireplace wood-burning?"

"No. It's electric, but I do have a backup generator that will kick in if the power should go out."

Kieran couldn't help but chuckle. "Okay. That's good."

"Does your mom have somewhere to go if she loses power?"

"Not specifically. I'm on my way to a meeting with the mayor and other officials. We do have a few contingency plans for the more vulnerable people in town like families with small children or the elderly. Some people are prepared like you are with their own generator, or they have a wood stove or fireplace, but not everyone that needs them has them."

"If your mom needs a place to go, she's welcome here. Just call me if the power goes out, as I might not be aware of it if I'm sleeping."

Feeling relieved that he wouldn't have to worry about his mom if the power should go off, Kieran said, "Thank you. I really appreciate that."

"As long as your mom is okay spending time with me," Cara said, her voice subdued.

"You don't have to worry about that," Kieran assured her. "She has no problem with your past."

"Okay."

Kieran pulled his Jeep into a spot in front of the building housing the mayor's office, guessing at where the parking lines were since the snow had long since obliterated them. "I gotta run. I'll talk to you later, okay?"

"Yep. I hope everything goes smoothly."

"That makes two of us." Kieran turned off the Jeep, picking up his phone as the call switched over from the car's Bluetooth. "Take care of yourself."

"You too."

The call ended with that, and he sat for a moment, saying yet another prayer that God would grant him another chance at a relationship with her. He knew he didn't deserve it, but that didn't keep him from wanting one.

CHAPTER TWENTY-NINE

Bracing himself for the blast of cold and snow, Kieran shoved open the car door and got out. He walked quickly to the glass double doors that led into the two-story building that was across the street from the police station. He headed for the stairs that led to the second floor and the board room where the meeting would be held.

He could smell coffee as he neared the room, and he couldn't wait to get his hands on a cup of it. A glance around the room as he stepped inside showed that there were a couple of people who hadn't arrived yet.

"Hey, Kieran."

Turning, he spotted Stuart Price walking toward him, a cup of coffee in his hand. The large man with a shaved head had been the fire chief for the last twenty years. He'd grown up in New Hope, and he was devoted to the town. His oldest son had recently joined the fire department, determined to follow in his father's footsteps.

Stuart's deputy chief was there as well and greeted Kieran with a nod. Carter Ward was close to Kieran's age, and by all accounts, he was good at his job. He'd moved into town a few years earlier, and though he attended church fairly regularly, he didn't get involved in any of the programs.

Carter was a man of few words, however, and rarely initiated a conversation, but Kieran had learned to never underestimate the man's ability to communicate when needed. They'd both spoken at events at the schools and had worked together on training exercises. When he needed to, the man was able to communicate very well.

"Guess I'd better get myself a cup of that before you two finish the pot," Kieran said with a nod to the cups the men held.

Carter gave him a half-smile as he lifted his mug and took a swallow.

"I have a feeling it's going to be a long night," Stuart said with a sigh as he moved toward the large coffee urn. At least it wasn't a twelve-cup pot. That probably wouldn't have been enough to get them through the meeting.

After getting his coffee, Kieran greeted the others in the room as they waited for the mayor to show. He'd just gone back for a refill when she arrived.

"Good evening, everyone," Bailey Patterson said as she headed straight for where Kieran stood next to the urn.

"Leave some for me?" she asked with an arched brow. Even at this late hour, she wore a suit, and had her hair pulled back in a bun similar to what Cara wore.

Kieran wasn't sure if it was because she was young that she felt she had to keep a professional appearance whenever she was in her mayoral role, or if she really did like wearing suits that much. Though he realized that, except for the person in charge of the municipal buildings, they were all wearing their official uniforms.

"Half a cup, maybe."

"You'd better hope there's more than that," she said as she reached for a cup. "I have a feeling we're going to need it."

Unfortunately, Kieran had the same feeling. Before going to the table, he snagged a couple of cookies from the container next to the coffee urn, fairly certain that Stuart's wife had sent them with him.

The mayor settled into the seat at the head of the table. It didn't take her long to get the meeting underway. Even though she was younger than almost everyone present, no one there questioned her authority because, over the past two years since her election, she'd proven herself more than capable of leading their town.

She quickly moved them through discussions on how they would tackle everything from emergencies to road cleanup to power loss. This was the first major snowstorm she would be facing as mayor, but having lived in New Hope Falls her whole life, she'd been through a few.

Throughout the meeting, the lights flickered, but it wasn't until they were near the end that the electricity actually went out for more than just a couple of seconds.

"Well, it looks like we might be putting the worst-case scenario plan in place," Bailey said. "Because of the way the temperature has dropped, if the power stays out for more than an hour, we'll have to alert people with vulnerable persons in their households about where they can go if they feel it's necessary to relocate."

The power was still on when the meeting adjourned, but they were all braced for the worst. After saying goodbye to the others, Kieran made his way across the street to the station, leaving his Jeep where it was parked. It already had a healthy layer of snow on it, so he'd probably need a shovel in order to dig it out later.

If he could overlook the dangers that came with significant wet snowfall, the scene around him was kind of pretty. The blanket of white gave the town an eerie brightness under the moonlight. The Christmas lights on Main Street had been removed a couple days previously, but they would have made the night even prettier had they still been up.

Inside the warmth of the station, he greeted the two officers who were on duty. He gave them a rundown on what had been discussed at the meeting then retreated to his office. Though he didn't necessarily need to stay the whole night, he wanted to be there if the power did end up going out.

He called his mom to check on her but resisted the urge to call Cara again. Even though their conversation earlier had gone fairly well, he didn't want her to feel like he was taking advantage of the situation to force contact between them.

Instead, he focused on the weather reports, finding it a bit amazing that cities and towns to the west of New Hope weren't getting the snowfall they were. Places to the east definitely were, though. Some of them worse than New Hope.

The heavy wet snow put them at risk for downed branches and powerlines. They weren't really prepared for snow like that, but thankfully, it appeared that warmer temperatures would follow quickly behind the storm, melting most, if not all, of the snow within a matter of days.

Around ten, Kieran decided to head for home. The lights had continued to flicker but had stayed on, so he was hoping they would stay that way.

Back out in the cold and the snow, it took Kieran a while to get his Jeep cleaned off. By the time he climbed behind the wheel, his face felt half-frozen, and his lashes were damp from having to blink away the snow that had kept falling on him.

He drove past his mom's, not too surprised to see that her lights were on. She tended to be a night owl even on the best of nights. He was sure she was seated in front of her fireplace, knitting while she watched something on television. Though he contemplated stopping, he decided to just head for home and give her a call once he got there.

He'd just turned the corner to his street when all the streetlights went off. By the time he'd reached his place, they hadn't come back on. He pulled into his garage because he didn't want to have to clear his car of snow yet again if he had to go back out.

As soon as he was in the house, he called his mom.

"You okay there?" he asked.

"So far, so good," she said. "I turned the heat up earlier, so the house is toasty warm at the moment. Hopefully it will stay that way."

"Cara has offered for you to stay with her if your place becomes too cold."

"She has? You've talked with her?"

"I talked with her after church, but then we spoke again this evening."

"Did you talk about getting back together?"

"I did, but I'm not sure she's interested."

"Ah, sweetie. Don't give up on her too easily. Just give her some time to get used to the idea. Things ended rather harshly between the two of you."

"My fault, I know," Kieran said. "I wouldn't blame her if she didn't want to give me another chance."

"We'll just have to pray that if a relationship between you is God's will that He will change her heart like He's changed yours."

Kieran knew that if this was ever going to work, God had to be the one in control of how things progressed from that point on. He hadn't prayed at all before ending their relationship so abruptly. Hadn't even taken the time to determine if it was God's will that he end things with her. This was a tough lesson on how badly he could mess things up when he acted impulsively rather than seeking God's direction.

Not sure that he wanted to discuss things any further with his mom, he said, "Anyway, she has generously opened her home if we need it. If things start to get too cold, let me know."

"I will. Love you, son."

"Love you too, Mom."

After their call ended, he called the station to make sure their backup generator had come on, which it had. Next, he followed up with the senior care home to make sure they had power as well. Then the countdown began as to when they'd have to make a decision to open the community center since it was the largest place with a backup generator.

Knowing he wouldn't be able to sleep, Kieran decided to head back to the station. At least there he'd have coffee. Something that seemed pretty important for surviving the night.

The power was still out a couple of hours later, and the temperature had continued to drop to unseasonably cold levels. With the electric company telling them it might be several hours yet before their workers could restore power, the contingency plan was put into motion. Kieran texted his mom to see how she was doing, not wanting to wake her with a call if she was still warm enough to sleep.

When she called him back, Kieran quickly made plans to pick her up. At one point in time, the fireplace at his mom's had been wood-burning, but when she took over the home after his uncle's death, she hadn't wanted that hassle. Now he wished they'd left it alone.

Before leaving the station to get his mom, he took the time to phone Cara to make sure she was still okay with his mom staying with her.

"Kieran?"

"I'm sorry to wake you."

"Is the power off?"

"Yeah. It's been off for a couple of hours now."

"Really?" He heard rustling on her end of the phone. "Why didn't you call me sooner?"

"Mom wanted to wait until her place got too cold. Plus, we kind of hoped that the power wouldn't be off for long. But we're at the point now where we're opening up the community center for people who need it. My mom could go there if you prefer."

"No, bring her here if she's okay with that."

"Okay. I'm not sure how long it will take me to get her to your place. The roads are a mess."

"No worries. I'll unlock the front door. Just come up when you get here. All my alarms will be turned off."

"Thank you. I really appreciate this," Kieran said. "I'll see you in a bit."

What should only have taken ten minutes ended up taking close to forty-five by the time he got the vehicle cleaned off and slowly made his way to his mom's. When he finally pulled his Jeep to a stop in front of Cara's place, he noticed that there was a light illuminating the main floor.

He helped his mom from the Jeep then took the bag she'd packed from the back seat. As promised, the door was unlocked when he pulled on it. They tracked in some snow, so his mom insisted that they take their boots off in the entryway. Kieran led his mom along the hallway, listening as she exclaimed over the pictures of Cara hanging there.

The door to the apartment opened as they made their way up the stairs, and Cara greeted his mom with a smile.

"Welcome to my home," Cara said as she stepped back so they could enter the apartment.

"Thank you for allowing me to bunk down here. I hope it's not an inconvenience."

"Not at all." She was wearing a pair of floral leggings and a dark blue sweatshirt. Her hair was in a messy bun with tendrils slipping free against her cheeks.

"I'm going to head back out, Mom," Kieran said as he set her bag down. He wanted to stay, but he needed to be available at the station as they fielded calls from people wondering about the power outage. He'd probably have to make his way to the community center at some point too.

"Stay safe," his mom said as she gave him a hug.

"I will." He turned to Cara. "Thanks again for letting Mom stay here with you."

"You're welcome. If you still have the key to the front door, you can just lock it. If not, I'll come lock it behind you."

Kieran looked down at his key chain and saw that it was still where he'd clipped it earlier when he'd come by to give it to her. "Sorry. Guess I forgot earlier."

"No worries. You can use it to let yourself back in again later."

He nodded his thanks, then headed back downstairs. For the time being, he left his Jeep parked in front of Cara's. It was close enough that he could come back to it if need be. If they left the police station for some reason, they'd take the police vehicles.

As the hours passed, he survived on coffee and stale cookies that he'd found in his desk drawer. When the sun finally rose just before eight, he was fighting the exhaustion that came with having been up for twenty-four hours. The problem with daylight was that people were beginning to attempt to move around town even though they'd been told to stay home unless they absolutely had to go out.

The police station began to field calls from people who were either stuck or who had been in an accident, and it took all of Kieran's patience not to lecture people each time they had to deal with the aftermath of an accident. By noon, the power was back on, and he knew he had to get some rest, or he'd be the cause of the next accident.

After making sure the guys at the station had a handle on things, Kieran wearily made his way to Cara's to check on her and his mom, struggling, at times, to keep his footing in the drifts of snow. There were other people out and about. Some of the businesses were working to clear the snow from in front of their buildings.

He chatted with a couple of them before he reached the studio door. After unlocking the door, he took his boots off and headed up the stairs to Cara's. The apartment door was open, and the aroma drifting out made his stomach growl.

"Hello, darling!" His mom came to meet him with a wide smile, wrapping him in a tight hug. When she pulled back and looked at him, she frowned. "You look so tired."

"I am. It was a long night, but the snow has let up some, and the power's back on, so here's hoping the worst has passed."

"Come eat something," she said, tugging him toward the table.

It seemed a bit like his mom had taken over Cara's apartment. "I don't want to impose."

His mom glanced over to where Cara stood, stirring something on the stove. Without looking away from what she was doing, she said, "It's no imposition. We made plenty."

"In that case," Kieran said as he sank down onto one of the chairs, "I'd love something to eat. Stale cookies just didn't cut it."

Cara moved away from the stove to reach up into a cupboard and pull out some dishes. She set three bowls on the table, giving him a small smile before turning away. Thankfully, she didn't appear to be upset or tense around his mom. He'd worried about that, but it was good to see that she seemed relaxed.

"Your mom made us some beef vegetable soup," Cara said as she returned with the pot from the stove. "And some biscuits."

"One of my favorite winter meals," Kieran said, his tired gaze following Cara as she moved. He couldn't keep himself from watching her. Exhaustion had lowered his defenses, and all he wanted was to be close to her.

When they were all seated at the table, his mom said a prayer for the food. Kieran was hungry, and he knew that if he didn't eat, he'd wake up starving, but it almost took more energy than he could muster up to lift the spoon to his mouth. When he did manage to get it to his lips, the taste of the soup made it worth the effort.

Normally, he would have polished off two bowls and a couple of biscuits, but that time, he was done after one bowl and one biscuit because it was enough to take the edge off his hunger, which meant sleep rose to a higher priority. He gave them a brief update on where things stood for the town, but then gladly went to sit on the couch while his mom helped Cara clean up.

He planned to take her back to her place then go home to crash. If he were lucky, he'd sleep until his alarm went the next morning, barring any more storm-related catastrophes that might require his attention.

CHAPTER THIRTY

Kieran wasn't sure what woke him. He wasn't uncomfortable, but he knew he wasn't in his bed. Had he fallen asleep at his mom's? The room was cloaked in shadows, making his waking slow.

He stretched then looked to his side. The sun had set while he slept, but the soft glow from a nearby lamp cast enough light for him to recognize that he was still at Cara's.

With a groan, he pushed up into a sitting position. He leaned forward, bracing his elbows on his knees as he scrubbed at his face. While the bone-deep exhaustion had eased, he was still tired. It chafed at him a bit that he'd been in Cara's apartment for a few hours, and he'd spent them sleeping.

"How are you feeling?"

Kieran lifted his head to see Cara sitting in a chair near the window. Her legs were pulled up, and her arms were wrapped around them. He hadn't even noticed her there because the lamp that was on was in the opposite corner of the room.

He straightened then sighed. "Still tired but better than I was. Has the snow stopped?"

"Yep. Pretty much. The wind is still tossing it around a bit, though." She turned her head to look out the window. "A plow went down Main Street a bit ago."

Kieran groaned. "I'm guessing I have a nice pile of snow behind my car."

Cara laughed softly. "Yeah, I think you do."

"I probably should go," Kieran said, even though he didn't make a move to get up.

Frankly, he didn't really want to leave, but he knew he needed to. He was sure he'd already overstayed his welcome by falling asleep on her couch. He pushed back the soft blanket that was covering him and glanced around. "Where's Mom?"

"She went across the street to *Norma's* a little while ago."

"*Norma's* is open?"

"They opened around four."

He glanced at his watch and saw it was a little before five. Maybe he'd stop by there to pick up some food before heading home.

Cara leaned forward to turn on a lamp on the table next to her chair then she got up. "Do you want some more soup? There was lots left over from lunch."

"That's probably because I only ate one bowl instead of the two or three I usually do."

Cara headed into the kitchen and opened the fridge, seeming to take for granted that he'd stay even though he hadn't said he would. Kieran got up and stretched, trying to ease the tightness in his back. His uniform shirt was wrinkled, and he wasn't feeling all that comfortable in his clothes right then.

As he turned toward the kitchen, he saw that Cara had a large container on the counter and was ladling soup out of it into a couple of bowls. Apparently, he was staying, and he definitely wasn't upset about that.

"Can I help with anything?"

"I think I can manage. Just sit yourself down." She put the bowls into the microwave, then filled a couple of glasses with water and brought them over to the table. "How long will it take the town to recover from this storm?"

"Not too long, partly because the weather is warming up in a couple of days. That will help to melt the snow."

"I'd kind of forgotten what it was like to have a significant snowfall."

"I suppose you got quite a lot of snow in Chicago."

Cara nodded. "I loved it as a kid until I realized that I didn't get snow days off from school like other kids did since I was home-schooled. Of course, my mom caved after I protested having to do schoolwork when other kids had the day off. She spoiled me."

"I'm glad to hear that she spoiled you. My mom tended to spoil Sean and me too."

She brought the bowls over to the table then sat down across from him. After a moment's hesitation, she asked him if he'd say thanks for their food. He was happy to do that and took the time to pray for those who had been negatively impacted by the storm.

After the prayer, she nudged a container in his direction. "We've got left-over biscuits too. Your mom was such a sweetie to make all of this. She's a great cook."

"She is," Kieran agreed. "Did she make any cookies? They are terrific."

"No cookies, but she did manage to find enough ingredients in my pantry to make brownies."

"Oh, I hope there are some left."

"She managed to protect a few for you."

Kieran broke one of the biscuits and dipped it in the soup. It was his favorite way to eat his mom's biscuits when she served them with soup. "I hope it worked out okay to have her here."

Cara took a spoonful of soup, then she said, "It was fine. I'll admit, I was a bit worried, but I needed to see for myself that what you were saying about her attitude toward my family was true."

"And did you?"

She nodded. "We had a really good talk. She told me how she worked through her feelings about my dad, and then she asked me more about my mom and him and my life with them. I don't know how our conversation left her feeling, but it was very cathartic for me. I haven't had anyone that I could really talk to about that part of my life for a long time. Though I told you bits and pieces of it, the details I left out were things I needed to be able to talk about."

"Like your dad being in prison?" Kieran asked.

"Yes, that, but also how it was losing my mom the way I did and being forced out of my career. Though I'd known I wasn't going to stay with the ballet company forever, I'd always assumed I'd be able to leave on my own terms. My mom's death took away my control of so many things."

"One of the things my mom reminded me of was that you didn't have any control over who your parents were and that probably by the time you understood who your dad was, you'd already formed a close, loving relationship with him."

Cara stared at him for a moment then nodded. "I want you to know that I have never felt that my dad was innocent of what he was accused of or that he was misunderstood. I had to separate him in my mind. One part of him was a part I didn't know. That was Marco Moretti, the mafia boss. The other part was the one I did know and love. My papa. He gave up everything for me, so while I know people might think otherwise, I know he was capable of love."

"I've come to understand that," Kieran said, because he truly had. "I'm just sorry it took me so long. I had seen him as a monster for so many years that I couldn't fathom viewing him in any other light."

"If you think I'm mad at you because you broke things off between us," Cara began, "I'm not. I wasn't able to automatically reconcile his two sides when I learned about his life in New York. And it wasn't just the mafia part. I didn't understand how he could love my mom and me and yet not divorce his wife so that he could be with us. So I understood why you couldn't accept who I was. I never blamed you for that."

Kieran wanted to ask her what that meant for them now that he was willing to accept all parts of her life, but he'd promised not to pressure her. Even though it felt like that conversation had taken place ages ago, it really had only been a little over a day since they'd talked about it.

"I really wasn't sure that you could get to the point where you wouldn't resent me for loving the man that had hurt your family so badly. In fact, I was fairly certain that wouldn't be possible."

"But now?" Kieran needed to hear her answer even as he was a little afraid of what it might be.

"Talking with your mom helped me realize that it was possible for you to get to that point. Never once did I get the feeling that she was viewing me through the lens of my father's actions. And she told me that it pleased her to hear that he had become a Christian, and it just reinforced even more for her that forgiveness was the right choice. If God could forgive my dad for his sins, then it wouldn't be her place to hold unforgiveness in her heart toward him."

Kieran nodded. "She told me the same thing."

"She also said that she understood that it might be difficult for me to trust that you could really change how you felt about my dad."

His heart sank at her words, yet he also understood. He'd just hoped she might be able to have faith in him.

"I do want to trust you, though." Her lips curved in a gentle smile. "I want us to try again to see if we can make this work. You see, I love you too, and having to accept that what we had was over before I even had a chance to tell you that, was very difficult for me."

Kieran stared at her in shock. He'd hoped that she'd give him another chance to show how much he loved her and that in time, she'd come to love him. But he hadn't expected her to tell him already that she loved him on top of being willing to give him—give them—another chance.

"Really? You love me? Even after what I did? What I said?"

"Even then," she said, her smile growing.

Kieran abandoned his soup and got up from the table. He went to where Cara sat and sank to his knees beside her chair. She shifted so that she could look down at him as he reached for her hands. "I love you so much, Cara. Thank you for giving me another chance. You have no idea how much I want this to work."

She lifted one hand and ran her fingertips along his cheek. His eyes closed briefly, relishing the feel of her touch once again.

"I think I do have an idea because I very much want this to work too."

"Promise me that you'll always be open and honest with me about what you're feeling. Please don't try to hide things from me because you're worried about how I'll react. If this is going to work, you need to be able to express yourself freely. You need to tell me if I say or do something that upsets you because that's the last thing I want to do."

"I will, but it works both ways, you know," she told him. "I need to know what you're feeling as well. I don't want to cause you unnecessary pain, so you have to tell me if I say or do something that upsets you too."

It was a bit harder for him to promise her that, but in the end, he nodded. "I will keep seeing Pastor Evans during all of this, and if you want to join me, I'd love that."

"I think that might be a good idea."

Feeling like a weight had been lifted from his shoulders, Kieran got to his feet and pulled her up with him. Relief flooded him as he wrapped his arms around her and felt hers go around his waist. The feeling was so familiar, and something he'd missed so much in the weeks they'd been apart.

He buried his face in her hair, inhaling the familiar scent of her shampoo. "I've missed you so much."

She tucked her head into the crook of his neck and tightened her arms around him. "I've missed you too."

When she moved her head a few moments later, he looked down at her face, his heart pounding at the emotion he saw there. Lowering his head, he pressed his lips to hers. He was so grateful to have her in his arms again when it had been possible that he might never have had another chance.

He knew they had a lot to deal with, but because of God's grace and mercy, Kieran was confident that they would be able to overcome everything together.

Cara shifted in her seat, her stomach a mass of nerves. She wasn't sure when she'd last been this nervous.

"Everything okay?" Sarah asked from across the table.

"Yeah. It's just a bit nerve-wracking to have Kieran meeting my brother without me there."

"Why *aren't* you there?" Sarah scooped up a forkful of the slice of fruit pie she'd ordered.

Cara was asking herself that very question. She should have insisted. "Kieran offered to pick him up then take him to tour the seminary he's thinking of attending."

Sarah's eyes widened. "Your brother is moving to New Hope?"

"Possibly," Cara said, eyeing her friend. She hadn't given Sarah the details about the past she and Gio shared, only that he was her half-brother, and that they hadn't met until after their father's death. The truth of their past would remain a secret known only by a few.

"Is he single?"

Cara stared at her for a moment then laughed. "You want to know if my brother's single?"

"I'm trying to...you know...move forward." Sarah shrugged and sighed. "So, is he?"

Cara gave her friend a sympathetic look before answering her question. "Well, last I heard, he was single, but I'm also not sure he's looking to change that status at the moment."

With a sigh, Sarah slumped back, stabbing her pie with her fork. "Probably just as well."

"So, are your only standards for guys still that they be single and nice?"

"I've added a few more things to the list," Sarah said, a slightly dejected tone to her words. "Things like not being obsessed with money, and I've decided that local guys are probably best."

"Or at least willing to relocate." Cara hated to see her friend upset, but she understood how she was feeling.

"I think maybe I should steer clear of dating for awhile."

"Well, don't let one bad experience turn you off completely."

Sarah stared down at her pie as she continued to jab at it with her fork. "Yeah, I know, but maybe I'm not as ready for a relationship as I thought I was."

"Well, I don't think we necessarily have to feel ready. Goodness knows I didn't feel like I was ready when I met Kieran. Sometimes love shows up when we least expect it."

Sarah shrugged. "After seeing Eli and Anna then you and Kieran, I wanted something like that for myself. It just kind of sucks that my attempt at finding love didn't have your happy outcome."

"Just remember that for a time, I didn't think my attempt had either. Now it's my turn to pray for you."

"Did you feel a bit frustrated when I told you I'd pray for you and Kieran?" Sarah asked. "Because that's kind of how I'm feeling at the moment."

"Not frustrated. It was more feeling like it was hopeless, but who was I to tell you not to pray."

Having found love with Kieran, Cara couldn't blame Sarah for wanting that too. Though their relationship hadn't always been easy, it had definitely been worth pursuing. At first, she'd still been a little reluctant to talk about her father or let Kieran see her grief, but he hadn't allowed her to hide.

Every other day or so, in the course of their conversation, he'd slip in a question about her parents. Whether it was just asking what their favorite colors had been or something more significant like a favorite memory she had from a particular summer. Whatever it had been, he'd encouraged her to respond.

She'd answered him as honestly as she could, understanding even as she did so, the toll it might take on him. Learning those humanizing things about a man he'd only ever viewed as a monster. Her love for him grew as she saw the strength it took for him to accept her view of her father. That, more than anything, revealed how much he loved her, and with that realization, she was able to let go of the last lingering bits of reserve she had about trusting him.

He'd held her when she cried on the first birthday she celebrated without her father, then he'd taken her to a performance of *Beauty & the Beast* performed by a ballet company in Seattle. It wasn't the only time he'd held her as she cried, but those moments of sorrow had gradually lessened as the months passed.

In wanting to learn more about her father, Kieran had brought back the happier memories, easing the grip of her grief. And in the midst of it all, Rose had loved them both, offering her support without question. She had taken on the role of mother for Cara, and it had made her realize just how much she'd missed that connection.

And later that afternoon, they'd both be there for her as she carried out one of her father's final wishes. It had taken her too long to get to this point, but she'd wanted Gio present as well, and he'd only just finished giving his testimony in the trial of his brothers.

"If I'm going to try again, I might have to resort to using a dating app."

Cara wrinkled her nose. "Would you really want to do that?"

"Sure. Why not?" Sarah said with a shrug. "Lots of people use them nowadays."

"I know, but they're not always safe." Cara thought back to the few dates she'd gone on with men from a dating app and wrinkled her nose. "And a lot of times, they don't present themselves in an honest manner."

"I'd take precautions, of course." Sarah sighed. "But I probably won't go that route. My mom would likely have a heart attack if I did."

"Well, just promise me that you will tell me if you do decide to meet someone. Kieran and I can go to the same restaurant to keep an eye on you."

Sarah laughed, a bit of her sadness lifting momentarily. "Having the police chief supervising my date might be the only way my mom would let me meet someone through a dating app."

"Seriously, though, Sarah," Cara began. "I'll be praying that God will bring you the man He has for you, or that He'll give you peace in your current situation."

"Thank you. I know the Bible verses about being content, but I'm really struggling with contentment right now for some reason."

"Rose always says that our struggles are just opportunities to learn to lean more fully on God. I know that sometimes that's easier said than done."

"Sometimes?" Sarah asked with an arched brow. "Feels like *most* the time."

"Yes. I would have to agree with you there."

When Cara's phone chirped, she picked it up off the table and glanced at it.

Kieran: *Just finished at the seminary.*

Did it go well? That wasn't really what she wanted to ask, but those questions would have to wait until she saw him later.

Kieran: *I think so. He seemed to like what he saw.*

She sent him back a thumbs up, then a kissy face and a heart. When he answered with a heart-eye emoji, she smiled.

"Kieran?" Sarah asked, then groaned. "Like I have to ask."

"Yeah. He and Gio are finished at the seminary."

"How long is he staying?"

"I'm not entirely sure," Cara said. He was staying at the same hotel he'd stayed at with Doug. She'd thought of having him stay at the lodge, but she hadn't wanted the McNamaras to get caught in the crossfire if anything should happen. Plus, from what Sarah had said, they were booked solid. "If he's decided to move here for school, he'll probably want to take the time to look around."

"Would you like it if he was closer?" Sarah asked. "Considering you didn't meet him that long ago?"

Cara had thought about that question a lot over the past few months, but ever since he'd accepted her invitation to come out for that day, she found herself more open to having him live close by. They'd built a bit of a foundation for a relationship through sporadic calls and texts over the past six months, and it hadn't been as difficult as she'd thought it might be.

Her main concern had been Kieran. It had been one thing to accept her father, considering he was no longer alive. It would be something else altogether to have a living, breathing Moretti in his life. In the end, however, it had been his suggestion to invite Gio out, and he'd offered to take him to the seminary on his own.

"I think I would like to have him a bit closer. To have the chance to get to know him."

"Then I hope it works out for you," Sarah said with a smile. "And on that note, I should probably head back to the lodge. I promised Mom that I'd be there to help with some cabin cleaning and then supper."

"Thanks for keeping me company."

"Anytime." Sarah picked up her purse and phone. "Let me know how the visit goes."

"I will."

Cara didn't linger at the table once Sarah had gone. She took care of her bill, then headed back to her apartment to wait for Kieran and Gio.

An hour later, she heard the security beeps to let her know that someone had entered the building. Kieran had his own key for the front door, so she went to open the apartment door for them. This visit was a world away from Gio's previous visit when she'd barely been able to handle him being in her building, let alone her home.

When he walked into the apartment, Kieran drew her into a tight hug. Cara let out a sigh of contentment at having him back in her arms. He lightly pressed his lips to hers then let her go, moving aside so she could greet Gio.

"It's so good to see you again," Gio said as he bent and kissed her cheek. "You're looking well."

"I wish I could say the same for you," Cara said, her brow furrowing as she took in his drawn and gaunt appearance. "You look exhausted."

He dragged a hand down his face. "Yeah. I haven't been sleeping all that well, but I hope that will change now that the trial is over."

"You should probably spend a couple of days just eating and sleeping."

One corner of his mouth tipped up in a half-hearted smile. "I might just do that."

"Did you want anything before we head to the cemetery?" Cara asked. "Something to eat or drink?"

"I'm good," Gio said. "We grabbed something on the way to the seminary."

Within minutes, they were on their way again, heading for the small cemetery outside of town where, with the help of Pastor Evans, she'd made arrangements to have her parents' ashes interred. He and Rose would be meeting them there for a short service.

The early July day was warm, though the sun was currently playing peekaboo through the clouds. It was a day both of her parents would have enjoyed. Cara was just glad it wasn't raining.

When they got to the cemetery, Pastor Evans was already there with Rose and the cemetery caretaker. After they joined them at the plot that had been prepared, Kieran made the introductions. Pastor Evans shook Gio's hand while Rose hugged him. Gio seemed surprised then a little emotional as he stepped back from the embrace.

Cara looked at the headstone she had chosen. In death, her parents would share what they hadn't in life. A last name. It had required Doug's help once again plus a change of urn for her mom's ashes since the original one had her real last name on it. After a few conversations with Doug, they'd decided to use their middle names along with the last name that Cara now used. The one that Gio had also decided to share.

It felt, in some ways, as if she was wiping them from existence. No one would ever find them under their birth names. But she and Gio would always know who they were, regardless of the names that were engraved on the headstone.

Pastor Evans led them in a very short service, and as she stood there with Kieran's arm around her, Cara allowed her tears to flow unchecked. She hadn't expected to feel such emotion, but when it came, she didn't bother to hide it.

When Kieran handed her two roses to lay on the container that held the urns, Cara leaned against him for a moment before stepping forward to place them on top. Gio also had a rose that he laid alongside the two Cara had put there.

Even though she'd now been without her papa for almost nine months and her mom for much longer, this somehow felt like the final goodbye. And yet, she knew it wasn't. Pastor Evan's words at the graveside had reminded her that given their professions of faith, she would see them again.

The family she'd had for most of her life was gone, but she was building a new one. She and Kieran had talked about a future together and what that would look like. And now she had a brother, as unlikely as the possibility of that relationship had seemed when he'd first come to see her. Even Pastor Evans had come to play an important role in her life, that of spiritual mentor...almost a father of sorts.

Once the service at the graveside was done, Cara took a final look at the headstone before she allowed Kieran to lead her to where the cars were parked.

"Gio, why don't you come with me?" Pastor Evans suggested. "Kieran mentioned you are interested in going into the ministry. I'd love to chat with you about that."

"Sure," Gio said with a nod. "That would be great."

"I'll drop Rose off, then we can go for a coffee and some pie."

"Thank you," Cara said, appreciating that the man understood that she and Kieran needed some time alone together. She looked at Gio. "We'll see you a bit later."

"I look forward to it." Though he still looked tired, his smile appeared genuine.

Once they left the cemetery, Kieran turned the Jeep in the opposite direction of the town. Cara didn't question where he was going since she trusted him to know what she needed right then. It wasn't long before he was pulling into the small parking lot at the river spot where they liked to come when they had the time, and the weather was nice.

Since it was the middle of the afternoon in the middle of the week, it wasn't busy. Kieran led her to a table near the water, and Cara let out a long breath as she sank down on the bench facing the river.

"Thank you," she said as Kieran sat down beside her and wrapped his arm around her. She leaned into him, resting her head on his shoulder.

"You don't ever have to thank me for taking care of you," he said softly. "It makes me happy to be able to do this for you."

She tilted her head back so she could look up at him. "I love you."

He turned toward her and took her hands in his, turning them palm up and lightly brushing his thumbs across the insides of her wrists. Though she usually wore foundation to cover the tattoos there, she'd left them visible for that day, given what it held.

Not long after they'd gotten back together again, she'd told Kieran about them and what they meant to her. In that same conversation, he'd confessed to having watched her dance by accident. Neither revelation had been a negative thing, and in fact, they had brought them closer together.

"I love you too," Kieran murmured before he leaned in to give her a gentle kiss.

It may have been a tough day for her emotionally but sitting there with Kieran felt a little bit like perfection.

~ * ~

Kieran shifted in his seat, his hands tightly gripping the steering wheel. His mom reached over and patted his hand, drawing his attention briefly from the road.

"I don't know why you're nervous," she said. "It's not as if there's any chance she's going to say no."

"I know that. I'm just wondering if the timing is right. Today might not be the best day to do this.

"Oh honey, I think today is the perfect day. What better way to take a day of sadness and turn it into one of joy?"

Kieran considered her words then said, "You don't think it's too soon, do you?"

"Maybe if you were both younger and hadn't gone through what you have, I might agree with you. Might." His mom hesitated. "You both chose to rekindle your relationship, knowing that it wasn't going to be easy. Knowing that you had difficulties to overcome. You knew that and still chose to be with each other. You wouldn't have done that if you weren't committed to a future together."

Kieran knew she was right. Of course she was. He could also acknowledge that part of his nervousness was because he still remembered how well things had started out with Toni, only for them to go so horribly wrong in the end. This did feel different, though. The connection he felt with Cara was deeper and more tightly woven between them. Certainly they had a stronger spiritual foundation than he'd had with Toni.

"You're right. I want to be with her, and I truly believe God wants us to be together. I've definitely felt His hand at work through all of this."

"Then trust yourself," his mom said. "And trust Cara."

Kieran loosened his grip on the steering wheel as he pulled the Jeep to a stop in front of Cara's building. He got out and headed for the front door of the studio. He'd barely stepped inside when Cara appeared. She wore a light blue sundress with wide straps, a fitted bodice, and a skirt that floated around her as she moved gracefully toward him.

"You look beautiful as always," he said as she approached him.

She smiled and lifted her face for his kiss. "And you look very handsome."

"Why, thank you." He'd chosen a pair of black slacks and a gray short-sleeve button-up shirt, wanting to make more of an effort for this special dinner than his usual out-of-uniform outfit of jeans and a T-shirt. "Are you ready to go?"

At her nod, he took her hand, and together, they left the building. As they neared the vehicle, he could see that in the time he'd been inside, his mom had moved into the back seat. He opened the door for Cara then closed it once she was seated. She and his mom chatted as Kieran backed out of the parking spot and headed for the hotel where Gio was staying.

Seven months ago, he would never have imagined he'd willingly be sharing a ride with one of Marco Moretti's sons. But God had definitely done a work in his heart, as much as He'd done in Marco's and Gio's. He could now look at Gio—who looked an awful lot like his father—without feeling a wave of rage rising up within him. It hadn't been easy getting to that point, but he knew without a doubt it had been worth the effort.

He hadn't just had ups and downs in his personal life during the past half-year, there had been plenty in his professional life as well. They'd finally received an identification on the body found in the woods, and now one family had an answer to what had happened to their daughter. Well, sort of an answer. They still didn't know who had killed their child, but at least they could lay her to rest.

The lack of answers with regards to Sheila's disappearance was aggravating for all involved in the case. He continued to pray that they would find answers for Pete and Coral. It wasn't his case, but that didn't mean he wasn't invested in it. Since it impacted members of his town, there was no way he couldn't be worried about it.

Thankfully, the case that had brought him and Cara together originally, had had a decent—if not happily-ever-after—at least a temporarily happy resolution. When one of his guys had shared about the underage cat burglar and her motives with his family, they'd stepped up and offered to foster the younger girl.

Mary and Cara had gone to court on the older girl's behalf, and Andy had read a letter from Drake, all asking the judge to be lenient on her. When the judge had let her off with community service, the foster parents had taken her in as well. It wasn't the perfect solution, but it would at least get the girls off the street while they figured out what to do next.

"I texted Gio, so he should be waiting out front," Cara said. "Where are we going, by the way?"

"To a restaurant down at Port Gardner Bay. I asked for an outside table."

"Oh, that will be lovely," Cara said. "Maybe we'll see the sunset."

"I figure this might help Gio decide to move out here if he's still on the fence with that decision."

When he felt Cara's hand on his arm as he slowed for a red light, he looked over at her. She gave him a soft smile, her love for him shining bright in her eyes. "Thank you."

He covered her hand with his and gave it a gentle squeeze. "Anything for you, love."

It didn't take them long to get to the hotel, and as promised, Gio was waiting for them. As he climbed into the back, he greeted Kieran's mom. From the hotel, it took another half an hour to get through the traffic to the restaurant.

They were seated at a round table that looked out over the marina, giving them a great view of the islands and the water surrounding them. The evening was balmy, and though there were a few clouds in the sky, there wasn't any rain forecast.

The restaurant wasn't one that Gio or Cara had been to before since it was only located in the Pacific Northwest. They all ended up ordering seafood and spent the evening talking about pretty much everything except for the trial. As time passed, the nerves Kieran had been fighting earlier gave way to excitement.

Though he had debated doing this with just the two of them, he'd decided not to. Given that their families had shrunk so much, Kieran had felt it was important that they all be together for this important occasion. Once they'd finished with their desserts, he glanced over at his mom, and she gave him an encouraging smile.

As the evening had slipped past, people had come and gone from the outside eating area, and now there wasn't anyone seated at the tables nearest theirs. Kieran looked over at Cara, taking in her smile and the way she laughed at something his mom had said. His heart expanded with love for her. She was the one he wanted to spend the rest of his life with, and he felt confident that it was also God's will.

With that in mind, he reached into his pocket for the small ring box he'd placed there earlier. With just one hand, he managed to open the box and slip the ring onto the end of his pinky.

He glanced at Gio, and the man's smile broadened. He knew what was coming. In the absence of her father, Kieran had asked Gio for his blessing. Not that he wouldn't have proposed without it, but if they were building a future as a family, he wanted the man to know that he was welcome in their lives.

When he reached for Cara's hand, she looked over at him, her smile growing as their gazes met. With slow movements, and never letting go of her hand, he slid from his chair onto one knee. Cara's eyes widened, and her mouth opened as if she was going to say something, but then she snapped it closed.

Kieran had tried to rehearse what he wanted to say, but the long speech slipped away, so he just went with the main points. "Love, though we've had our ups and downs through the time we've been dating, all they've done is show me that you are the one I want to be with. The ups, the downs. The good, the bad. I want it all with you. I love you. Will you marry me?"

Cara reached out to lightly touch his cheek with her fingertips, blinking rapidly against the moisture that suddenly made her eyes gleam like silver. Her fingers lingered on his skin, a gentle touch that became firmer as she slid her hand to cup his cheek before she bent forward so their faces were closer.

"I love you, Kieran. So very much." She gave him a soft kiss. "I would love to marry you."

Kieran couldn't keep the smile from his face as he slipped the ring from his finger. He took her hand in his and slid it into place on her finger. Once it was securely in place, he lifted her hand and pressed a kiss to it before getting to his feet, drawing her up with him.

As he wrapped his arms around her, Kieran said a prayer of thanks that out of the darkest moments of both their lives, love had grown. And though it had taken time for him to accept Cara's father's role in those dark moments, he also knew it was because of him that they had reached this point of committing to a future to-gether, and that was something he never wanted to give up.

Each of them had faced tremendous loss in their lives, but Kieran hoped that the past was behind them now. That their love marked the end of the darkness that had dominated their lives, al-lowing them to accept the past without it dimming the light that now filled their hearts and would guide them into the future.

ABOUT THE AUTHOR

Kimberly Rae Jordan is a USA Today bestselling author of Christian romances. Many years ago, her love of reading Christian romance morphed into a desire to write stories of love, faith, and family, and thus began a journey that would lead her to places Kimberly never imagined she'd go.

In addition to being a writer, she is also a wife and mother, which means Kimberly spends her days straddling the line between real life in a house on the prairies of Canada and the imaginary world her characters live in. Though caring for her husband and four kids and working on her stories takes up a large portion of her day, Kimberly also enjoys reading and looking at craft ideas that she will likely never attempt to make.

As she continues to pen heartwarming stories of love, faith, and family, Kimberly hopes that readers of all ages will enjoy the journeys her characters take in each book. She has no plan to stop writing the stories God places on her heart and looks forward to where her journey will take her in the years to come.

Printed in Great Britain
by Amazon

26480210R10199